HIGH PRAISE FOR BRAM STOKER–AWARD FINALIST W. D. GAGLIANI!

WOLF'S GAMBIT

"*Wolf's Gambit* is that rare accomplishment in horror of a sequel that not only surpasses the power of the original, but turns your expectations against you at every turn. His writing has never been crisper, his suspense never more nerve-wracking, and his dry humor so consistently refreshing. Gagliani is fashioning an epic werewolf cycle here, one filled with terror, passion, violence, surprisingly affecting sensuality, and enough fantastical twists and turns to satisfy even the most jaded horror reader."

—Five-time Bram Stoker Award–winner Gary A. Braunbeck, author of *Far Dark Fields*

"A great big bloody beast of a book that enthralls the reader on multiple levels. Vicious, gory, sexy, fascinating—part supernatural thriller, part police procedural, pure dynamite!"

—Edward Lee, author of *The Black Train*

"*Wolf's Gambit* is the equivalent of a North Woods roller coaster—with each brutal twist the body count rises, but you never want the ride to end! This one goes for the throat over and over again, and as you slip through the slayings with Detective Lupo in a desperate race against time, the pages seem to turn themselves! I couldn't put it down!"

—John Everson, author of *The 13th*

"If you're looking for the same-ol'-same-ol' werewolf story, W. D. Gagliani's *Wolf's Gambit* is definitely not for you. Gagliani takes a rehashed theme and breathes new life into it with a cast of memorable characters and relentless suspense. *Wolf's Gambit* is one book you won't put down, and it's a story you'll never forget."

—Deborah LeBlanc, bestselling author of *Water Witch*

SURROUNDED BY THE PACK

The howling stopped suddenly, and Lupo knew why.

One of the wolves reached the prey sooner than the others and brought him down in a crash of limbs and brush. The fugitive gave a single long yelp of pain and surprise, but it was a tired one, and then he screamed as the snarling increased in volume and the scream was cut off.

The bastard's torn out his throat, Lupo thought, gripping the Glock as hard as he could manage with the silver burning his palm and fingers, guilt washing over him in waves for allowing the fugitive to be taken almost under his nose like that.

Lupo almost stepped out once again, but then his sensitive ears picked up the sounds he dreaded.

Soft padding of paws on the forest floor. An occasional snap of a twig.

One of the other wolves, a maverick, was approaching Lupo's hiding place, sniffing loudly as he caught some sort of scent . . .

Other *Leisure* books by W. D. Gagliani:

WOLF'S GAMBIT
WOLF'S TRAP

WOLF'S BLUFF

W. D. GAGLIANI

LEISURE BOOKS NEW YORK CITY

A LEISURE BOOK®

July 2010

Published by

Dorchester Publishing Co., Inc.
200 Madison Avenue
New York, NY 10016

ISBN 10: 0-8439-6348-4
ISBN 13: 978-0-8439-6348-9
E-ISBN: 978-1-4285-0894-1

Visit us online at www.dorchesterpub.com.

ACKNOWLEDGMENTS

Once again, this book is for my Mom and Janis. In loving memory of my dad, Alda Gagliani, and Aldo DiCorato.

Thanks are due to all the many writers who always inspire me to continue scribbling, including Tim Powers, James P. Blaylock, Robert B. Parker, Lawrence Block, Donald Westlake, Edward Lee, Richard Laymon, Joe Lansdale, F. Paul Wilson, Gary Braunbeck, Brian Hodge, Tom Piccirilli, Deborah LeBlanc, Douglas Preston and Lincoln Child, Michael Slade, Barry Eisler, Lee Child, David Morrell, Robert R. McCammon, A. G. Kent, and some from my youth, including Alistair MacLean, Harry Patterson/Jack Higgins, Desmond Bagley, and Duncan Kyle. This is dedicated to all of them for inspiring me when it counted most.

Thanks to the entire crew of the Starbucks at 8880 S. Howell in Oak Creek, WI, where large portions of *Wolf's Gambit* and *Wolf's Bluff* were written—friendly service, good music, and good tea made it a great place to write.

I'd also like to dedicate this book to the memory of five legends who've recently left us, Donald Westlake and Richard Wright (Pink Floyd), Stuart Kaminsky, Robert B. Parker, and Eric Woolfson (Alan Parsons Project)—*Shine on, you crazy diamonds . . .*

AUTHOR'S NOTE

The real Eagle River is located in the southern part of Vilas County, in northern Wisconsin. The real Wausau is in Marathon County, a ways southwest of Eagle River but still far north of the state's center. Once again I have altered these municipalities geographically, socially, and with regard to local city and county organization in order to suit my purposes. All characters in the alternate Eagle River and Wausau are either fictional or used fictitiously and should in no way resemble their real-world counterparts. However, some things are unalterably true. If you drive up Highway 45 or 51 from Milwaukee, and find yourself in the North Woods just past dusk, you might notice shadows keeping pace with you from the undergrowth crowding the side of the road. The pines are set claustrophobically close together, but these shadows seem to move effortlessly between them. If you look up, the moon's silvery sheen might be filtering through the high treetops. If you roll down your windows, you might hear the howling.

Don't roll down your windows.
And don't stop the car.

WOLF'S
BLUFF

PROLOGUE

What mountain?

Jared Bloom snorted derisively and picked up the pace. Shouldn't have been any trouble for Tim to keep up, because this wasn't much of an incline. Not much of a path through not much of a forest, scattered over not much of a mountain. Apparently somewhere nearby, a ski hill (man-made, of course) had opened and they'd christened the result something else, something more adventurous, something more *expensive*. But Jared's map was a little out of date and it still showed the entire area as the near-majestic-sounding Rib Mountain, except Jared had a sense whoever had named it had never actually *seen* a mountain. A real one, anyway.

Jared heard Tim puffing along not far behind him on the path. He chuckled. Maybe it was a bit more of a climb for the doughy Tim, whose exercise regimen had not too long ago consisted almost entirely of leaving the couch for snacks. Snacks and sex. And whenever possible, snacks and sex at the same time. Snacks, sex, and television, and Tim was happy.

Jared had put a stop to that. He liked his DVR as much as anybody, but he'd designed a real exercise regimen, as well as a schedule rounded out with plenty of sex, and now a new Tim was beginning to take form out of what had become sluglike and sedentary. Hell, even in bed Tim had been sluglike and sedentary. Now he was turning into the kind of partner Jared felt he deserved.

Jared smiled. He'd have to tell him that just to goad him a little. Hurt his feelings just enough, then console him with good old hotel sex. Nothing wrong with that!

"You keeping up, Tim?"

"Yeah, yeah, this isn't all that challenging a hike, Mr. Healthwise."

"And yet I hear you puffing," Jared called back, laughing.

"Because you saddled me with all the supplies!" Tim protested. "Who packs wine bottles and freaking glasses?"

"Somebody with a pack mule," Jared mumbled. "Somebody who can't wait to share the picnic basket with his lover," he amended, mostly for Tim's consumption.

Tim's footsteps were heavier, but they were steady. He was just out of sight on the part of the path that wound ever so slightly around the so-called mountain's slope. Jared heard him trying to conceal the puffing and smiled again.

The smile froze on his face when he heard Tim call out suddenly.

"Hey, what's the big—?" There were more words, but they seemed muffled, as if Tim had swallowed them instead of speaking. Tim's voice rose sharply, but the words were lost in the trees.

Jared turned and faced the way he had come. The path was clear, but he saw Tim's shadow lengthening at the far end, where he should soon appear, his overfilled backpack hulking over his shoulders and neck. "Tim?"

Tim didn't respond.

"What kind of game are you playing?" Jared called out.

"Jared?" Tim's voice had a quaver in it that Jared had never heard.

"Jared?" Tim repeated. "There's something—there's something following me. Something stalking me from the woods."

"Yeah, right!" Jared said. He wanted to laugh, but Tim's tone was spooking him. "It's the off-season, it's a weekday, it's not even a holiday. There's no one—"

The growling must have started out softly, because it wasn't sudden. Jared realized that he'd heard it along with Tim's voice just now, but he'd ignored it. But now it rose in volume and raised the hair on his neck and back just like fingers on his damned old-fashioned classroom chalkboard.

"T-Tim?"

"Jared, there's something big getting closer to me. In the trees. It's growling. I think it's—I think it might be a bear . . ." He stopped, and there was loud rustling from the underbrush. Tim gasped, but it was cut off.

The bloodcurdling scream that suddenly came from below was barely recognizable as Tim's voice. It ended with a wet gargling sound that chilled Jared to the bone.

"Tim!" he shouted, panicked now. "Timmy!" He stumbled crazily down the rock-strewn path to try and see what sort of fate had befallen Tim, half-convinced the boy was putting him on. Still, there was that growling. And now, *other sounds*. Almost losing his balance, Jared rode a few rocks down like a surfboard, pulling up short and grabbing a tree to break his free-fall descent. Rocks and pebbles followed him down and spread out under his boots like jagged marbles.

He turned and faced the slight bend in the path and stopped short, his eyes fastened on what lay before him, his brain racing to catch up and focus the image.

Tim was stretched out across the path on his back, his head lolling back like a grotesque deflated balloon. His throat was a mass of torn gristle and meat, a bloody hole through which it seemed gallons of blood had already gushed and soaked into the ground below.

"Tim!" Jared shouted, his body suddenly trembling all over. The shock literally halted his breath for a moment, then quickened it nearly to the point of hyperventilation.

Details began to sharpen and he saw that Tim's light blue North Face parka had been ripped open along the wind flap. The blubbery chunks of sausagelike tubes gathered up like obscene meat in a bloody serving bowl were Tim's intestines, slightly steaming in the cool air.

Jared felt his knees sagging, comprehension just eluding him beyond the obvious.

Tim is dead. Massacred, butchered.

But what—?

Then a blur of gray fur caught his eye—the corner of his eye, really, just off to his right. He turned, and there it was, impossibly, emerging like a ghost from among the tightly packed pines.

A large gray animal, a wolf—it had to be a wolf; they'd made a comeback, hadn't they?—stepped onto the path just a couple yards away. Jared stared. The animal's eyes seemed to glow, but that had to be a trick of the light. Its jaws worked at something. It was chewing and swallowing, its red-flecked muzzle trailing a streamer of bloody links.

The smell hit Jared all at once.

The wolf is chewing a piece of Tim's intestines.

Jared never realized that his bladder loosened and a stream of warm urine dribbled down his leg.

The wolf growled, chewed one last time, and swallowed again, then shook its head, and the remaining bits of intestine went splattering into the brush lining the side of the path.

Then it approached Jared, its eyes holding his all the while in a ferocious primeval stare.

Jared stepped back, forgetting the incline of the path, and tripped over his own feet, sitting painfully back on the rock-strewn trail.

The wolf's fangs were impossibly huge when it growled and snapped. Jared held up a hand, as if to ward off the attack he knew was coming. "Jesus, no," he mumbled. "No!"

The wolf lunged and landed on Jared's chest even as he tried to roll away at the last second. The weight of the beast drove his back painfully into the hard ground. But by then the wolf's jaws had closed on his exposed neck and started ripping out chunks of throat.

Jared's screaming was also lost in the gargling, bubbling sounds of his blood gushing into the wide-open maw of the monster. By the time those same jaws ripped through his clothing and started in on his entrails, his eyes were already glazing and memory of his past life had not flashed through his brain, as he would have expected. All that had flashed through his brain was the pain of being devoured alive. His death caught him somewhat by surprise and left him with an expression of wonder on his face. Wonder that a perfect day like this had turned out to include his end, and wonder at the forces that had brought him to this place at the same time as the monstrous animal now chewing through his flesh and organs.

A while later, its hunger sated, the wolf stepped from the path and melted into the thick forest cover. It ran with abandon through the woods, letting the cool air dry its bloodied muzzle. By the time it reached the creek and dipped its jaws into the cold water, it was fully content, with its stomach full.

After drinking, the wolf padded back down the slope to where another path snuck through the undergrowth and eventually crossed a picnic area and parking lot carved into the hillside. There was a vehicle tucked away toward one end of the lot. If anyone else had been parked there, they might have heard the sound of a woman's laughter rippling through the trees.

CHAPTER ONE

LUPO
SOMEWHERE IN GEORGIA

Grimly, he checked the load in his Glock.

The magazine was full, as it had been the last time he'd checked, so he slid it back into the grip until it clicked home. This was a clean Glock, unregistered and untraceable, procured by a friend of a friend, whose inventory was full of such clean pieces. He'd loaded the magazine, and the spares in his belt pouches, while wearing latex gloves to make sure there would be no prints on the brass. There was a second magazine on the dash, loaded in the same careful way but with special rounds, riding in a pouch he would hang from his belt at the last second.

Lupo sat in a borrowed Honda that also had no paper, though it could survive a cursory look. The legit plates and registration would only fall apart if followed too far down the paper path. But his source for clean cars was almost as good as his source for clean guns. As a cop, he had access to a directory of people whose businesses resided on the fringes of the gray areas of the law.

"You know you're asking for trouble, Nick," Sam said from the passenger seat. He was fidgeting with his hands, rubbing down his aging fingers, trying to straighten them against the arthritis. "You can't keep crossing the line without being seen. You can't keep walking into trouble by yourself."

"If I caused the trouble myself, I can," Lupo muttered.

"Look, I had to get rid of that petty robber. Sure, I should have known better before that, when I chased him down and—"

Sam waved him off. "I know, I know, that was maybe a necessity, but this—this I'm not really sure of. You're here, far from home, driving a ghost car—"

"And packing a ghost piece," Lupo interjected, holding it up.

"Right, the piece means you plan on doing some housecleaning down here."

"No, that's what the other stuff in the other magazine is for. And the trunk."

"Ah, all the silver. So you think there are more of them here? Those three might have been the proverbial bad apples."

"Sam, isn't it obvious? I can't believe there were only three of them in the entire world, first of all. Besides me, I mean. Suddenly we're a group of four. That means there's no end to the possibilities for more. And if there were three bad apples working for Wolfpaw Security, then why not more? A place like Wolfpaw strikes me as the perfect hiding place for bad apples, not to mention a natural way to, uh, 'wolf out' without too many people catching on."

"You're talking about the Iraq connection?" Sam looked out the passenger window before turning back to Lupo. "You think there was more to it?"

"Listen, from what I've found out, these guys killed their way through a bunch of in-country assignments. Nobody would have noticed, official or otherwise. Talk, rumors, whispers maybe. I was able to track down one source who says, off the record, mind you, that he remembers hearing rumors of weird animal attacks—all fatalities—following these guys throughout Baghdad, Karbalā, and Basra. Nothing that anyone official ever cared about, what with all the bombings and assassinations and ethnic cleansing. What's a few more unusual deaths? Maybe starving animals were responsible. Maybe it didn't matter. After all, these people were subhumans, so why care?"

"You're being harsh on the Wolfpaw management."

"Am I?" Lupo snorted.

"Think the management knows about the creatures?"

Lupo frowned. "That's the million-dollar question. Maybe the whole company's rotten with these things. Maybe they don't just tolerate them, they encourage the behavior. Maybe it explains the corporate name and logo."

"You mean instead of werewolves being drawn by the work and the name, it actually symbolizes their, uh, 'nature'?"

"Sure, why not? I became a cop partly due to the enhancements this condition gave me. I would have washed out of the academy, if not for a few subtle advantages. So these guys, maybe they figured why not make the best of our abilities, make a ton of taxpayer money in government contracts, and eat as many live humans as we can get our paws on? And if you thought that way, where else would you go?"

"So this is the answer? A midnight raid?"

"Not a raid. More like a recon mission. I want to see from up close what these guys do in their off time. And what their training facilities look like."

"You know they're probably gonna get decommissioned in the next year, right? They're gonna get pulled out of Iraq. Too many unprovoked killings."

"Doesn't that make my point?"

"I'm talking gunfire deaths, Nick."

"Sure, but those are the visible deaths. It's those undocumented killings I'm interested in."

Sam sighed. "I guess. I know you may be right, but do you think you should risk everything—*even risk Jessie*—just to ease your curiosity? You know how she feels about your obsession with Wolfpaw."

"We can't be completely safe until I know. And until

things are taken care of, even if I have to be the one to take care of them."

Sam was silent.

"Sam?" Lupo turned.

There was no one there.

Lupo blew out a long breath. The hair on the back of his neck tingled.

Shit.

He racked the Glock's slide.

JESSIE

A late outbreak of the flu on the reservation had kept her at the clinic for an extra shift, so by the time it had quieted down again, she wondered if she should even bother going home. A couple more hours and she would be back in the car, driving to work to face another whole day of sniffling, miserable kids and their parents. It wasn't much to look forward to, and with Nick out of town there was nothing to draw her home, either.

Jessie turned out the lights and settled into the plush futon on which she'd recently allowed herself to splurge, back in the private little room behind her office. It was far better than a cot, much softer, and wrapping the long green and gold Packers fleece blanket around herself would keep her warm and cozy until it was time to reopen the doors.

She warmed up some cold tea in the microwave, broke out an emergency bag of Doritos, and checked her small bookcase for something good to read. Thrillers had lost their sheen for her after she'd become involved with Nick Lupo, a man who came with his own thriller life. She'd had enough of real-life thrills. No, maybe a nice locked-room mystery, a civilized "cozy," would be perfect for the cold weather and the way she wanted to feel under the fleece.

She selected a thin paperback and cracked the cover with

little interest but to distract herself just long enough to let sleep claim her. The words swam before her eyes and she began to let them, preferring to allow her mind to wander. She couldn't help it. She and Nick had argued about his trip, and she'd lost. He was stubborn, a typical Italian, as he would often admit, which galled her even more because it proved he knew he was galling her but then going on to do it anyway, which gave his decisions an element of premeditation she resented.

Jessie had wanted to let things settle down before getting involved in some kind of terrible business all over again. The mercenaries and serial killer combination that had complicated the previous few months had proven difficult to explain and cover up, and only because Sheriff Tom Arnow had been personally aware of all the facts had they been able to drag a virtual tarpaulin over the whole sordid affair.

Mayor Ron Malko had turned out to be a serial killer with a long résumé, and they had been able to manufacture an aura around him which they used to explain some of the killings that otherwise had been perpetrated by his employees, mercenary types recently home from a long and apparently enjoyable legalized killing spree in occupied Iraq. The gruesome difference was that these mercs had preferred devouring their victims after playing with them.

Nick had been shocked to learn there were others who shared his "condition," as he called his lycanthropy. Though she'd often reminded him that logic dictated there would be more, given the fact that Nick knew at least two others had existed before him: Sam Waters's son, and the neighbor boy who had bitten Nick and ruined his childhood—and life, to hear *him* tell it.

Jessie felt the jury was still out on whether Nick was cursed or blessed, but it was certain (and she was forced to agree) his luck had been running rather in the negatives in the last couple years.

Her thoughts ran to luck because the bright lights of the new casino across the way blinked on and off all night long, painting her drawn shade a kaleidoscope of neon colors. The casino didn't face the clinic. Its raised ski-lodge-style facade dominated the main street in from both directions on U.S. 45. Jessie's clinic—really a well-equipped small hospital—faced the next street over, but the building's squat footprint occupied the entire block, and the room she lay in now, trying to rest, was located at the rear of the building. The bland rear wall did face the casino, however, with its winding drive and valet-parking lot leading to the three-story log atrium topped by huge replicas of stretched Indian blankets, their jagged designs recalling the worst stereotypes Jessie could think of, but apparently nobody cared as long as the money rolled in. Actually the lobby and its atrium were understated compared with the much greater crimes perpetrated inside the casino proper.

The roar of buses accelerating after dropping off loads of elderly casino hounds seemed to punctuate her thoughts. What time was it? Had to be after 2:00 A.M., and people were just arriving.

The council must be happy.

Just a couple months of operation and the money had to be rolling in. Sure, there were construction costs to cover, and payrolls, and training, and a million other things. Jessie's clinic had seen a spike in routine physicals, forced by the employment agreements for all new casino staff. Construction was still ongoing next door to the casino, where the hotel and convention center was slowly taking shape.

The evil pond that had caused all the recent trouble had been drained and its secrets divulged. Bodies had come out of the black water by the dozen, weighed down by everything from chains to cinder blocks and boat anchors. The newer victims had been zipped into strong canvas Christmas-tree-storage bags, but older remains had settled into a sort of organic sludge even veteran medical-examiner staff members could barely stomach. Bones and other remains had been scooped out of the mud like twigs. The stench had been over-whelming for weeks, until the tribal council had held a public cleansing and burned various bonfires in a sacred ceremony specifically geared to helping the reservation purify itself physically and psychologically of the evil that had been done on its border.

Then the casino itself had risen from the previously cursed site and taken shape, and the surviving members of the council fast-tracked the casino and convention center project. Rick Davison had inherited the reins of the council and, sworn to secrecy about what he had witnessed, had led the tribe's effort to reinvent itself and bring prosperity to the downtrodden community.

Jessie had to give Davison some credit. For the most part, he had managed to navigate the fine line between heading toward the distinctly cheesy and keeping some semblance of tribal honor and self-identity.

The fact that he tended to avoid her whenever possible rankled her, however. It wasn't her fault their world had been invaded by evil forces who had upended everyone's lives. But Davison seemed to hold her responsible for bring-ing Nick Lupo into their lives, despite the fact that Lupo had vacationed in nearby Eagle River for over a decade be-fore her relationship with him had transitioned from that of landlord to friend to lover.

But she understood the tendency to associate the trauma suffered by Davison and his family with her and with Nick Lupo, even though they had helped Sheriff Tom Arnow van-quish the threat from four vicious killers—hell no, they were the *reason* Sheriff Arnow had succeeded. Without them, there was no telling when Eagle River and the rez would have broken the bloody chokehold. How many more would have died if Nick's intervention hadn't occurred when it did?

Jessie put the paperback down and stared at the flashing behind the shade. She hated to admit it, but the casino was fascinating to behold. Maybe it was the whole psychology of it, the way people who could ill afford it were drawn to throw their money into machines that for the most part were designed to gobble it up, spitting back an occasional win just to spur the rest of the so-called players into donating more of their paychecks.

Maybe it was her love of the Alan Parsons Project 1980 album *The Turn of a Friendly Card*, which explored the gambling addiction from a medieval-tinted progressive-pop-music perspective, that still seemed to hit the mark all these many years later. The fact that this love was shared with Nick had helped draw them together after years of friendship.

But now Sheriff Tom Arnow's face was in her mind. She shook her head, almost as if wanting to deny it, but the image was there.

She could see the angular planes of the tough sheriff who'd come to Eagle River by way of Daytona and Chicago, where he'd been a hard-nosed cop before deciding to find an easy path to retirement. Eagle River had not been it. She smiled a bit sadly to herself. She'd hated to see Tom go. He was interested in her, she could tell, maybe from the very beginning of his tenure as sheriff, but he'd backed off when he realized she was with Nick Lupo. And then Nick had decided to reveal his terrible secret to Tom, and that had made him more than just aloof. His world had been rocked, that was certain.

Nick had been right, though. Arnow would never have listened to them without solid proof, and the best proof was a clear look at Nick Lupo changing from man to wolf, dangerous as it was. He would have stood by and watched as more and more victims were either devoured by the pack of mercenaries Ron Malko had hired, or disappeared at the hands of Malko himself. There was no way Arnow would have believed Nick's version of what he was up against, and the alliance that finally overcame the mercenaries would never have existed.

Nick's decision to blow his secret to someone he only hoped he could trust had been borne out as a wise one in the end, but it had led to Arnow's hasty departure when the last of the paperwork was filed, after the state and federal authorities were satisfied that Malko had simply gone around the bend and hired trained killers to do his dirty work. The discrepancies between what was said and what some of the forensic evidence showed had been either ignored or written off as errors caused by the "backward" conditions of the provincial—*hick*—crime labs available locally.

She glanced at the wall clock. Two forty A.M., and there was a full house across the street. As there was every night. The cars and SUVs stretched out in a long line off the highway, snaking through the parking lots or into the parking structure. Jessie unrolled herself from the fleece and stood stiffly, hovering on the brink of a decision that made little sense. The room was slightly illuminated by the brightness of the flashing lights, and she could see the familiar outlines of her furniture. She avoided the sharp corners and approached the window, feeling the pull through the shade and the glass panes. The pull of the casino.

Not the gambling, not that. The environment itself seemed to draw her toward the warmth of that giant barn they'd erected in the center of her reservation. In essence, she felt it was valuable research she should do. She cast about in the dark, finding her North Face jacket mostly by feel. It was still cold in the North Woods, even though winter's back had finally been broken by the reluctant sun and its minions, warm southerly winds that were nothing if not unseasonable. But in the middle of the night, winter plotted its comeback, and the chill would take the breath right out of you as you crossed wide-open spaces between buildings even here in this small but growing community.

Before she was quite aware of it, she had zipped up the coat and edged toward the door, feeling fatigue slide away as a growing glow of excitement began to warm her insides. She took the stairs down to the ground level, passed the rear nurse's station with a wave at the overnight staff, and was soon pushing through the exit door near the loading dock, where she stood overlooking the small surface lot and its smattering of vehicles illuminated by the strobelike casino lighting. Night staff and maintenance crew, perhaps an overnight patient or two, and a couple security guards. Her old Pathfinder was in the corner, parked in its reserved slot. She could just click the remote and head home after all; just a few steps away was the means.

She stepped down the concrete stairs and crossed the lot with quick steps, ignoring the temptation of the Pathfinder. She felt a strange emptiness in the bottom of her belly, probably because she missed Nick, probably because she knew he was very likely in danger at this very moment. The emptiness gnawed at her, but as she approached the—

The cathedral, she thought. Eric Woolfson, who'd penned the lyrics for the Alan Parsons Project, had gotten it exactly right.

The casino *was* a cathedral of sorts, and a steady stream of pilgrims made their way to its doors, some helped by walkers and canes, a few in wheelchairs. Perhaps they thought the cathedral would cure them of their ailments. A bus was currently disgorging some right now, and they were shambling like zombies toward the light. Like insects to the zapper.

She approached, stepping over curbs and through the still-unfinished landscaping islands, and joined the nightlife throng as they made their way to the revolving and automatic doors. An elderly lady who could barely walk without someone taking her elbow struggled with the door. Jessie opened it for her and the woman mumbled thanks, barely able to change the focus of her determined entrance. The inside of the casino called to them like a siren leading a ship to the reefs, and they went without protest.

Jessie followed the old woman into the atrium and looked up, as she always did when she entered.

CHAPTER TWO

LUPO
SOMEWHERE IN GEORGIA

He had hiked a mile or more from the road, following a narrow path he suspected might be traveled occasionally by armed sentries. He'd been training himself to catch and follow scents without forcing a Change, though when he managed to do so, they still weren't as strong in his nostrils as they would be when he was in wolf form. He often wondered how much more there was to learn about his condition. It was late and there was no moon, so he thought he had the edge on any sentries.

Unless they're wearing night-vision gear, a voice whispered inside his ear.

And he knew they might well be.

But they probably wouldn't risk all the whispers and speculation likely to come from nearby communities when people realized the compound was treated like a fortress. Lupo was gambling that the outer rings of the perimeter, at least, would be free of too-visible security measures. For instance, he'd been surprised by the lack of a fence of any type. Only red and white NO TRESPASSING signs spaced about a hundred yards apart warned the curious there was any danger at all waiting beyond the tree line. The signs spelled out the fact that there was security in place, but did not make specific threats.

He planned to only penetrate a certain distance and survey the situation. He was willing to gamble he'd spot enough evidence to support—or destroy—his conclusions, before being forced to breach the main defenses.

The hike hadn't taken much out of him, but the pouch flapping on his belt seemed to sear his skin even though he had planned for a thick layer of multiple fabrics between him and its contents. Unfortunately, he'd learned the hard way that there wasn't much more he could do. The very same silver that protected others from him could protect him from others, but the cost was pain. The deadly impact came when a bullet shattered inside a body and sent a million sharp, searing fragments through one's internal organs. Lupo had tasted that pain and knew enough to avoid it, but here he'd had no choice but to prepare in case his suspicions were confirmed.

The Wolfpaw compound was set on a couple hundred acres of woodland surrounded by hilly scrubland giving way to a swampy corner, bisected by several narrow waterways. Reachable only by one major two-lane paved road that was bound to be patrolled and gated, plus airstrip and helipad, the twenty-building spread resembled a rural college from the air, complete with a bare quad-cum-parade ground, a sports complex with Olympic pool, and various exercise and training facilities carved from the wooded areas. Word was that a biathlon course even wended its way through the "campus," as the locals referred to the compound, helping to promote its benign college image. Lupo was willing to bet biathletes weren't training for the Olympics, but for cold-terrain warfare. The several standard outdoor shooting ranges were so situated among quarries and dug-out trench systems that virtually none of their sound carried off-compound.

Lupo avoided the marked path, traversing instead the narrow ravine that flanked it. The underbrush grabbed at him and snagged his black clothing like grasping claws, and he made his way slowly into the heart of the preserve, keeping his eyes peeled for cameras and booby traps. Although not blessed with a wolf's night vision while in human form, Lupo's eyes were still keener than average in the dark, and all his other senses were also supernaturally enhanced. It had taken him a lifetime to learn some control over his gifts (or curses, as he usually saw them), and he was still learning. After what he had learned about the three mercenaries he'd faced recently in Eagle River, it was safe to assume Wolfpaw werewolves would have complete mastery of their abilities, and that was why Lupo was willing to let the silver loads on his hip give him second-degree burns. He would heal quickly from any painful weals they caused, but he could defend himself if discovered.

He continued over the uneven terrain, picking his steps carefully. About a half mile more into the brush he began to spot the early defenses. A trip wire crossed the path down low, painted in green and brown camouflage splotches to make it disappear. Only his sharpened vision picked up the metal post around which the wire was wrapped. He followed the wire up a straight pine trunk and saw a brown plastic camera housing mounted a dozen feet above the ground.

That's rather old-fashioned of them, he thought, avoiding the spot easily. But the systems would likely increase in sophistication. Another half mile and the post he spotted held a photoelectric or laser cell—he couldn't tell for sure, but either way it was a beam he could easily spot. He dropped down low and examined the ground before him inch by inch.

There it is.

Another set of beam transmitters, these mounted just *off* the path in order to catch stealthier visitors such as he.

He smiled grimly.

They'd be getting trickier the farther he went from the highway. Did that mean there would be mines and automated guns as he approached the citadel itself? Were they willing to *terminate* intruders, rather than just neutralize them? Lupo felt frustration building. It was eminently possible he'd made the trip for naught. He wanted to penetrate and observe without being observed. It would do no good for him to be caught or wounded. And even being killed now seemed possible, if he wasn't careful. And they would know just how to do it.

Lupo considered making his way back to the car and abandoning his quest. There would be other ways. He had a contact who was checking into Wolfpaw's finances, but it was a delicate process and would take time. He had put out feelers for ex-members to contact him—a bogus version of him— "for a business opportunity." He'd considered an ad in *Soldier of Fortune*. But maybe it was best to stay under the radar, as far as Wolfpaw was concerned.

Lupo decided to chance another hundred yards or so. He moved off the ravine, left the path behind, and slowly wove his way through the tangle of brush, checking his wrist compass to make sure he wasn't wandering in circles but was, indeed, still heading for the headquarters quad, even if in a roundabout path.

Halfway through his determined distance, his ears picked up the sound of faraway undergrowth, crashing.

Someone running.

Jesus, this was more like it. Lupo focused on the sounds and tried to analyze what he heard.

Two sets of running feet.

Out of control.

Panicked running, uncaring about generating telltale sounds.

Running for their lives.

Lupo melted into the shadows cast by a thick clump of evergreens whose branches had intertwined like malformed arms, creating a sort of woodsy cupola just large enough to shelter his form. He was grateful for having recently learned about Ghost, the human scent neutralizer used by hunters to disappear, because it was the only way he knew to keep other wolves from scenting him out. He had sprayed himself and his gear thoroughly before leaving the car.

The sounds of running approached from east to west, not far ahead of where he was, perhaps around where he had decided to cut short his recon mission.

He heard panting, rapid breathing from two panicked runners, and then it sounded like they were separating, with one heading slightly toward where Lupo hid in his shelter and the other veering off farther away, roughly at the point where Lupo had determined he would quit.

The sudden *crump!* and flash of an explosion lit up the dark night and the woods where the farther of the two fugitives had headed. Shrapnel zipped through the underbrush like a scythe and Lupo made out the crash of a mutilated body flipped in the air coming back to earth in a heap of bone and tissue. He didn't have to see it to imagine it.

A mine. Pressure sensitive, probably.

Christ, he'd been right. And if there was one mine, there were bound to be others. Now the terrain around him took on a completely different aspect, dangerous and deadly.

The nearer fugitive crashed to a halt, his breath rasping like an out-of-control locomotive, a sob torn from his mouth as he also interpreted what had happened to his companion—and maybe saw a preview of his own fate.

He had to be barely a dozen yards away, catching his breath and sobbing, mumbling incoherently like an escapee from an insane asylum. Blubbering.

Lupo started to leave his shelter, figuring he could drag the helpless runner into the shadows and somehow avoid capture from whoever was pursuing.

The sound of the explosion had barely faded when he was suddenly very aware of who the pursuers were.

The howling reached both Lupo and the fugitive at exactly the same moment.

Not far. And a pack of them.

Wolves.

The fugitive cried out, a moan of fear and dismay, pain and resignation. He crashed forward a few feet, unsteady on what had to be rubbery legs after all the running, and moved away from Lupo's hiding place, effectively ruining Lupo's chances of helping him.

Lupo melted back into the shadowy wood coffin and prayed the Ghost spray would hold. He drew his Glock and ejected the magazine by feel, then worked his gloved hand into the leather pouch and fumbled out the sizzling metal of the silver-loaded magazine. He screwed on a silencer his source had recommended as one of the best, re-racked the slide, and held the pistol as it heated in his grip, the silver beginning to sting even through the layers of gunmetal and ABS polymer. It was pain he could bear, for a short while.

But was he crazy? Could he afford to jump into the radar like this? He'd wanted proof, and now he had some—to his satisfaction, for sure—but would it lead to his murder right along with the two unfortunates the pack was running down?

Scratch that. The *one* unfortunate, for the other was now a pile of body parts. Not that the wolves would mind the just-killed game. It just saved them some effort.

Lupo could tell the pack had split up, some apparently

tracking the one who'd tripped the mine. The others, maybe two, were approaching the survivor quickly but with practiced stealth, and were perhaps only moments—and yards—away. Lupo heard the fugitive stumble away, but any rhythm he'd managed in the headlong flight was now broken and his will was broken, and he was resigned to being caught and torn apart.

Lupo could sense it from his hiding place. He'd felt the same sense of resignation from his own prey, everything from rabbit to deer to—

Glock in hand, he prepared to defend himself if the wolves caught his scent, or simply tripped over him in their own rush to bring down their prey.

JESSIE

Huge square timbers swept upward above her as she stood inside the doorway, six of them converging to a point three stories high. Huge triangular opaque glass panels set between the timbers let in soft white light during the day, but now they were black. The interior of the hexagonal entry was ringed with fanciful, Indian-themed carvings fashioned from driftwood. Horses, bears, wolves, and other totems seemed to dance over the heads of the pilgrims who streamed in through the main entrance. Off to the side was a tall counter staffed by three burly security guards. Jessie smiled at them and waved, thinking that *burly* would describe pretty much every security guard in the place.

"Hello, Doc Hawkins!"

She turned to see yet another blue-suited guard approaching from the building's side wing, where the offices were located.

"Hey, Bobby! Nice to see you."

"Nice to see you, too, Doc. Gonna do some late-night gambling again?"

Jessie frowned, but forced herself to smile over it.

Bobby Burningwood was a local who had risen to the rank of lieutenant in the reservation police, but had left the force when the casino administration had advertised in an effort to beef up its security force. Bobby was an ex-marine who'd easily passed his test and risen again to head of the night-shift security. He'd seen her a lot, lately.

"Maybe," she said, noncommittally. He was close now, and she reached out and grasped his hand. Dry, firm, a man's hand. She wasn't sure why she enjoyed touching him. It wasn't something she did often, but Bobby was such a good guy, she didn't feel guilty.

And right then she was a little annoyed with Nick, wherever he was.

Hell, she knew damn well where he was. He'd discussed his suspicions with her for two months. They'd argued about what he wanted to do. They'd resolved nothing. He'd decided to follow his hunches. So on top of the usual danger their relationship engendered, she could see Nick adding to his troubles willingly.

Neither of them had healed after Sam had turned the shotgun on himself that terrible night on the beach, when a werewolf bite had sentenced him to a double life full of blood and lies. He'd taken the silver loads as the ultimate antidote to the curse before it could even set in, and in so doing had abandoned his friends, who had come to rely on his wisdom and guidance.

Both Nick and Jessie felt the hole in their lives, and it had begun to eat at their relationship. Except for the lovemaking, which was still phenomenal and connected them in deeper ways than they even admitted, their few days a month spent together had become an endless series of sniping and bickering. Over nothing, sometimes. Over life and death, other times. Last month, there had been a blowout over this one.

"I'm taking a few days off and going down to Atlanta," Lupo said in the middle of dinner.

She chewed the bit of steak she had sliced from his slab of rare meat. Often she made one huge steak and sliced a few strips off the done end, letting Nick enjoy the rest of it the way he preferred, charred on the outside and barely warmed on the inside. It was a concession to his wolf side, eating as close to the earth as possible whenever he could.

After chewing, she looked into his eyes. They could be cruel. She'd seen it. But they were not cruel this night. They were hardset, maybe a bit too straightforward. He knew she'd fight, try to talk him out of it.

"Why do you feel you have to pursue this?" she asked. She already knew the answer, but what else could she do?

"I think Sam would agree with my concern. I have to follow the trail. I have to find out more than what we already know, and there's no one else to deal with the consequences."

She expected his line of reasoning. She even agreed with it in principle.

But why did it have to be him? Ever since they'd found each other, found their deep connection, life and his "curse" had spit bad luck and trouble at them every chance it had. They might never had gotten together without Martin Stewart's revenge spree, true, but she wasn't very likely to give the monster any credit. She hoped he was rotting in whatever hell existed, and indeed she hoped one existed just for him. If ever somebody deserved the classical torment of the fiery circles, Stewart was it.

She reached across the table and took his rough hand in her own smooth fingers. She marveled at how gentle his coarse hands could be when they massaged her skin, her nipples, her secret places. She wanted to lean over and kiss it, to take it and place it over her heart to prove to him that he was toying with her emotions by once again threatening to drag them into dangerous times. She thought he would feel her heart's fear-flutter. She hoped he would. But would he ignore what he felt?

"Nick, I know you want closure, but this is the kind of thing that never ends. Every layer leads to another layer. We barely managed to make it out of the last one. Tom—look at how Tom Arnow couldn't handle it."

She knew she'd made a tactical error as soon as she said the words.

His lips curled in sarcasm. "Tom Arnow didn't have to run away from it. He could have faced it, the way you did, the way Sam did, the way even that idiot Davison managed to face it."

"He's an idiot because he's on the council?" She felt the need to defend Rick Davison, who had taken the lead on the council's stalled casino plans and had finally driven them to near completion. "He's an idiot because—"

"Let's not talk about him," Nick pleaded. He took one last bloody strip from the steak, swallowed it almost whole, then pushed his plate away. "I know it's hard for you. But I have responsibilities. As a cop, sure, but also as a—as what I am. Sometimes I can't even say it. I feel cursed not only by what I am, but also by the fact that I'm stuck setting things right. I can't just dial the phone and palm off the problem. Believe me, I wish I could."

Another dinner ruined.

But then his eyes held hers and she fell into the depth of his sincerity.

She was being a bitch, accusing him as if he chose to disrupt their lives. She knew he wanted a stable life as much as she did. His hadn't been anything like stable, so he lusted for stability. It was just that, well, everything always seemed to blow up in their faces and tear them asunder.

"If you go down there, will you be satisfied with just observing?" She touched him again, reluctant to let him go both physically and metaphorically. "If you go, will the knowledge be enough?"

He was silent for a moment. "No," he said. "If what I suspect is true, then I'll have to act. I'll have to do something. I'll have to—"

"You wouldn't have to do anything. Just let things be. You could. You wouldn't have to put yourself in danger again. You could find another way."

"There is no other way, Jess. You know that." His fingers pressed hers. He wanted her to understand. "This isn't something you call the cops for."

She smiled sardonically. "Unless that cop is Nick Lupo. Then you can call him. Right?"

He laughed once. "Right. Like the movie. 'Who you gonna call?' Who else?"

"Doc, you okay?" It was Bobby's voice, and suddenly her whereabouts swirled back into focus.

"Huh?" She had wandered away for what seemed like a long time. Hopefully it was only a few seconds.

"I was asking if you were okay." The big man smiled disarmingly. "When I asked if you were gonna play a little, your eyes kinda seemed to look far away."

She tried to laugh it off. "It was a long day today, a double shift. I guess I'm more tired than I thought."

"Yeah, I heard that flu's going around. It's a bitch, too. Half the boys are down with it. Some of us are pulling three straight shifts. But some guys, they *never* get sick."

She shivered a little. Maybe it was the night's chill, finally getting to her. Maybe it was the proverbial walk across her grave. Maybe it was something happening to Nick, *right then*, that very moment.

"Are you feeling okay?" she asked, trying to turn the conversation away from her. She'd seen a couple other of the rez casino guards come in for something to relieve the flu symptoms, but not Bobby.

Damn, that insistent "casino note" was incredibly loud to her ears tonight.

It was like the Muslim call to prayer. She wondered if there was something subliminal about it, calculated to draw weak personalities to the slots. To any of the tables, for that matter.

"Yeah, I'm like a bull. That's what my daddy used to say."

"Good for you." She nodded, almost forgetting what her question had been. She'd better hit a slot or a table soon. The itch was coming back. She started to edge away.

"Oh, hey, I almost forgot," Bobby said. "There's a couple shows coming up you and Nick might like."

"Yeah?"

"Kansas, in July. They're on tour with both violinists, and rumors are, Livgren's gonna join 'em. And the Alan Parsons Live Project's coming in September. That's your thing, isn't it?"

"Sure is! Good memory. Thanks, Bobby."

Nick would be thrilled about the Kansas news, and Jessie couldn't think of anything better than hearing her favorite Project songs performed live. The casino theater seated about six hundred and had started to suck acts from their national small-venue tours, and fans had begun to stream north to see them. The hope was that concertgoers would get there early, gamble, see the show, then eat in one of the casino's restaurants, then gamble some more. It was win-win for the casino, if they could draw people through their doors who rarely gambled. Or get them to stay overnight—though the hotel was still under construction.

The original casino-complex site had been abandoned after the pond was drained and all those bodies pulled out of the black water, lined up like grotesque mummies on the gravel beach. That photo in the local paper had killed everybody's enthusiasm for the casino in its original location, and the new council had moved fast under Davison to grant the project space in the center of the reservation in order to rescue it from the superstitious. And what gambler isn't superstitious on some level?

That was how the Great Northern Casino had come to shine its light into the rear of her hospital, right in the center of the main business district. Nobody wanted the vibe left by the serial killer and his several dozen decaying victims to underlay the foundations of a business that would depend on people's interpretation of Fate and Fortuna. There wasn't a Death card in a traditional deck, but as modern cards were derived from the tarot, the reaper's shadow wasn't so easily dismissed.

Jessie cursed the day the council voted to relocate the entire project, dumping it into her backyard.

She made a mental note to tell Nick about the shows, then told Bobby to let her know when the tickets went on sale.

"You bet, Doc. I'll do that."

She thanked the big man and pulled away with a final wave and smile, heading through the maze of video-poker and slot-machine rows, straight ranks of roulette and blackjack tables, and the many cashier's cages tucked into the woodsy decor. The interior of the casino proper was like a barn with faux trees as pillars and imitation Indian cultural icons and animal totems spread on ledges along the outer walls. The crowd wasn't huge, but unused machines were hard to spot. Only a few gaming tables were covered and out of action, and not many empty seats greeted her at the others.

Jessie angled toward the wing tucked adjacent to the theater doors, found a quiet block of quarter slots, and slid onto the red vinyl barstool perched in front of one colorful slot machine. The machine's screen came to life as if it knew its next victim had arrived.

Jessie glanced around and spotted no acquaintances. Then she took the Dreamquester's Club card from her pocket and slid it into the lit-up slot. The window blinked and showed her credit line, automatically converted to quarters. Almost five thousand of them.

Over a thousand dollars.

She didn't worry about the fact that the casino took money and intentionally reduced it to simple numbers, allowing people to slowly disassociate the two until losing the one didn't seem as bad as losing the other.

Nick would have called it a mind-fuck.

She pressed the 3 CREDIT button and watched the virtual dials spin dizzyingly. A few seconds later, three different pictures lined up at the end of the "spin."

Lemon. Cherry. Dollar sign.

Instantaneously, three credits—three quarters—were subtracted from the total on her card. She hit the button again and watched the entire sequence repeat itself, trying to focus on the dials and their multiple pictograms as if she could freeze them in place and make each spin a winner.

Every time the reels ended their simulated spinning, the pictures were a different combination.

Jessie's eyes glazed over and her hand hit the PLAY 3 button automatically, ignoring the vestigial lever on the side of the machine. Most accomplished gamblers ignore the "one arm" part of the slot machine—it's too slow.

If someone had stopped her between any two spins and asked, she would not have been able to answer the simple question, *Why?*

She let her fear of Nick's new intensity, and his new obsession, sink below the vaguely compelling need to watch the dials spin their cycles of futility.

She pressed the button and the rapidly shifting color bands reflected on her face.

CODENAME: WAGNER

Wagner watched from the bland minivan until the quarry left the house, then exited the vehicle and broached the high-security door and alarm with a series of devices from a black shoulder bag.

Black-bag job, Wagner thought. *Aptly named.*

The luxury condominium was everything Wagner expected, and maybe a bit more. Every room, every corner, yielded something about *her* that couldn't be learned from her patented television image. There were interests, likes and dislikes, all arranged for anyone to discover who could also analyze. And Wagner was good at analysis. Very good indeed. While employed by Wolfpaw Security, Wagner had become a top field commander of "special shock troops," as they were sometimes euphemistically known.

Wagner had taken the operatic name—it was from Richard Wagner, the composer, not *Robert* Wagner, the B actor—because it matched the worldview that included a history set deep into the proud ashes of the Third Reich. But this was rarely talked about and acknowledged. It was merely there, lying in the deep background of the company's roots. Useful when needed, but generally left unconfirmed and uncommunicated. General recruits had no need to know. And Wolfpaw subscribed to the need-to-know doctrine.

Now Wagner moved through the woman's lair like a ghost, touching little with the latex gloves worn as precaution. Wagner checked the freezer and the trash bin and nodded. There were clues if one knew where to look for them.

Twenty minutes were all it took, and the door was resecured, the alarm rearmed, and the ghost was gone, past the oblivious doorman on duty.

Now Wagner had worked up an appetite.

The nearby Barker Island park was like a smorgasbord.

In the deep thicket, a likely subject huddled under a ratty blanket and a couple of tattered overcoats. Paper bags were situated around his emaciated body as a windbreak. Even Wausau had been reintroduced to the homeless after the long-spiraling economy.

The bags were no protection from Wagner's claws and jaws.

What the ghost left behind were the torn-apart remains of yet another homeless man. His half-gnawed intestines were strung around him and over the park bench like semaphore flags on a sloop.

This made the third such set of remains found in a city park.

Not counting the series of hikers who would never share pictures of Rib Mountain with anyone again.

After the meal, the howling caused every other homeless man and woman within hearing range to dig deeper into their makeshift shelters, clutch their homemade weapons more tightly, and pray to a god they had proof didn't exist. Or at least didn't care about them.

The howling went on and on.

Later, it was replaced by sirens.

Wagner disappeared again, tonight's work done.

CHAPTER THREE

LUPO
SOMEWHERE IN GEORGIA

The howling stopped suddenly, and Lupo knew why.

One of the wolves reached the prey sooner than the others and brought him down in a crash of limbs and brush. The fugitive gave a single long yelp of pain and surprise, but it was a tired one, and then he screamed as the snarling increased in volume, and the human scream was cut off abruptly.

The bastard's torn out his throat, Lupo thought, gripping the Glock as hard as he could manage, with the silver burning his palm and fingers, guilt washing over him in waves for allowing the fugitive to be taken almost under his nose like that.

Christ!

Lupo almost stepped out once again, but then his sensitive ears picked up the sounds he dreaded.

Soft padding of paws on the forest floor. An occasional snap of a twig. Sounds too vague to be heard if he weren't as sensitive as he was.

One of the other wolves, a maverick, was approaching *his* hiding place, sniffing loudly as he caught some sort of scent. Had Lupo forgotten to spray something? Mentally he took inventory.

Shit, my gloves. They'd been in his pockets.

Idiot.

It was almost too late, but he shoved his gloved hands under his armpits in a last-ditch effort to hide the alien scent. Not far away, he heard the sounds of at least two wolves feeding on the carcass of their prey, who was now probably already disemboweled and half-devoured.

But a low growl came from nearby, and Lupo's eye was close enough to a gap in the gnarled wood of the cocoon that housed him to see a large gray wolf circling. It growled continuously and its fangs dripped as it drove itself into a half frenzy, trying to catch the scent of the intruder.

Lupo considered his options. There was no saving the two fugitives, and at this point making his own exit from the infiltrated portion of the compound was not a given, either. One wolf would alert the others and the pack *would* run him down. He couldn't fight them all, and he couldn't outrun them all. His only choice lay in the element of surprise, and the load in his Glock—though even the pistol had become almost too sizzling for his skin to tolerate the burning. He forcibly locked the pain out of his mind. Life and death trumped any temporary discomfort, and his healing powers would take care of the burns afterward.

If he survived.

His hand—especially palm and fingers—sizzled as if he held it in an open flame, and it was all he could do to avoid screaming, dropping the pistol like a naked torch, and finding a way to cool his burn.

Lupo bit down on the pain and mentally separated himself from the sensations shooting up his forearm to his brain. He waited for the hunter wolf to turn his back on him and edge a bit closer, and—at just the right moment, if he timed it right—he would make his move.

Not far from them the feeding continued. The sound of fanged jaws ripping into the hot flesh and working at the limbs and torso was unmistakable.

It reminded Lupo of his own hunting.

But it could sound like his death.

Hand blackening, skin sliding off the bone like overdone poultry, he blocked the intense pain from his brain and waited for the right moment.

JESSIE

It was later, and she was taking a break from the slots.

She stood near one of the snack bars and drank passable coffee from a cardboard container. Anything to make you feel at ease. Coffee, tea, juice, soda. Booze, for the high rollers. All comped so you could spend your money without distraction.

She watched.

There was a general flow of people moving like a gentle eddy across the vast casino floor. The Native American art motifs dominated walls and pillars, which were covered to resemble primitive tent poles. Faux stretched animal skins made of cloth or rubber were used as screens to separate a row of slots from a row of busy blackjack tables. In a corner, round poker tables were occupied by serious, squint-eyed men and the occasional woman. Guards made sure spectators kept outside the roped area. In the center of the gigantic room, eight roulette wheels on tables stood as a clump. They were crowded even though it was well-known that roulette's odds were the worst in the casino. There was something about watching the wheel spin.

O, Fortuna!

The green field on which people lost their stacks of chips seemed so damn prosperous.

Jessie finished her drink and nodded at a couple of the blue-suited security guys she knew by sight. They patrolled in easy walks, checking for unusual behavior. Occasionally they accosted people on cell phones and gently, tactfully, relieved them of the devices, which were banned. A receipt would be handed out and the phones kept at the security counter.

She found a new slot machine and watched its slot swallow her card and reward her with a happy little electronic tune that seemed to escalate until she finally pushed the BET button.

Within minutes she was engrossed in the action on her screen—the rolling reels, the pictograms snapping in place with electronic thunks and bleeps, the flashing lights that washed over her in waves.

The number in the card-slot window dwindled dangerously and occasionally jumped with tiny wins intended to encourage further play. It hovered around the same figure, but trended downward. Jessie didn't worry about it. There were still plenty of credits, and the night was young enough.

The incipient headache she ignored, as she did the growling in her belly. The smell of sweat and smoke wafted over her as the stools nearby changed hands and new gamblers replaced the old.

Well, they were interchangeable. She glanced at them and half-smiled. They were almost comical in their ordinary predictability.

Where the hell was Nick right now?

Goddamn him, where was he?

Nick! Why aren't you here? With me?

I need you, too.

She pressed the MAXIMUM BET button and watched yet another empty spin.

LUPO
SOMEWHERE IN GEORGIA

The scent of sweat-wet fur momentarily suffused his nostrils and he felt the Creature—*his* Creature—slide up, close to the surface, and hover just underneath.

He suppressed. He talked the Creature down because he knew, Lupo *knew*, that in this case his Creature wasn't up to the task of losing the pack, or fighting them. Survival meant human and Creature working together, and he didn't have a good record of that. Not yet.

Always a first time.

The snuffling of the curious wolf was merely feet away, outside the wooden cocoon. The intruder was clearly puzzled by the hint of a scent surrounded by a complete dearth of scent—the Ghost doing its thing, but Lupo's gloves giving him away like a softly tolling bell.

Four paws softly trod the needle-covered ground. First one, then two, three. The fourth paw stepped gingerly down on some low undergrowth and the wolf was almost past.

But then he stopped. A soft growl emerged from the sharp muzzle.

Lupo ignored the maddening, blazing sear of the silver-loaded pistol and set his legs, his muscles tightening.

The wolf had found the chink in Lupo's Ghost armor, the human tang that hovered around his damnable gloves.

Before the wolf could process the direction and turn his head to check the gnarled tree trunk that seemed thick but was instead hollow and filled by a human, Lupo hurdled the beast like a horse without a saddle and straddled the wiry body.

The wolf reacted quickly, attempting to buck his unwanted rider upward, jaws snapping back from side to side, looking for purchase, but Lupo dug in and—while still in motion—swung the Glock's silencer-bulbous muzzle right to the rear of the bucking wolf's head and ground it into the fur.

He squeezed the trigger, once. Twice.

No silencer can truly suppress the sound of a gunshot, because the gas escapes in an explosive rush, the bullet slamming through the barrel to its target. But the sound of Lupo's two gunshots was muffled by the wolf's fur and the head itself. The slide's harsh backward clacking as it loaded the next round (and again) seemed impossibly loud to his ears, but he could do nothing about it. With his other hand, in the meantime, he ground the wolf's muzzle shut, enough to stifle the monster's squealing.

The two silver slugs tore through the wolf's cranium and blew out brains, eyeballs, and most of its jaws.

It was a miracle Lupo hadn't shot his own hand off in the process.

The squirming body beneath him sagged onto the ground as the bullets expanded and blew the head apart.

Lupo flew over the dead wolf's deflated corpse as if it were a bicycle he'd braked too suddenly.

He landed in the brush, warm blood and bone coating his hand and most of his clothing.

Behind him, the corpse flickered from wolf to human

countless times in a second. Finally it settled into the form of a naked male human with most of his head missing.

Lupo pulled up, half on his knees, and made sure the enemy was indeed terminal. From what he could tell, the rest of the pack had not heard their companion's execution. The searing, blinding pain in his hand and arm continued to jab his brain like a scalding blade. He avoided giving in to it and shrieking uncontrollably only by force of will.

Beyond the circle clump of close-set pines, the other wolves barely paused in their snarling feasting, clearly too occupied with the fresh carrion to notice.

He was about to stand upright, when the nearby undergrowth rustled again. He dropped down onto the forest floor and ducked behind the corpse. From out of the woods came another wolf, advancing slowly. His eyes locked onto the body of the dead werewolf.

Lupo had already extended the Glock. As soon as his eyes met those of the wolf, he squeezed off five shots in rapid succession.

Lupo smelled the wolf's sizzling flesh and his own. The wolf flopped around like a grounded fish, the silver doing its worst to his insides. But his jaws opened and he struggled visibly—he would manage to raise the alarm even if it took a single howl. Lupo still gripped the Glock, his hand burning up as if he'd held it in an open flame for hours. He squeezed the trigger again and again until the slide locked open with a loud metallic click. The wolf's head disappeared in a burst of crimson gore. He hadn't been able to make a sound.

But now Lupo was out of silver ammo.

He had a minute, no more, to make a decision.

He stood and stumbled to his just-vacated shelter, tossed the Glock gently into the tree trunk, and stripped off his clothing as quickly as he could. Thankfully, even though his gun hand felt as if he'd shoved it into a blast furnace, it began

to tingle with magical healing as soon as the silver was separated from his skin.

He slipped a thumb-drive-sized black plastic housing from
a pocket and plucked off a paper strip covering one side,
flicked a tiny button on the front, then stuck the unit onto a
branch just above the bole of the tree, where it seemed to
disappear. He made sure the exposed rubbery cement held it
securely against the bark and stepped away.

As soon as his clothing was likewise tossed into the hollow tree and he stood shivering in his bare skin, Lupo called
upon the Creature. He visualized himself on four paws, his
body rippling with muscle and covered with smooth fur. So
close to the surface was it hovering, that he felt himself going over immediately and he froze for a moment in his wolf
skin, trying to meld his human side and the Creature's side
more quickly than usual, the transition still causing him a
certain discomfort when the two psyches met and attempted
to combine, clash, separate, and finally coexist.

The human with the monstrous.

Man and wolf.

Lupo exerted control over the primordial wild brain, convincing through mental images that the enemy pack was
too close, too well trained, and too great in number for him
to stand and fight. The pain in his hand translated as a
sharp ache in his paw, but it was a diminishing pain as his
blood flowed to the area burned by the silver. The pain
would disappear quicker the longer he spent in this form.

For once, the Creature did not resist his human handler's
imperative. Often Lupo was forced into a battle of wills.
This time his fur ruffled with alarm and anger and survival
instinct. He gathered his four strong legs under him and
bounded away in the direction of the road, where, the Creature knew, awaited the means of their escape.

Behind him, the other wolves continued to feed, oblivious for now to what had happened nearby.

But Lupo knew they'd finish their feast any moment. They would miss their companions. They would easily sniff out the death struggle, and then the corpses.

Then they'd sniff an interloper, another wolf.

And the hunt would begin anew.

He didn't wait.

HEATHER

She looked at herself in the full-length mirror mounted on the closet door. The walk-in closet was almost as large as her bedroom. It was so large, it had its own closet. That was where she kept some of her toys.

She looked at herself carefully. She was gloriously naked. She cupped first one breast with a strong yet delicate hand, then the other. She scanned her perfectly-shaped nipples. She moved one hand down her flat stomach, past the big dimple of her belly-button, and down farther. Her pubic mound was smooth, hairless. She could see her engorged labia peeking out from between her lean, muscular thighs.

She touched herself and tingled.

Then she half-turned so she could catch a view of her buttocks.

Need another mirror, she thought. *To complete the picture.*

From what she could see in this one mirror, she was perfect.

She had shortened her natural blonde hair so it didn't cascade down her back anymore. The station had received dozens of e-mail complaints.

She smiled at herself, basking in the perfection of her face, her features, her teeth, her flashing eyes. All natural. No enhancements, surgery, Botox, anything. Even if people thought so. She wore no makeup.

She was fantastic. When she put effort into it, she was beyond spectacular. She had always been, of course.

But now she was even more fantastic. Now she had become a creature of myth.

She thought the words that way: *a creature of myth.*

It had improved an already-perfect package. It had heightened, tucked, muscled, and streamlined what had been already superb.

She touched the skin on her shoulder. The scar had healed long ago, but she remembered the ripping, tearing, and the blood. She had been locked in the throes of sexual abandon, her beautiful young lover—the mysterious Tef—snuggled deep inside her, when she'd reached back and felt fur sprouting along his skin. And then he had growled while driving into her, and he had Changed *inside* her. *His erection had Changed.* She had felt ecstasy mixed with shock and surprise. And then he had taken a bite out of her shoulder, his teeth turned into fangs, his body no longer human. She *knew,* even though she couldn't see him. She had screamed, and she had felt his no-longer-human body tense for another great, tearing bite.

And like a sitcom cliché, his cell had rung and he'd been forced to take the call, and she had barely managed to hold him off while locked in the motel bathroom.

It wasn't long before she'd thrown in with two cops and a woman doctor and an Indian, and the night was a blur, but she had shot Tef three times with silver-tipped bullets, and one of the cops had finished him. She had watched the two men turning from human to wolf and back again as they struggled for supremacy, but Tef had been mortally wounded, and the cop emerged victorious, if a little the worse for wear. She had known, even then, what she was becoming.

And a little clear-eyed thought had made it *all right.*

Now it was all good.

She felt the growl work its way up her throat, but suppressed it.

She had learned fast. She'd had no choice. But learning had been . . . fun.

She made a pirouette in front of the mirror, then set about dressing for work. Work *and* play.

CHAPTER FOUR

LUPO
SOMEWHERE IN GEORGIA

The wolf crept away from the scene of his momentary lapse of reason, quietly putting some distance between him and the frenzied wolves.

Lupo steered the Creature as gently through the pines as possible, knowing too much rustling of the undergrowth could bring the pack down on his back. Plus there were clearly other wolves present on the compound. The Creature's ears picked up more howling from far away, perhaps the center of the complex. If he'd been in human form, he would have laughed sardonically. He'd wondered if there were other wolves at Wolfpaw. Now he had reason to wonder if there were Wolfpaw employees who *weren't* werewolves.

Jesus Christ, they'd named their damned company after themselves, like a fucking joke, and he'd been too blind to see it. What did they have to do, come calling in cartoon wolf masks to get him to see the way things were?

His paws stepped carefully through the greenery rendered black by the deep night around him. Through the Creature's eyes, Lupo suddenly saw that on his way in he had barely missed several trip-wire cameras and even a few mines. The telltale triggers winked at him from below layers of pine needles scattered to conceal them. The Creature's paws avoided these easily, and Lupo wondered if he had merely been lucky, or if his wolf's instincts had been operating in his human subconscious. Or perhaps he had set off some security unmonitored cameras that could be checked later for his image.

Damn, he thought. *Maybe Jessie was right.*

Behind him, somewhere nearer the center of the main compound, a second pack seemed to be on the verge of meeting up with the first. The howling intensified, driving him farther into the shadows. Adroitly avoiding booby traps he'd missed earlier, the Creature ran when the running was good, and crept cautiously when the pines closed in or their branches seemed to reach down and try to snag him for the hunters.

The two packs converged, and the howling turned angry and aggressive.

Lupo figured they'd found their murdered companions. A few seconds of confusion passed quickly, and then the sudden silence turned ominous. They were clearly getting on his trail, checking for his scent in widening concentric circles.

A minute later, ragged howls reached his ears and he knew the game had turned against him. From the variety of voices he could identify, he calculated maybe a dozen full-grown individuals, all in wolf form, all after *him*.

His only advantage was past, the silence in which he had done the killing and slipped away. Now the distance between him and his potential killers was nearly irrelevant, as they knew the terrain and he didn't.

He felt the Creature heating up, the uncontrollable rage ratcheting exponentially, his instincts setting off alarm bells as the hunters made themselves known. A set of three—a "squad," Lupo thought—seemed to be approaching more rapidly, more directly than the others. The experts, the teachers. The deadlier ones. *Shit.*

Lupo felt the Creature begin to alter his response, his brain switching from fear to aggression. Adrenaline flowed, twanging through his veins like lean lava. As if he might turn and fight the pursuers.

No!

Lupo brought more of his hard-fought control of the Creature's brain into play, forcing the more primitive thought process aside and reinforcing the new priority.

Escape.

Fight another day.

Standing and fighting would simply give the rest of the pack time to close in and surround him, so even if the odds of three to one proved somewhat desirable, it was a fool's errand and he'd regret it when the remainder of the pack arrived to sink their fangs into his belly. Lupo fed the Creature an image of death and pain he hoped would change the new inclination.

Slowly, wasting at least a few precious seconds he couldn't regain, he felt his human will making the desired impact on the Creature's escape instinct. His paws picked up their rhythm again and he began to gallop, the scent in his nostrils that of the highway and the car he'd left hidden around a curve in the road. The Creature was now committed to leading him there.

But the hesitation, however brief, proved costly. The Creature's ears pricked up—

Too late, much too late . . .

—when there was a sudden crashing in the nearby undergrowth, and two black figures broke through the greenery and entered his field of vision, their snouts open, fangs bared, snarling and foaming as if rabid.

The Creature snatched control from Lupo and whirled to attack the new threat.

Lupo might have considered that his wild side believed a good defense to be a true offense, but he simply did not have the time to formulate the thought. Adrenaline and instinct took charge of muscle and fang, and all he could do was get out of the way.

The two attacking wolves were taken by surprise by the Creature's sudden switch from escape to fighting mode. Their own aggressiveness was blunted as the muscular black wolf closed on them with incredible swiftness. His fangs tore and ripped through the snout of the first opponent even before the other wolf could howl for reinforcements or signal his own fear.

Lupo's Creature snagged the opponent's jaws with his own and ripped sideways, tearing through bone and muscle, taking chunks of pelt and tossing them aside in a red mist. Without any hesitation at all, his eyes on the second hesitating wolf, the Creature dipped back toward the devastated opponent and clamped jaws onto its neck, ripping out his throat with one more economical motion of tearing teeth.

The wolf was dead before its body sagged onto the pine-needle-covered forest floor.

The Creature turned toward the other wolf, but he was already retreating, running for its life. The approaching pack, led by the third outrider, was still moments away.

Lupo let the Creature turn its attention to the remainder of the distance yet to cover. He flew toward the road, the taste of wolf blood sweet on his palate, the roaring of victory making his veins sing.

Lupo lost himself in the Creature then, giving himself over to his wolf side with no remaining hesitation.

Paws made fleeter by the easy kill, enemy blood tingling on his tongue, Lupo and Creature united and soon reached the outer edge of the Wolfpaw property. The howls of rage seemed to fade behind them.

Lupo skidded onto the road, his nails raising sparks as he ate the distance to the vehicle the human had left parked in a copse just off the concrete.

Lupo thought through his transition, and within fractions of a moment he was opening the car door with the keys left hidden in their magnetic holder. Forethought he had almost not even realized had become second nature.

He was on the road when he sensed the wolves reaching the outer perimeter of their property, forced to stop and watch his taillights recede in the darkness.

Only then did he acknowledge the fact that it was cold, and he was naked, shivering on the car seat.

"So, was it worth it?"

Lupo shrugged. "I think I know more than I want to know," he said. "Shit, I think they're *all* wolves."

"As you suspected," Ghost Sam said, reaching for the heater knob. "You really *knew*, deep down inside."

"Yeah."

"What will you do about it?" The Indian pointedly faced forward, as if giving Lupo a modesty perimeter.

"I wish I knew," Lupo whispered after a long pause. The wheels turned rapidly beneath them, heading for town, leaving the Wolfpaw compound behind. But an armed pursuit could even now be nosing onto the highway.

He took the stubby receiver off the dashboard and flicked it on. And listened.

Perhaps his course of action would be decided by what, if anything, he heard in the next few minutes.

He was in luck. Angry voices filled the car. He tried to pick out individuals, but it was difficult. There was a confusion of voices speaking over each other, until the voice of an officer cut through them all.

"—fucking bastard—"

"—shot his head off—"

"—goddamn murderer—"

"—never had a chance—"

"Not true. Shut up, all of you. They had their noses. They failed. He got the drop on them, and he never should have. What else?"

"The silver indicates he's human, sir. No wolf could handle silver. I'm hurting just being near it."

"You fool, I can still smell his skin broiling. He has a tremendous threshold for pain. He held that pistol even while his hand was melting."

Grumbling and muttering from farther away, indicating the group was huddled around the corpses.

The fucker's turned it into a lecture. He's dangerous.

Lupo imagined them standing naked around the scene, shivering in the chill, their teacher taking them through the lessons they should learn. He was almost jealous. Nobody had ever helped him with his condition, or its consequences. No one until Caroline Stewart, anyway. The first great love of his life.

And he had killed her.

"—got away in a fucking car."

The officer barked, "Beta Squad, report!"

"Checked the highway perimeter, sir. The scent is like us, as you expected. Nothing else to report."

"Nothing else? What about perimeter cameras?"

"Officer of the watch is checking the digital recordings, sir, but he reports it looks like the guy parked out of sight of any cameras. About two dozen vehicles drove past, so it's impossible—"

"Get on *all* of those. We'll run plates, work through the list. We'll get the bastard."

"Sir!" a voice shouted near the transmitter's mike.

Rustling sounds obliterated the rest of the voices for a few seconds.

"Jesus! The bastard's been listening to us—"

A loud crash, a fraction of a second of raised voices, and then another crash, suddenly cut off.

Lupo sighed. They'd spotted the bug, smashed it. Then he chuckled. That officer would bite somebody's head off. Rather than destroying it, they could have used it to track him. Or at least fed him some false information useful to them. But an overzealous and angry young pup had clearly acted with typical brashness and wiped out their best chances.

Outside, the dark outskirts of Eatonton came into view and he slowed down. Wouldn't do to be stopped for speeding while driving in the nude. He had a motel room on the far side of town. He would stop there and dress, grab up his few belongings, and be on the road in minutes. He wasn't worried about their ability to spot his car from the camera recordings, because the car's plates could never be traced to him. They were a dead end, as was the car itself.

"You're not surprised, are you?" Sam said.

Lupo shook his head. "Well, a little. I thought werewolves might have infiltrated the ranks of Wolfpaw. But I'm convinced all of Wolfpaw is—"

"Like you?"

"Yeah."

"Now what?"

"Heading home. I think they'll come after us, Jessie and me. Maybe Tom."

Ghost Sam nodded and left Lupo to his own thoughts.

There was planning to do.

The road narrowed as he traversed the sleeping town, then widened again, and he followed the main road to the turnoff, then made a couple unneeded turns just to check for any surveillance. There didn't seem to be any.

Lupo saw the motel sign. The neon vacancy sign fluttered red in the darkness. The long, old-fashioned, L-shaped building was a throwback to the fifties. A semitrailer took up half the lot, but a small BMW and a couple nondescript sedans were the only other vehicles. Lupo drove to the end unit, parked, and waited to make sure no one was in evidence lurking about.

He put his head in his hands and considered his options. None of them were desirable.

From the Journals of Caroline Stewart
November 30, 1981

The shadows are deepening. Winter's coming. I'm shivering at the mere thought of crossing the Mall from the Union to Enderis Hall when the gale-force sharp-as-knives winds off the lake lash the wide-open space. Madison has an underground tunnel system perfect for such wintry expeditions—why, oh why, don't we? I've heard there are tunnels, but not for public use. They're probably creepy.

I think these days my shivers are related to more than just the coming cold. As much as I look forward to keeping warm in bed next to Nick, I also dread the worry that assails me from the moment I wake up to when I finally succumb to sleep again. It's true, between those times there's some very satisfying lovemaking. But . . .

The dread and worry arise from doubts I have about my original assessment of Nick's condition. Although there were signs of his nascent ability to control his "episodes" from the beginning, it was also true that most often the moon was the only influence and he could not refuse its imperatives. On the nights of a full moon, Nick is no more—the "Creature" takes over. Instinct and appetites, the needs of a wolf, take control. But over time, we were able to determine that Nick's mind can be active even while the Creature roams free. And if that was true, as indicated by fragmented memories Nick had of his episodes, then the possibility of control could not be far off. Clearly, if Nick could begin to exert control, then what he once considered an illness, a disease, would begin to look more like a gift. But recently there have been setbacks in our experiments.

Jerry Boone's suicide is the latest and most worrisome development in the backslide. Dr. Boone was one of the best local proponents and practitioners of regression therapy, and his off-the-books session with Nick seemed promising to us. Whatever occurred during that session may have led to Boone's suicide. He was found with a self-inflicted gunshot wound to the head amid the shambles of his office, all his books knocked to the floor, apparently by Boone himself. This was indicative of a man who suddenly felt his knowledge, his training, had let him down. He must have felt useless, and what could have reduced him to this state could have been the revelation of Nick's alternate nature. Boone was grounded in reality, and if his reality was shaken enough—or his conception of reality, I suppose—then he might have become suicidal.

But here's where I start to feel some doubt.

What if he didn't become suicidal?

1978
NICK

The money changed hands quickly, invisibly, in the library. Nick took the cash eagerly and it disappeared into his pocket in a folded-up wad. He rummaged in his backpack and came up with the package wrapped in tissue and sealed in a Baggie, like a sandwich. He handed it over to Josh, whose hands seemed like arthritic claws.

"Remember," Nick whispered so none of the other kids at nearby study tables could hear, "you never got those from me. You use them and get into trouble, I don't wanna get dragged into it."

"That was the deal, man. I got it." The packet disappeared into Josh's backpack and he zipped it shut.

They shook hands solemnly.

The deal had been struck a month ago, during the bus ride home. The bus had just pulled out after its ten-minute layover at the school.

"Hey."

Josh had startled him as he read his book. Nick looked up. "Hey," he said. Now what? He hated being interrupted during those short periods when he could read his preferred stuff, not what some teacher deemed important. He raised his eyebrows. Josh Gowan often shared the same double seat on the afternoon bus they rode home.

It was always the same. The social outcasts tended to be loners who sometimes huddled together for the purpose of warding off the attention of those who would prey on them if given the chance. The jocks, the hoods and toughs, the stoners (usually they kept to themselves), the socialites, the weirdos, all would sometimes form alliances and pick on the outcasts because it was safest to pick on them. The other groups were all large enough to provide protection for each member. But when somebody wanted to bust some heads to impress buddies, or make time with some chick who liked to watch pointless tough-guy behavior, the nearest outcast was immediately marked by invisible but altogether too-real crosshairs.

Josh and Nick had formed a temporary alliance of their own. The early bus was crammed full of loud, thuggish boys and the fake-tough girls who liked them. The boys liked to show off for the girls, who laughed at others' misfortune like hyenas watching a lion kill. There was hardly ever a seat on the early bus. You had to stand, desperately hanging on to the overhead bars, balancing on the pitching floor and avoiding the stretched-out legs of toughs who relished an excuse to pound you for touching them, no matter how unintentional the transgression might have been.

Both Nick and Josh had scoped out the potential for poundings and chosen to remain in the emptying school later than necessary in order to hop the later bus. This had improved the odds, because the majority of kids wanted out fast, but it also made the two of them stand out more when a group of the toughs somehow ended up on the later bus. So Josh had taken to sitting near Nick, in theory creating the illusion of being a tougher nut to crack. Most rides were uneventful, and the two had struck up something of a friendship based on the half-hour ride and the shared outcast status.

Nick never considered confessing the strangeness of his secret life. Josh had, however, confessed that his looks, clothes, and tendency to read whenever opportunity allowed had resulted in a rumor that had spread throughout the school. *Josh Gowan is a fag.* Didn't matter what Josh had to say about it, what was real, what was obvious to anyone who watched him interact with girls, or what he'd paid a few kids to spread as a counter-rumor. No, he was labeled and had become a pariah.

Josh knew damn well that having been so labeled would one day lead to a pounding by some jerk from one of the cliques, someone looking for respect and adoration from idiot peers.

Josh told Nick of his incipient problem. It was apparent that Josh would require some sort of protection. It didn't matter to him, but Nick also knew Josh wasn't a fag because Josh had confessed undying love for one of the most popular girls in school, Sherry Ludden, a pretty if vacuous cheerleader type who wouldn't have even been aware of Josh if he hadn't tripped her in the cafeteria one day. (Nick suspected it wasn't an accident.)

Amazingly, Sherry had taken to spending a few minutes with Josh now and then, or sharing a table at lunch, and one could almost hold out some hope that Josh stood a chance with her—all of which caused him more trouble, because when an outcast (and a "fag," on top of it) seemed about to break out of his boundaries, it was noticed by the other groups and observed in the same way a delinquent might stare at insects with a magnifying glass—just before charring them with a ray of magnified sunlight.

So now the rumors had begun to mention that there might be some payback for Josh's reckless attempt to gain access to another clique through his unlikely—*imaginary*—friendship with Sherry Ludden. Word was, there would be some physical punishment to be meted out to Josh when he least expected it. Which meant that he walked around school always expecting it, and had begun making plans for altering the odds so they'd be in his favor.

Thus the original bus meeting, followed by another such meeting in the library and the clandestine browsing of a catalog most adults would have been shocked to know belonged to mild-mannered, quiet Dominic Lupo.

It was a U.S. Army–surplus catalog to which he subscribed, and it included numerous pages of the borderline-illegal items the average survivalist, KKK, and Aryan Nation member, or budding anarchist, and maybe also rogue cop, might have considered useful additions to their arsenal. Josh had caught a glimpse of Nick browsing the catalog in the library, and had convinced his friend—likely the only friend he had in school—to let him pick out something to "improve the odds" when the inevitable happened and somebody from one of the offended groups decided it was time to pound the fag.

Nick was sympathetic, but also worried his own interest in such fringe gear would come to light. After swearing Josh to secrecy, Nick had opened up the surplus catalog and watched as Josh drooled over the commando knives, garrotes, nunchucks, and other dangerous weaponry available for mail order. Josh settled on one item and pointed at it after glancing around to see if a librarian was nearby.

"I want two of those."

Nick flipped the catalog around to his side of the table, holding up a notebook with which to camouflage the illicit material if a librarian or fellow student happened nearby.

"Brass knuckles?" he said. "Are you sure?"

"One for each hand." Josh made fists. *Zam! Pow!*

The knuckles were impressive, cast in brass and made to break teeth and jaws and noses. You laid the heavy brass implement on your palm, then stuck your fingers through the metal bands and positioned them so they protected your knuckles when you made a fist. Besides protecting the knuckles, the brass put a metal edge into each blow landed on an unsuspecting opponent. The weight of the knucks themselves would help increase the blows' impact, thereby making their user a much more effective fighting machine.

Of course, Nick thought, even with the knucks, if one had the misfortune of being overwhelmed, then all bets were off, as the opponent might well turn the tables and use the knucks against *him*. He suspected Josh would find himself in such a predicament all too quickly.

But Nick did require some cash to fill out his collection of Executioner books. And in this transaction, Nick saw the way to make a profit. The knuckles were a bargain-basement ten bucks apiece. Plus shipping, another five bucks.

"Sixty bucks," Nick blurted out. "I'll order them for you, but you have to take that to your grave, man."

"Don't worry, I will." Josh looked pained. "I'm tired of being afraid. I just want the chance to defend myself. Those assholes aren't gonna just open up their arms in a hug and ask me into their fucked-up little club. We both know that."

"Sure, but that don't mean we have to get ourselves

arrested." Nick looked around to make sure no one was eavesdropping. The coast seemed clear. "The cops catch you with these, you're in deep shit. And if you use 'em, they're gonna go after your source. That's me."

"Man, you know I'd never rat on you. If these things save my life, I don't care if they lock me up for a while. Better than getting the shit beat out of me."

Nick nodded. "Okay, I'll order them. You pay me half up front, then when I get 'em, you pay me the rest."

"Deal!" They had shaken on it and gone their separate ways. The initial cash was handed over on another bus ride, and Nick had dutifully mailed in the money order.

When Josh took delivery of the merchandise, they were sitting at the same library table. After Josh made the packages disappear, they shook hands again.

DICKIE KLUG

He was drunk again, but it felt great.

Ever since he'd been a kid, hanging with his cousin, he had always liked the feeling of being just slightly buzzed. He had given up doing the breaking and entering while stoned or buzzed, because he knew he'd get careless and goofy, but that didn't stop him from finding a reason to be buzzed whenever he could. Well, tonight it felt great because it messed with his memory just enough to give the illusion things were cool.

But things weren't all that cool, were they?

Fuck no.

Ever since he'd fished that woman out of the lake, he had found a reason to be buzzed all the time.

God fuck it, what had he gotten himself into?

He should have taken an oar and bashed in her brains. And let her sink out of sight forever.

But would that have even been enough?

Not so deep down, he knew it wouldn't have been *near* enough.

All of a sudden, being drunk no longer felt *great*.

It felt *desperate*.

He wiped his face and forehead with one meaty hand, dragging it across his skin as if it were a towel. He made a gargling sound. He leaned up against the brick wall and waited for the world to stop, or at least slow down. And he waited for the hot, sour taste of vomit to retreat from the back of his throat, where it threatened to bubble up. He tasted half-digested onion pizza down there, and thinking of that sweetly sour taste just about clinched it.

He waited for the potential cramp to pass, listening to the rhythmic throbbing of his blood echoing in his ears.

Eventually he traversed the length of wall, hanging on to it. He had to get inside and clean up. Outside the lobby door, he fumbled with his keys and squinted at the key ring in the lamplight. The keys flickered and winked at him, and he finally selected the right one and found the lock after jabbing a few times to no avail. Inside, the narrow stairs almost defeated him, but he was able to muster the will to heave his bulk up toward the light, using both walls and handrails as guides. And lifelines.

Eventually he was inside his place. He flicked on the overhead lights and almost caught himself marveling at how nice it was, even though it wasn't his style.

As if he even had a style. His style had always been Early American mobile home, or fishing shack.

This was one of those pricy converted factory lofts, not as much of a high ceiling as some, but long and narrow, with one brick wall running the length of the place. There were a couple sections of stuccoed wallboard breaking up some of the open space and giving the bathroom and bedroom some privacy, but the bulk of the square footage was taken up by the long living space and the galley kitchen at the rear, next to the bedroom. Even though his head spun, he still glanced at the big-screen Samsung TV and the leather couch and the big armchair and wanted to feel something like pride.

But he couldn't. And the alcohol made him almost weep now, right when he could least afford to.

It was his place, but *she* paid for it.

He shed his leather jacket and left it where it fell, then kicked off his shoes and stumbled toward the little wooden bar near the sofa. Hands shaking, he poured himself a drink, straight Grey Goose, and gulped it. It made him sputter and cough, but the burn going down felt right.

Even this, everything in here, everything he touched, it was hers. She'd had it here all waiting for him when she'd come back for him, finding him hiding in his hunting shack in the middle of Fucking-A Nowhere, Vilas County. She had warned him to stay away from people, and he had mistakenly thought he could hide from *her*, too. But she'd knocked on his door and had been there, middle of nowhere, a look in her eyes that said, *Do what I say or you're fucked.*

That was his interpretation, anyway.

And now he was here, in this prison he called home. He had a debit card with all the funds he needed. He hadn't tested its limits, but he'd bet there were limits. The utility bills went to *her*. The cell phone on which she called him at all hours was *hers*.

His *soul* was hers.

His intercom bleeped and he put down the drink and went to press the button without checking. He was coming around, feeling better. Hell, he had almost canceled the appointment. But now that the chick was here, he felt his groin respond.

She'd better be what I asked for.

He threw open the door, and she was *exactly* what he had requested from the Class Act agency.

Slender, golden hair, heavily made-up, popping gum. Dressed like a slightly too-old cheerleader.

When he smiled at her, something in his eyes must have caught her attention. Fear crossed her otherwise-bored features.

Dickie liked that. He liked it a lot.

CHAPTER FIVE

JESSIE

She went to the door, hesitated, then pulled it open. The doorbell still echoed through the house.

Nick stood outside, a Packers cap slung low over his face.

"Do you have a warrant?" she asked. She wanted to smile, but she knew the kidding words had come out colder than she had intended. Why hadn't he used his key?

Idiot! Because you didn't part on the best of terms.

They'd fought before, but this time it had been . . . somehow more traumatic. After that meal, which had ended well enough, they'd gotten into a discussion of what he thought his plans might turn out to be. It had become obvious to Jessie that his obsession would put them both in danger. If Nick's theories panned out, anything he did would be fraught with peril for everyone he knew. Anyone either of them knew.

Now her words lingered in the air between them.

Then she noticed his hand. It looked as if it had melted in a fire.

She knew what that meant.

He found wolves. He had to use the silver.

"Nick," she said. Her voice caught. His eyes were hooded, sleep deprived. *Haunted.*

She opened wide the door.

He stumbled in, still silent.

"Have you slept?" He shook his head. She took his arm, helped him toward the leather sofa that faced the fireplace, and felt him sag into it.

She couldn't look at his hand.

"Jesus, Nick, talk to me."

"They're *all* wolves," he mumbled. "The whole goddamn group. They'll be hunting us soon. I—I'm sorry, but I think I've brought them onto us, like a curse."

"Are they following?" She glanced at the door. She knew all too well what it meant to be hunted. They'd kicked in her door, the Stewart gang. Had wanted her as bait. As more than bait. She shuddered. She knew what it was like. *Leave it at that.*

And now Nick had stirred up a hornet's nest.

"Not following right now. They've got a bunch of dead ends to track down first. But they'll know it was me. They'll suspect. They'll send somebody, sometime."

Jessie felt her pulse begin to throb loudly in her ears. "When?" she asked.

He shrugged out of his coat and tossed the cap aside. "Not just yet. We have time. They can't be too obvious. Those other guys, they were renegades. They were mercenaries out on their own, not representing the company. I think Wolfpaw's had enough trouble in Iraq and Afghanistan. They're under scrutiny, probably because of idiots like those three, who overstepped their bounds."

"Then again, they're cold-blooded killers," she whispered, still shivering. She wished she'd started a fire.

"Yeah, there's that." He put his good hand on her hip. His other hand he hid as well as he could. She was standing over him, looking down and wishing they could go back to the early days of their relationship, before Martin and the rednecks, before the Wolfpaw killers and Malko the serial killer. She placed her hand on his hand, felt the heat pass between them.

"How about a fire?" she asked.

"That would be nice."

"And some food? You look hungry." He looked *depleted*.

"Sure. I drove straight through, but I took a roundabout route in case they'd tracked me. I wanted to be sure."

"No sleep?"

"Not for a couple days now."

"I'll start the fire, then get you something—"

He groaned. His hand flipped and caught hers, and he pulled her down to him. She let him. Their mouths found each other and the fires raged between them, many words unspoken. It was a while before she pulled away to light the fire and turn on some music, and after she did they huddled in its warm embrace and made their own warmth.

Jessie undressed him carefully, and he let her, and then he watched as she shed her jeans and man's shirt, and she stood before him, glowing, with the firelight behind her. The damp wood snapped as the flame slowly spread, the light eventually growing to dispel the darkness outside the windows. Naked, she turned away long enough to close the blinds around them.

She remembered the feeling of being watched from outside, from the dark.

She turned back to him and the need they'd built up finally burst.

Nick nuzzled her neck and to Jessie it was almost like the first time. His stubble tickled and scraped her skin, and she felt the need overtake her, and after he took his mouth away from her neck and covered hers with it, she reached down and took him in her hands, grabbing gently, possessively, displaying her need with the urgency with which she handled his flesh.

He groaned and their tongues met in a hot, moist ballet. She moaned with desire, looking into his dark eyes, and she thought she saw a flicker of the primeval there, a glimpse of the Creature, a hint of his wild side.

She found it exciting, she found him exciting, his touch and his lips.

He had grown hard, cradled in her hand, and she felt her readiness and his tingle jolt through her. She straddled him in one smooth motion, her lips still attached hungrily to his. She felt him enter her easily when she sat lightly on his lap, his own need driving him deep into her. She thought she would faint at the pleasure of his reach, her flesh taking him in greedily and not letting go.

The fire's flickering light reflected in the glass around them and dappled their sweat-slicked skin. The image melted when they slowed their feverish pace to flow into other configurations.

They touched each other reverently, their past anger forgotten in the heat of their passion.

He took her from behind after she rolled over and opened herself to him, and then she arched her back and leaned her head so their mouths could meet again. The rhythm rocked them both until she thought she would erupt, but then he slowed and gently brought her around so she could face him again and he was still inside her, the rhythm overtaking them until they rode the crest together. Then the orgasm rippled through them while their tongues met, their eyes wide open and staring into each other's soul until the heat started to cool on their skin.

When Jessie could hear again, the strains of something baroque by Handel seemed to melt into the fire's gentle snapping.

It's the perfect moment, she thought as he slid out of her and their bodies melded together in the sweet afterglow. The music's quiet, lilting majesty painted the scene golden.

She wanted that moment to last forever.

But then she remembered everything he had told her, and now if she thought about it, she could smell the dangerous determination in his sweat, as if it had leaked from his pores to foul their lovemaking. It was as if the adrenaline of his hunt, his chase, whatever he had done, had somehow poisoned his body and now it was enveloping her, too.

The beauty of the Handel piece faded in her ears and she felt her heart pounding instead. She placed her hand in his, and though he took it and brushed it with his lips, she turned away and wouldn't meet his eyes. Even when he pulled her hand gently to his face, she stared at the window beside them as if she could see through the blinds.

What was circling around them? Were the woods even now crawling with killers? What new horror had Nick brought back in his stubborn crusade?

She turned to face him, and before she could stop herself, she slapped his cheek with her wide-open palm.

The Handel ended at that exact moment, so the smack of her hand on his skin seemed louder in the new silence.

He stared at her in stunned shock, saying nothing.

"What have you done now, damn you, Nick?"

He was silent for a long moment, letting her question hang in the air between them. Finally, when he spoke it was with a soft voice. The pain was evident in it.

"Jessie, I'm sorry. You can't imagine how sorry. How much I want to hang on to this moment and keep the outside world out. How much I wish I could afford to forget about Wolfpaw and what I know, deep inside, they would have done anyway."

She recoiled from the name of the company that had turned their world into hell again. "You didn't have to go down there and poke the sleeping dog," she said accusingly. "You could have left it alone."

He put his hand on her face and gently turned it back toward him. "But that's just it, they wouldn't have left us alone."

"How do you know?"

"Because I think there's a werewolf operating in the Wausau area, and it's just a matter of time before the Wolf-paw people catch wind of it and come to finish the job, tying off loose ends. We are a loose end, Jess. Our names are connected to this thing."

Her mind reeled. Another werewolf? In Wausau? That wasn't very far away. That was where—

"Wausau?" she said, her eyes boring into his, her voice nearly spitting the words. "Isn't that where . . . what's her name . . . where *she* was from? Where she worked?"

He nodded.

"I thought she was dead!"

"I did, too, and she did disappear for a while. After that night, when she ended up in the lake."

"But then?"

He hesitated. "But then she reappeared. She survived, stayed out of sight for a while, kept her name out of the story at first. And—"

"And?"

"And then she showed up on the news again a couple or three weeks later."

"And you couldn't tell me?"

"It wasn't good to talk about it. You know that. We tried, but it was better to move on. We had our own wounds to heal."

The silence hung between them again. Jessie wished the baroque disk would start over. Anger bubbled in her veins, and despite the warm glow of the lovemaking she wanted to throttle him.

"How did you find out about—*her*?" She tried, but couldn't keep the bitterness from her voice.

Now he turned away from her.

"I suspected. At first it was just a thought, but it bothered me. There were a couple suspicious deaths a month later. I monitored her television station. And then she was back on the air. A month after the first murders there were two more. They were called bizarre animal attacks. Then there was an animal attack a couple weeks later. Less time between them. Some were kind of explainable. There were some disappearances, too. Runaways, they said. A couple homeless men. Then—"

"Yes?" She *knew* what he was going to say. She was still shocked when he confirmed it.

"I started to keep an eye on her."

"You what? *You what?*"

She heaved herself up and off the sofa, away from his warm skin, and snatched up her discarded clothes with sharp little motions, as if she were ripping them to bits. She stood over him, accusing, angry.

Hurt.

"I've been keeping her under surveillance in my spare time," he said, softly.

She knew he was trying not to antagonize her. Trying to soft-pedal the truth, knowing how she'd take it.

"Surveillance?" she spit at him. "What kind of *surveillance?*"

"Following her, staking out her apartment, that kind of thing."

She heard the beginnings of defiance in his voice.

Doesn't he have a right to do these things?

"No," she said, answering the unasked question. "No, you don't get to just slip that past me. You started to hang around Wausau? While you were telling me you were busy on the job?"

"I *was* on the job . . ."

His face reflected his knowledge of how it sounded, now that she said it. It sounded like *deceit*.

She threw her clothes across the room and stalked, naked and magnificent, to her bedroom. She left him there, bathed in the glow of the fire, the moment destroyed, the air that had been swollen with their passion—their *love*—now tainted by her anger. And by his deception.

She slammed the door. As soon as she reached the bed, the tears came.

LUPO

He ran with the night creatures and they gave him a wide berth, understanding that this time he wasn't hungry, he was just angry and spoiling for a fight.

Muscles loosened during the run, his fur steaming and his breath even. The run was therapy, play, and a desire to forget his human side's preoccupations.

A rabbit bolted through his field of view and the Creature played with it, catching it but letting it go, once swatting it with a single swipe of one powerful paw. But *It* lost interest in the game quickly, and the rabbit rolled to a stop at the base of a pine, its back broken.

The Creature snorted. *Not even a good game tonight.*

He went off to seek other challenges, and a long howl loosed from its throat.

A warning.

Don't mess with me tonight.

From the Journals of Caroline Stewart
December 8, 1981
We made slow, wonderful love last night, and afterward we lay together, content to compare days while letting our sweat dry on our skin even while the light from the

streetlamps outside bathed us in burnt orange. I thought I was being subtle when I brought up his one aborted session with Jerry Boone, but I should have known better. Nick is very attuned to nuance, for his age. I felt his muscles stiffen as if electricity jolted through them. His heart started to race. I could tell because my head rested on his chest at the time. I pretended not to notice.

"I thought it would be helpful if we talked about what happened in the session," I said.

"Helpful to who?"

"Helpful in general," I said. "But certainly most helpful to you. I'm helping you with your quest to understand, so you'll gain the most, but if I can better help you, then it's good for me to find it helpful, too."

He shifted his position so he could look at me. I turned my face up and kissed him lightly on the lips.

"We don't have to do this now, if you don't want to," I said.

"No, maybe you're right, we should. He was a good friend of yours, wasn't he?"

"Yes. I think he might have had some feelings for me. I considered him a close acquaintance, a good colleague, but I guess we weren't friends."

"It must have been a shock," Nick said.

It had been a shock to me. When I told Nick right after I'd talked to the police, he'd seemed distant. Surprised, sure. And that sense of relief. Maybe relief that he wouldn't have to bare any more of his secrets to anyone.

Except me. I figured I was still welcome to rummage around his past and his condition.

"I still can't believe it." I shook my head lightly and my hair washed across his chest. "Maybe if I'd been a better friend I would have known what might make him take his own life."

"Maybe," he said.

"So what happened during the session? Did you have some success? I had always heard his methods were somewhat unorthodox, but I wasn't sure what that meant. It's way out of my area."

"Don't you know? You talked to him."

"Well, yes, but he was bound by doctor-patient confidentiality. He would never have told me."

I had asked, but Boone clammed up. Rightly so, of course, but still it had been frustrating.

Nick shifted on the bed and I felt his sigh.

I couldn't help wondering why he was so reluctant to tell me. But then I found out.

"I don't really know how he did it," Nick said, "but Boone put me under. I remember thinking, 'This is bullshit!' and then I think it wasn't bullshit at all, because whatever he did, it relaxed me and he started asking probing questions. I don't remember the questions, but at some point I started to feel nervous. You know, anxious. Then I—I can't be sure about this, but the session started to feel bad, wrong, I don't know."

I didn't say anything. I was suddenly afraid to breathe, and afraid to interrupt him or stop him somehow. Nick started to shiver. It was subtle at first, but then it felt as if his body was developing a fever and his skin started heating up.

"Caroline, I—I think I might have Changed during the session. I think I may have flashed back and forth, you know, man to wolf and back again."

"Jesus," I said. I couldn't help myself. I wondered what somebody like Boone would have made of that. Could that have made him seek a way out? But why? Why allow it to bother him so much that he couldn't live with the knowledge?

"What happened afterward?"

Nick was silent for a long time, and I thought he wasn't going to answer. But then he did.

"Thing is, I don't really remember. I think about it, and it makes me nervous. It scares me, and I get the shivers."

"Like now?"

"Like now. I remember my clothes being loose, like I'd taken them off, put them back on fast. But I don't know for sure. He looked shaken. Pale."

"Whatever happened must have been traumatic."

"Yeah. I had that sense of having flashed back and forth, but he wouldn't say it, would barely talk to me. He just dismissed me and locked the door after I left."

"That was the last time you saw him?" I asked.

"Yes," he said. But he paused just a beat, hesitated long enough to make me wonder if he was telling the truth.

I'd never questioned that before.

"Okay, Nick." I decided to let it go for a while.

I caressed his stomach muscles, which were bunched and strained under me. I let my hand turn in a lazy circle, feeling his hot skin with my fingers. I imagined what went on under his skin when the Change hit, how his organs Changed, how the fur grew so suddenly on the outer surface of his skin. Slowly, he seemed to loosen up and start to respond to my caresses. Not long after, he turned my face up to meet his and put his lips on mine, and we kissed and then time was immaterial again for quite a while. We were both excited, both hungry for more of each other, but I felt that some kind of barrier had been defined.

For the first time, I was surprised to find I didn't believe him. I think he remembered more than he said, and that he had seen Boone again after the one session.

But what should I do about it?

When we shifted positions, he drew me on top of him and I was ready, too.

*We made love, but there was a desperate quality about
it. A little pent-up violence. It was as satisfying as it had
always been, but it was disquieting, too.*

1978
BRAD SCHNEIDER

The two geeks shook on it. Whatever *it* was.

They didn't notice Brad Schneider, hiding behind the
stacks, looking for whack-off material among the women's
magazines, spot them shaking hands.

He snickered aloud despite himself, wondering what
the two faggy-boys were up to because he couldn't quite
hear them. He promised to remind himself to mention this
when the gang met up behind the school in the Wiener
Woods, which was what they called the thick grove of trees
that made a semicircle behind the school's running track
and baseball diamond. It was actually known as the Vienna
Woods, but the other name was much more apt.

Schneider was one of the ragged-edged group formed by
the intersection of the hoods and jocks—one of a few who
could get away with pretending to be a jock because of his
athletic abilities, but who secretly preferred being in charge
of a group of even more aimless thugs. Thugs who as often as
not did his bidding, as if they'd voted him their spiritual
leader.

They had started the rumors about the Gowan kid partly
because they really thought he was a fudge-packer, but also
because he'd taken to hanging around Sherry Ludden, who
was the best friend of Susie Brown, Brad's current main
squeeze.

After giving Brad a particularly wet, sloppy blow job in
the thick of the Wiener Woods one night, Susie had pes-
tered him with her newest and most annoying obsession—

the absolute conviction that Brad had to rescue her friend Sherry from the gay-boy before it was too late.

Brad had barely been in the mood to listen, since her vacuum-like mouth had just about blown his mind as well as his wad, but she pointed out that she'd swallowed his entire slimy load, and he owed her.

"You owe me for that blow job, Brad, and for every other time I put out in the back of your 'Cuda, or in the basement of your parents' house, or in Karen's pool—*hey, right while people stood around just a few feet away!*"

And she went on, her voice rising in volume. He owed her for every time she'd let him fill her ass with his curved pecker, which, she reminded him, she could tell everyone about and then *just see* how much ass he'd get!

He owed her for all of it.

Brad was addicted to the sight of that blonde, curly head swirling around his dick while she sucked him out like a pro—*Who wouldn't be*, he wondered—and he wanted nothing to do with the idea of losing her *and* also maybe losing out if she followed through with her threat. He'd always been embarrassed by his unusually curved member, and only the fact that Susie claimed it made him unique had kept him from being forced to keep it in his pants for two years.

But now Brad had a plan that might keep him wallowing in shapely ass—Susie's round and perfectly shaped ass, to be specific, and maybe some of her friends'—for a very long time. Right now, keeping himself in poontang was the priority that made opening his eyes in the morning worthwhile. Having to put up with his dipshit parents and idiot siblings was almost tolerable when he was fucking some new cheerleader or getting blown by one of the gymnasts behind the bleachers. Everything else pretty much faded into insignificance.

Right now, watching those two marginal boys in the library

passing love notes or whatever they were doing, shaking hands, touching, he shivered with feverish expectation. All it would take would be a word or two whispered in the right ears, a few bucks blown on some supplies, and who knew, maybe the whole thing would be epic in nature. He wasn't one for book learning. He knew that and skated through most subjects because of his well-known athletic abilities and because most teachers were probably vaguely afraid of him, but he recognized he had an innate sense of the mob mentality and the myriad ways it could be molded for his own uses.

Brad saw himself as a "godfather" type. He was adept at manipulating others into doing what he wanted.

Tonight was a Friday, prime party night for sure, and there would be various parties on Saturday for anyone who could drag his sorry hungover ass out of bed long enough to start drinking again.

"Hair of the dog," like the song said.

But next weekend was a long weekend, and Brad had grand ideas. Seeing the fag and his nonentity friend got the mental gears rolling, that was sure.

"Hey, Rollie," he called out as he turned the corner into the long hallway that led to the gym and the locker rooms. It was where he lived, practically. "What's up, man?"

Rollie stopped his swaggering walk long enough to wait for Brad to join him. "Nada, man. Well, except for the party tonight." He wagged his very long Gene Simmons tongue at Brad and they both giggled.

"Muff!" said Rollie.

"Divers!" said Brad.

They giggled some more.

Roland Hawthorn II was known as Rollie, a nickname which had started out as *Roll-y* for the rolling papers he was never caught without.

In fact, he'd single-handedly increased the school's access to pot due to the almost limitless freedom his father, owner of Hawthorn Brokerage, conferred upon his delinquent kid. Of course, Hawthorn senior didn't quite realize the extent of young Roland's nefarious activities, and it was a good thing he didn't—as the kid's penchant for blackmail of other well-off kids served to funnel business to his dad's brokerage. Rollie could be very convincing when he negotiated with some hapless victim who didn't want his mommy and daddy receiving Polaroids of the apple of their eye with young cheerleader snatch attached to his curly tongue or impaled on his royal scepter.

Or worse.

Therefore most rich kids went through hell trying to line up their daddies' business for the elder Hawthorn. If their effort could be independently confirmed, then Rollie and Brad were like as not willing to negotiate a compromise punishment that would prove sufficiently painful and de-grading. It was testament to their abilities as punishers that *no one* ever chose the second option easily.

If one of the "undesirables" ended up caught in their web, a kid whose family lacked a fortune or means by which to pay off the blackmailers, then their punishment often made them accomplices in other "actions," the result being a long rank of lowly henchmen with nothing to lose. The brilliant scheme had evolved over time and turned into an ongoing criminal enterprise only hinted at in rumors at once whis-pered and denied in the halls of Grover Cleveland High School.

Drugs, sexual services, money, silence, and cooperation flowed back and forth in complex arrangements carefully balanced to elude teacher and administrator observation.

The swirl of kids between classes around them might as well have been a cone of silence.

"Listen, Rollie, I got a real hard-on for that faggy kid in your history class."

"Really?" Roland arched an eyebrow in best John Cleese fashion.

Brad frowned. "You know what I mean."

"I'm afraid I have a pretty good idea." Now he was Groucho Marx, brandishing an imaginary cigar.

"Quit it, Rollie. I'm talkin' about the Gowan fag and gettin' him good, once and for all."

"What will our reward be, pray tell?" Roland rounded on him and drove him back first into the wall lockers with his physical presence, his nose ending up only inches away.

Rollie was about the only other GCHS student who could do this to Brad without incurring the athlete's wrath and some sort of public retaliation. In the ranks, total obedience was the rule. But the two masterminds could deal with each other any way they chose. Such was the prerogative of rank and privilege.

Rollie noticed the hall seemed to have emptied and looked straight down, where Brad's muscular hand had suddenly grabbed hold of his testicles and squeezed gently but with insistence, a reminder that increasing the pressure—and thereby crushing tender male tissue—would be easy.

Rollie's eyes roved back up and met Brad's.

"Do you have something to say or are you just happy to see me? If you're gonna start, why not finish me off, lover?"

There was some measure of disguised rage buried behind the sleazy words. Brad got a hint of it, but wasn't sophisticated enough to decipher what it meant.

Brad gave Rollie's scrotum one hard squeeze and then released him. He rolled his eyes and grinned like a Halloween skull.

"Our reward will be doing *that* to him, except we'll just go on squeezing till we make peanut butter out of his balls."

"Whyn't you say so from the first, Bradley, me boy?"

Rollie could roll with the punches, adjust to a changing situation, and retain his above-it-all demeanor.

Even Brad knew that Rollie could always retaliate against him at some later date, when he least expected it. There was always someone willing to move up in their organization, so all Rollie would have to do was put the word out on Brad and somebody would step up, willing to do his bidding in order to gain favor. Gaining favor might mean the difference between being laid for the next couple years and being considered a social leper.

There would be takers. He was sure of it.

Brad only wanted to show Rollie the value of his plan, and to remind him he was no pushover. It was a calculated risk, but he'd had no intention of following through. On the other hand, now he had Rollie's undivided attention.

Brad had contracted for a couple of his flunkies to clear the hallway long enough to keep the transaction private, so Rollie wouldn't lose face.

"What's your plan, Stan? Come on, Bradley, me boy."

Brad suddenly backed out by squirming from between Rollie and the lockers. His discomfort grew. Rollie could do anything, if he became angry enough. Brad wanted an interested, engaged Rollie—not a vindictive one.

"Let me tell you about next weekend," Brad said. He waved off his sentries. Slowly, the hallway filled around them.

Brad talked for a long time. Rollie listened, the smile growing on his angular face.

CHAPTER SIX

KILLIAN

He closed his office door and stood inside for a minute, taking time to process what he'd just learned.

His gaze swept over the room's utilitarian furniture and file cabinets lined up along one wall. A trestle table along another wall held ungainly stacks of folders and files arranged in crooked rows according to their importance and age, a system only he understood.

The only nod to comfort and style was a leather chair and a relatively new cherry computer desk and hutch holding his flat-screen monitor, with a computer CPU buried underneath. Even his two rarely used guest chairs were spartan in design and dusty, one of the two covered with a teetering stack of folders. Along the same wall as the door was a short credenza that held his coffeepot and a tiny microwave where he could warm up the convenience-store burritos he admitted were his one unexplainable food vice. Yet another file cabinet took up the rest of the space alongside those. Along the far wall, behind the desk and below the office-wide window, was another low table laden with papers and crooked stacks of books.

Killian grimly surveyed his domain, reminded again how the "system" viewed him and his role. How the hell could he have known that accepting the Internal Affairs promotion would make him a pariah among his fellow officers? Sure, the movies always portrayed IA cops in exactly that way, but he'd never put much stock in movies and television shows. Turned out he should have paid attention and carefully considered before taking the work.

The irony was that Killian was good at it. He had closed down some pockets of small-time graft and institutionalized shakedowns that once plagued the department, but had later made his name and career investigating the numerous high-profile incidents of excessive force that had led to various shake-ups of the department's entrenched administration. Stuck in a traditionally white, semi-Germanic way of thinking, and often seen as racist and out of touch, the MPD had caused its share of controversy over the years through several chiefs and administrations sometimes considered to be as parochial as those of New York, Los Angeles, and Chicago. And Griff Killian had himself come from New York and somehow become this department's go-to guy in a controversy, a closer.

Problem was, in so doing, he had also sealed his fate.

Never quite accepted by the tight-lipped Midwesterners, he had found his steely New York persona both a help and a hindrance when dealing with the delicate matter of police policing themselves. He was straight enough to want to do a good job, and dogged enough to seem driven by the devil himself to bring a bad cop down, which made him seem to enjoy what he did and made him a target for resentment among other cops. Occasionally, in the dark of the night, he regretted his rise in this particularly disliked aspect of police work, regretted his pit-bull mentality when faced with the code of silence that encouraged cops to cover for their fellow cops, and regretted having allowed himself to corner a niche no one else wanted. It had cost him friends, companions, at least two women, and probably a half dozen promotions.

Griff Killian was a hated man within the department. When he walked the halls of the downtown precinct, it was said the Grim Reaper was out recruiting for hell. When he walked the halls of outlying precincts, veteran cops took cover and avoided him until he was reported to have left. Doors closed down hallways he took, and he was certain some administrators had even locked themselves in their offices rather than see him.

Killian was equally amused and dismayed by this response to his diligence, but he was just as likely to use it in his investigations by leveraging one cop against another, which was what happened when they feared he had turned his judgmental gaze on them.

Right now, he had turned a judgmental gaze on one cop, his pet project for the last year. He stood inside his office door and spotted the file in question. It was flagged in red, a bright slash of color sticking out of its side. Sure, he was all for computers and machine-readable forms, and retro projects that would enter all archived files into various databases, but he was also old-school enough to prefer working with paper. He hit PRINT every chance he had, making sure he had a hard copy of every file, form, rap sheet, bio, and report he ever saw. He'd been around the block enough times to see files disappear overnight, sucked out of the database through shady means and relegated to the black hole of cyberspace. By printing everything, Killian liked to believe he was a step ahead and at least not likely to be caught flatfooted when some tiny bit of evidence disappeared from under his nose. It was just this kind of file he had flagged in old-fashioned fireman red.

Dominic Lupo's file.

He walked to his desk and sat behind it, staring down at the file. He didn't have to open it. He knew its contents very well.

Heroic homicide detective. Decorated member of the Dahmer task force and, more recently, the gang-violence task force. Well liked by most cops who'd worked with him. Partner of one murdered veteran homicide cop, Ben Sabatini, and one recently promoted, Richard DiSanto. Dominic Lupo was a model cop, on paper.

But not on Killian's paper. No, Dominic "Nick" Lupo was a maverick. He wasn't really a team player, but he pretended to be, and that pretense was what had snagged Killian's attention.

And there was strange stuff, as Killian put it when he'd conferred with the department psychologist, Dr. Julia Barrett. He had dug up some questionable actions, some strange absences, and the occasional insubordination—all of which were noted in Lupo's file. And then there was the Eagle River fiasco, the Martin Stewart connection between murders in Milwaukee and an apparent home-grown terrorist cell in Vilas County, far up north. Dr. Barrett hadn't quite broken the confidential seal of her sessions, but she'd hinted—more than hinted, really—at her suspicions about him and his involvement in the killings. There were too many pat solutions, too many unconvincingly tied threads.

Then Julia Barrett had confided in Killian that she was placing Lupo under some sort of unofficial surveillance. Killian had questioned her approach. What was she doing? Following him around? Staking out his apartment? But she had claimed she was seeking some evidence of his activities. Then she had taken a leave from the department, presumably followed him north to his hideaway, and . . . well, apparently she'd had the misfortune of stumbling over yet another batch of up-north backwoods types, who had killed her and mutilated her body.

There was some hush-hush crap going on, because Killian still hadn't been able to learn much about what had happened to her. Word was she'd been partially *eaten* by the serial killer who had imprisoned her in his dungeon.

What the fuck was going on up north? Killian had snorted with disbelief when he heard some of the details, although they were still unsubstantiated. Sounded like what people back home said of New Jersey's Pine Barrens. Cannibalism, bizarre killers, inbreds, whatever the hell they said, it sounded like northern Wisconsin could give the Pine Barrens a run for their money.

The whole thing smacked of amazing convenience.

And who'd been at the center of all that crap up there that had indirectly led to Barrett's death? Why, Dominic Lupo, of course. Killian could have put money on the connection, except he wasn't much of a betting man. But his personal warning bell had gone off again. Sabatini had died, Barrett had died. Maybe these deaths were indeed convenient for Lupo. Maybe if they were convenient, they weren't coincidental.

What he had just learned was another puzzle piece, and he wanted to put it on the board. He fanned the papers he'd carried in with him onto the desk, next to the print file. Later he would scan them and store them on his hard drive, but he would also clip the sheets together and save them in the paper file.

The papers were the medical examiner's report of an autopsy. A routine autopsy, as it happened. Kid was a gang-banger from the south side, one of those busted as part of a gang of jewelry-store robbers who used fast motorcycles to rip off more than one store at a time. He'd been busted after a high-profile stakeout operation just a few days before Barrett had gone and gotten herself killed. Then the kid had made bail, and within a few days after that somebody had filled him full of lead as he sat in the passenger seat of a parked car.

Well, that was the weird part, wasn't it?

They hadn't filled him full of *lead*, exactly.

The medical examiner said it had been a blend of metals. More *silver* than lead.

Silver ammunition?

That was a new one.

So who'd shot Julio—or Juan, or whatever his name had been—Ortiz? And something with a J. Jesus, maybe. Go figure.

And what about the silver slugs? The Lone Ranger had killed the kid? Well, that was bullshit.

Who'd busted the kid in the first place? Detective Dominic Lupo, of course, as part of the gang task force. He'd chased the kid down while the two gangbangers rode a motorcycle down an alley. Then the kid had claimed he'd been attacked by a guard dog, had been ripped up enough that he'd been treated at the hospital before being dumped into the county jail. Weird enough, sure. Nobody'd ever found the dog, or even seen it. Lupo had brushed it off, and it had been forgotten. But the attending ER doctor had tested the wounds the kid had suffered that night, and he'd identified what he called "canid" DNA. It was weird, his report implied, but it wasn't exactly *canine* DNA. It was as if the DNA had been twisted somehow and rendered almost unrecognizable. Something had attacked the kid between when he'd fallen off the bike and when Lupo had cuffed him, but *what?* The doc's report had concluded that the DNA sample had been contaminated and it had been a dog as the kid claimed, and the note had been filed away and forgotten.

But not by Killian.

It was another weirdness in a long list of many.

And then the kid came up dead shortly after making bail. Killian couldn't even find out how the kid had posted bail in the first place, though he was working on it. But either way, the kid hadn't lived long. *Days.*

And he'd been killed with *silver slugs.*

Killian had dug. He liked digging. It made him good at his job. It also made him a pariah. But in any case he'd dug and found silver slugs mentioned again in the system.

Oh yes, he'd said. Oh, yes.

A gunsmith had been shot and killed with silver slugs he

had apparently made for the very same Martin Stewart, who'd then caused all that mayhem up north, and here, with the escorts killed in malls. Martin Stewart, who'd gone head-to-head with—you guessed it—*Nick Lupo*.

Jesus, it was too many weird connections.

Big coincidences.

As the TV show once said, *There are no big coincidences and little coincidences, there are only coincidences.*

No, these were *big* coincidences.

Killian tapped his pen on his lip and cast out his thoughts. Maybe he could understand what it all meant. He glanced out his window at the gray, overcast Milwaukee spring sky. The answer was out there, hovering around his perception, but he couldn't snatch it from the air. The cold air. Didn't it ever get warm here?

He reached into the tiny fridge in the corner and selected a colorfully wrapped burrito. Already knowing the instructions, he popped the rolled snack into his microwave and nuked it the prescribed amount of seconds. His belly did a flip in advance rebellion. He ignored it. As he waited, he went over his new information again. What the hell did it all mean? The micro dinged and he reached in. He unwrapped the hot burrito gingerly, blew on the gnarled end, and took a small bite. Chewing the pulpy mass pleased him, not that he could explain it.

He would pay for it later, he knew with certainty. Yet every heavenly bite paid off in its own way.

As he chewed, his mind worked. He wiped his hand on a paper napkin and picked up the phone. He dialed an internal number.

"I think we need to talk," he said when the other end was picked up. He paused and listened. "No, we really do."

He hung up and took another thoughtful bite.

His stomach gurgled.

LUPO

They walked into the Pirates' Cove and found it empty. It was the off-season and the economy was slow, and the weather wasn't all that good.

Of course it's empty.

Jessie had been cold to him all day. Yesterday he had dressed after their blowout and walked home, to his cottage, alone. He had showered for a full hour, washing away the rest of their passion and the grime of his long trip, and the sleepless time surrounding it all. He had shaved, naked, while in the background Fish sang about the deadliest weapon being truth.

Shit, I have a knack for this, playing just the right music to jab me right in the heart.

When he was dressed he turned off the music. The big Scotsman's poetic lyrics tended to speak right to Lupo's soul, and sometimes that was too painful. *Too damn direct.*

He sat in his armchair and stared out onto the dark channel. It was like a long black slash on a black velvet painting, with the tree line hazily poking upward into the lighter sky.

Jessie's face hovered in his mind's eye. Funny, he'd never noticed, until Rich DiSanto told him once, how much she resembled the model Cindy Crawford. *Minus the famous mole,* DiSanto had said. *You know, near her mouth.* Lupo had laughed, but then he'd realized his partner was exactly right, and he felt foolish because he had never noticed. Not all those years he paid her rent and they were friendly but not involved romantically, and not even later, when he spent so much time falling into those eyes, and tracing the curves of her cheeks with his scarred hands.

He'd never noticed the resemblance. The hair was cut differently, but it was nearly the identical shade. She filled her jeans the same way, and wore her makeup more lightly, but still in the same style as the model. He'd been aware of Cindy Crawford's covers—what male in the eighties and nineties hadn't noticed that dark-eyed gaze?—yet he'd been myopic when faced in his own life with someone so perfect. Probably he'd been too dazzled by the contrast between them. And he'd never mentioned to her what DiSanto had said, unsure how she'd take it.

Now, as he slid onto a barstool next to her in the Cove, he wondered again how he'd never seen it. Maybe everybody but him had noticed. He might not have admitted he was looking for neutral ground, but the empty tavern was clearly that, and afforded them a certain privacy cocoon even if other drinkers showed up. Maybe he hoped they were less likely to argue in front of an audience. The woman tending bar served them almost reluctantly, a brandy old-fashioned with a cherry for Jessie and a rum and tonic for him, then went back to sitting below the high-mounted television and some sort of racy soap opera.

"Tell me about Wolfpaw," Jessie said after sipping her drink.

"I wanted to keep you out of it," he said. He wrapped his glass in his fist, but made no move to drink. Even as he said it, he knew how silly the words sounded.

"I'm already *in* it, Nick. As soon as you're in anything, I'm automatically in. From the day you were forced to let me into your secret world, I've been forced to come along." She waved her hand to forestall his complaint. "I'm not saying I regret that. I'm just saying, keeping me out of anything is naive."

Lupo nodded. She was right. Maybe it was a latent medieval ideal of chivalry he felt obligated to act out, ever the knight in shining armor.

How silly is that?

But his folks had raised him to follow a sort of gentlemanly ideal—*Make fun of it if you will,* he thought—and it was ingrained enough that he tended to do it without much thought. He'd met cops who were convinced he was faking, but he wasn't, and he didn't care if they doubted.

"See, it's like I can't get the genie back in the bottle. It was bad enough when I couldn't quite control my own, uh, urges. Now that I'm not alone, I'm even more unable to control anything." He wasn't sure she could understand. Hell, he wasn't sure he understood, either.

"It's what happened to Tom, isn't it?" Jessie said.

"Probably." He drank. "He realized how little control he had over his world, once things like me were in it. Couldn't face it, I guess."

"That's sad."

He drained his drink, nodded at her, and waved at the soap fan for another round.

"So, what about Wolfpaw?"

"They're a private security firm, sometimes called a security contractor. They're really a private army employing former service members from all branches. They'll go anywhere, do anything. They're modern mercenaries. I checked their website. They even have air and naval services, though those areas tend to concentrate on patrol capabilities, not actual combat."

"They have their own planes and ships?"

"Yeah, a small air force made up of fighter planes and surveillance craft. Plus a whole squadron of drones. The naval unit's made up of a dozen destroyer- and frigate-sized ships, and a fleet of high-tech patrol boats. But they're not the part of Wolfpaw I was interested in."

Jessie said. "No, you were interested in the soldiers, the ground troops."

He looked at her with pride. "Yeah. They had, like, twenty thousand troops in Iraq, at least until they got into trouble for being trigger-happy."

The woman served their new drinks, took money from what Lupo had set out, and returned to her show.

Jessie lowered her voice. "They can't all be . . . like you."

"No, I don't think so either. But those trained down in the Georgia compound seem to be. Maybe they have a battalion. Maybe the top brass is wolf. They seemed to have the run of the compound."

"You saw them?"

"In action. They murdered two men they were hunting. Like a training exercise."

Jessie covered her mouth, her eyes widening.

"And I killed two of the bastards."

"Oh, Nick," she said. Her eyes went to his hand, which looked better, but hadn't quite healed yet. Then she understood. "Oh, shit."

"Hornet's nest, Jess."

"Wasn't it dumb to go in there?" She turned away. Angry now.

He spoke carefully. "In retrospect, I could have observed from farther away. I could have been more—"

"*Careful*, Nick, the word is *careful*."

"Yes."

"And now we're—"

"Yeah, we're in trouble."

FALKEN

Detective Sheila Falken picked up her quarry as she left her building at the edge of downtown. She had time before her shift, and she wanted to keep the woman in sight.

It wasn't difficult.

The woman was tall and blonde and familiar to just about every male in the Wausau area. She was not likely to give Falken the slip. From where she was parked, she watched the woman walk a block to a Starbucks coffee shop, disappear for five minutes, and return to the sidewalk with a covered soft cup in one hand. She made her way back to her building, entered the lower-level garage door with a swipe of the card she held, then disappeared again.

Falken started her car, an unmarked Chevy, and waited. Sure enough, Heather Wilson's silver Lexus SUV poked its snout out of the garage entrance a couple minutes later and turned into the thin traffic.

Falken swung the Chevy in behind the Lexus after letting a few cars squeeze between them.

Her mission was personal, but as a detective she had use of the car pretty much on demand, so she didn't worry about it much. Keeping the Lexus in sight wasn't difficult in the smallish downtown area, and she could guess where the woman was headed. She was more predictable than Falken had expected when she began the tail.

Maybe that would make Falken's job easier.

She rolled down the window and let the cool air play through her hair.

She tingled with anticipation.

KILLIAN

They met at a café that tried hard to be trendy because it was located in the heart of Milwaukee's trendy East Side. Killian knew of at least eighteen perfectly adequate bars within walking range of where they sat, but Marcowicz had insisted, and now they sat across from each other. Between them were two glasses of iced tea. Marcowicz sipped nervously at his, using the straw almost daintily. Killian ignored his.

David Marcowicz was the police psychologist who had replaced Julia Barrett after her murder. He alternated sipping with quick glances all around.

"You realize," he said, "that I could lose my job. And my license."

Killian ignored this.

"I have to be discreet."

"You called me, originally."

Marcowicz nodded quickly. "I did. I did. I heard—There was a rumor you were interested in nailing Detective Lupo, and I got a vibe from him I just never liked."

"So you don't like Detective Lupo?"

Marcowicz sipped and swallowed as if his mouth had dried up in the last few seconds.

"No, it's not that," he explained. "He's likable enough. For a tough cop. Got commendations and medals, awards, you name it. Kind of an old-school cop, you know?"

"So then, what?" Killian glanced at his watch.

"So it's that there's *something* about him I don't like. Something hidden. Something, I don't know . . ."

"You're the doctor here," Killian pointed out helpfully.

"Yeah, but I'm still new. I haven't known these guys that long. I have some of Barrett's files, though. She wrote things about him, and I started following her leads."

Killian sighed. "Can we get to it?"

"Okay, look, Lupo's been involved in some stuff—"

"I know about it. I have his file. I need to know what you know that's not in his file."

Marcowicz sighed. "I give the guy the benefit of the doubt on the incidents, okay? But since the last one, he tells me he's been . . ."

"Yeah?" Killian prodded.

"He had this friend up on the reservation, Sam Waters. An elderly, uh, Indian, you know. Got killed in the shootout."

Killian wanted to strangle him, but he pretended he was patient.

"Lupo didn't really want to talk about it, but I use a few relaxation techniques—"

"Hypnosis?"

"Not quite, but I can get the patient to a very relaxed state that is almost like mild hypnosis. Patients sometimes open up before they realize what they've confessed."

"Go on."

"Lupo was slightly under, very relaxed, when he started to talk about this Sam Waters who was killed. He says he's been talking to him. Having visitations."

Killian snorted. "Shit, are you telling me Lupo sees dead people?"

"Uh, no. As far as I know, he sees exactly *one* dead person."

It was clear the idiot Marcowicz didn't get the reference and that just made Killian dislike him more.

"This Sam Waters comes to him and converses with him, argues with him, about Lupo's plans, his job. The same way he might argue with his partner. It's not that unusual, especially in cases of stress-induced trauma. He's had some of that. Probably just a way for Lupo to talk out issues with himself, except he thinks he sees—"

"You tell anyone this?" Killian interrupted.

"No! I shouldn't even be telling you. But if you go back far enough in his files, farther than even what you have, you start to see some patterns. Detective Lupo has had some strange coincidences in his life as a homicide cop, even as far back as his rookie days."

"You found out all this?"

Marcowicz shook his head, then swallowed some tea. "Barrett. She was obsessed. I mean, she hated the guy. Accused him of faking his foot injury."

Killian tilted his head. "I saw the original med report. His foot was hacked off. He wears a prosthesis."

"Right, but she swore that sometimes he forgets to limp."

"He either lost a foot or he didn't. Pretty hard to fake that kind of injury."

"True, but Barrett was stubborn. She seems to have been sure of what she knew."

"I'll keep an eye on him. Why don't I have the complete files?"

"Department's still trying to do retro work, going backward through all files and converting to MRF. Machine-readable form. They're just way behind, always understaffing the data-entry group."

Killian grunted. He'd suspected there was a reason his file was truncated. He hadn't gotten around to tracking the rest of it down yet.

"More iced tea?" Marcowicz stood and snatched up his cup.

"No." Killian still hadn't touched his.

He watched the bowlegged doctor approach the counter and ask for a refill. He thought about Lupo. If what the doctor said was accurate, then maybe the cop was more deeply traumatized by the recent events than anyone realized.

Or, he thought, *he's into some kind of scam and I'm going to take him down.*

When Marcowicz returned, Killian asked a series of questions that kept them there for another half hour. Marcowicz displayed a strange combination of reluctance and eagerness to toss Lupo's confidentiality aside. Killian wondered what he stood to gain from throwing suspicion onto Lupo, but he couldn't think of anything. Even though he was gaining knowledge, he felt a thinly disguised disgust for the doctor, who was supposed to protect Lupo's secrets. But by the time Killian left the café, he felt certain Lupo had something to hide.

In a cop, that usually spelled trouble.

CHAPTER SEVEN

LUPO

He sat in his car and watched her apartment, a rooftop condominium in a new building vaguely resembling a warehouse with an octagonal corner tower, just across from the wide-open square around which flowed Wausau's main business district.

On the horizon to the right, its spearpoint tip visible behind a massive commercial block and high-rise parking ramp, stood Dudley Tower, the city's tallest building. It was now officially the First Wausau Tower, according to his research.

When he scanned the Paladin condo block, he could see the twenty-foot glass panels of her corner tower windows, but he couldn't see inside. The glass was tinted and reflective.

He scrubbed his face almost brutally with his hands and tried to wipe away the fatigue.

And maybe more.

The guilt?

He looked at his hand. The skin was healing, the areas that seemed to have melted now returning to normal, with his coarse black hair sprouting again. The pain was a distant memory.

Too bad all pain can't be a distant memory.

Three months before he'd been parked in almost the same spot, after following her Lexus SUV from near Rib Mountain State Park, where she had apparently spent the night.

He thought he knew what it meant, he thought he was right in his suspicions, but there was still a niggling doubt.

Could he act, with doubt?

Would he?

Ever since she had reappeared on television as the high-profile anchor and occasional investigative reporter, Heather Wilson had haunted his dreams. There was the long absence, of course. A call to her station manager produced the automatic lie of a leave of absence. The last time he had seen her, disappearing under the dark waters of Cranberry Lake in the middle of the night, he assumed she'd drowned. Another reporter had strung out meaningless sentences regarding the story of Ron Malko and his decades of serial killing, but it wasn't Heather. She hadn't returned until two weeks later. In the meantime, Tom Arnow had grown cold and somehow more bitter, detaching himself from the job half the city council had accused him of doing poorly anyway.

Lupo suspected Tom had developed a *thing* for Heather. He had mourned her death, only to see her reappear without any apparent trauma, or back story. She hadn't returned to make a statement. She hadn't contacted anyone at all. Tom hadn't lasted long after that.

But Lupo had begun to wonder about Heather and her disappearance, and how she had survived. Then he had heard about the other disappearances, and then the animal attacks. They were mostly transient homeless men, a couple runaways, and some hookers.

And Lupo had almost accidentally traced someone from Eagle River, a petty thief whose name he recognized, and who had seemingly disappeared the same night. It was Dickie Klug, hillbilly cousin of the bastard who'd thrown in with Martin Stewart. Dickie was a petty thief, not very successful, as well as a sometime handyman and pot dealer. Lupo had first formed a theory about that, but then he'd found the guy living in Wausau in what was a completely impossible living arrangement. Lupo had begun to shadow Heather on his days off, thwarted by the long drive from Milwaukee. Eventually he had started taking vacation days, and then sick days, milking his physical trauma, and maybe his psychological trauma, too, he thought.

Lupo cursed the way werewolves couldn't sense each other while in human form. If there were ways, he didn't know them. There had to be clues, hints. But he couldn't convict and execute Heather Wilson on a hint or a hunch.

So he had waited for her to leave in order to invade her space. The lobby was probably covered by hidden cameras, but he went for the elevator like a resident. There was no live lobby guard, so security would only respond if something happened.

The apartment's lock yielded to his special pick and he was inside, clearing the wide hallway before any curious neighbors could step out and spot his face.

She was working. He had checked her schedule, confirmed it with a voice-disguised phone call, and watched her ride with a driver in a news van to the site of a story being reported from city hall. So he had doubled back to her apartment with the practiced driving of someone well acquainted with the directions.

Her apartment was on the sixth floor of the new condominium block in downtown Wausau. *Hell, it takes up a third of the sixth floor.* Glass, exposed red brick, and marble seemed to form every angle in the cavernous loft. Leather furniture—comfortable rather than simply stylish, he noted—made conversation pits here and there, some facing a massive LCD television perched on a huge stand filled with related components, others facing an equally impressive fireplace. Modern art mostly reigned on the pastel walls, though here and there a contrasting Renaissance painter grounded the whimsy of the avant-garde. Bronze nude sculptures in various poses implying sexual pleasure added a vague erotic sense that clashed with everything else, but was probably more her personal style.

Her alarm had been easily defeated, but it was a temporary bypass, and he knew there would be a malfunction signal sent to the security company in approximately ten minutes. The device he used was experimental, unavailable to the general public, but his source had guaranteed it would look like a power surge–related hiccup they would note but most likely neglect to report to their client. In the meantime, her motion sensors sensed nothing at all as he stalked like a ghost through her bedrooms.

He found her sexy underwear, her secret stash of sex toys, her sex sling (swinging limply in the current of heat kicked out by the guest-room register, professionally mounted to the ceiling joists with weight-bearing anchors), and a porn collection that would have put most men's to shame, mostly well-organized rows of DVDs lined up on shelves behind the false back wall of a smaller closet within her walk-in closet.

He shook his head. He'd suspected she was promiscuous, but perhaps she was actually a sex addict. Her bedroom smelled musky and sensual, with a strong perfume undertone. Was that his imagination, the musk? Just because he knew she was sexy?

He nosed into her desk drawers, file cabinets, and plastic bins stacked in a corner of her office, which was a third small bedroom adjacent to her master bath through connecting doors. She had framed journalistic and television awards and certificates, and various mounted articles about her television work. A cursory inspection of her files showed a near-anal tendency to save everything and anything, but also the inclination to keep it orderly. Unfortunately, there were two smaller file cabinets with combination locks that he couldn't breach. Her computers, a desktop Mac and a laptop, with a space cleared next to it for another laptop, would have been a target of his attentions, but he had too little time, and not enough expertise to leave no trace of his intrusion even if he could manage to copy the contents of her hard drives.

Another day, maybe, he thought, looking at the hardware with longing.

What was he looking for, really?

He left everything the way he found it, but moved stealthily and quickly to the kitchen. The freezer proved to be virtually identical to his, with packages of red meat overwhelming any other foods. Not much fruit or vegetables to be found anywhere, but was that really enough evidence? Sure, he knew his own needs ran to rare meat, especially when he couldn't hunt, but as much as he thought it a possible hint of her lycanthropy, he couldn't very well assassinate her on such flimsy circumstances. Still, he filed away the thoughts for later. Her trash was empty, recently dumped into the incinerator chute, probably.

Damn it, that might have helped.

Minutes later he was back in his car, waiting to see if the alarm-monitoring company would show up to check on their hiccup. Sure enough, a pseudo–squad car pulled up in front of the building and two uniforms got out. He figured they'd already been told the problem had passed, but would check the master circuitry anyway.

Not long after, they left, shaking their heads and laughing about the easy call.

Lupo muttered a curse. Had he learned anything, except that Heather Wilson was a sexually overcharged person?

"Hell, I knew that when I met her."

"I remember," Sam said. He was in the backseat.

Lupo looked in the rearview mirror and caught his gaze. It was so much like *An American Werewolf in London*, he thought. Except Sam always looked the same. He was grateful for that.

"What do you think, Sam?"

"You need some help. Can't be with her twenty-four/seven, can you?" He slid back onto the seat so Lupo couldn't see him anymore.

"Yeah, help would be good."

"Not Jessie."

"No, not Jessie, for sure," he said. He pictured her anger when he'd copped to his off-the-books stakeouts. Of course, being unable to confide in Jessie was a hindrance because she already knew werewolves existed. He needed a partner in the know.

"Let's go over the list," Sam said from the backseat.

Lupo was already doing that.

FALKEN

She didn't use her badge to get into the athletic club, but instead filled out a registration form and paid with a credit card.

As she suspected, a pro shop within the exercise complex carried everything she needed to begin using her new membership. About the only thing she couldn't have done today was reserve a racquetball or handball court. That would take a one-day notice. Otherwise, she bought the bare minimum in sweats, shorts, soap and a towel, and even a lock for her new locker, all from a bored teenager who didn't look "pro" at anything but slacking.

She wasn't worried about losing her quarry—there were only so many corners of the complex to hide in, and by all accounts and by her own observation, the person she was tailing made routine visits that lasted at least a full hour.

Once changed into the generic sports clothes, Detective Sheila Falken began to stalk the halls and stick her face into the pool room, the tennis courts, the cavernous shedlike great room filled with ranks of stationary bikes and treadmills, flat-screen televisions flickering a few feet apart on every available wall surface. She started to worry about finding her quarry after all, but then Falken checked the weight room and there she was, a glowing halo of health surrounded by sweaty muscle-bound guys whose eyes strayed to check out the celebrity among them every chance they had.

Falken stepped into the room confidently and half-smiled as some of those eyes shifted toward her. Her image in the wall mirrors wasn't half bad, she allowed, and even though she wasn't the celebrity her quarry was, she deserved the attention. She was deceptively muscular, in the sense that in sweats her muscles looked sleek and toned, but if she wore a dress—not that she did *that* often—the muscles didn't seem outrageous or out of place.

Her dark hair pulled into a ponytail spilled confidently down her back, and her rack seemed to have attracted as much attention as her booty, which was round and full yet spectacularly shapely (if she said so herself). Her face was unlined, not showing her actual age. She wore plenty of makeup, partially so people would remember it and her face, and when she went without the lipstick and mascara and slipped on a pair of her old-fashioned glasses, her appearance changed completely. It was a simple form of disguise, and it had been effective more often than she could say.

Falken flexed a little and smiled when she spotted a few appreciative glances, the eyes diverted from the star of the room. At her age, it was gratifying that she could even compete with somebody like local television celebrity Heather Wilson and her million-watt body.

Falken found a vacant universal and pumped iron absentmindedly, keeping her eye on Wilson in the mirrors. The two women were almost exact opposites in terms of complexion and hair, but the pair provided more than enough eye candy for the lifters spread out on the mats and at the other machines.

Heather Wilson seemed oblivious to the attention her curves garnered, and Falken had to give her credit for really working up a sweat with the weights. She wasn't faking, showing off for the horn dogs, as Falken had expected. No, she was lifting serious weight for her body size and clearly spreading out a credible workout complete with sweat and wrinkled clothing. None of which lessened the impact of her camera-friendly looks one tiny bit. Falken smirked and added her admiration to that of the slobs around her, though she hid it well. Within minutes she was lost in her own workout, content to keep an unobtrusive eye on Wilson in the mirror.

Detective Sheila Falken was on Heather Wilson's trail, and she would stick like the proverbial glue until it was time.

She lifted a couple hundred pounds of metal bricks without too much trouble. She could sense eyes on her. She felt herself getting wet, aroused beyond belief. She couldn't help it; exercise and testosterone turned her on. She smiled at the closest males who probably smelled the musk on her and gave them more to look at and fantasize about. Meanwhile, she studied Wilson with her cold, dark eyes.

Measuring.

Wilson was unaware, spending her time watching mostly herself, and making sure the men were watching her. And most of them were watching, dazzled by the blondeness of her hair and the lush curves of her lean tigress's body. She seemed to be wearing her bold on-camera makeup. Falken thought she should be sweating some of it off, but she didn't seem to be.

They probably make television personalities from a completely different mold, she thought, smirking.

Still, most of the men seemed to salivate over the goddess in their midst.

One man set a barbell down carefully and then approached Falken. She watched him come closer, the muscles on his muscles rippling in time with each confident step. His neck was like gnarled wood, and his arms seemed to have been carved from granite. He had a goofy smile on his ugly face.

Falken continued to lift, keeping Wilson in the corner of her eye.

"Hey, lookin' good, babe," he said when he arrived close enough that she could smell the steroids filtering out through his pores. His voice was gruff.

Falken saw that Heather was heading for the door. "Back off, asshole," she said.

Her eyes followed Heather through the door; then she looked at the offended lifter. His eyes were wide, his brows dark and scary. Anger flushed across his features.

"Ain't no call for that, missy," he started to say. But then he stopped because Falken had grasped his wrist and bent it back so far that he went to his knees, his face contorted.

"I said, back off. I meant it." She gave him a push and he flopped over onto his side, his wrist broken. He started to howl in pain. *Very unmasculine*.

"Next time, listen," she said. Then she followed Heather into the long hallway to the locker room.

CHAPTER EIGHT

DICKIE KLUG

Every time he opened his door he felt his heart pound, expecting *her*.

This time, he opened the door and it crashed in on him, bashing him in the face—or what would have been his face, except he managed to raise his arm and his wrist took the brunt of the door's swing.

"Hey, you can't—" he shouted as he backpedaled into his living space, falling flat on his ass. The door shuddered open all the way, and Dickie blinked at the figure standing in the doorway.

"What the fuck—?"

"Shut up, Klug."

He stared at his intruder. Recognition hit a second too slow. But he knew who it was. At one point he had pinned a photograph cut out of the local newspaper on his wall. Time had passed, but he recognized the long hair, the smirk, and the wild look in the man's eyes.

"You—you're that cop killed my cousin!"

"Not technically, scumbag."

"The fuck you doing here?"

The cop stepped all the way in and closed the door behind him with exaggerated care. There was a crack in the plaster where the doorknob had connected with the wall.

"I want you to know I'm on to you and your game." He scanned the room. "No way you're paying for this yourself, scumbag. What's your deal? What's your arrangement with her? Is it what I think it is?"

"The fuck?" Dickie sputtered, but it was a halfhearted effort. "You got no juris—*jurisdiction* here! I'm gonna—"

"Gonna what?"

The cop's smirk turned meaner. Dickie thought he saw murder in his eyes. He shut his mouth.

"So who pays for this? You never made an honest dime in your life."

The cop towered over Dickie, and he couldn't get up without presenting too good a target. He sat.

Dickie's mouth was dry. He tried licking his lips, but it might as well have been sandpaper on brick.

"I—I inherited the money," Dickie said. "I got proof."

"I'll bet you do," the cop growled. "I'm sure she got you some crackpot paper-fuck of a cover. But I know what's going on, and I'm gonna shut her down. I'm telling you so you can get your sorry ass out of town before the shit hits."

Dickie wondered what the cop's real play was. Why was he coming here, intimidating him? Why send out a warning to her? Didn't the cop know he could just pick up the phone and call her?

But then Dickie realized that he wouldn't call, and the cop seemed to know that. Dickie was too afraid of her.

"Whattya mean? The fuck's going on you're gonna shut down?"

"The murders. She's not getting away with it. I know what's happening, and when I catch her at it, she's done. You're done, too."

Dickie was still sitting on his floor. He shook his head as if clearing it. "Shit, man, I don't know what you're talkin' about." He thought fast.

Heather Wilson had returned to work only after she had learned to hunt the homeless men and women Dickie corralled for her. They were easy, willing to follow him anywhere for the promise of work or a meal or even, occasionally, sex. Willing to go anywhere, even with him, in his rattrap old Dodge, as long as there was some sort of payoff at the end of the road.

What they found, however, was the end of the road for them. He took them to various deserted picnic areas and waysides, kicked them out of the car, and watched them stand around clueless until *she* came charging out of the woods. A sleek and muscular gray she-wolf, bloodlust in her cold eyes, she came out of the cover of the woods and lunged at them. Some ran a few yards before she brought them down like wild game; some stood petrified and managed to simply wet their pants. Others screamed and tried to force their way back into his car.

He watched them, let them bang their fists on his glass and hood, until the wolf reached them and dragged them off. He watched as the wolf took some immediately, and toyed with others for a while, depending on their response. He watched as she tore them apart, strewed their intestines all over the grass, ate chunks of them with sloppy tearing and swallowing like a dog nosing into a bag of kibble, and then howled her victory while staring through the glass into his eyes, reminding him that only her grace allowed him to live.

To live and to serve.

That had become his lot in life, making sure he could continue to live by feeding her "game." She treated the whole thing as a game, too.

Sometimes she had allowed him to watch her turning back into a human, into the woman newscaster Heather Wilson, the same statuesque blonde that made male pulses race all over the Marathon County. When she chose to grant him a view of her, he would stare mesmerized at her extraordinary figure, the upthrust breasts and the smooth hairless pubic mound, the long legs ending in perfectly shaped buttocks, and the mane of glowing hair that cascaded down her bare back. She was a goddess, and he was smitten while yet still afraid of her, of what she was, what she had become.

Then she would run past him and sometimes turn back into a wolf, other times simply disappear into the woods, the blood of her victims still staining her cheeks and lips like grotesque makeup.

But after a dozen or so such hunts, which was what she called the exercise in which she simply murdered helpless old men and broken-down women, she had come to some realization and he had been granted more and more free time between hunts, even though his rent was still being paid.

At night, every night she was on, he watched her reading

the news on his wide screen and masturbated to the memory of what she looked like naked.

Now with the recent events swirling through his thoughts, Dickie Klug saw that the wild man wasn't going to act like a cop with official business.

"You got no jurisdiction here!" he repeated. "You can't just barge in—"

"I just did. I want you to disappear, Klug. Just walk away. I want her to call you and find no one home. Get me?"

"What? Are you fucking crazy?"

"What's wrong? You afraid of her? Big man like you?"

Dickie licked his lips. He had to be careful here. Not give anything away. If the bastard was gonna kill him, he'd be dead already. He was just talking, throwing his weight around, so Dickie still had a little leeway.

"I got a legit job here," he said, trying to be earnest. And he *did*, though she had set it up so he didn't have to do much but check in occasionally. She had *connections*. But this crazy cop was gonna piss all over his situation. "I can prove I got work in this area."

"I don't give a fuck," Lupo growled. "You pick up and move yourself on out of town. Otherwise you'll get in my way. And you don't want to do that."

Dickie stared into the dark eyes and agreed. He'd seen eyes like that, intense like that, before. *She* had eyes like that.

Lupo advanced on him and stood over him, and Dickie felt an embarrassing warmth spread in his shorts.

The cop's nostrils flared and he grinned a smile that held no mirth whatsoever.

"I think we understand each other," he said.

And then he was gone.

Fuck, Dickie thought. *Fuck fuck*.

Who scared him more? He was gonna have to think about that. But first he had to change his pants.

LUPO

From an angle-parking slot across the street he watched her leave her place in the middle of the afternoon. He was still tracking her movements.

He followed Heather to a series of downtown bars, where she ordered drinks, and he watched as men looked at her hungrily. She enjoyed the looks, it was clear, and Lupo became one of the lookers without too much trouble. After the first bar there were others, an itinerary of sorts, and at some point he found himself getting closer and closer to her, somehow tricked into thinking he was invisible. But he wasn't sure when he realized that he was no longer the watcher, that *she* had become the one who kept tabs on him.

Even though he kept to the dark corners of the crowded bars, he sensed that she had made him. Her head tilted his way and he caught her smiling into the bar mirrors as she sipped her liqueurs or harder booze. She ignored most approaches by starstruck males and smiled as if repeatedly hearing a private joke.

Lupo nursed a beer in each place, trying to avoid being obvious. She seemed oblivious to him and most other men, though her every move was a pose.

Finally she led him out to the street and he was able to swing into the light traffic behind her, keeping a few cars between them at all times.

When she pulled into an old-fashioned no-tell motel out on the strip lining the old north stretch of Highway 51, he wasn't even aware of watching her park in front of an end unit and enter it after digging into her purse for a card key.

In fact, he was barely aware that he had eased out of his car and clicked the door shut quietly, and that now he was approaching her door. There was no plan. Maybe some surveillance through the plastic curtain, maybe just a recon pass and then a hasty retreat for a stakeout. He wondered vaguely whom she was meeting, or who would show up. He kept to the shadows and read the number on her unit, suddenly realizing how close he was.

He wasn't aware of anything except that she threw open the door, naked, her breasts thrusting out at him, her shaved-smooth sex glistening with desire. He was close enough to reach out and feel the electric charge generated upon the contact of their skins. Her musk surrounded him and the next thing he remembered he was on his back on the motel room floor with her astraddle, facing his feet and using him to impale herself, her flesh grasping him hungrily and forcing him deeper. Then he was kneeling behind her and pulling the golden hair as if it were the reins of a beautiful thoroughbred.

Click, whirr . . . His mind went blank for a while.

And then he was lying on the bed as she knelt between his thighs and engulfed him with her experienced mouth. He came in a gush and the lights of the room seemed to make her eyes glow as she held his gaze, the corners of her mouth upturned in a tight smile of conquest and superiority.

Jesus, what have I done?

It was much later, when he asked himself. But he had no answer. He had no excuse, no rationalization. It just *was*. He had been following her, and then he was in her. As if there had been nothing else stretched between the two moments.

And he promised himself it would never, *could* never, happen again.

But he knew it would.

They had never talked throughout the feverish coupling and uncoupling. They never spoke about what had happened that night on the beach, with the Wolfpaw mercenaries and their hostages. Lupo tried to gauge whether she had turned wolf, but even though he felt hypnotically attracted to her, he could not determine if she carried the werewolf gene. Damn he wished werewolves could sense each other as humans.

Would have led to too much territorialism, probably.

Heather was an adroit, controlling, insatiable lover, and he wasn't surprised. He was malleable to her desires, consumed with the sense that at some level he had always known this would happen. Just not when.

At least I know where she is at every moment, he thought with the crazy giddiness of someone on the edge.

And where she was right now was particularly stimulating; what she was doing with the tips of her fingers and her tongue sent electric shivers up and down his brain stem. He surrendered to her attentions again, and lost the thread of his thoughts.

And still they didn't talk. Their communication was in the form of animal grunts, moans, and panting.

They never talked, because Lupo had started the day tailing her and ended it fucking her as if she'd become some sort of drug he couldn't explain, but that he had to have.

She used him, and he let her.

From the Journals of Caroline Stewart
December 15, 1981
I need to start being honest with myself.

Jerry Boone's death weighs terribly on my mind. It's sadness at a promising life and career cut short, and at the loss of a friend and colleague. He was someone who enjoyed my company and conversation, and I felt the same way.

It's sadness, but it's also guilt.

I can't help feeling that my insistence on attempting regression with Nick somehow caused Jerry's death. Perhaps if it had been someone else, the results would have been the same. But it's no comfort to suspect someone would have had to pay a price for trying to help Nick. I've paid only a small price, but as Nick was attracted to me from the beginning, there's a feeling of immunity. Of anyone in the scientific field that Nick could conceivably have contacted to demonstrate the depths of his problem, I was perhaps the only one who would have been willing to accept the unacceptable, the unbelievable.

Did Jerry kill himself because he couldn't handle what he saw? (Supposing he saw a manifestation of Nick's condition.)

Did he give up on life in this world because of suddenly realizing its rules had changed forever?

I've been thinking nonstop about this. Did he kill himself because of something Nick said?

What if the truth is more complex?

What if there was a manifestation, Nick explained it away—or acknowledged it—and over two months' time Jerry learned something else?

Jesus. Is there some other explanation?

1978
BRAD SCHNEIDER

"Sure, why the hell not?"

Rollie liked intrigue, and this sounded like fun.

Brad called a kegger for the Vienna Woods.

Wiener Woods.

So much clandestine sex went on in the acre-wide grove of trees that Vienna had given way to Wiener among those in the know, who nevertheless did not realize it was correct, if mispronounced, German.

Rollie giggled. A kegger in the Wiener Woods was always fun. And this one was shaping up to be the most fun.

Their friends began to gather early.

Someone carted the kegs into the clearing, setting up near a rickety picnic table that had dispensed plenty of splinters to naked buttocks and knees.

The crowd started to gather when a chosen few dropped off cardboard boxes filled with bottles of heavy booze.

Word spread quickly that something special was going to happen tonight, if a certain fag boy showed up. The mood was anticipatory. Jocks and thugs licked their lips as they discussed what they hoped would happen to teach the pervert a lesson.

Girls giggled, and stroked boys' egos along with their biceps. Some snuck a grope at tight groins. Horny jocks saw their opportunity and patted rounded buttocks.

Brad stood proudly with Rollie at the keg station, watching as the electricity began to hum in the air between cliques. The mood was something like what it must have been early in the evening at a Roman Bacchanalia.

Brad pictured some of the scenes of *Caligula*, the true version he'd been able to see at a bachelor party last year. He felt his groin tightening at the thought.

"All the guys ready?" Rollie asked, leaning over so no one would hear.

"Yup, everybody's waiting for the signal. He shows up, he becomes the show."

"That's great," Rollie said. "I like the way you think, Bradley." Rollie hunched over in a sweeping, elaborate bow.

"There's nothin' to it." Brad blushed. Rollie's thanks could be effusive.

All it had taken was a few words spread amongst all the organization's lieutenants. Everybody was on board. Kids from all cliques started showing up, hanging out together, laughing it up. Some of the groups intersected other groups and Brad noted with amusement that some of the jocks seemed to have little trouble interacting with the stoner girls.

Maybe they gave great head, he thought.

Whatever.

He enjoyed his handiwork for a while, watching the kegger get into full swing. Most kids drank beer from Dixie cups. Crushed cups started to show up underfoot throughout the clearing. A braver few were at the table, mixing themselves "adult" cocktails: Seven and Sevens, whiskey sours, rum and Cokes. Easy, sweet, knock-your-head-off drinks, if you had a couple or ten. Rollie's endless credit had supplied them with enough booze to drown a herd of elephants.

Everywhere Brad saw evidence of the orgylike atmosphere that would eventually turn the party into something truly memorable. And it was all him, wasn't it?

Brad was standing around sipping rum and Coke and chewing the fat with Rollie.

Rollie bragged that he'd managed to bribe a couple local cops to turn their backs on the gathering.

"Yeah, how'd you manage that?"

Rollie pointed.

In a far corner of the group, two uniformed cops sipped drinks and chatted up a small group of the cutest socialite girls, who seemed to be hanging all over the cops' uniforms, their hands touching biceps and patting their gun belts seductively.

"Brilliant! Those guys probably got woodies they could pound nails with."

"Those girls are on 'em like flies on shit! That's their assignment as long as the fuzz is here. Their shift change is comin' up, so we'll be cop-free for a good long time, since they ain't gonna report us.

"Plus," he added in a whisper, "I got some Polaroids of them cops with the chicks. They're gonna keep quiet."

Brad nodded his approval of the whole strategy.

The jocks stood around in groups, flexing and drinking, laughing uproariously at their idiot jock jokes. Brad was part of the group and made his share of in-jokes with the different groups, but he was truly a fake—an impostor whose interests lay in the manipulation itself more than the results or the status that made Rollie such an attention hog.

When the pervert finally showed up with his entourage of losers, signals flew from group to group.

The level of drunkenness was high, and Brad stood back and hoped to watch his handiwork unfold. He had turned as many of his friends and connections into Josh haters as he could, constantly undermining the geek by calling him names guaranteed to enrage the mental midgets who made up the majority of the Brad and Rollie network.

Brad licked his lips and melted into the background for now.

The trigger had been squeezed.

It was time to watch the bullet hit the target.

And obliterate it.

CHAPTER NINE

LUPO

He was lying with Jessie and feeling her breathing next to him after their lovemaking.

Though sated, he felt unrest, and the guilt washed over him knowing that even when he and Jessie had made love, sometimes he found himself thinking of *her.* He didn't choose to, but the thought would start and the images would come, and then he had come and it had been very good for both of them, and only he knew Jessie wasn't as much on his mind as she should have been.

Later he felt her shift position next to him, her sinewy body stretching along the length of his and wrapping protectively around him, a hand slowly reaching around his back in a sleepy embrace, and he had the vivid thought that he should eat the muzzle of his Glock, it hurt him so much to have lied to her and betrayed her like this. And yet he had done it.

He swore to himself he would stop. No more Heather Wilson. What had happened was an aberration. It wasn't him, his style, whatever it's called. He knew he loved Jessie because his destiny had become so much intertwined with hers, as if their togetherness had been decreed by some greater power.

"Nice way to show her your love," Ghost Sam said.

He was sitting in the club armchair Jessie had placed next to the fireplace. Lupo could just make out Sam's features in the soft glow of the dying fire.

"Leave me alone!" he said, his voice a hiss.

Jessie stirred and muttered in her sleep, so he shut up and made his breathing match hers until she was asleep again. When he next squinted at the chair, Sam was gone.

Guilt and conflicting emotions kept him awake until dawn tinged the walls with gray light.

DICKIE KLUG

He stared at the phone she had given him. A prepaid TracFone. No records, she had told him. No eavesdropping. It was his only link to her, or her to him.

Should he call her and tell her about the wild-eyed cop?

Not wild-eyed, really. But his eyes seemed to change colors. Maybe that was just a trick of the light. Or maybe it was more than that.

He reached for the phone, but stopped midway.

Maybe this was a way to be free of her. Not warning her.
Did he want to be free of her?

He stared at the phone.

WAGNER

Wausau was rightly proud of its parks system, and Wagner
was happy to bask in the pride. Every other week, Wagner
had begun hunting in a different gemlike park.

Sometimes rare homeless people and even an occasional
family came in handy. Sometimes it was a late-night jogger.
Sometimes a dog walker. The dog would end up in the
pound, traumatized out of its wits, the owner either mauled
by the mysterious animal or simply gone from the face of the
earth. Wagner made sure half would be found, and the other
half never.

Tonight Wagner stalked a lone figure wearing a hooded
sweatshirt. His muscles showed clearly even through the
dirty gray cotton cloth with a faded college name screened
on the front. He was walking through a tiny corner park
near city hall.

A weight lifter out for a breath of air? A criminal stalking
his own prey?

Wagner didn't care. Stalking a stalker was just as much
fun, and maybe more.

When the dude felt eyes boring into his back and whirled,
he was faced with a large wolf, which in the dark he took to
be a dog.

They were near a fountain with a water-spouting cherub
perched atop its two basin levels.

The hooded guy grinned. "Nice doggy," he said.

From the tone, Wagner deduced the man wasn't a friend
of animals. In fact, the man had a small, flat semiautomatic
pistol held in one hand in his pocket. The muzzle poked out
like a black eye.

"Come here, doggy," he said, trying to smile.

Wagner approached, knowing that in the dark a wolf would look like a dog to an unsuspecting dipshit like this guy. The semblance to a canine served Wagner well at night.

"Com'ere, ya mutt," the man grunted under his breath. "I got somethin' for ya. Come on."

Wagner approached, sniffing, *faking dogness*, then gathered and leaped, going straight for the throat.

The man tried desperately to unstick the gun from his pocket, but all he did manage was to shoot through the sweatshirt fabric and jam the slide in the material.

That's why you always use a revolver with a shrouded hammer if you want to shoot through a pocket, idiot.

Wagner's powerful jaws tore through the man's windpipe and jugular while the two bodies crashed to the ground.

A mewling cry erupted from the man's throat but was cut short when his blood spurted out in a series of jets.

Wagner growled and dug farther into the thick neck, teeth and fangs sawing tissue and bone while muscular legs collapsed the prey's chest.

The struggling slowed and came to an end as the thug bled out.

Wagner fed. Then dragged the remains into a thicket near a set of faux Roman columns, where they would be found soon, but not immediately.

The only witnesses were the dark windows of a small office building that bounded the park on one side, and a darkened old church across the quiet street.

A good night's work, all in all, Wagner thought.

CHAPTER TEN

LUPO

The early-morning Midwest flight to Atlanta was not quite full. Lupo found his seat and tossed his carry-on in the bin above his seat. An angular woman in a dowdy grandma coat who was coming down the aisle stopped short when she saw him.

Not him. It was his pistol. His leather jacket hung open long enough to give the woman a good view of his holstered Glock as she squeezed past.

He looked at her and grinned, curious as to what she would do. Her seat was two rows back, and after she sat she pushed the call button set into the plastic cowling above her head. She leaned over and whispered something to the younger, pretty woman who was already in the window seat next to hers. The pretty woman leaned out a bit and glanced in his direction, then spoke softly to the dowdy woman. The younger, dark-haired woman shook her head gently. She was thin and wore a peach blazer and khaki pants and caught his eye as he craned to see what was happening.

When a flight attendant arrived, the older woman whispered in her ear as well. Lupo had to face left to be able to see them in his peripheral vision. The attendant listened intently and whispered back something, but the passenger interrupted, gesticulating. The woman in the blazer seemed to keep out of it forcefully. Finally the attendant spoke too loudly.

"He's a police officer, ma'am! He's allowed to carry his weapon. Now, please fasten your seat belt."

The older woman glowered at him and he smiled crookedly at her. The woman in the peach blazer seemed to have been amused, because she also smiled slightly, but at him.

She was far more than just pretty, he noted, amending his earlier assessment.

The flight attendant winked at him when she went past. He smiled at her, too. Damn, she was one of the cute ones.

He checked back and the older woman passenger was now blushing, embarrassed. He nodded to the beat of a song in his head and smiled in her direction. Then he glanced at her seatmate and included her in his smile. She gave him a sardonic eyebrow and grin. He felt her eyes on his back through the preflight and then the perfect takeoff.

He settled back and thought about the woman in the peach blazer briefly, then allowed the routine flight's gentle motion to rock him to near sleep until the imminent landing was announced. When it was his turn, he deplaned without a look back.

Atlanta was the usual crazed pandemonium. Soldiers in camouflage traveling in clumps, an NBA team towering over a group of fans and everyone else around them, beeping carts, and streams of antlike passengers.

Lupo hated it. He didn't really mind traveling, but this reminded him too much of the days when he would fly to visit his parents. Bad memories were attached to many of those trips. He shrugged and hoofed it to the end of the terminal, rode the airport subway along with thousands of harried travelers, and was amused when he spilled out at the destination terminal and spotted a flash of peach material.

Sure enough, it was the dark-haired woman from his flight.

Great, she's heading to the same plane.

It wasn't likely, was it?

Yes, it is.

From behind, he had to reassess again.

Not thin, actually, but lean. Very athletic, graceful. In fact, she had a very pleasing look from behind. *A nice ass.*

A sliver of guilt made him uncomfortable, so he looked away, up at the endless rows of directional signs. Easy to fall prey to sexist thoughts in the heart of the Atlanta airport, where most women seemed to be blonde and attractive. And friendly, too, in his experience, often striking up conversations on airplanes or at gates. This woman stood out by nature of her dark hair, when apparently most women in Georgia had to be blonde, if all he had to judge by was his experience flying through.

Silly thoughts. He combed his long hair with his fingers and bore down on the long walk, still keeping the peach material in sight.

He reached the connecting gate a minute after she did and followed her to the only empty seats available for waiting. Coincidentally, they were across from each other. The woman's eyes grew wide when she spotted him slipping into the black seat across from her. Lupo nodded and smiled, and she looked way. But she was smiling, too.

When the seat next to him was vacated by a sullen teenager who reluctantly joined his family elsewhere, the woman suddenly stood and crossed the aisle, sitting so she could touch his arm.

"You shouldn't mock the concerned passenger. You could have been a hijacker," she said.

Lupo grinned. "The day's young. Maybe I'll hit the next plane."

She chuckled. "Are you really a cop? Let's see your badge."

Lupo searched her face for humor. She was half-smiling, not letting him see whether she was serious or not. It was a nice face, he noted, from up close. Wide, sensuous mouth.

Long, straight nose upturned at the end. Her eyes crinkled when she smiled. *Half-smiled.*

He showed her the badge on his belt.

"All right, then I feel safe."

He nodded, happy to comply. "Too bad your seatmate never did."

"So what's your story? Extraditing some crazed serial killer?"

"Been there, done that," he said.

"Following a crime boss or his flunky?"

"Old hat."

"Vacation?"

"What's that?"

"You don't want to tell me?" she said.

"It's important police business."

"So important you can't tell me?"

"Something like that."

She searched his face for humor and he gave her a glimpse, otherwise he'd scare her.

"What's *your* trip about? Vacation, sipping margaritas by the pool?"

"I wish," she said. "I'm a contract killer."

"You kill contracts?" he said.

"Silly!" She reached into her purse and flashed a badge. "I'm on the job too. Sheila Falken, Wausau Police."

He could honestly say he hadn't seen that coming.

JESSIE

She left him a snarky voice mail when he didn't answer his phone. It wasn't very nice of her, suddenly complaining about his unexpected trip. But he'd barely come home, after probably causing a problem with those Wolfpaw people that would lead to who knew what sort of trouble, and then he'd left her a note about taking an early flight back south.

She'd lost her mind, for a minute.

He could be so *infuriating*! So sensitive and solicitous on the one hand, but so lizard brain ruled on the other. So protective and careful at some times, and so foolhardy other times. He seemed to radiate contradictions.

But she sensed that his conflicts raged within and ate at him despite his best intentions.

She dug through her bag for the gaming card.

Lately, it seemed she craved *The Turn of a Friendly Card* for all the wrong reasons.

Maybe she needed to take up the tarot.

LUPO

They chatted and compared notes up until their flight boarded, and then they were able to negotiate a seat change and Falken ended up in the window seat next to his. He felt the touch of her thigh on his and pulled away a little, encroaching on the aisle enough that the flight attendant's cart smacked his arm several times on its way through the cabin.

Lupo found himself talking comfortably with the fellow cop, their conversation ranging from stories about being on the job to the occasional personal revelation. She was too easy to talk to, and in the back of his mind he saw Jessie's face. She'd be jealous if she knew he was having such a good time on a flight he would normally have hated.

"I remember you now," she said. He had just mentioned the Martin Stewart gang. "Jesus, that was you, uh?"

He nodded and drank some of his water. Talking about the incident made him nervous.

"There was something else up there in Vilas more recently, wasn't there?" she said.

"Might have been," he said.

She laughed. "You're so reticent."

"What's that mean?"

"Well, I don't know why you might be," she said.

"No, what does *reticent* mean?" he said.

"Reticent?" Then she saw him smiling. "I get it, an old *Seinfeld* line. You got me."

He liked that she recognized the joke. In fact, he rather liked her.

"You ever think of making the switch to the big city?"

"New York?"

"Ha ha," he said, fake-laughing. "Less big. Milwaukee. We always need good detectives. You a good detective, Falken?"

She looked over her water cup. "I get by."

"I bet you do."

She grinned. Looked out the window awhile.

"So how many homicide cops can Wausau actually support?" he said later.

She grinned again. "Well, I'm a detective, but it's homicide-vice-bunco-you-name-it. Our detective squad's eight out of eighty-odd uniforms and civilians."

"Pumping up the job title, eh?"

"Name of the game. Homicide sounds better, doesn't it?"

"Indubitably."

"You work homicide exclusively?" she said.

He grimaced. "Right now I'm on a fucking gang task force. Enforced rehab leave."

She nodded in sympathy. "Not much gang activity in Wausau, but we're seeing the beginnings."

"What're you up to in Daytona?" he said. "If I may ask."

"Routine. I'm attending a deposition for an open case I got a stake in. Boring. You?"

"Visiting an old, uh, friend."

"Oh, okay, I get it. Butt out. No problem."

"Nah, it's just . . . a sore spot."

"I got those, too."

They sat in companionable silence until the plane started to dip. Atlanta to Daytona Beach is barely more than a hop, and Lupo pondered the fact that the best seatmates he'd ever had were always on the shorter leg. The Milwaukee to Atlanta leg always drew less interesting characters.

While they were on approach, Falken braved the quivering cabin and refreshed her makeup and he watched from the corner of his eye.

She's flirting, no doubt about it.

She was monitoring his reaction from the corner of her eye as she finished up her lips with gloss and checked herself in the compact.

He thought back to her little charade with his pistol on the previous flight. He saw through that, now. She would have made him. She'd been getting his attention. Despite the friendly talk, had she been tailing him?

He hadn't forgotten she was a Wausau cop. What were the odds?

He smiled blandly and didn't let his eyes betray his thought patterns. Why would a Wausau cop tail him?

Unless she'd seen him tailing Heather Wilson.

That might be problematic.

"When you going back?" she asked when she'd put her makeup away and they awaited the long approach. In the background the cabin attendant droned out a few connecting gates. The Daytona airport is small, so there weren't many.

"Tonight or tomorrow. You?"

"Couple days, I hope. It's been a long time since spring break in Daytona for me."

"Yeah," he said. "Same here."

They deplaned in silence as people around them chatted on cell phones and filed out slowly. At baggage check, Falken plucked a light folding suitcase from the grinding carousel.

"Can I drop you somewhere?" Lupo asked. "I've got a car at Avis."

"Thanks, but I'm being met by a local cop. I'll just wait until he gets here. Maybe I'll see you on the return flight."

She smiled at him, squinting in the bright sunlight that dappled the airport proper through the many panes.

"Maybe, Falken, maybe. Have a good trip either way."

"You, too."

They shook hands, and he felt a spark of something when they touched.

Dangerous, he thought.

He watched her walk toward a row of black chairs, then went to claim his rental.

Definitely dangerous.

WAGNER

Another set of eyes among many wouldn't set off the quarry's internal alarms.

A safe distance went a long way to making that set of eyes anonymous.

Wagner watched. And learned.

And adjusted the plan as needed.

But mostly watched.

LUPO

He wasn't sure why, but he sat in the white Buick at the far end of the lot and waited. He had no particular hurry. The weather was splendid, as always, with the early-afternoon heat battling the car's AC and almost winning.

A half hour later Falken exited the terminal from the doors at the end of the rental-car alley. She went to a black Camry in the lot and dumped her bag in the back.

That's weird. Had she lied about the ride?

Then again, maybe her ride had crapped out on her.

Curiosity engaged, he pulled out of the lot a ways behind her just to make sure she was heading toward Daytona proper.

And if she was tailing *him*, why had she let him go first?

He shook his head. Secrets. He hadn't been entirely candid with her, so why shouldn't he expect the same?

He watched her head straight for International Speedway, then swung away and traversed various back roads until, twenty minutes later, he turned left on A1A, the ocean briefly in front of him with its intense blueness. He passed brightly colored, high-priced beach houses on the right, some of them hidden by walls and ranks of wild Spanish bayonet and saw palmetto spikes. Here and there, an older and more modest home still squatted on a smaller lot. Awaiting the wrecking ball, some of them—when Florida real estate rebounded, these houses would be the first to go and cede their beachfront to the nouveau riche.

Sparser real estate on the ocean side gave way to a long stretch of sand beyond a ridge of dunes topped by scruffy vegetation, with occasional wooden walk-outs leading to the monitored beaches. On the landward side of the highway, family restaurants and bars and curio shops in the requisite Florida pastels jostled for attention between the three- and four-story condo complexes with names like Vista Marina and Playa del Mar.

After passing the sign for Ormond Beach, Lupo kept an eye on the cross streets. At the intersection of U.S. A1A and Kathy Drive was a tan condo building with long, private balconies looking seaward. It turned out to be the building he wanted. The rest of the street was made up of neat, very well-maintained Florida bungalows and ranches.

The condo he wanted was on the upper floor, facing the ocean. It was at the end of the hall. He rang the doorbell and waited.

There was a chance nobody would be home, but it was a weekend, and it was worth trying here first. Lupo had the secondary address, if he needed it.

A shadow crossed the door on the inside. Lupo could see

the twin shafts of light from the sun filtering into the apartment.

There was a long pause in which Lupo looked directly into the peephole. Finally, he heard the lock disengage. It even sounded reluctant.

"Goddamn it, Lupo," Tom Arnow growled. "What the hell do you want?"

"Hi, Tom," Lupo said, nodding. "Can I talk to you?"

Arnow stood in the gap between the door and the jamb. He stared at Lupo. Not with dislike, Lupo thought, but with conflicting emotions. Hell, he was an authority on conflicting emotions. He understood.

"I don't suppose you can talk from there?" Tom said, sighing. "Not sure your neighbors want to hear any of it."

"Yeah, I guess not." Arnow stepped aside and back and waited for Lupo to cross the threshold.

Lupo felt it immediately.

Silver.

Nearby. It was like heat and a rash and a fever all rolled into one. Strong, pungent, and weakening. He staggered a little, caught unawares. Behind him, Arnow closed the door. He pointed at the shotgun he had propped up in a corner of the foyer.

"Any reason I shouldn't just pick up that scattergun and blow you away? Might be for the best. For me, anyway."

The apartment behind him seemed neat and comfortable, masculine, well decorated.

But right then all Lupo could think of was the proximity of the silver.

"Tom, I just want to talk. We're in trouble again."

"Oh, great, that'll make me change my mind." He did pick up the shotgun, but he backed away from Lupo and stowed it somewhere out of sight, at the rear of the apartment.

Lupo felt his singed skin starting to cool as it healed. Wherever the gun was now, the distance was sufficient.

"You'll hear me out?"

"I have work to do later, but what the hell. You came a long way. I wouldn't want you to go home empty-handed."

Arnow's voice betrayed his bitterness. Lupo wondered whether he was more bitter about Heather . . . or about Jessie.

The former sheriff of Vilas County gestured at the French doors leading out to the balcony. "Let's sit outside."

Lupo followed him to a white deck protected by white stucco walls, giving the building a two-toned look. Colorful hibiscus in planters lined the sides and railing, providing a semblance of privacy. Wooden deck chairs faced the ocean. A table stood between them; a half-empty bottle of cheap VSQ brandy and a glass attracted a hovering bee.

"Don't worry," Arnow said, "all my neighbors need hearing aids."

Lupo nodded at the bottle. "Early to have a drink."

"Sure. Join me?"

"Shit yeah."

"Bar time somewhere in the world."

"Exactly."

"I'd have figured you for rum."

"The Midwest is stuck in me, I guess."

Arnow went inside, rummaged in the galley kitchen, and returned with another glass. "Rarely need two," he explained. He poured three fingers into each glass and shooed away the curious bee.

They drank in silence for a while, looking at the waves rolling into the beach across A1A. A few people walked along the water barefoot, their hair flailing in the ocean breeze. The water was very blue. Lupo sipped the dark golden liquid and wondered whether Arnow would ask, or whether he should begin.

In a while, Arnow said, "I have a stakeout planned for tonight." It was a way to move things along.

Lupo nodded. "I won't be long. Your PI business doing well?"

"In Florida, PI stuff always does well. Lots of divorces, insurance-fraud cases, cons, the occasional missing person, missing dog, you know. Except here, the missing dogs often end up down some rogue alligator's gullet."

"Nice work if you can get it."

"Having been a cop here before helps." Arnow drank his brandy. "Ice?"

"Nah, I'm good."

He nodded. "Here everybody wants to put everything on ice."

"I can see why."

"So what's the deal, Lupo? Why are you bringing back the past? I rather liked forgetting all about it."

"Not with that silver-loaded shotgun in the corner."

"Yeah, well, there's a whole new world of bad guys out there. You should know, of all people." Arnow smirked. "You made my life a whole lot more complicated."

"Wasn't my first choice. Listen, those Wolfpaw guys knocked me for a loop, too. I thought I was the only one afflicted."

"Interesting choice of word." Arnow gulped more brandy, then splashed a couple shots into each glass. His hand shook.

Lupo frowned. "I've considered it a curse ever since I, uh, contracted it. It's a disease."

"Those guys—"

"Those guys used it, wallowed in it. I always found it a problem. Everybody I've ever loved has suffered because of my disease."

Arnow glanced at him sharply. "Jessie Hawkins?"

Lupo forced a slight smile.

If I needed proof.

"She's fine, Tom. For the moment, we're both fine. But here's the thing. What I came down to talk to you about." He drank. It was good, increasing his courage, albeit artificially. "Those three we had to deal with. Bad as that was, and old Malko's pulling their strings. Pretty fucked up. But they're not the only ones. There are more in Wolfpaw. I verified it myself."

Arnow was silent a long time. Seemingly a long time. Then he sighed. "That's why I made up a big batch of the silver slugs, Lupo. Once out of the bottle, I knew the genie wouldn't go back in."

"Funny, I just used that analogy."

Arnow didn't seem to have heard him. He nodded, almost to himself. "I knew I wasn't done with it. I knew it would come back to haunt me. I knew—"

"There's more," Lupo said.

When Arnow turned back to him, he looked haunted. His eyes were weary, wearier than Lupo remembered.

"I think Heather Wilson became one of us," Lupo whispered.

"One of us, or of *you?*" Arnow said bitterly, as if he knew the answer.

Arnow just wanted to put off the inevitable, or maybe even just fool himself into not believing. Lupo could tell. The response was typical of someone in denial.

And I know all about denial.

CHAPTER ELEVEN

ARNOW

They were still on the balcony, still drinking, but had fallen silent. The ocean water was blue and hazy. Across the way, a group of children played in the surf. Adults ignored them from nearby. A squadron of pterodactyl-shaped pelicans glided past in perfect formation. One of them released a long string of feces across the beach like bombs from a B-52. His sleek saurian head seemed to be grinning.

Arnow watched the panorama to which he'd become accustomed and took small gulps of his drink and tried to work up some anger or disdain for the cop who shared his space.

"I'm a PI now," he said finally, "because I didn't want to work for 'the people.' Just specific people."

"People who can pay."

Arnow sipped and nodded. Gestured as if to say, *There you go.*

Lupo held off a minute, then said, "I can't prove Heather's turned wolf. I've been trying to do surveillance, but Wausau's a pretty long drive from home, and the Milwaukee PD put me on this gang task force, so my time's not my own. On homicide, you make your own hours, you know that. But now I'm stuck as part of a team. DiSanto's my shadow whenever I'm in town, and my vacation days are getting stretched. I just can't stay in Wausau to tail her everywhere."

"What makes you think she's *turned*," Arnow prodded.

"Animal attacks. Marathon County's been keeping them pretty quiet due to the tourism thing. Rib Mountain's a gold mine for us, hiking and birding and all that, and in winter the ski resorts need the visitor dollar. But every couple weeks there's been a mauling. That's what they call it, but it's really bad stuff. They let out word, got some doofus DNR and University of Wisconsin 'experts' to say on camera that we may have a mountain lion, or a cougar. Somebody floated the possibility it's a wolf, since their comeback in the state, and people always hear that coyotes are getting more brazen. The DNR's hiring some hunters to maybe hunt it down, but so far it's all talk. I'm sure at some level there's a sense something weird's going on."

"But no one's saying anything specific."

"No."

Arnow couldn't help being drawn in. "Where are the attacks happening? What about the vics?"

"Yeah, I figured you'd catch on. Some attacks occurred in the national forest a county away, Taylor County, but most are in the Marathon state and county parks. And now city parks. Vics are mostly homeless, transients, bums. Some old folks still ride the rails, you know. And I'm convinced some supposed runaway situations, missing persons, and so forth, are actually more vics."

"Just haven't been found yet."

"Right. There's been a few hikers found in pieces, but most are folks wouldn't be missed."

"Carefully selected?"

"Most of them, you'd say. Or lucky coincidences."

Arnow sighed.

Another low pelican formation zoomed past, this one almost overhead. Not for the first time, he wondered whether he should duck. So far he'd been lucky.

"So what do you want from me?" he said.

Lupo swished his drink and looked through it at the sea. In a bit, he sighed, too. "When we lost Sam Waters, we lost a wise ally. I could use someone to spell me on the surveillance gig in Wausau. On Heather Wilson. And it has to be someone who knows the truth."

"Surveillance? On Heather? Shit, Lupo, you're asking a lot. Then what? I'm supposed to put her down with a silver slug?"

"If she's killing people indiscriminately. Yeah."

"Fuck you."

Lupo put his glass down. "I understand, Tom."

"Do you?"

"I get what happened. I know how you felt when she went into the lake. But I suspected that Tef guy, they called him Tef for Teflon ammo—clever bastards, eh?—he was the one bit her, passed on the DNA. They were doin' each other. Heather's not—she's not *monogamous*, let's say."

Arnow wondered if Lupo was talking from experience. "I sensed she's a wild one," he admitted.

"But you liked her anyway."

"Given the opportunities available, she was a likely choice for a kind of infatuation." Arnow held his glass wistfully, tilting it. "Maybe the experience would have, uh, tamed her a bit."

"Yeah, except instead it made her into a monster."

"Shit Lupo, that seems like a crappy thing to say, coming from—"

"I know, a monster like me. I feel that way most days. But I don't revel in my affliction. I'm trying to control It instead of letting It control *me*."

"Easy to say. You ever kill anyone else while . . . *under the influence?*"

Lupo turned away. "Yeah."

"Anyone who didn't deserve killing?" Arnow rounded on him. "Anyone you just didn't *like*? Can you draw the line and walk it?"

Lupo swallowed what seemed like gravel. "I haven't always been able to do that."

LUPO

He was sitting in one of the black chairs with his back to where the Delta plane was maneuvering toward the Jetway, ignoring a limp magazine held loosely in his hands.

He smelled subtle perfume and looked up just as she slid into the chair next to his.

"Hey, Falken," he said, nodding.

"Detective Lupo, nice to see you again."

She had changed her clothes. Today she wore a light leather blazer over a red blouse and black jeans. Comfortable suede boots. She'd done her makeup bold, red lipstick matching the blouse. Her dark hair looked good over the leather. Her eyes flashed amusement at his lack of surprise.

"Got it all done yesterday," she said, explaining. "Thought I'd get home on the first possible flight. So here we are. Your trip go well?"

He had never told her what he was doing. Was she on a fishing expedition?

"It went. No, I wouldn't say it went well. Let's say it could have been much better."

"Sorry about that."

"Not your fault."

"No, you're right. Mine went as well as I could expect, and now it's over. So I get to haul my ass back home." She paused, measuring her words. "Get back to work. And a kind of private case I'm chewing on. Off the clock."

"Oh?" he said. Curious. *Too curious?*

"Yeah, I think I'm on to something weird, but there's no way I can write it up, put it on the books. It's so far-fetched, so fuckin' bizarre, I'm not sure I'm even sane, thinking what I've been thinking."

"Yeah?"

The PA crackled. Their flight was called along with the boarding order. They compared boarding passes and saw they were in the same section, a few rows apart.

Lupo watched her as they waited. Her look was intense, and she was clearly nervous. Whatever she wanted to tell him was making her uncomfortable.

Jessie would hate knowing I negotiated another seat change to stay close to her.

Her fragrance, whatever it was, smelled good.

The plane was two-thirds full, so they managed another seat switch. When they were winging over the calm hyper-blue water and curling back over land to head north, he loosened his seat belt.

"You were saying?"

She hesitated. "You're gonna think I'm crazy."

"Why would I? You seem as sane as any cop I know," he said.

She emitted a short bark, a manly laugh. "Thanks, I think."

"Seriously."

"Okay, seriously, I think we've got a serial killer in Wausau."

"Haven't heard anything official coming out from Wausau," Lupo said with care. *What does she know?*

She nodded. "My point exactly. If it's a serial killer, it's one who hasn't hit the radar yet." Then she added, "I'm onto something, but I can't go to the brass because it's so ridiculous."

"Try me," Lupo said.

She tilted her head and gave him a thoughtful look. He glanced past her through the porthole. Clouds were fluttering past amid sharp sunbeams. He gave her time.

Lupo felt his own heartbeat in his ears. The roaring of his blood. The cabin pressure seemed to heighten the effect.

He was responding to—to what? Her perfume? Her intense, attractive face? The coincidence she was presenting him with?

Finally she spoke again.

"You can talk me down anytime," she said. "Cause I know it's going to sound crazy."

"You keep using that word."

"I do," she said, "because it is. If I'm right about the killings being connected, the killer being the same, then I think my main suspect is a local celebrity."

His pulse pounded in his ears.

"Come to think of it," she added, "you actually know her."

"Her?" His voice was hoarse, his throat parched. He wished he had some water, but the cart hadn't reached them yet.

Falken nodded, her look uncertain. She seemed to hesitate again, then make up her mind. She pressed her lips together, steeling herself.

"I think it's Heather Wilson, the news anchor." She nodded once, decisively. "There, I said it. Now you can start laughing at me."

Lupo searched her eyes. They seemed iridescent in the low cabin lighting. They were big, mysterious. Attractive.

Damn.

"Watch yourself." Sam Waters leaned in and whispered from across the aisle. "What the hell are you doing? Think of Jessie." He made a clucking noise.

Lupo ignored Ghost Sam, turning his back on the aisle as much as he could. Unfortunately, this meant he was almost facing Falken. Her head was close to his. Her red lips parted. She smiled tentatively.

"Crazy, huh? I *told* you."

He still hadn't said anything, but he felt Sam's disapproval behind him, across the aisle.

"Maybe not so crazy," he said.

Her relief was obvious.

"What about the murders? How many?"

She thought. "I can't be sure. See, I think whoever's doing it is disguising them."

He made an interested, inquiring look by raising an eyebrow.

"Going to sound crazy again," she said. "There's been this spate of animal attacks."

"What kind? Maulings?"

He wasn't going to let on that he knew.

"Worse. Deaths. Victims torn apart. The media's caught on to it, but only locally. We haven't released details, like the fact that some of the victims were partially eaten."

"Geez," he said, because she would expect him to.

"Yeah, and the chief's been on television talking about a mountain lion or cougar. You know, they sometimes wander down from up north, Canada even."

"Sure."

"Or coyotes."

"Makes sense."

"So he stands in front of the cameras flanked by a DNR representative and an animal expert from the zoological society, the university, or whatever."

"But you're not on board with that?"

"No, not hardly."

He took a chance. "DNA?"

"Inconclusive," she said. "ME's waffling. Seems as though the DNA's some kind of weird unknown canine strain. The usual outrage about pit bulls and such just creates more noise. More like, these hicks don't know what they're doing."

"Hicks? Aren't you from there?"

"Chicago born and bred," she said, smiling.

She had a nice smile.

"So they're beneath you."

"Didn't hear that from me."

"No. You'd never say that."

"Never."

He didn't want to appear too agreeable. "So anyway, you think your serial killer's killing people and making it look like animals did it?"

"I know, I know. Crazy. But I can't explain it easily any other way, either. Discount the DNA for now. Wilson's behavior recently has been, uh, erratic. She has some strange connections. And she seems to be sexually predatory."

"How did you amass all this information, and why?" he said, and a niggling sense of worry started tickling the back of his neck.

"Well, it's a long story, but some strange stuff Wilson did came to my attention. Long story, short flight."

"We have a second flight," he pointed out.

Their arrival into Atlanta's Hartsfield Airport was announced, so they relaxed as the cabin attendants cleaned up after the drinks. Lupo caught himself watching her profile from the corner of his eye. She was striking, that was certain. She was confident. Probably a good cop. She was messing with something she couldn't possibly handle on her own, though.

A dilemma for him. Or an opportunity.

Their layover was nearly nonexistent, so they spent it chasing the crowd to their next gate in a different, faraway terminal, barely making the Milwaukee plane before it taxied away. The flight was full this time, and the chief attendant was older and frowned on their seat-switch request. He was in the tail, she was over the wing, so they parted reluctantly and the flight was eventless.

At the arrival gate, Falken's cell rang and she motioned him to wait. When she was finished, he asked if she wanted to have a drink and finish their conversation.

"Love to," she said, "but I have a puddle-jumper flight into Wausau, and it leaves in about three minutes."

She sat in one of the waiting chairs and dug into her bag. "Here's my card, we'll talk."

Lupo gave her his card and nodded. He didn't want to seem too interested in her case, but on the other hand he'd wanted a partner for the Wilson surveillance. She was better than a liaison to the Wausau police, because she was already ahead of the game. "Be in touch, for sure. Meantime, watch out for those mountain lions."

She smirked. She dug in her bag again and spent a minute refreshing her lipstick, then dabbed some subtle color onto her face. He felt grimy from the flights, but she looked spectacular. Soon her new flight was called and she headed for the stairway down to the runway, where the tiny commuter jet waited.

He waved and she waved back, winked, and smiled widely at him.

CHAPTER TWELVE

ARNOW

After Lupo left, he mixed another drink and let the rest of his business slide for the day. Another reason he liked being his own boss.

The nerve of the guy, coming here to ask for help.

After what he had done to Arnow, Arnow's job. Arnow's *world*.

He swirled the ice in the drink with his finger and watched the sun blazing away until it was past the edge of his roof. A slight breeze came in off the ocean, cooling the air a few degrees so that the balcony now was a comfortable place to sit. He sipped the drink and thought about the next one. He still had half to go, and already lusted for the one he would pour soon.

Definitely a problem developing.

He finished the drink, went in, and made another.

On a whim, he snatched up his laptop and carried it outside to the table. He drank, then booted up, opened a browser and connected to his Wi-Fi network. He went to Google and thought, then he typed in *Wausau animal attacks*. The list of results was longish and mostly recent. Some were duplicates, some were obvious nonhit misfires, but about a dozen were solid stories filed for local media. He bumped up the size of the browser text—*Aging sure sucks*, he thought—and started to read.

KILLIAN

From across the squad room, he stared at Rich DiSanto's back.

The detective was working on his computer, hunched thoughtfully over the keyboard, playing a fast version of hunt-and-peck with the keys. The kid always seemed to have Lupo's back, that was for sure. Several of Killian's attempts to engage Lupo's partner in conversation had resulted in smooth brush-offs, the kind available only to somebody convinced he was clean.

Nobody treated Killian that way if he had a skeleton—even a single fibia—in his or her closet. *Nobody.* So the kid had to be pure. *As the driven snow,* DiSanto would have said.

He ducked into his office and kept the light off, observing the squad room from the darkened recesses of his own space, hiding behind the partly open blinds.

He could hear the rolled burrito in his fridge calling out to him. And the heartburn that would follow was already making itself known. It was almost as if he somehow punished himself with the worst food possible, he mused.

Some kind of Irish Catholic guilt thing.

Maybe a kid named Griffin Killian had to have developed a few complexes, what with all the sinning by thought, word, and deed that had been shoved down his throat.

Maybe that was why he felt such an intense sense of outrage when somebody did wrong, especially when they were supposed to "serve and protect."

Nick Lupo was a strange case, all right, because Killian's inquiries seemed to portray Lupo as both some kind of rogue cop, and also one of the most solid and loyal partners on the detective squad.

So why did his gut tell him there was something just not right with the big Italian cop? Why had Barrett been so intent on pinning something on him? And why was Marcowicz following suit? Why did he make them uncomfortable?

Killian shook his head, closed the blinds, and finally turned on his light. On his desk lay a few printouts he had been shuffling around, looking for a fit.

There was Barrett's file on Lupo, which he wasn't supposed to have. Not officially, anyway. There was a file with Marcowicz's notes, courtesy of Marcowicz himself, who was most likely in defiance of some regulation Killian wasn't about to look up. And there were some ME autopsy reports.

The strange canine DNA bothered him. Actually, it was *canid* DNA, to be accurate. He'd done some research online, just enough to get the terms straight. The domestic dog is *Canis lupus familiaris*. The wolf, direct ancestor of the dog, is *Canis lupus lupus*. Both are canids. There are differences in the DNA, but they are altogether more similar than not. And they are distinct.

So far, so good.

But there the reports caused Killian more heartburn.

Because the ME who had done the report on Barrett's remains had concluded there must have been a lab error. What he'd found was a strange variation that hovered somewhere between dog and wolf, like a mutation. Separate strains of the same DNA. So the doctor had been attacked by a pack of wolf-dog hybrids? There was such a thing, when wolves got together with farm or stray dogs, but were these hybrids running around in packs? Wolf dogs were illegal to breed and own, so they'd have to be wild.

And it didn't explain why the DNA wasn't exactly one or the other, even though the ME seemed to think it should have been more definite than that. But the trauma to the poor doctor had been so extensive, mostly perpetrated by the serial killer Malko, that there was little reason to figure out what had happened to her body afterward. The ME had written an eloquent shrug into the report and left it at that.

Killian sidled over to his fridge and pulled out one of the burritos that were calling his name. He unwrapped it, laid it on a paper plate, and slid it into the microwave. Nuked it for the appropriate time.

Then the Milwaukee County ME's report on the gang-banger provoked its own questions. Killian remembered from the transcripts of the post-bust interrogation that the thug had insisted some of his wounds had been caused by a large phantom dog no one had seen. The ER doctor on duty had assented that the guy's wounds appeared consistent with those that could be made by a dog, but nobody'd tested it.

But the county ME had done an autopsy after the thug had been gunned down while sitting in an idling car, and—this was what got Killian—he mentioned in the report that there had been some of the same weird DNA in the thug as in Barrett's corpse. Another paper shrug, given the cause of death—four 9-millimeter slugs.

And then it got even weirder, because the ME had added that the body had apparently spontaneously combusted after being shot. No other way to explain the significant burns.

Except for traces of silver the ME had also listed as being present in and around the wounds, inside the thug's torso and head, and throughout the exit wounds. Only one of the slugs had been recovered from inside the car's metal frame, and it had tested positive for silver alloy.

The damned silver slugs bothered him.

Silver bullets?

Killian wasn't as superstitious as some of his ancestors, but what was the deal with the silver?

A Lone Ranger complex?

The microwave dinged and his mouth started watering.

Damn this compulsion, he thought. He burned his mouth

on the first bite. It was so good, so gooey. Melted cheese dribbled on his chin.

How did all this connect?

Killian might have been cynical, but it almost tested even his level of disbelief.

Nick Lupo is the connection.

Lupo was Barrett's patient, and she had followed him to Eagle River on a mysterious mission. To warn him, they said now. But her notes made clear her dislike of Lupo, so warnings were unlikely.

Lupo was one of the Milwaukee thug's arresting officers, part of the gang task force. The same thug somebody had executed using silver slugs.

Killian had tried very hard to get his hands on the autopsy reports done on the three ex-Wolfpaw mercenaries Ron Malko had hired to do his political killing. But somebody had put the lid on those.

Lupo? Did he have that much clout?

Instinct told Killian this part of the deal was greater than Lupo. Maybe Wolfpaw, which, even though it had been decommissioned from its long-term Iraq involvement, still swung considerable political weight. Their troops were said to have been more *on leave* than *former members*. As if only death could remove them from the ranks. Maybe that was true.

Eating the burrito's last bite, Killian ran through the last parts of his weird case. Maybe chewing the mushy processed food gave him clarity (before the heartburn). Either way, Killian wondered if his IA case could ever be wrapped.

He'd cleared his blotter for this one. He was damn well going to try.

LUPO

After picking up his bag, he hoofed it out to the parking structure, found his car, and drove out after surrendering a couple twenties. It didn't even occur to him to flash his badge and declare police business to avoid paying for the parking. He'd heard other cops did it.

"So now what are you going to do?" Sam said. He was in the passenger seat. Lupo noted he was not belted in. *Why would he be?*

"Do about what?" Lupo muttered.

"About this cop, Falken. What else?"

"What do you mean, *do*," said Lupo.

"You tell me."

Lupo rolled his eyes. "Geez, can't I get some peace?"

"Up to you," said Sam. "You're heading for trouble. We both know you're going to throw in with her sooner or later. Not much peace in that. Might as well admit it."

Lupo swung onto the freeway, then headed for his apartment on the lower East Side.

He was silent for a while. Then he said, "Falken's got the right suspect, but no clue what's really going on. If I don't help her, Wilson's going to eat her alive. Literally."

"She's a very attractive woman," Sam said.

Lupo drove in silence.

Sam snickered. "You did notice. I know you did. You're like that character in the Parker books you like so much, Jesse Stone. You notice all women, what they look like."

"So what?" Lupo said. "Sure, Falken's okay."

"Don't get upset, I'm just saying. If you were Bond, you'd be on her already."

"Yeah, like Bond's more real than Jesse Stone. Anyway, I'm not James Bond. Never said I was."

"My point exactly."

Downtown rose around them as he swung away from the lakeshore. Lupo fumed, his lips set tightly.

"What about Jessie?" Sam said. He picked dust motes off the dashboard.

"What about her?"

"I asked you first. What's going on between you two?"

"Nothing."

That was it, maybe they'd been stifling each other. Jessie had shown her jealous side when Lupo first met Heather Wilson, and she still seemed to think Lupo harbored some secret lust for the telegenic news anchor. Now that Lupo was trailing Wilson, it was easy for Jessie to interpret things the wrong way.

"Wrong way? You sure?"

"Stop reading my mind."

"Stop being so obvious."

Lupo clamped his mouth shut.

How long would Sam haunt him? How long did one's ghosts continue to torment those who had led to their deaths? Lupo understood, intellectually, that Sam was here because of his own feelings of guilt. He was surprised he'd even mentioned it to the shrink, but it had been a moment of weakness, and the guy was so unassuming—not at all like the imperious Julia Barrett had been. He'd barely batted an eye at Lupo's disclosure, which was privileged information anyway. No way Marcowicz would spill to anyone. The sessions were taped, but he was bound by law to keep whatever they discussed private.

Sam was leaving him alone now, so he sighed and headed for home. A quick shower, a change of clothes, and a bite to eat at his second home, the diner down the street, and Lupo was rolling into the squad room an hour and a half later.

DiSanto lurked over his desk when he approached.

"What's up?" Lupo asked, and his partner jumped, startled.

"Sorry, Nick. Uh, didn't expect you back just yet."

"So then it's open season for anything on my desk?"

"No, just checking for a note I wrote out yesterday for you. Wanted to add a second note."

Lupo waded past DiSanto's angular frame and dropped into the old office chair. When the department had upgraded furniture a year ago, laying out a thousand dollars a chair for some avant-garde technological marvel of a new ergonomic design, Lupo had left his in the carton and had it dumped into storage, preferring to keep his old but comfortable, less-than-ergonomic padded leather captain's chair.

He scanned his desktop, a sea of file folders and stacked papers. Sure enough, a couple yellow Post-its were curling on top of some unfinished report copies. Like most cops, Lupo still preferred to deal with paper first, transferring information to the online forms only when he was satisfied with their content.

The top note was covered with DiSanto's scratching.

Lupo grinned. "I can't read it. Just tell me."

DiSanto looked around. Other detectives sat at their computers or moved back and forth between desks and offices. Nobody seemed to be taking notice of them. The row of offices that took up one wall, where the captain of detectives and other administrative honchos hunkered down, was mostly dark. *Long lunches.*

"Killian's been asking around about you."

"Oh yeah?" Lupo kept his expression neutral. "Wants to be friends, does he?"

DiSanto made a sour face. "Hardly. I trust that guy as far as I can throw 'im."

DiSanto was a lover of clichés and used one whenever he could.

"So what?"

"Nick, you know IA doesn't shine around unless they've got wind of something. And this Killian guy, they say he's a pit bull crossed with a crocodile. Won't let go and likes to swallow people whole."

"Wouldn't that be some kind of snake?"

"Whatever. You know what I'm saying."

"Sure." Lupo glanced down. "What were you gonna add?"

"Huh?"

"The note. You said you were gonna add something."

"Oh, yeah. Killian asked me about you twice, and the second time he asked how long since you'd been in."

"And?"

"I told 'im you were following up some leads and were out of town, like we agreed."

"And?"

"And he didn't like it. Looked like he swallowed a whole trout. He wanted to know if you tended to stay out so much. Oh, and he asked about your injury."

Shit.

Lupo realized that sometimes he forgot to limp a little. It was all he needed to do, but it was easy to forget. He couldn't let this knowledge bother him too much.

DiSanto slid into Lupo's guest chair and went on. "I told him you have good and bad days. Some days you don't gotta limp as much, is all, with the humidity level and all. What you think it's about?"

"Don't know. Maybe they're nosing around to see about my retirement. If I'm about to, or maybe they want to nudge me." He didn't believe that at all.

"Shit, why would they? You're not impaired. Anyway, detectives got different standards for disability than uniforms."

"I know, but Killian's got hold of something. He wouldn't be asking questions otherwise." He booted up the computer and watched the hated Windows routine churn through its many steps before his desktop came up. He checked his e-mail, saw one from Jessie and a couple others he'd have to answer. And there was one from Falken.

Shit.

DiSanto's face confirmed that he agreed, even though he wasn't saying. "You do anything you should be worried about right now? You bopping his girlfriend?"

Lupo grimaced. It wasn't a particularly good time for him

to deny involvement with somebody, even if the person was someone different from DiSanto's stab-in-the-dark choice.

"No," he said, making it clear it was a ridiculous proposition.

"Okay, maybe he wants to review that whole up-north thing I got you out of."

DiSanto had led the cavalry, all right, but they had gotten there too late.

"Yeah, right, you were spectacular."

Lupo clicked open a couple of the unrelated e-mails and scanned the text. Boring routine stuff in one, an enigmatic one from the police psychologist, Dr. Marcowicz. Wondering if he'd like to come in more often. Lupo tapped his fingers on the desk, feeling heat rise to his face. Hair started to sprout on his forearms and he shoved his hands under the protective cover of the desk, hoping DiSanto hadn't noticed.

Anger sometimes provoked "manifestations," as Caroline Stewart had so many years before begun referring to those incidents where the wolf wanted to come to the fore on its own.

He needn't have worried. DiSanto was checking out a woman another detective had hauled in. She seemed to be a victim of something or other, but she was dressed in a revealing silk blouse and tight-fitting jeans. When she turned to sit on the cop's desk chair, DiSanto muttered his approval.

Lupo clicked open Falken's e-mail.

Hey Lupo, nice meeting you on the plane. Sorry we didn't get to finish—I've got more to tell you. Maybe you can drive up some time. I think my dept's really on the wrong track. You have experience with weird stuff. This qualifies. Call me when you get the chance. See ya, Falken.

He hesitated, then opened Jessie's e-mail, which had an attachment symbol. *Now what?*

She said,

Nick, I'm so sorry we parted unhappy. Hope I can make you happy again soon. Love, Jess.

Then he grinned. The attachment was a small but very sharp digital photo of Jessie Hawkins topless she had clearly taken herself. She was looking into the lens and licking her lips. *And is that a wink?*

He closed the e-mail quickly, before DiSanto could see it. *Damn,* he thought. *Damn damn.*

From the Journals of Caroline Stewart
December 19, 1981

Ever since I started to think about another possible explanation for Jerry Boone's death, his suicide, I keep going back and forth on whether to open up with Nick about my fears. About whether he remembers more than he says, knows more than he admits.

But I've always found Nick to be an honest and up-standing young man. He's so tortured by his condition, by some of the things he's done . . . He's in a world of torment, and I hate to add to it. He needs understanding and friendship. And love. Not paranoia and suspicion.

I haven't been able to draw him out on some of those things he says he's done, and I admit that our relationship keeps me from wanting to really delve too deeply into his past. What I know is enough to indicate he needs careful handling, and he needs trust as well as love.

I'm willing to give him those things.

I want to give him those things.

If only the incident with Jerry Boone hadn't happened and we could go back to just his more deeply internalized problems.

But now that Nick might have had something to do

with Boone's death, the niggling doubts keep me up nights even after the satisfying lovemaking. He's in need, and he surely senses my own needs—thanks to my evil family— and he's so sweet and willing to give me what I need . . .

How can I refuse to give him what he needs?

How can I push him where he doesn't want to go?

It's nearly Christmas and that holiday always brings back nightmares of my fucked-up family life.

Can a professor say fucked-up?

Anyway, Nick has his own Christmas demons and we hope to help each other slay them.

I plan to start concentrating on some of these bothersome questions. Maybe after Christmas, after we've given each other the gifts we both need so much.

I hope waiting won't make anything worse.

1978
NICK

When they reached the cleared-out part of the Wiener Woods preferred by the kids, the kegger was in full swing.

Twilight had just fallen and darkness was beginning to tinge the clearing floor, lengthening shadows and turning the knots of drinkers into shadows themselves, nearly impossible to recognize.

Josh waved at a couple people he recognized despite the waning light.

Or maybe he's just faking, Nick thought.

From what he could tell, when kids turned to watch them entering the clearing, they seemed to be laughing. They nudged each other and pointed or tilted their heads, gesturing as Josh and Nick walked past.

Maybe they were looking at Sherry Ludden, who had tagged along. She was pretty hot.

Maybe they were looking at Nick Lupo, the outcast, trying to decide why he'd bothered to show up.

Maybe the three of them *were* the entertainment.

Nick felt a rumble deep down in his belly, a portent of
something bad to come.

The Creature stirred somewhere within, too.

Nick considered his options. He could melt away and
disappear. No one would notice. Or he could stay and help
Josh if something weird happened.

Why were kids deep in the middle of conversations stopping their yammering to stare?

*Damn it, Josh, why'd you insist we come to this thing? These
people hate you.*

Nick sensed it. Maybe Josh didn't. But Nick noted that
Sherry seemed to get the same vibe he did. She looked
around nervously, nodding at acquaintances. Unfortunately,
they also seemed to laugh and snicker as the three walked
past.

Sherry was wearing a frilly white blouse and the same
kind of hot pants most other girls wore, jeans cut to barely
cover the buttocks. She looked great in hers, Nick thought,
and he couldn't help but wonder why she had somehow
struck up this friendship with Josh, who had become the
ultimate outcast.

Damn it, Nick knew he was jealous. It wasn't the first
time he'd suffered the fate of the outsider, but seeing someone like Josh, who was farther outside than he was, getting a
girl like Sherry . . .

Well, it hurt. He shouldn't have let it, but there it was.

By the time they reached the keg and the picnic table
that served as the drink station, Nick knew something
was up.

Basically every group broke out laughing after Josh passed
by, their faces bizarrely distorted by the weird lighting. It didn't

seem to be Nick they were looking at, and some of the jocks and thugs stared at Sherry with drool practically dripping from their tongues, but it was Josh they made faces at.

"Hey, Josh," Nick said quietly, "let's get outta here. I got some beer at home." He did, too. Frank Lupo drank the occasional beer and, in keeping with his Old Country roots, didn't care if Nick had one occasionally. By the age of sixteen, Nick was able to drink at home as long as he didn't overdo it. So when he offered beer, he really was able to. But Josh blew him off.

"Fuck that," Josh said. "They got beer here!"

"Sure, but—"

Roland Hawthorn nudged his way over.

"Welcome, Lords of Geekdom!"

"What?" Nick said, barely sure he'd heard the snobbish bastard right.

"Yes, step right up. Bradley, pour these gentlemen and their 'lady' a drink."

Brad stepped up to the tap and grabbed a Dixie cup. He held it out and some nameless jock nearby hawked up and spit a wad of slime into the cup. Then Brad filled it with beer.

"One faggot special, coming up. *Coming*, get it?"

He handed it to Josh, who took it.

Didn't Josh see the spitting?

Everybody within sight of the keg laughed uproariously, watching to see what would happen.

Despite Rollie's orders, nobody bothered to offer Nick a drink, and he didn't care. "Josh . . ."

"Josh," Sherry said, "Nick's right, let's go."

Josh shook his head and stepped forward, bringing the cup closer to his lips.

Everybody watched. The entire crowd seemed to hush as one.

Josh brought the cup slowly to his lips and seemed about to drink the disgusting cocktail, but at the last second he tossed it into Brad's face.

And that was when everything went to hell.

CHAPTER THIRTEEN

LUPO

He reached out to Falken and waited while somebody tracked her down and transferred his call to her desk phone.

"Hello," she said, a slight impatience in her tone.

Lupo smiled. There was a decidedly coplike sound to her voice. Forceful.

"Nick Lupo."

He thought about how he needed an ally, without Arnow here to back him up. But he would have to play this carefully, since he wasn't about to tell Falken everything about Heather Wilson.

No, they'd have to catch her as a traditional suspect, not as a wolf. Even if he was right, he had to maneuver the situation so he could put her down once and for all. Falken's theory of Wilson's crimes was close, but too dangerous for her.

"What's up?" Falken said. Her tone made a subtle change and he thought she sounded pleased.

"Just checking in. Your, uh, private case. How is that going?"

She was circumspect. Clearly, other cops were within earshot.

"Let me call you back," she said.

His phone rang in a few minutes and he saw the call came from her cell. Probably she'd stepped out of the squad room.

She's careful, he thought. *Doesn't want to be linked to her quarry yet.* This would help him, too.

She filled him in with more details.

The animal attacks seemed to be continuing, but they were fewer than the unexplained disappearances. Wausau police were stumped on the disappearances, officially blaming the declining economy for leading otherwise-stable people to run away from their lives. But not all the disappearances were stable people. In fact, most were homeless men and women caught between shelters.

"You don't buy the official word your bosses are putting out?" Lupo asked.

"Nah, I can smell cover-up. They may or may not be connecting the missing people and the attacks, but they don't know anything about either."

"So let's go back to your suspect, the Wilson woman. How did you latch on to her? What's your evidence?" He hoped she wouldn't say she'd been staking out the loft.

If she has been, she might have seen me doing the same. Or going in.

Jesus.

Falken made a sighing noise. "I don't have evidence. I have hunches and innuendo and some weird behavior. I can lay out some of it, but we should do it in person."

"Okay," he said, suppressing a sigh of relief. "I got a situation here, but I'm heading north in a day or so. I can swing by and we can meet."

"Sure, fine. Let me ask you a question, since you've got your own suspicions about this woman."

"Fire away."

"What do you think would make this Wilson woman such a predator? I mean, if she is, where does it come from?"

"Well," he began carefully, evading all of his suspicions, "when I met her she seemed to have a strong sense of entitlement, almost superiority. Serial killers always feel superior to their victims. Who knows what happened in her childhood?"

"She seems to have been something of a sexual predator, from the notes I've been able to cobble together," Falken said. "You have any ideas about that?"

He felt his face warm in a typical blush. Ever since his youth, he'd embarrassed easily. He was grateful she couldn't see him. But was there a humorous edge in her voice? Was she toying with him?

"She was involved with one of the killers in the casino case. And there were rumors she'd been banging her cameraman, among others, but he turned up dead. I don't know anything about her before our paths crossed."

"There have been, uh, rumors and innuendo ever since she came to town."

"Okay then, but sexual predation doesn't connect directly to serial killing." He didn't want to appear too eager to convict her.

"No, course not. But it might show predisposition to obsessions."

"Sure."

"So, we barking up the same tree? What's your interest, and where does it cross mine?"

He had to tiptoe through his explanations. "I have connections to the northern part of the state, as you know. Your disappearances hit my radar, and I remembered she was a dogged reporter. Thought she might be on to the story. Then I stumbled onto the possibility she might *be* the story."

"How?"

"Story for another day," he said evasively, using her own strategy. "In any case, her behavior caught my attention.

Like you, I figured you can't finger her without some careful planning, a solid case. Celebrities are hard to pin down, and she's about the biggest one you guys have."

She sighed. "Yeah. So we teaming up?"

Lupo thought fast. Without Arnow, he was hampered in his attempts to tail Wilson, and now that he was compromised as one of her conquests, it might be best to have a local contact. She might be unofficial, but she could always make it official. Although Lupo might need to take extreme measures. Until then, somebody to help keep tabs on the woman had to be a plus.

"Why not?" he said. "You just tailing her?"

"When I can. We can coordinate. Mostly I work nights, so the days are my own."

Perfect, he thought, grateful they'd missed each other so far. "Fine, let's divvy up the time."

They made arrangements and he rang off after they said their good-byes.

"Catch you on the flip-flop," she said, and he wondered if she was mocking him.

Falken was a strange fish. But he couldn't help liking her.

KILLIAN

What had people done before search engines? He wondered about that as he Googled animal and dog attacks in Wisconsin.

Out in the squad room, DiSanto was lounging while Lupo, who had finally put in an appearance, was yakking on the phone. Killian had a fleeting thought about employing federal domestic eavesdropping to spy on Lupo's calls, but even he found that particular opportunity distasteful. If there was an IA case to be made against the cop, then Killian would make it using old-fashioned police work coupled with his gut instinct. *And heartburn.* No illegal spying, please, even if politicians had managed to make it pseudo-legal by bending laws and their intent.

And it was likely the feds wouldn't help a mere local cop with this bizarre case, anyway.

Killian watched as the search hits piled up into the thousands. And the top couple pages were current.

Wausau. Eagle River. Milwaukee.

Wausau was the clear winner, but he knew nothing about it.

Jesus. Why hadn't he heard anything about all those stories listed in local media?

They had somehow not gone national, for one thing. He read as many as he could, scanning the text and moving on to the next in somewhat reverse chronological order. The police and DNR up there, wherever Wausau was, were floundering about, messing with vague and illogical zoological explanations.

Maybe it was time to get on the horn. Or in the car.

Killian read on and felt his fingers tingling. He lusted for another burrito, maybe a beef one this time. But he held off and kept reading.

He looked up and saw that DiSanto was heading for the bathroom, which was at the end of the hall. The trip would take him past the offices, including Killian's.

He set out on an intercept trajectory and was standing in his doorway when DiSanto came parallel with his office.

"Hey, DiSanto," he called out. "See you a minute?"

DiSanto had guts, Killian had to admit. The younger cop glanced at his watch, a huge silver and black diver's thing with a gigantic screw-down crown protruding from the side, and then looked at Killian with a smirk.

"Got a minute, sure."

Killian gestured toward his chair, but DiSanto waved him off.

"Got an appointment."

"Okay. Just a follow-up. You mentioned earlier that you and Detective Lupo were following up some leads out of town."

"Uh, yeah." He seemed uncomfortable. Resisted the urge to look at the watch again.

"Where exactly?"

A flash of something crossed DiSanto's face. He didn't want to rat on his partner, but it was a reasonable question from one of the administrators, and it could be checked anyway.

"Wausau and vicinity," he said.

Bingo.

"Thanks, that's all I wanted to know."

Now DiSanto didn't look so eager to escape.

"No more questions, Detective."

DiSanto nodded and slinked out.

Killian smiled. Maybe he'd have that burrito after all.

Sure, DiSanto had probably already told Lupo about Killian's questions, but that just made the game all the more exciting.

Killian closed his blinds again and considered whether his stomach could handle more gut bombs.

Live on the edge.

Kind of like following Julia Barrett's footsteps.

JESSIE

She felt a tickle when she thought about that little photo she'd snapped on an impulse. Sure, it wasn't really her style. Kids were "sexting" all over the place according to the news, but she was an old lady—a sexy old lady, she hoped, but still too old to indulge herself like that.

But it had felt naughty and fun, and she hoped it caught Nick just right when he opened it.

She had been on the verge of sending a conciliatory e-mail when she'd spotted her camera just within reach on the shelf next to her desk. She felt flushed and more than a little horny already, and the camera lens was so inviting. She set up the short desktop tripod and experimented with the angle and lighting.

Then, before she could change her mind, she stripped off her top and undid her bra and let them sag to the floor. A quick flick of the camera's timer setting, and she was staring into the shutter and making a face like a porn star.

Nick's friend who was murdered by Martin Stewart had been an escort who was expanding into porn. Jessie had watched some of Corinne's DVDs when Nick wasn't home, without his knowledge, trying to get a sense of the girl whose death had sent him into a spin. Corinne was an exuberant exhibitionist, clearly enjoying herself on camera, and the sex had been—well, it made Jessie blush even though she had been alone. But it had definitely awakened her a little to some tricks she'd tried on Nick, who clearly approved, even though he had no idea where they'd come from. After they'd killed Martin Stewart, Nick had never watched the videos again.

Anyway, Jessie had realized that one thing she hadn't done yet was use the camera in sex play.

Well, why not?

She and Nick seemed to be growing apart. There it was, a miserable cliché Rich DiSanto would have loved, but it was true. Whenever she could, Jessie used her looks and what she was learning to try and make Nick settle down, not in the traditional sense of the term. He was a werewolf—there was nothing of the traditional in *that*—but he seemed to draw trouble like a magnet. She had gotten used to the wolf stuff, but now if only she could keep him from poking too many hornets' nests.

She figured she might as well throw herself at him to try and keep him occupied.

Occasionally she was reminded that women found him

quietly attractive, though, and it set off a jealous response in her of which she was embarrassed, but powerless to halt.

She wondered if he strayed.

He didn't seem the type, really, but he also seemed helpless around women. Ever since Caroline Stewart, his first lover and confidante, whom he had murdered unintentionally and traumatically, he had become—no, he had *forced* himself to become—unable to let himself love, lest the loved one end up paying a steep price for knowing him.

So far, women who got close to him had indeed paid a steep price. The steepest. Except Jessie, who had managed to survive due to her own abilities. *And a little bit of wolf love,* she thought.

Now they made the perfect couple.

If only she could convince *him.*

Enough people had hinted that she was still attractive, comparing her to an earthy version of some former supermodel.

Well, she thought, *let's see if they're right.*

She ended up snapping a series of photographs, maybe thirty, and selecting the best one. So much for impulse!

She walked into the Great Northern, waved at the guards on duty, and was sinking further in debt within minutes. The numbers that represented quarters just kept diminishing like tiny countdowns to the end of her life. Or of her credit line, whichever came first.

As she pressed the slot-machine buttons over and over, triggering lights and sounds and precious little winning, she tried to ignore the burning she felt in her heart.

DISANTO

By the time he returned to the squad room, Lupo was gone. He found a brief e-mail asking him to cover as long as possible.

"Goddamn it, Nick," he muttered. "Jesus Christ on a stick, you ask a lot."

Killian was sniffing around, trying to catch them at something. DiSanto was all for giving the guy the runaround, but there was no point prodding him into some sort of formal action. Clearly, he was like a dog with a bone.

So Lupo was out to Hicksville again, following his nose on some new crazy thing he didn't want to share with him. At least not yet. He'd end up needing help eventually, like last time, and then both of them would get raked over the coals for infractions that would run the gamut from taking too much time off to who knew what.

DiSanto looked back over his shoulder surreptitiously.

Looked like Killian was in there, cackling over another one of those nuked burritos he polluted the air with. If the guy had to have a food fetish, couldn't it have been for pizza and calzones?

Shit, frozen burritos! The lowest of the low on the fast-food totem pole.

Yeah, sure enough, the guy was huddled over his desk, munching out. It was a wonder he hadn't ballooned to four hundred pounds.

DiSanto had an inkling the guy was going to follow Lupo around at some point, like that idiot Barrett. He would keep an eye on Killian and blow the whistle on him.

Gotta have Nick's back, whatever the hell he's into.

Plus, nobody really liked Killian. If he was against you, you suddenly had lots of allies. It was like that.

DiSanto suspected Lupo was like an iceberg, a little tiny peak visible on top and a whole lot of jagged ice hidden underneath.

For some reason, though, he wanted a look at that underneath part.

He glanced at Killian's office and whistled a tuneless version of a Sinatra song.

The park formed a corner, the intersection of Fifth and Mc-Clellan streets.

McClellan, Grant, Washington, Jackson—they sure love their generals up here.

The white marble of the rear of city hall overlooked the park and its memorial fountain.

Buds were beginning to sprout on the trees, mostly oaks and maples. A short row of evergreens was black in the twilight, the space around them a pool of thick shadow.

Wagner stalked the shadows behind the evergreens on two feet. Actually it was two outsized wolf paws, picking their way carefully over the needle-covered ground. A light wind whispered through the fanlike branches and masked the rustle of the dead needles being disturbed. Though Wagner was very careful, sound carries at night and people in lonely settings after a certain hour tend to get jumpy when they hear unexpected sounds. Stealthy sounds.

Wagner was stealthy. The person on the other side of the evergreen rank was walking on the narrow concrete path that snaked diagonally through the park in the historic district. Beyond the tree line, the shadows of faraway downtown buildings hunched over the darkening horizon. The path wasn't a great shortcut, but it shaved a few minutes from walking the square corner. People heading home from work at city hall walked it all day long.

This particular person was a woman. Wagner smelled perfume—a lancet to the nostrils. High heels clicked on the concrete, short rapid steps. Wagner paced her from the shadows, saliva pooling inside wicked jaws.

This is the best part of the hunt.

She must have sensed or heard something in the wind, carried on the wind, because the steps stopped suddenly. Wagner stopped in midstride. The smell of the woman's fear—sweat and adrenaline—layered onto the perfume, a bitter cocktail that aroused Wagner most pleasantly. The steps began again, increasing their rapid tempo until the woman seemed to be running as fast as the impractical heels would allow.

Wagner howled once.

The woman's breath caught as she gasped, stopping for a fraction of a second. Wagner could see her now, only yards away, bending down to strip the heels and setting off at a dead run in her bare feet. Her short skirt hampered the running, however, and her pace was still slow and awkward.

Wagner didn't bother to switch to four legs—what was the fun of that?—pacing the prey on two paws but aided by an impossibly long gait. When the angle of approach brought Wagner within reach, a single lunge took the massive wolf through the air and its front paws punched into the screaming woman's back hard enough that the sound of her spine snapping echoed through the empty park.

Wagner rode the dying woman down to the concrete, where her face was flattened below the sharp claws that bit into the flesh of her back and sides, tearing clothing as if it were paper. She was done now, dead or dying, and Wagner's jaws made sure with a quick tear to the right and to the left. The woman's head virtually fell off the twitching shoulders, blood cascading over the dark concrete. Wagner batted it away, the last shreds of skin and cartilage snapping like rubber bands.

Then Wagner fed on the hot flesh and remaining blood.

CHAPTER FOURTEEN

HEATHER

She looked down at the top of his head and was grateful he hadn't turned out to be one of those guys who were balding but managed to hide it well until it was too late. He had a thick head of hair that almost reached his collar, and no bald spot.

Right now, he was proving that what he'd whispered to her in the booth where she'd slid next to him after a long stare-down was indeed the truth.

He had a very talented tongue, and he employed it well in her favor. He held her folds open with his long, piano player's fingers and tasted her in just the way she liked, traversing from one orifice to the other, making tiny swirls and occasionally probing with his disproportionately long, slick tongue, which she hoped indicated length elsewhere, too.

Sometimes a woman could be grateful for the up-close detail shown in porn, which she assumed taught a few men at least what women preferred. *Some women.*

She shuddered with pleasure as he found her spot and obliterated it with his contortionist tongue.

What was his name again?

Greg something?

She'd barely paid attention during and after the dance they'd engaged in in the darkened pub where she had caught his eye right while it roved toward hers. He was a lithe, not too muscular jogger type. Not a bodybuilder or anything, but she'd tingled at his voice, his touch, and it didn't take her much beyond that when she was in need.

She'd always been that way, but even more so since her *alteration*. It was like being in heat, and she lusted for male companionship a large part of her day. Currently, the sports guy at the station was a regular Thursday-night rendezvous, and one of the line producers an occasional, when he could shed his clingy wife.

Right now, she knew she was bathing Greg's tongue with her juices, and he lapped them up with gusto. A long finger found her puckered hole and probed, and she groaned with need, pulling away and repositioning herself for his entry. To his credit, Greg had no problem responding to her nonverbal commands.

Perhaps they were on the same page.

When he finally dropped his briefs, she saw that the mythical correlation between tongue and penis was not so mythical. He entered her with a single thrust she welcomed with verbal agreement, and he rode her to another plateau. Moments later, she orchestrated a switch and he was right with her, withdrawing and reentering with barely a stroke missed.

Compared to her last pickup, Greg was turning out to be a keeper.

She felt her flesh sizzle with ecstasy and melted all over the wrinkled bedspread again, and then encouraged him to increase his pace.

Heather thought of herself as a thoroughbred, trained to pace herself and still come in first. Greg was a worthy jockey. When she insistently flipped him and changed places, she proved she could ride him just as well.

It wasn't long before they spent their passion like an ocean wave whipping itself to bits on a rocky shore.

Heather liked the metaphor. She lay across his sinewy body and let him soften inside her. But to her surprise, he didn't lose much. He winked at her and she leaned her face into his and let him know how much she appreciated him, and then she started riding again.

They had barely spoken at all.

Later, when both were spent, she watched the light fur come surging out of her forearm pores in tufts. A growl worked its way up her throat and she suppressed it. She felt the wall between her human self and what she became growing thinner now and again, as if someday she might just go over and become the lovely wolf and never return.

It had been like that on those first full-moon nights when she had learned what had happened to her, when she had no control, and knew no better.

And if she did turn wolf with no turning back, she had no doubt she would sooner or later devour the flesh of any lover who lay with her, no matter how much he had pleased her. Now she understood Tef, the lion-haired mercenary who had melted her insides as a lover, but who would have probably ravaged her body and consumed her flesh and organs. He had begun to do just that, but had been interrupted.

She had learned that the wolf side was slave to its lusts and desires as was the human side, only the compulsions were a lot more deadly.

God help anyone who got in the way.

She caressed Greg's groin and took his penis in her hands. She watched her hands Change. Her fur sprouted dark and coarse, nails growing into claws that could disembowel him in a moment. Asleep, he shifted under her rough caresses and she almost lost control.

The wolf wanted to tear off his genitals. And gorge its appetites in that other way.

Heather fought it, this time, and won. Greg snored on, content and unaware.

Next time, she wasn't so sure she'd win.

Lupo

He was just swinging the Maxima off the business leg of Highway 51 and into Wausau proper when his police radio caught the call.

The lit-up tip of Dudley Tower stood sentry in the distance. The other squat downtown buildings around the square were mostly dark and abandoned for the night, except for residential blocks.

After checking his map, he found a quick way to the crime scene, a ways east from where he was. The evening air was chilled and even the sun's last rays of the day promised more cold as he stepped out of his car near the edge of the park.

Lupo approached a cop stringing yellow tape and flashed his badge. The cop looked gray, pale, and embarrassed. If he cared the badge wasn't local he didn't say so, simply pointing toward the sparse trees. "Over there. Christ, it's bad."

Lupo nodded in commiseration, then stepped onto the grass and followed the sounds of activity and the halogen light trees somebody was setting up to illuminate the crime scene.

A sergeant looked up. "Detectives on the way—Hey, who're you?"

Lupo flashed the shield and introduced himself.

"Milwaukee, eh?" The older cop said his name was Dell'Onore. "Got a brother there. Useless piece of shit. You guys had some animal attacks, too, dint you?"

Lupo wasn't sure what he meant but nodded agreement. Better to let him think Lupo had a reason for being there.

"Damndest things, these attacks," Dell'Onore said. "Suddenly we got a trend, you know? This mountain lion's days are numbered, know what I mean? But we got every available man on the job and no one's even seen 'im."

Lupo spotted chunks of raw organ meat and a coil of torn human intestines nearby. The stench was unbearable even to him. Dell'Onore had clearly seen a lot during his life—he stared at another clump of bones and torn flesh nearby.

A human head, male, lay like a flattened soccer ball on its left cheek. The nose was bitten off. The eyes had burst out their sockets, trails of blood and gore trailing from the blackened holes.

"One swipe, probably," the grizzled cop said. He seemed energized by the duty.

An ashen Asian man in an overcoat parted nearby branches and stepped out, wiping his forehead.

Dell'Onore chuckled. "That's where this guy's equip—er, *genitalia* are. ME's not quite settled in the job yet."

Lupo made agreeable cop noises. The young medical examiner seemed to be collecting himself before heading back into the breach.

Back into the breach. That was more DiSanto's kind of line, wasn't it?

Dell'Onore cleared his throat. "The Mod Squad's here," he muttered.

It was Falken. She stepped into the brightly lit area. She raised an eyebrow at Lupo, then addressed the old cop. "I got it, Dell. You work the perimeter."

"Sure," he said, clearly annoyed at being dismissed.

"Oh, by the way, Officer," Falken added, "I'm neither *mod* nor a *squad*."

The cop walked away, shaking his head. Maybe he didn't like what she'd called him; maybe he didn't like women cops telling him what to do. Lupo put his money on both. But maybe he just wondered how she'd heard his comment from so far away.

He grunted a greeting. "Fancy meeting you here."

"Took the words right out of my mouth," she said. "Scanner?"

"My partner would love you," he said, not bothering to explain. "Uh-huh. On my way to do some surveillance on our person of interest."

"Looks like we're too late. If it's her."

Falken looked great in a distressed-leather blazer and tight black slacks. Her dark hair was trapped in an unruly ponytail. Her lips were as dark as wine and her eyes elaborately made up as if she'd been interrupted while on a date.

Lupo tried to concentrate on the evidence instead of looking at her. It was no mountain lion or cougar, he knew that. The teeth marks were obvious, and they would nearly have matched his. He thought he could still catch some wolf scent, but it was wispy, masked by the grue and all the humans traipsing around. In moments it would fade to nothing.

"So?" she said. Her large eyes pinned his in the harsh light.

"Coyote not likely," he said. "No mountain lion or cougar. Wolf maybe. Or—"

"Or what?"

"Or we should talk."

"You think it's *her*?"

He shrugged. "She lives nearby."

"How does she do it?"

"Let's grab a coffee when you're done here."

"Yeah, let's," she said, eyeing him. Then she stepped away and started ordering some new uniforms around. A photographer came, and EMTs in no hurry. The ME had recovered and he directed the collection of the remains. Other cops scoured for evidence. Lupo stayed out of the way, watching Falken's take-charge attitude. She didn't seem affected by the victim's gruesome condition. *Tough one.*

No need to check on Heather now. She'd be snug in bed, well fed and happy.

It occurred to him he looked forward to that coffee.

WAGNER

Dominic Lupo dominated the crime scene even though he didn't belong there. The uniforms deferred to him subconsciously, and he stood near a twin halogen portable tree that blasted cold light over everything, turning blood black.

Wagner grinned, remembering the blood. How it tasted going down, coating the palate.

Now Wagner watched Lupo carefully, seeing not only the confidence of experience with crime scenes, even messy ones, but also the *knowing* in his eyes. Wagner was close enough to see his eyes. The Milwaukee cop wasn't shocked by the violence here.

Wagner nodded, convinced.

Lupo has seen it before.

He knew about werewolves. His stamp was all over what happened to Tannhauser and his men. Wagner had needed to confirm.

Now Wagner was certain about at least *one* enemy.

There were others to seek out, but Lupo and Wilson might well lead to them.

LUPO

The restaurant was more than a coffee shop and it wasn't an old-fashioned Wisconsin supper club. It was a newfangled high-class steak and lobster establishment around the corner from Wilson's condo, but they'd checked her windows and it appeared she wasn't home.

Working or stalking, Lupo figured.

Falken ordered pasta primavera and Lupo had a steak that, if he'd wanted it cooked perfectly by normal standards, would have disappointed. He requested it medium even though the Creature wanted it very rare. It came rare enough to make them both happy, though he didn't say so.

They laughed about the mediocre food at trendy high prices.

"Most people would think we were sick to eat at all after that crime scene," Falken said as she broke a piece of bread in two. "I find that it makes me hungrier for some reason." She nibbled at the bread.

"People gotta eat," Lupo growled in a gravelly voice like Dell'Onore's and they both laughed.

Nice laugh, he thought.

"True." She paused pensively.

He drank a long sip of flat draft beer. Another disappointment for such a nice-looking place. Maybe they'd have been better off at the dark pub around the corner.

"Yes?" He said. "But . . . ?"

"True, but that *was* pretty terrible. Can't say I've ever seen anyone torn to pieces like that. You?"

He nodded. "A few. A bomb blast once, one of those nail bombs. Took the guy's head off and bounced it down a staircase. Rest of 'im sat down in a convenient chair and bled out."

"Bizarre."

"See, the way it was angled when he set it off made it into a claymore. The nail pattern took his head off and didn't make a mark on the rest of the guy at all."

"Anything else?"

He could have mentioned the Eagle River tribal-council killings, but he decided to hold off for now. He shrugged.

"Assorted stuff. Nothing quite that, uh, drastic."

"Gunshots?"

"Pretty bad, some of 'em. Goes with the territory."

"Gangs?"

"Those are usually straightforward. Anyway, I'm usually homicide. Gangs is until I'm rehabbed." He pointed at his foot and shrugged again. He sawed at the steak ineffectively.

"You don't limp much."

"I'm getting used to the prosthetic. Eventually, they tell me, I won't limp at all."

She nodded. "That's great. Any other horror crime scenes?"

"More than I can count," he said evasively. He'd have to come around to telling her his suspicions about Heather Wilson, but carefully. Probably not yet time. Wilson was his prime suspect, of course, but he'd have to take it slower with Falken than with Arnow. Would it get easier? Would he start telling anyone and everyone about his condition?

No.

On the other hand, he would have to prove that Wilson only really worked as a suspect if the rest was real. If she had turned wolf. And he was ready to bet she had.

Falken ate some pasta, lips pursed as she sucked in the long strands, big eyes above looking into his, almost batting her lashes. Uncomfortable, he ignored her flirty approach.

"So," she said after swallowing. "Any others you can tell me about?"

"Some serial killers leave pretty gruesome stuff behind. I was a new detective when the Dahmer case broke. I helped collect the evidence. His trophies."

"Wow. Must have been . . . awful."

"Awful enough. Couldn't get the smell out of my nose for weeks."

"And yet here we are," she said, spearing some vegetables. "Both obviously unwilling to give it up."

"Here we are," he agreed.

He drank flat beer and wondered just when to come clean. Jessie would never agree. Tom Arnow had been enough, and she *liked* him. No, this was his decision, but it was best to keep his cards close to the vest for now. He could always clue her in if it seemed necessary. Right now he could continue the charade of Wilson having some weird way to fake animal attacks.

Like the fake Loch Ness monster "claw" murder weapon in an old episode of The Saint.

Wilson was crazy for drawing attention to herself like

this. But then, maybe she was traumatized by what had happened to her. She wasn't thinking clearly. Not realizing her spree was showing up on somebody's radar. But maybe she just didn't care. She had seemed headstrong and willful.

Not for the first time, he wondered when Wolfpaw would catch up to him. Jessie had been right. He had flown right up into their radar.

But he hadn't expected so many goddamn werewolves.

Let me take care of this one first.

They discussed the crime scene a while longer, but he was forced to play dumb, so it wasn't very fruitful. He was unwilling to get into the teeth marks and other aspects. He wanted to assess Falken's receptivity to things of a strange nature, but couldn't find the opportunity.

Mostly Falken flirted with him, looking at him over her glass with amusement at his discomfort.

"Do I make you nervous?" she said, misreading his reticence.

"No. Ah, well, I'm just with . . ."

"With *someone?*" she said, laughter obvious in the curl of her lips. "Attached, committed? *Married?*"

"Not married, but yeah to the rest," he said, and she laughed her laugh again.

"Good for you."

He couldn't tell if she was mocking him. Mocking the idea he was unavailable to her, if she was determined to get him?

His discomfort began to manifest itself where he hid his hands under the table. He felt fur sprouting up and down his arms and along his spine. He cleared his throat to mask any unintended growling. The Creature didn't like to be toyed with, and sometimes it reminded him he wasn't completely alone.

No wonder he had hated his condition as a kid. No wonder he would have done anything to be rid of it. Except for those times it allowed him to have revenge.

Then it had come in handy.

> From the Journals of Caroline Stewart
> December 25, 1981

There was a beautiful snowfall in time for Christmas.

A white blanket enveloped the city, bringing with it a bright country stillness worthy of a Currier & Ives.

And then the gifts . . .

Dear Lord, we gave each other gifts last night and today. We gave again and again and again. We spent almost every minute of the last eighteen hours in each other's arms, and when we weren't, we were being naughty in some other way.

I haven't had so much sex in my entire life!

And I loved every moment.

Nick Lupo is the best thing that ever happened to me.

I know there's something dark lurking there, in the corner where we don't see it—where we try to pretend we don't see it—but I think we deserved this vacation from the realities.

This has been my best Christmas ever!

I feel like Scrooge having been shown the good parts of Christmas Present. I'm sad about all those Christmases I never enjoyed, but so grateful to Nick for having made this one so memorable.

And it's not over yet . . .

1978
BRAD SCHNEIDER

Sputtering, Brad wiped his face with his shirttail.

The fuckin' faggot!

It was a lucky shot. It splashed him perfectly in the face and he could taste the bitter snot-and-beer mix on his tongue. He could barely keep from heaving.

He stepped up, his face beet red.

But before he could grab the faggot Josh by the neck, good old Rollie had given some sort of signal and a half-dozen jocks had already done so.

Josh struggled to get loose and managed to tear one arm out of somebody's grip. Somehow he ended up with one of his brass knuckles in his fist, flailing about and connecting here and there.

Brad shouted, "Get the fucker!"

His face was red now with the feverish lust for blood that had driven him to mastermind the entire thing.

It worked. Josh's arm was twisted and the brass knuckles ripped from his fist.

Brad's breath came faster as the faggot's body became a punching bag for just about everybody in his organization.

He licked his lips.

This was better than getting blown.

Better than getting new cheerleader ass.

Better than anything in his life, ever.

The power coursed through his veins like a potent blend of heroin and speed and testosterone, giving him a monster erection.

He whispered something to one of his minions and gestured at where Sherry Ludden was struggling weakly.

He was a master manipulator, and now was the time to enjoy the result of his labors.

He felt the blood engorge his penis and reveled in the feeling of power, lusting for the release yet wanting this power trip to go on forever.

The minions started to separate Sherry's struggling form from that of the faggot kid.

It was two separate things, after all.

Brad smiled.

CHAPTER FIFTEEN

LUPO

"So, tell me about you," she said over a rich chocolate mousse, the best part of the meal.

He shrugged. "Academy, uniform, homicide, now gangs, soon hopefully homicide again. That's about it. Boring."

"Well! You left out Dahmer—"

"You already knew about that."

"And the Martin Stewart case. Others, I'm sure. Couple commendations. You're too humble."

"Blame my parents. Humble immigrants. Taught me humility. Italians are often portrayed as arrogant Tony Soprano types, and some are, but many more are quiet and unassuming."

"Nick Lupo, you are not unassuming!"

"I try to be. Okay, what about you? Your name Irish?"

She laughed. "Sounds like. But I have a deep, dark secret. You and I are probably related way back in the old country."

He was shocked. "No way! You're Italian."

"Almost pure wop. Family name was Falcone. My grandfather dropped the *e*, maybe was pressured to, maybe it was a sound financial decision, who knows? So we became Falcons. Like the bird. When I was old enough, I decided to be less obviously ethnic. I changed it to Falken, with K-E-N so nobody would know what it was. My father disowned me. Well, there were other reasons, too."

"How'd the Sheila come about?"

She grinned. "Australian mother."

He chuckled. "Italian-Australian?"

"Yup."

He considered her straight face. "Bullshit?"

She bobbed her head in an exaggerated nod. "Yeah."

He let it go. If she wanted to tell him the truth, she would. "Chicago, you said."

"Right. Lots of dirty politics. Father and uncle and a brother are all cops. Another uncle's a fire chief. I made my way north after starting out on a beat in the city. Made detective here a lot sooner. I think they like me!"

"I bet they do," he said, smiling.

When to broach the subject?

She made the decision for him. "See, also boring. How about we discuss my suspect?"

"Sure. You planning to continue surveillance?"

She nodded slowly. "I think so. She's bound to make some mistake. Soon."

"How did you come to suspect Wilson?" Maybe her answer would determine his approach. Could she handle it, the way Arnow had? Of course, later Arnow had allowed his acceptance to corrode.

"Pure chance. I was first at the scene for several of the animal attacks, and she was there already. Beat me to the scene twice. It made me wonder. Then I stuck some pins in a city map and saw that a bunch of the city attacks were like a circle around her apartment."

"Would she be so stupid?"

"Criminals are arrogant, stupid bastards usually. She probably thinks she's golden because she gets face time on television. Too good to be caught."

The check came and he paused to pay the waitress, who disappeared again into the back. The place was emptying out, he noticed for the first time. Falken had taken up all his attention.

What time was it? He checked his watch.

Damn, what am I doing?

He needed to get out and about. Maybe the Creature could stumble onto a scent, or the rogue animal itself. It had to be Heather Wilson. Who else would poach the Wausau area?

Jesus, would Falken freak if he told her the truth? It seemed as if they were dancing around the truth because they were both afraid the other would react with ridicule. But did she know something or didn't she? She'd said *strange* with regard to what she knew, but then she'd backed off.

Her phone trilled and she excused herself.

Fuck, Lupo swore under his breath. *What to do?*

"Gotta go," she said after taking the call and speaking a couple monosyllables. "Some kind of problem with a gang thing."

"Gang? Need a hand? My current area."

She shook her head. "Nah, thanks. This is an ongoing thing, not high profile. We cover all the bases here, as detectives."

"I know when I'm not wanted," he joked.

She fake-pouted. "Now you'll hold that against me forever."

"At least."

They parted at the door, promising to be in touch about the Wilson surveillance.

Nothing resolved, nothing accomplished. Just verbal sparring and flirting.

He watched her walk away quickly. He almost decided to follow her, remembering how she'd lied in Daytona. But it was probably a white lie. And he knew he really should get on the road to Eagle River, if he wanted to get there before morning.

Jessie was probably waiting for him, wondering where he was.

He could also check on Heather Wilson.

He ruffled and combed his unruly hair with his fingers. How had he managed to get himself between *three* women?

Christ, he was due for some payback. He was sure of it.

The sad thing was, he deserved it. He'd slipped up big time. And all he could hope was to somehow keep the three in separate orbits.

Good luck, idiot.

Oh yeah. Idiot.

HEATHER

She ran on wolf legs, her eyes rolling in the silver moonlight. It was only a sliver of moon, a quarter or less, but the light seemed to be aimed directly into her eyes. She smiled with her fangs, which were still dappled with blood and flecks of bone from her recent kill.

She paused at a creek and dipped her muzzle into the cool water flowing there, first drinking to slake the thirst caused by the salty food, and then to shake her snout and clean her whiskers. The tiny creek wound through the park like a casually dropped piece of rope, usually drawing other night creatures for a drink. But when the wolf was present, the deer and the rabbits stayed away.

Then she ran again, feeling the moonlight on her back fur and enjoying its caress.

WAGNER

Wagner sat in the near dark, waiting. The laptop screen was the only light in the room. The phone was plugged into the computer's USB port. There was a double click and a connection sound not unlike the old-fashioned modems once used, but also at the same time different. Then the software on the screen jumped to life with three rows of sound waves.

The software had, once upon a time, been based loosely on Pro Tools, a program used by musicians to record their voices or acoustic instruments digitally and store the data on a hard drive. Since then such recording software had become commonplace, used in podcasting and similar applications, and was often downloaded free of charge. But some developers had other ideas. The software Wagner had open was identical to software open on the computer and phone at the other end of the call, and it accomplished several tasks simultaneously. First it altered the speakers' voices, then it scrambled the phone signal, which was sent over the Internet phone to phone. It also identified each speaker by comparing the voices to on-file voiceprints, so both were convinced they were speaking to a specific caller. There were also several panic features built in to allow a caller held at gunpoint who might be compelled to speak to also covertly alert the other caller of the situation.

Right now Wagner was speaking and the caller was listening. Then the waveforms on the screen danced and Wagner listened. The altered, scrambled voice came through the Trac-Fone in flat metallic tones.

"Your report is incomplete," said the robot voice.

"Time isn't of the essence—"

"For you."

"Yes," Wagner said, concurring. "For me. I am closing in on one and using the subject as bait for the others. We don't know how many there are, but only that there are others. Once they are all identified and gathered, they can be harvested."

"You're certain the, uh, harvesting will be final."

"That's what is taking some time," Wagner said, staring at the sound waves on the screen as if they would coalesce into a picture of the other speaker. Clicking a camera icon would have done just that, but neither caller wanted to see the other in this case. "I have to balance my baiting with trying to avoid too much civilian interference or under-standing."

"A difficult process."

"At best. But the timeline I predicted is still viable. And our measured response will also allow us the payback we seek."

"Revenge is secondary," the robot voice said.

"True, but highly desirable."

"There is some agreement from the Committee, but you must keep the prime objective in mind at all times."

"Tell the Committee that the task is well in hand."

"Your skill is well-known." The waves stopped for a second. "Your results are guaranteed. There is no room for failure."

"There won't be any failure."

"See to it. Carry on. *Heil!*"

"*Heil*," Wagner said, and closed down the connection along with the software.

Before shutting down the laptop, Wagner opened different software and ran through a series of commands, clicking through a half-dozen menus until one double click brought up Nick Lupo's computer desktop. A few more clicks and Nick Lupo's e-mail program lay unwrapped like a virtual onion.

Wagner scanned the list of new e-mails, opened and read a series of them, and then when they were closed they appeared as unread again. One, sent by Jessie Hawkins, elicited a chuckle because it included a risqué photo of Lupo's doctor friend. *Lover*, clearly.

JESSIE

Bobby greeted her from the security counter, where they stored confiscated cell phones, checked bags, and monitored the entrance. There was a high-tech security office behind the scenes, well-stocked with multiple flat monitors rotating camera views from everywhere in the complex. The counter at the entrance was the low-tech public face of security, designed to make them seem like benign cops.

"Hello, Bobby," she called out, returning his wave.

The place was humming. One o'clock in the morning, and it made no difference to the gamblers, who fantasized about getting lucky just once—one big score was all it took. One big score was always potentially waiting for that next spin, deal, or pushed button.

She hadn't heard of any big scores lately, so the seasoned gamblers were on the lookout for one, when the odds would finally favor a player instead of the house. Jessie figured, even then the odds were really in the house's favor, but it was a nice myth to promote.

She found one empty slot machine and slid in her card. Several thousand "credits" showed up in the window.

She pushed the button for maximum bet and watched the reels spinning like a hypnotist's wheel in an old horror movie.

Infuriating, she pondered, that she knew she was wasting her money, yet couldn't stop. Didn't want to stop.

What would a shrink say? She could always find out, couldn't she? Plenty of people went into therapy for less. If anyone had a right to feel the need for some therapy, it had to be someone who was dating a werewolf. A werewolf with issues. She almost snorted with a sardonic laugh.

On the other hand, he had a right to issues. He did. Nick was a thoughtful guy who'd had some bad breaks, and he seemed to love her unconditionally, so she owed him the same. But not only had he dragged her into his life and his "condition," but he'd drawn them into trouble. If that Wolfpaw company was suddenly gunning for him, it was the result of his inability to let go. His inability to let things slide.

She pushed the button and watched more money flush down the toilet that was the slot machine.

She wanted to stop, but she was unable to let go.

Ironic, wasn't it?

The noise level was distracting. Voices blended in with the constant C-major chord the machines emitted as a sort of cattle call. She looked around and saw old people hunched over machines, cigarettes gripped in wrinkled mouths—mostly women, she noted, who did the cigarette thing—a look of desperate determination on their faces.

Would she look like that one day?

Hell, did she look like that *now*?

She shrugged and pushed the button.

"Hey, Doc." The voice behind her threw her out of her reverie. It was Bobby, the security guy. A good, solid rez man, who'd been a good cop. Nice family. He was making good money here. A friendly, beefy bear of a man with a ponytail. She'd liked him on sight.

"Yeah, Bobby? How are you?"

He hesitated. "Eh," he said, punctuating with the standard so-so tilt of the head, willing to tell the truth if she asked. "Not bad, I guess."

She liked him too much to avoid his obvious attempt to tell her what was on his mind.

"What's wrong?" she asked. The hell with the machine; it was a dud, anyway. She took her card back and stepped away. A cronelike elderly woman swooped in and shoved her way onto the stool.

Jessie grinned and stepped toward the side, near the free-drinks counter. Bobby followed, seeming to wrestle with himself.

"Now," she said, once they were away from the crush of gamblers, "what's wrong? Is it your health?"

"Not really," he said. He hesitated. "It's work. I mean, it's kind of the council and work."

"What is it?" He really seemed troubled. He looked down, embarrassed to be unloading on her. Yet he'd approached her. "Bobby?"

"Doc, I don't know what's up with the council lately, but Davison's been acting weird. And now he's just laid off some of the boys. A third of the security staff's been let go."

"Is business bad? The economy's affecting everything. Maybe they need budget cuts?"

"That's just it. According to the newsletter, business is booming. Actually going up."

"Bobby, you didn't lose your job, did you?"

"Not yet, Doc, but I can see the writing on the wall. I think I barely survived. Maybe 'cause I tend to work extra shifts all the time without complaining. But the others, they're family men and they're younger, so their wives want them home."

"Did management give any explanation for the layoffs?" she asked, intrigued.

Davison had been the voice of reason when he'd taken over. Sam Waters would have been a shoo-in to head the council, but he was gone and Davison had had little trouble gaining the votes he needed from the shrunken council. He also knew about werewolves, having seen plenty that night on the beach of Cranberry Island, but he had made it plain he wasn't ever going to talk about it, even with Jessie or Lupo, or Sheriff Arnow. It was classic denial, and now here he was, perhaps acting irrationally.

"It was bullshit reasons, Doc," said Bobby. He looked at the cameras dotting the high ceilings in their blue bubbles, as if worried that there would be a record of his talking to her. "These are all rez guys, and now we're shorthanded. Why would he take jobs away from our own people?"

"What were the reasons the council gave?"

"Like I said, bullshit. Like how the department is over-staffed. It ain't. And how some were observed taking too many breaks. Not even true. And something about modern-izing the surveillance, but we're still spankin' new, so what's to modernize? Bullshit."

Jessie nodded. "Doesn't sound like he was being truthful."

"Nope, and I think they been telling different people different stories, too."

She was intrigued enough to forget about losing more credits. "I'll check into it," she assured him, touching his arm. "I see Davison fairly often. I just didn't know."

"Just happened, Doc. No way you could have known. Thanks for lookin' into it. I'd like a straight answer at least."

She edged toward the corridor that led to the theater in one direction, the restrooms, and in the other direction wound up at the foyer, where an escalator disappeared into the upper level, where the restaurants and bingo halls drew their share of visitors. He walked her to the door and opened it for her.

Outside, it was just before dawn, light beginning to tint the sky over the pines that hugged the sides of the complex.

Jesus, how long had she been in there?

She glanced at her watch. *Three hours!*

She *had* to get some help.

She waved at Bobby and set off across the lot. A couple buses filled with weary, poorer players pulled out. A shiny new casino bus pulled in from some nearby retirement community.

What the hell was up with Davison?

And what the hell was Nick doing?

She smelled the smoke and sweat of the casino on her skin and clothes and felt her gorge rising. She needed a shower.

LUPO

He went there anyway. He drove to her building almost automatically, barely registering his own actions. If she was there right now, then perhaps she wasn't guilty.

But then, who was?

Lupo wasn't sure whether he wanted to find her or not. Which would make him feel better?

The windows he knew were hers were all dark. She was either gone or in bed. She'd had enough time to hunt and return home, but he knew from experience that after a hunt he wanted to run through the woods, soak in moonlight if there was any, and just take in the joy of freedom on four paws. If she was the same, then she'd still be out.

Then he'd check her place. The trash. Any other clues. A quick in-and-out trip, then he'd get on the road. He rationalized it knowing he would make it up to Jessie somehow. He owed her.

He slipped into the quiet building unobserved, then let himself into her place using the alarm-bypass device. About ten minutes was all it gave him. He waited a minute to let his eyes attune to the dark. Bare street light gave the loft a soft glow. In the kitchen, he checked her trash and saw the remains of numerous empty meat containers.

You knew you'd find this already, he told himself.

You just wanted to be careful.

On the other hand, the containers might indicate someone who wasn't eating fresh human meat. Was actively avoiding it.

He slipped into her bedrooms, his eyes now sharply able to see details. She wasn't home. Her beds were made. Another inconclusive clue. He checked her "playroom," where the sex swing hung limply.

No one there either.

He turned to leave the premises and had reached the outer door when she threw it open and stood before him, her features twisted in anger.

"You! What the hell are you doing here? How did you get in?"

She was formidable in her rage.

The attraction he still felt for her after their one strange tryst made itself known to him. And she sensed it.

Her eyes became slits and the corners of her lips turned up in a sly smile that immediately overtook the anger at finding an intruder inside her wolf's den, as it were.

"You want me," she whispered in a throaty voice.

He wondered if she still tasted the raw flesh she'd eaten earlier.

Her eyes locked on his and held them captive.

She approached him, slowly dropping her jacket and starting to unbutton her dark blouse. She let it slide to the floor and then wriggled out of her black bra and shed it like a snake's skin. Her skirt magically loosened and dropped, and the frilly panties followed.

Lupo watched the display with a mixture of lust and dismay. His groin made the lust all too clear.

Was it a sexual advance, or was she about to Change?

Could he finish her here?

The Creature in him bubbled up to the surface. He felt it clamoring to be set free.

Should he bring her down?

If she isn't a wolf, then the Creature will kill her.

If she is and Changes along with me, then our fight might be a draw.

Silver would make it a sure thing, but he had none. He hadn't prepared for a face-off.

Innocent building residents might be hurt.

He made his decision quickly, regretfully. He suppressed the Creature and barged past Heather Wilson even as she reached for him, naked and magnificent, her lusty flesh only inches from his. He felt the heat emanating off her skin.

She grabbed his clothing and tried to draw him back playfully, but he shrugged her off.

He edged into the hallway, her mocking laughter following him seemingly all the way out to the street.

Retreat.

The better part of valor? Wasn't that cowardice? Or discretion? DiSanto would know. Nick grunted bitterly.

Almost as if under hypnosis, he found himself sitting in his car, moving out of town. He wasn't even sure how he had gotten there.

He heaved back onto 51, speeding openly, and soon swerved crazily off on 17, driving hard for Eagle River, humiliated and more than a little pissed off. She'd made a fool of him. Worse, she had played him to a stalemate.

CHAPTER SIXTEEN

WAGNER

The park lay sprawling outside the southern edge of town, groves of trees in clumps hunched over winter-bare picnic areas full of still-upended wooden tables.

In the dark, the ranks of tables near a fieldstone and timber storage shed resembled a strange Victorian architectural nightmare right out of a Dickensian London slum.

Wagner knew a small group of homeless men and women had made a shelter in the lee of the up-tilted tables. Who knew where they had come from? Perhaps they were local victims of the ruined economy, or seasonal workers left without work, or old-style hoboes on the road.

Wagner didn't care. At the moment, the homeless people were the next item on a long list of actions designed to flush out those who knew too much about shape-shifters, and perhaps about specific ones.

They had tacked cardboard panels to the sides of the

tables to form a windbreak, and more panels had been connected with scrap two-by-fours to form a sort of lattice roof over the walls created by the upended tables.

The scent of unwashed bodies, sweat, and greasy food—some of it apparently cooked on a series of ramshackle portable grills—hung over the encampment. Local police would surely roust these people if they noticed them, but so far they hadn't.

And that made them a gift to Wagner.

The wolf prowled the edges of the temporary shantytown and luxuriated in the various scents—men, women, and a couple children. Perhaps they were a group of related families. Their scents were intertwined in intriguing ways. Stalking the humans was a pleasure in itself, but Wagner could already taste the hot blood and greasy flesh before arriving.

Circling ever closer, the wolf first took a child who sat huddled by herself, two ragged dolls in her tiny hands.

An *appetizer*.

Wagner was almost humane, killing the small human without undue torture. No one could accuse Wagner of lacking empathy of a sort.

The taste of blood drove the wolf on, and in a minute sharp teeth and jaws and slashing claws landed in the midst of the group just as a meal was being shared. Wagner took one man's head with one swipe of a gigantic paw, then ripped out the throats of two women who ran screaming for cover before they could reach the outer edge of the makeshift camp. A man screamed in pain and rage and charged the wolf, a clutched blade glinting in the grill-fed firelight.

Wagner felt one knife slash parting fur and skin, but there was no pain and the sensation of magical healing immediately spread through the wolf's organs.

The man watched as his killing blow barely slowed down the huge wolf, then his scream ended in a gurgle as the steel-like jaws clamped onto his neck and sawed through bone and flesh with inexorable determination. His blood geysered into the wolf's throat, but the animal was already turning to pursue several others still trapped between the back wall made by the tables and where the snarling animal waited.

Screaming only stimulated the wolf's bloodlust.

The rest of the people died one by one, chased down and disemboweled like stragglers in a herd.

In minutes it was over. Wagner sampled the goods before they turned cold.

Then it was away into the shelter of the trees.

Wagner howled in pure joy, satisfaction, and the glow of a job well done.

The cop Dominic Lupo would now have no choice but to bring in his cohorts. The endgame was in sight.

Job well done.

LUPO

Miles went by as he aimed northeast, pine trees lining the roads except for the hickish little unincorporated towns that flashed by like phantoms in the night.

The police radio had been sputtering for a while, picking up a sudden surge in traffic he ignored for a long stretch, too busy berating himself for his weakness.

Lupo knew he had all too often given in to his weaknesses, which ended up causing others pain. Usually people he cared about. People he *loved*.

He heard the words *animal attack* and almost swerved, one hand reaching for the volume knob. The dispatcher's voice filled the car with a strange combination of awe, disgust, and excitement.

Goddamn, this sounded like a mass murder, except it was still being referred to as an animal attack.

Fuck!

Turn back?

They were stretching everyone's credulity by invoking more animal attacks, yet what else could they do, given their refusal to look to the supernatural for their answers?

Had his spurning of her advance caused her to take out her anger on innocents?

He smacked the wheel, giving in to the infamous Lupo temper yet again.

His indecision and weakness was leading to deaths. In his mind, he flipped through options.

Lupo watched for a signpost, and when one appeared in his headlights, it told him he'd already traveled three-quarters of the way. Turning back would just get him nowhere at all. Plus now he *needed* to see Jessie, to find a way to cleanse himself of his sins without hurting her.

Anyway, he imagined Falken had already made the crime scene her own. *There* was another goddamn problem in the making. He *had* to bring her aboard soon. Even if he had to show her proof of his claims, as he'd done with Arnow.

He saw a wayside come up on the right and flicked the wheel just enough to take him rocketing into the empty lot, pulling the Maxima to a ticking halt just beside the tiny stone outhouse and its Plexiglas-covered visitor map and signs.

He rolled down his windows, switched off the engine, and listened to the police chatter a few more minutes. Then he stabbed the radio and shut it off. The cool night's silence enveloped him and he sat in the dark, hearing the breeze ruffling the trees high up. He let the cold air play across his face and tousle his hair. Tears welled up in the corners of his eyes and the cold air made them sting.

Violently, he smashed his hands on the steering wheel once, twice, then more, again and again, until the pain in his wrists reminded him he couldn't afford to damage his car.

Heather had outsmarted him. There was nothing to congratulate himself for there. He had poked the Wolfpaw hive and stirred up trouble down south, too. Trouble that might well be on his doorstep any day now. And that pit bull Killian was nosing around his ass and catching a scent he seemed to like.

Fuck, fuck, and fuck.

Lupo wondered if it was part of his destiny to always get himself into things over his head. So far, he had managed to array all sorts of enemies at his throat, and no allies to speak of, unless he counted the flirty Falken, who wasn't quite an ally yet.

Ignoring the time, he wrestled his iPhone out of his jacket and dialed Arnow's cell. He didn't give a shit what time it was in Florida or anywhere else. He needed to get the former sheriff into the game, and he didn't have much time.

Clearly, some werewolf was targeting people in the Wausau area. This new near genocide of homeless people he'd heard about on the radio was almost like a slap, a gauntlet across the face. Either Heather had gone out after he'd barged out, just to get his attention, or somebody else had.

Maybe Wolfpaw is in town.

Arnow's phone buzzed a few times, then he picked up and grunted.

"Listen, Tom," Lupo said before the PI could wake up, "I'm in some kind of shit here and I could use your help."

"Yeah? You think?"

"Yeah, I hate to ruin your idyllic home life down there in heaven, but . . . could you fly up here?"

Arnow chuckled. "You don't check your voice mail much, do you?"

"Huh?"

"I took the last flight up. I'm in a motel across from Mitchell International. I got a car lined up. Just getting a couple hours' sleep, if I can, then heading up. Where the hell do I meet you?"

Relief flooded Lupo's body like a wave of fresh blood in

his veins. He felt almost light-headed with sudden energy. With Arnow around, he could approach Falken and prove his case without her dismissing him as a kook. The three of them could find a way to prove Wilson was their wolf, and act on it. The burden of being judge, jury, and executioner wouldn't rest with him alone.

"Let's make it Eagle River, Tom," he said, sighing with released tension. "I'm heading there now. There was a huge incident in Wausau, a group of homeless people . . . a fucking massacre."

"Was it Heather?" His voice cracked just slightly.

"I don't—I need help to figure it out. It could have been Wolfpaw."

"Jesus, Lupo."

"I know. But they don't really have a motive in this."

"Wow, I'm relieved."

"I'm their motive. These people have no bearing."

"Okay, where am I going?"

"You remember where Jessie lives?" He winced as he said it.

Arnow sighed. "Yeah, I'll start on my way up in a couple hours. I hate all those long stretches of dark county highways you got up there. Plus I have to wait for a UPS overnight delivery I sent myself, care of this motel. A heavy one."

Lupo didn't have to ask.

Silver ammunition.

"Tom?"

"Yeah?"

"Thanks."

They clicked off, and Lupo waited for the blood to stop rushing through his face and hands. The call of the woods was strong, and he had the urge to Change, right there, and go for a run. Maybe later, he thought. Better to get back on the road now, see Jessie, make amends. *Something.* Something had to go right.

A few minutes later he started up, closed his windows, and pulled back onto the deserted road. Some weight had been lifted off his shoulders.

So why wasn't he feeling better?

LUPO

She wasn't at home, or at his cottage down at the end of Circle Moon Drive, so he jumped back into the car and headed a ways north to the reservation.

Chances were good he'd find her at the clinic, the rez hospital for which she had become default head. The tribal council had searched halfheartedly for a professional administrator who was also a physician, but had given up after a few candidates had proven unacceptable. Davison had turned to Jessie Hawkins, who had done well enough in the same role when the clinic was a tiny one-story bungalow. Now that the hospital was a new building several stories high and stocked with up-to-date equipment and an ever-expanding professional staff, Jessie could scale back her role as physician and run the place as an administrator who knew the score. It made sense all around.

Lupo always felt depressed when he entered the reservation. Although recently some improvements were obvious—probably related to the casino money that had begun rolling in—especially in the quality of the roadway itself and some of the new construction being carved from previously virgin pine forest, he still saw signs of the decades of poverty that it would take more than a quick cash infusion to cure. He drove past a few ramshackle fishing-bait businesses, a couple paint-flecked convenience stores, and also a new movie theater triplex. The contrasts, if you looked for them, were startling.

Lupo pulled into the hospital lot and smiled at seeing

Jessie's venerable old Pathfinder in its slot. He pulled up next to it, stiff from the long drive.

Maybe she can lock the office door and work the kinks out of my back.

He smiled. It wouldn't have been the first time. Since she'd cut back the doctoring and increased the "administrationing," as he joked, she'd sometimes been able to play naughty behind closed office doors.

Sure wasn't outside the realm of the possible.

He was excited at having Tom almost on his way. An ally would ease the pressure on him, smooth things with Falken as they brought her aboard, and give him another gun in his arsenal. He'd be able to keep Jessie out of it more. Since losing Sam, he'd had nightmares of his lifestyle—and its drawbacks—dragging her into deadly danger.

They paged Jessie for him when he found her office locked. Maybe she was in the ER, or visiting patients. Or maybe she was grabbing a bite to eat.

Lupo's pulse started to race. What if Wolfpaw had reached out and grabbed her? *Or worse?*

He headed back to the main desk and spotted a security guard he'd spoken to before. They nodded hello—Lupo had been to see Jessie dozens of times.

"Have you seen Dr. Hawkins? It's an emergency, and her car's parked out there, but nobody's seen her."

The guard was about to shake his head; then he took a quick glance around and leaned closer over the counter.

"Didn't hear it from me, but she might've headed to the casino," he whispered.

Lupo laughed. Then he saw the guard was serious. "The *casino?*"

"Yeah, she heads there sometimes, late at night, after shift."

"Serious?" Lupo's head spun. *Jessie? In a casino?*

He thanked the guard, whose name he couldn't remember, and headed outside. He stalked around the building and made for the garish monstrosity that hovered over everything in the vicinity. He waited for several buses to rumble past, wondering at the stream of people entering the building even this late.

Inside, he ran into a security guard he remembered.

"Bobby, right?"

The big guy's eyes widened in recognition. "Howdy, man! How goes?"

"Good. You see Doc Hawkins around?" Lupo almost expected Bobby to laugh and shake his head. The whole thing had been a mistake.

"Yeah, she's back there. Quarter slots, probably."

"Yeah?"

"Yup, her usual corner. Hey, she tell you about those bands we got comin'? Kansas, Alan Parsons. Stuff you two really dig."

"Uh, yeah. Thanks, man." He looked around. "You guys a little shorthanded?" The security counter was unmanned, and the usual knot of blue shirts at the entrance was missing.

Bobby nodded, a sad look overtaking his features. "Yeah, we had a bunch of layoffs. I was just tellin' Doc Hawkins about that a couple days ago."

"She come in often?"

"Uh, almost every night, an hour or two." He looked sheepish, as if he was worried about breaking a confidence.

Lupo nodded as if it sounded right.

But it didn't!

What the hell was this all about?

He shook hands with Bobby after commiserating briefly, then set off to hunt for Jessie. The noise of the slots and video-poker machines would have driven him crazy in a short while, he mused. And they'd joked about that more than once.

He shook his head.

It beat all hell out of him.

JESSIE

She watched her red number edge up—ninety-nine, one hundred, one hundred one, all the way to one twenty-five. Quarters. This was a little over thirty-one dollars.

Not a bad win.

Of course, she'd dropped about two hundred quarters to get there.

She snickered.

House always wins, even when they lose.

Suddenly she felt someone standing behind her, craning to look over her shoulder.

She whirled.

"Nick!"

"Hi," he said.

She jumped off the stool and snagged him into a big embrace, her lips seeking out his before he could speak.

When she let him go, he took a breath. "Checked for you at the hospital," he said. "Then I hear you like to come here *most nights.*"

She felt the heat of a blush washing across her face.

"Uh, occasionally," she said. She reached back and ejected her Dreamquester's Club card and pocketed it before he could see how much she had on it.

"I thought you hated gambling."

"Well, there's a lot of stuff we start out hating that we then end up liking. *And vice versa,*" she added.

"Whoa," he said. "What's *that* mean?"

She sighed. "It means I loved having you up here all to myself, but now you come with all this Wolfpaw baggage, and Heather baggage, and whatever else kind of baggage."

"So you come to gamble? That makes it better?"

"Maybe then I don't think about where we're going wrong!" she said, more nastily than she intended.

Ouch, she thought.

He winced.

"Okay," he said. "I can see we'll have to talk. But it's best if we go home right now. Tom Arnow's coming after all. I can use the help in both the Heather and Wolfpaw *baggage* handling."

She smiled despite herself. She'd always liked his sarcastic sense of humor. Even when she was sometimes the butt of it.

She followed him out of the building, waving at Bobby at the entrance, and they held hands as they crossed the street and parted in the lot.

He swept her into his arms and kissed her long and hard, and she felt comforted.

Okay, now he knows, and he's not dumping me. Yet.

She tingled all the way home, following his car and thinking about what she was going to do to him when they got there.

For a while, at least, she didn't want to hear about all the dangers he was bringing down on their heads. Again.

But was that a woman's scent she'd caught off his clothing?

LUPO

As soon as she let them into her cottage, he pulled her down on her leather sofa and nuzzled her neck just the way she liked.

She let him, her ardor apparently matching his.

Was she sniffing him? What was that about?

He kissed his way down her neck, down to her breasts, and slowly started to sneak her blouse out of her pants.

"Nick Lupo! You must be horny."

Or guilty. The thought lanced through his brain and he suppressed it. *Maybe just horny, thanks to Heather.*

He willed his inner voice to shut up. You never knew when it was going to use your mouth to start speaking suddenly, getting you in trouble.

He kept nuzzling the cotton until she helped him remove the obstacle, impatient for his lips on her skin. He complied, leaving a line of gentle kisses down her collarbone and over her brassiere. He fumbled with the catch and slipped it off down her shoulders at about the same time she helped him shed his shirt and then undid his belt.

"Ooh, Mr. Lupo," she whispered throatily into his ear, her hand reaching inside the front of his trousers. "You like me, you *really* like me."

He grinned into her soft skin and licked a line from one ripe nipple to the other while she handled him and gently freed him from the constricting material.

While he gently kneaded her nipples, she grabbed his shirt from where it lay crumpled between them and cocked her arm to toss it.

But instead she sniffed at it again.

And then she pulled away from him and held him off with her other hand.

"Tell me why this smells like a perfume I don't own, Nick."

He was stunned with the rapid cooldown. Her hand left him still tethered by his pants, and her nipples were suddenly far away, across a sort of chasm that had opened up between them.

"Jess, I have a job, I interact with people. Female people. I don't think—"

"I remember the scent, Nick," she said. "It's that Wilson woman's. I think it imprinted itself on my nostrils the very first time I met her. You seeing her?"

"I told you, I suspect her. I think she's Changing and causing those so-called animal attacks."

"We fought about this already. I should just accept that

you'll have her perfume on you because you're following her. Just how close do you have to get to follow someone?"

"She caught me. We had to interact. She was a little close, sure, but mostly angry at me for tailing her." Lupo knew it sounded lame. But he had done the right thing, at least that time.

Damn it.

He felt like turning the tables. *What about this secret gambling, huh? How much you been donating to the longhouse through their casino?*

But he held back. Maybe he could steer things back to where they'd been headed.

He said, "I only want to be with you."

"Isn't that a song lyric?"

There was a brief silence between them. Maybe he detected a few degrees' worth of warmup. They faced each other, half-naked, halfway to angry, but now it seemed ridiculous.

"Yeah," he admitted, grinning. "That doesn't mean it's not true."

Her lips quivered with suppressed humor. Suddenly she was about to cave. "Hit me with another one."

" 'I was born under a bad sign,' " he said without missing a beat. " 'There's a bad moon on the rise.' 'Ahooo, werewolves of London.' "

She couldn't help grinning.

And then they were tangling their limbs again, and this time Lupo was tugging her pants down and sliding her panties aside, and he was inhaling her musky scent, and before long she was indicating her pleasure.

"Jess, you know I'd never hurt you," he whispered into the soft skin of her inner thighs. She groaned in response.

He knew he was being truthful, but it didn't make him feel any better.

Things got better from there, at least for a while.

CODE NAME: ALPHA TEAM

Hartsfield-Jackson Atlanta International Airport processes millions of travelers, thousands of flights both domestic and international, and countless tons of cargo and baggage. With its beeping VIP carts, moving walkways, the People Mover subway, its own MARTA station, and endless numbers of cabs, limos, buses, and car-service autos, the traffic never ends.

Into this never-ending, always-changing stream of perpetual motion, the group of eight men made little impact. They wore nicely cut suits like successful businessmen and carried stylish briefcases, but anyone watching them with an analytical eye might have noticed their military bearing and precision walking formation. Anyone watching closely would have noticed that their ID tags, carried in flat cases hung around their muscular necks, allowed them passage through every TSA security checkpoint without any further question, search, or impediment. They did not remove shoes, belts, coats, or expose their briefcases to the scanning equipment. In fact, the men themselves were shown around the scanners and sent on their way with nary a second's delay.

Anyone tracking the luggage checked by the eight men would have witnessed a similar phenomenon. Their eight long rectangular flight cases, silver in color and reinforced at all corners, similar to those used to protect musical instruments, scientific instruments, and photographic equipment, slid through every checkpoint and scanning device between the airline counters and the parked airplane's cargo hold. Anyone who glanced at or examined the special tags prominently displayed on all sides of each case immediately cleared the case for passage, and in fact a special cart was used to transport them directly to the plane, where handlers with special clearance hand-carried them to the cargo hold.

At their destination, they would be handled in the same manner.

The eight men sat in four side-by-side groups of two in the first four rows of coach, but were treated as if they were occupying first-class seats. The offered service was lost on them, as they pointedly ignored any questions asked by cabin personnel, who learned quickly to leave them in peace. The flight crew considered them foreign nationals who spoke no English, and gave them a wide berth after repeated attempts to serve them drinks met with stony silence and blank stares.

When the aircraft finally landed at its destination and the eight were the first to deplane, every single flight attendant heaved a sigh of relief, as did all nearby passengers who had begun to consider the men's long silence and rude stares the possible hallmarks of a terrorist cell. More than a few of their fellow travelers that day made a silent prayer of gratitude that their aircraft was not a target of the eight creepy phantoms who flew with them.

ARNOW

His replacement was Leo McCoyne, a small-town cop from Indiana. He was a short hydrant-shaped fifty-year-old who seemed fat but was deceptively muscular. Arnow had met him briefly after resigning but before leaving Eagle River for good. The transition had been smooth despite the deaths of the deputies and the strange circumstances surrounding the events.

Now Arnow shook hands with McCoyne, asking for quick access to some files related to a case in Florida.

"Computer or old style?" McCoyne asked from behind his desk. It had been Arnow's desk. He missed it more than he thought he would.

"Both. Shouldn't take me long."

McCoyne pointed to the squad room outside. "There's a computer station out there you can use. All the old files are in a special room down the hall now. I got people scanning shit into the database. Most of it's useless, but you know everything's going 'green' and we gotta do our share."

"Thanks," Arnow said, standing and extending his hand. "I really appreciate it. I should be out of your way in a couple hours. Probably less."

"Nice seeing you again, Tom." The sheriff looked at his watch. "Hey, I gotta go. Help yourself around here. Need anything, just ask."

Out in the squad room, Arnow sat at the empty computer. He was prepared to do nothing for as long as it took to become part of the background. He hadn't seen any of his old deputies yet, and the new ones ignored him—after all, the sheriff himself had shown him the computer.

Arnow surfed around the department files and records, clicking names and taking notes. Then he stood and stretched. The dispatcher—the same pierced kid who'd been in training when he was sheriff—brought him coffee. He wasn't even sure she remembered him, but he smiled at her. He drank, then nonchalantly hit the can, then made his way deliberately to the special room as if he were lost and unaware.

He was in luck. The files were stored at one end of the hall, and at the other end was the evidence room, which was what he had come for.

His old master key still opened the door. He closed it softly behind him and started searching.

JESSIE

She did her rounds, but her mind wasn't on the patients.

Thank God there weren't many, and there weren't any in serious condition!

Damn it, why was life with Nick Lupo so difficult?

Sure, she'd signed on to something unusual, incredible even, when it had turned out that he was something out of a book or movie.

That hadn't been the most difficult aspect to deal with. It had been his baggage, and he continued to add to it.

Now he was poking the rabid dog of the mercenary outfit they'd read so much about the last couple years.

"Jesus, Nick!" she said, and kicked her file cabinet.

Ouch. Shouldn't kick hard things with soft shoes.

Sam Waters would have turned that into some old tribal rule, a mischievous grin on his wrinkled face. She missed him a hell of a lot, and she knew Nick did too, even though they had started out as enemies.

Sam had been a wonderful elder, a guy with a foot in both the tribal world and the white world that surrounded them. He would have made a perfect head of the tribal council, and it would have been his if hadn't been for the damned casino project, which had divided the tribe and ruined old friendships.

"Wish you were here, Sam."

She often talked to herself. But now she noticed that the nurses at the nearby nurse's station had stopped working to gape at her. She smiled crookedly and wondered how a *centered* person, as she had always thought of herself, could now talk to herself and kick things, and send her boyfriend a naked picture of herself.

She grinned despite herself.

ARNOW

Evidence was still collected in labeled bins and stacked on metal shelving mounted along the room's four walls and a range of free-standing shelving taking up the middle. There wasn't a lot of crime in Vilas County on the whole, so the shelves were half-empty. Everything was arranged by date, then alphabetized and numbered.

In a moment Arnow was at the six bins that held evidence from the second "terrorist" attack.

He chuckled drily. Homeland Security must have put an asterisk next to Eagle River, a red flag on the map. Two incidents of domestic terrorism in a relatively short time, plus vestiges of the Posse Comitatus, the KKK, and other weird militias still calling the rural areas of Wisconsin home. Somebody would be assigned to keep an eye on the news out of here.

But then why ignore all the animal attacks?

What was it about this area, lovely as it was, that attracted all the loonies—and now the damn werewolves?

Shit, he could remember when that would have been a ridiculous thought to have.

He riffled through the contents of three bins before hitting it on the fourth.

"Bingo," he muttered. He reached in, snatched up the very item he was looking for, and replaced the bins exactly as he had found them. He listened at the door, pulled it open, and slipped into the empty hall.

"Can I help you with something?"

The voice behind him almost made him jump. He turned to face a lanky deputy he didn't know, giving him a suspicious glare.

"Thanks, you got a bathroom around here?" he said loudly.

"Over there," the cop said and pointed. And waited until Arnow had gone in for his second visit.

He ran the water and flushed and washed his hands and used the scratched-up dryer. When he left, the suspicious deputy was nowhere to be seen. He felt a sheen of sweat on his brow. Nothing like being tossed into a cell in his own sheriff's office. His pulse pounded in his ears.

By the time Sheriff McCoyne returned, Arnow had finished with his spurious search and was just packing up. The item he had lifted was tucked down the back of his pants and covered by his loose Florida shirt.

"Keep in touch," the sheriff said as they shook hands, not really meaning it.

"Sure, thanks." Arnow wondered if Leo and his cops would get in the crossfire this time. Whatever was coming down would be messy, indeed.

He waved and headed out, thinking of Jessie Hawkins.

From the Journals of Caroline Stewart
January 6, 1982

Every good thing must come to an end, and our short vacation from the troubles of the world—and our troubles, too—is over. Back to school, back to the academy, back to the real world.

God, if only there was a time machine that allowed you to make a loop so you could relive just your best times over and over.

I've made an effort to avoid thinking about those secret thoughts, those suspicions that hit me just a couple weeks ago. Now that reality has reared its head, I have to set aside those fond memories Nick and I made during the holidays and start worrying again about his condition—and whatever may have led to Jerry Boone's death.

And when I mentioned it to Nick today, he turned eyes on me that I thought would blaze out of his head and envelop me in their iridescent fire.

For a second, I thought the Creature was there, staring at me out of those eyes.

Then they dimmed and Nick was back.

He was embarrassed at his reaction, but he had defi-

nitely gone away suddenly. And the wolf had manifested itself strongly enough to scare me.

I dropped it, but the incident started me thinking. Maybe thinking too much. Maybe thinking too many negative thoughts.

Nick, I'm starting to fear all our work and progress has been for nothing.

And I'm starting to fear Nick is more responsible for Jerry Boone's death than he admits. What if he killed Jerry intentionally?

1978
NICK

Nick jumped to his friend's defense, but four muscular arms grabbed him and held him immobile. Other arms gripped Sherry's biceps.

Someone whispered in Nick's ear. "Don't fuck with us and nothing's gonna happen to you. Brad and Rollie got a contract out on that Josh kid and you can't do anything about it."

Nick struggled to see who was dispensing this free advice, but he couldn't crane his neck far enough to the side while snagged in the jocks' iron grip. He struggled uselessly for a minute more; then he felt the Creature begin to rumble to life.

Jesus, no!

If the Creature could manifest without the moon's call, then who would stop the slaughter?

Nick wouldn't have any control.

The world would come to know his secret in the worst possible way.

They would hunt him down like the animal he was.

Frank Lupo and his Old World friends would go gunning for him with their silver-loaded shotguns.

Nick stopped struggling.

To his eternal shame, he stopped struggling and went limp. But the jocks' grip on him never faltered. Whoever it was, they wanted him to stay out of it.

Now he watched in mute horror as the mob made up of Brad and Rollie's enforcers continued to manhandle Josh. He'd been disarmed, his brass knuckles now being used against him, battering his chest and side.

The repetitive smack of fists and feet against his body drowned out his pain-filled grunts and groans.

The crowd had moved closer and hemmed in the fight zone so anyone entering the clearing might not have even noticed what was happening.

Nick still wanted to help, but it took all his strength to suppress the Creature. There was a week to go to the full moon, but the Creature didn't actually need the moon's influence to claim control of Nick's body.

All at once Josh seemed to give up struggling and just accept his punishment. Blood from various cuts and abrasions all over his face had rendered him almost unrecognizable. Bloody teeth fell in clumps from his torn lips. Still fists continued to rain on his battered body. Rollie seemed to have taken personal interest in Josh's punishment.

Punishment? For what?

A rumor that most likely wasn't even true?

And even if it had been true, how could he deserve such a beating?

Now Sherry, who had tried to break free of her captors, was being dragged behind the picnic table, her clothes in tatters. Her screams were obliterated by the mob's loud shouting in their irreversible bloodlust.

Nick started to struggle again, almost ready to cave to the inner pressure and let the wolf out, but a fist knocked him senseless and his eyes blurred.

He was dumped off to the side of the crowd.

Jocks and thugs were still pounding on Josh.

And then he heard Sherry screaming.

His vision was screwy, but he saw that Brad Schneider had gathered a few thug friends around him and was now ripping off the remainder of Sherry's clothes. Her breasts were stark white in the near darkness that had descended on the clearing. Her mouth was open in a scream somebody stifled with a wadded up rag made from her torn blouse.

Nick was still sluggish, but he stood and wavered until his senses returned, and rushed at Brad just as the bastard was in the act of dropping his pants while his thuggish minions held Sherry's bare legs open.

Jesus!

Nick started to feel the wolf clawing its way to the surface, coming as if from the depths of a deep, dark cavern in his soul.

The wolf was—

Crack!

Nick's jaw seemed to bounce like a ball on a string and he lost his connection with the Creature.

And he lost his connection to the conscious world, feeling his body reel sideways in an out-of-control Sam Peckinpah-style slow-motion flight, a flight that ended when his head smacked into a nearby tree trunk.

He sagged to the dirt and darkness swallowed him.

CHAPTER SEVENTEEN

HEATHER

The martini bar had become popular the very first week it opened in its central Wausau location, a couple blocks from the First Wausau Tower. Upscale to a fault, only those who found twelve-dollar martinis reasonably priced tended to bother entering, especially in conservative Wausau.

Apparently the crowd swarming the stainless steel and glass bar all felt the cost more than justified.

When she pinned up her hair, changed her makeup, and wore glasses, she was rarely recognized. Even still she had to be careful. This was why she lobbied so hard to land a network job. New York, Atlanta, LA, San Fran. Anyplace other than this shallow pool in the Midwest. *Upper Midwest*. But still . . . In those large markets, she could roam free, troll for mates whenever she wanted, never worrying about consequences.

Hell, now especially she didn't have to worry about consequences.

But here she was too visible, too exposed, too easy to spot and recognize. Hence the disguises, on nights she craved company.

That fool Klug had his uses, but he was out of his element even here, and there was a limit to what he could do for her. Which meant there was a *limit* for him. An "expiration date."

She glanced around this latest watering hole, at the available clientele, at her overpriced drink. Nothing looked very appealing. The men were too beefy, too cocky, too stupid, too dull. For a moment she pictured Tef, the one who had ensnared her with his iridescent eyes, incredible build, quiet intensity . . . and had she mentioned he was very well equipped indeed? Her shoulder tingled where he had unintentionally given her "the gift," as she thought of it now.

She saw herself as a lean, muscular wolf and almost went over, *just like that.*

God, she loved it.

It was almost like an intense orgasm.

No, it *was* an orgasm. It heightened every sensation to a spear point.

She had hated it at first, feared the strange changes, the uncontrollable lust for raw meat and blood, the fur. (She'd never been a *fur person*!) The weird cravings. But then she had begun to learn what she could do, remembering what she had witnessed, and soon she was emulating those others. It came naturally to her. Soon she was luxuriating in the obvious joy of being *two* instead of one. She had always been two; it was just in a different way. Her ambition fueled her desire to control this new aspect of her life, and in turn, this new aspect fueled her ambition.

The wolf liked being Heather as much as Heather liked being the wolf.

She signaled for a new drink. Another badly made mojito. They just didn't know, here. She considered and added Miami as a place to job-hunt.

Men continually tried to catch her eye. She didn't think they recognized her, not yet. She wore her semipunk disguise tonight, light-years apart from her TV look. She scanned the close-up crowd, wishing they weren't so tightly packed. A couple in the stools beside her suddenly stepped away, and before the gap was filled, she caught a pair of dark eyes that held hers with a smoldering look she felt way down below.

Holy shit, it's been a while . . .

It had been, but maybe it was time. The intriguing eyes were hidden again behind a trio of bloated salesman types, loud and crass, who were trying without success to engage any woman in their immediate vicinity. Loud, brassy women vied for attention yet ignored the men nearby.

Heather craned her neck forward, leaning slightly over the bar, and turned her head casually to the side, hoping for a look around the testosterone obstruction. She was startled to find those eyes again, fixing her with the same kind of stare.

Very nice eyes. Dark and mysterious. Hair so black it was almost steel blue in the bar's buzzy lighting. Red lips, parted to show even, white teeth, tip of the tongue poking primly between them. A curve of a smile. A raised eyebrow.

Heather found herself responding to the unspoken query with her own eyebrow.

Were they agreeing to ignore the loud men between them? She was vaguely aware their attention had split between her and the dark-haired woman. Or were they agreeing to something else altogether?

Heather felt a tingle right where it counted most.

Her instincts were almost never wrong.

The dark-haired woman spoke to the men and they looked at each other, shrugged with near-drunk overemphasis, and moved away.

Suddenly the dark-haired woman filled the gap left by the businessmen. She levered closer to Heather, conspiratorially, and whispered in her ear.

"I could tell they weren't your type," she said, impressively audible in the loud environment filled by pulsing electronica and chatter. "So I got rid of them. Hope you don't mind."

"Mind? Not likely. Let me buy you a drink."

"Sure. Double cosmo. It's the only decent thing they make here."

Heather flagged down the harried barman and ordered two, giving up on the mojito.

"Just out of curiosity, how'd you get rid of them so fast?" One more slug.

"I pointed out your prominent Adam's apple and told them we're both transsexuals."

Heather almost gagged on the last of the mojito.

"What! I don't have a prominent Adam's apple!"

The dark-haired woman smiled sweetly. "No, neither do I. But after I put the suggestion into their simple minds, they saw what they expected to see. Voilà—annoying jerks disappeared like magic."

The new drinks came.

"Shit, that's brilliant!" Heather toasted her new friend and they drank, clinking glasses. Something passed between them when their fingers brushed. Heather felt her pulse rise. Felt heat coming on fast. Felt . . . *intrigued*.

"My name's Heather," she said, forgetting all about her intended alias.

They shook hands. Something passed between them again.

"Erica."

They held the handshake far longer than necessary.

Another double cosmo and they had become fast friends, in a way Heather knew she could never be with a male. They compared careers, glass-ceiling limits and limitations, the disgusting groping of lust-filled coworkers, the uselessness of so-called stable relationships, and the joys of beating male chauvinists at their own game.

Two more double cosmos and they could barely keep their hands off each other.

Erica nudged Heather and tilted her head so Heather would look. Some of the men in the place seemed turned on by their display, but a growing number started to smirk and wink at each other.

"Looks like the rumor's spreading," Erica said.

Heather giggled. "Time to go!"

They left arm in arm, drawing stares from the confused crowd, and by the time they reached City Square Park they were ready.

Heather leaned in and hesitantly touched Erica's lips with hers, eyes open and waiting.

Erica opened her mouth and drew Heather toward her as their lips met, struggled together, then parted. Then their tongues flicked at each other, exploring, tasting.

Heather felt herself gushing and her breath hitched when Erica's hand gently cupped her mound. *As if she knew.* Their hands roved, their lips continued to dance, their eyes took in each other's face in the park's dim lamplight.

They necked like teenagers, sliding onto a nearby park bench with barely a pause.

The air was cool, but their skin felt hot to the touch.

Heather's breathing was rapid.

This was what she lived for.

Life, indulgent. Her attitude had only been magnified by the werewolf's bite.

KILLIAN

Animal attacks.

The phrase rattled in his mind and memory. The words had awakened something, something hazy from his childhood.

His family's farm in the States had been based on a blueprint the Killian clan had owned in the Old Country for hundreds of years. And when his father had started to lose livestock, there had been hushed conversations around the fireplace. In the dead of winter, Killian now remembered seeing the splashes of dark blood left where some animal had met a violent fate in the night.

Those discussions had included nearby farmers and even occasionally a county sheriff, and Killian remembered them loading guns and setting forth on useless hunts that found signs of more animal deaths, but never many clues to who or what had perpetrated these "animal attacks."

At least, Killian wasn't sure he remembered being included in the conversations, and his mother had certainly kept him from the hunts.

The men had huddled around the snapping fire and conversed in hushed whispers, and it wasn't until much later that Killian had realized little Griff had been excluded, tones softened when he was nearby, subjects changed when he naively approached his elders.

His grandmother's stories of griffins and other creatures had inspired his name, but he hadn't made the connection then.

No, he'd never cracked the secret of those "animal attacks" that seemed to occur every couple years on the Killian farm. And his father had warned him sternly to forget about them, even as he'd sat cleaning one of the long guns with which he had set out days before, slogging through the mud and snow. Distant gunfire had sometimes startled little Griff, but his mother had begged him to ask no questions.

And he hadn't, not until much later. But then it had been too late.

And now here he was, faced with mysterious "animal attacks."

And a cop who seemed fascinated by them.

As he himself was fascinated.

He crinkled up a burrito wrapper and tossed it thoughtfully at a waste bin. *Three points.*

What the fuck were these animal attacks?

He felt a stirring inside. It scared him, a little.

Heather

It was a haze. A dream sequence.

Heather remembered making out in the night's chill, walking rapidly into the night, holding hands, and then she was kicking aside her door and, moments later, her shoes and soaked panties. The dress followed.

Erica's mouth alternated between Heather's face and her most sensitive places, so Heather could taste herself as well as Erica's hints of jasmine and cinnamon, a woodsy flavor that made Heather's tongue tingle.

After a long session on the living room sofa, with Heather receiving Erica's increasingly loving ministrations, she tugged her new lover to the spare bedroom, stripped her, and introduced her to the sex sling. And to her prized collection of custom-made colored-glass phalluses, arranged like antiques in a plush case.

Heather selected one and went to work on Erica's levitating body, finding her special places and learning to please them with curved glass in hand and quivering lips. Erica's groans guided Heather's exploration and rewarded her with an explosive orgasm followed by others that shook Erica's body and set the sling to swinging crazily.

They changed places then, and continued to pleasure each other, reaching for other ridged or studded shapes, probing, melting together and separately, and finally ending up on the spare bed, spent, the covers tossed haphazardly to the floor.

Kissing passionately for an extended period led to a repeat session and further use of Heather's arsenal of strap-ons and bright, silvery, threaded-together spheres.

Some time later Heather lay beside Erica, amazed at how lively the dark-haired beauty had been.

"Just like me," Heather muttered.

Erica slept on, a contented smile etched on her classic face. Heather knew she'd been picked up, had allowed it to happen, didn't regret it. But she did wonder. She'd been with women before. She'd never had qualms about fulfilling her urges and desires. She'd been in threesomes, foursomes, and the occasional orgy. She hadn't realized she was in the mood for another woman's gentle touch until Erica came along, with her humor and outrageous beauty, and showed her.

She climbed carefully out of bed and padded to the living room. They'd disrobed willy-nilly, here and there. There were bits of discarded clothes everywhere.

Where had Erica dumped her handbag?

She groped around in the near dark, navigating by the lights from the street below shining through the tall windows.

There it was, next to the sofa.

Heather felt furtive but didn't care. She also felt suspicious. She reached for the designer bag, felt its weight, and started to open it.

The lights went on, blinding—and startling—her.

"What are you doing?"

Heather dropped the bag on the sofa. Before she turned away, however, she caught a glimpse of a small black pistol tucked inside.

She turned to face Erica.

CHAPTER EIGHTEEN

HEATHER

"What are you doing?"

Heather was blessed with natural camera-ready presence of mind. She was never rattled, never unprepared, never at a loss no matter what happened in the studio while she read a broadcast or one of her special investigative reports. Once a storm had driven a blown-over tree through a pair of studio windows, destroying a corner of the on-camera set. Heather Wilson had barely batted an eye, continuing her broadcast while most of the crew ducked for cover. She'd earned a reputation as a chick with steel nerves.

Now that reputation served her well. "I was looking for my bag," she said, smiling widely, completely innocent. "I picked up yours first, it's right here. But mine was right next to it." She held up her own bag, which she had scooped up at exactly the right moment. They were nearly identical. "See?"

Erica's face dissolved into a smile, too. "Thanks. I figured I should make my face presentable again before being on my way."

Heather tilted her head. "I just wanted to sneak a smoke. You have to go so soon? I have other plans for you. And anyway, we'd just mess up your face all over again."

Erica had slowly approached and they were now face-to-face, both naked, breasts thrusting at each other, the sweat still drying on both their bodies.

They leaned into each other and started kissing passionately again, the heat rising between them quickly, washing over them in a wave. They sank to the sofa, handbags forgotten, and soon they were deep into each other's pleasure.

As Heather lay back, Erica's lovely face and talented tongue slinking down to her sensitive mound, trailing cooling saliva, she nevertheless wondered about the gun she had seen in the handbag.

What was Erica's game?

Right now she didn't care.

But she couldn't help feeling she'd dodged something.

Dodged a bullet?

DICKIE KLUG

He was drunk off his ass when she called, but suddenly he felt sobriety filling his veins like ice water.

"I want you to start following me. Stay out of sight and watch. See if anyone's following me. For Christ's sake, be subtle."

"What?" He wasn't sure he had heard right. *What the fuck now?*

"Listen," she hissed. "I'll go over it once more." She did. "I want to know if anyone's keeping a tail on me. You're going to be their tail and tell me who it is, and what they're doing."

There was metallic silence on the cell line.

"Do you get me?"

"Ah, yeah, yeah. Got it. Follow, keep an eye out, see other tails. Got it."

"You're drunk again!" she said, voice rising. "What use are you?"

"I saved your life," he muttered weakly. *Whined*, really.

"And I've saved your worthless hide a million times by now. The wolf would have killed you on day one. The least I can expect is for you to be ready and able to do what I need."

"You got it. When should I start?"

"Now, you idiot. Get over here and start right now."

"Is there, uh, somebody there I should follow?"

"No, she's gone. But I want to hear about anyone from now on."

He muttered agreement and she cut off the call.

Jesus.

He stumbled about his mess, trying to find the clothes he needed for the cold night. He'd gotten lazy since she had yanked him from his normal life's work, and even though at first he had been forced to feed her "prey" to feast on, her demands had lessened and he'd grown complacent. Dickie didn't know the word *complacent*, but he knew what he'd become.

Then he'd started to wonder why she had begun taking her own prey again, without him as part of the equation. That cop's visit had rattled him, and he'd never told her. Maybe that cop was tailing her . . .

If that was the case, telling her now would turn him into wolf kill, wouldn't it?

He watched his hands shake as he got ready to leave.

ALPHA TEAM

The eight burly men with military bearing and baggage made up almost exclusively of long metal-reinforced flight cases boarded two identical black Ford Expeditions after stopping at the Avis counter. The clerk realized she'd held her breath the whole time they had stood rigid in front of her, waiting as she filled out the paperwork.

After checking the GPS, they set off on the road aiming north.

Their leader, Wilcox, occupied the passenger seat of the first SUV, filling it with his muscular bulk. There was no small talk among the grim men. They knew what they had been dispatched to do.

The driver was Blount. The two in back were Dix and Pollard.

In the second SUV, Santino drove and the passengers were Turner, Gradenko, and Barton.

This was all that remained of Wilcox's squad after that bastard had infiltrated the compound.

Not only had he sworn revenge, he'd been told not to return if the report would indicate the team had failed.

Not to return meant a death sentence. It meant, *Run!* And also, *Don't bother—we'll find you in the end.*

Everyone in the squad understood the instructions.

Wilcox flicked on a smart phone and waited for an answer.

"We're on our way," he said quietly into the phone. "We'll be in place by morning."

Wilcox turned to survey the other three in his vehicle.

"It's on," he said.

The others nodded. Their grins were filled with fangs.

From the Journals of Caroline Stewart
January 11, 1982

I had to let the thought sit for a few days. I'm not sure I can face it.

Could Nick have killed Jerry Boone, and faked the suicide?

Jesus Christ, Nick . . .

Could Nick have killed Jerry? To shut him up, to keep him from talking to others—or to me?

I'm deathly afraid to pursue this line of inquiry, but how can I ignore it? How can I live with myself if I don't get to the bottom of this?

1978
NICK

Later he realized that he had somehow reached the phone booth on the other side of the school and managed to dial the operator, who had sent the police.

He was bloody and ragged. Unsteady on his feet.

His head was cracked open and his brains were leaking all over his clothes.

Well, that's how it *felt*.

There was an egg-size lump on the side of his head, and his jaw felt loose.

He made his phone call, barely coherent, then stumbled away from school and away from the Wiener Woods and managed to reach the residential area opposite the athletic

fields when the sirens swept past him on the main thorough-
fare he had wisely avoided.

He kept to the shadows, knowing that if someone, anyone, especially a cop, spotted his battered form, he would be
swept in along with whomever they were able to corral from
that clearing.

Christ, he couldn't clear his head of the images.

That bastard Brad Schneider has lost his mind.

The last thing Nick remembered seeing was Brad's hairy
thighs obscuring Sherry's while his thugs either held her
down or cheered him on.

And Josh had been battered to a pulp.

Nick could only imagine what had happened after he was
knocked out.

He remembered the faces he had seen before losing con-
sciousness and wondered how he could ever see them again
as anything but the monsters they'd become.

He considered himself a monster, the Creature inside
him an evil he would have done just about anything to
exorcise, but what he'd seen felt as if it would scar him
forever.

A sudden growl worked up from the frustrated Creature,
the wolf who had been nearly summoned and would have
laid waste to the fuckers who had beaten and raped his
friends.

Jesus, beaten and raped.

A loud siren marked a cop cruiser just around the corner
and Nick lunged for a nearby overgrown hedge. In the house
beyond, a dog started barking.

Nick saw the cruiser prowl past, its searchlight sweeping
for him along the sidewalk. He hugged the shadows and
tried to burrow into the dirt below the hedges.

Nearby, the dog was going crazy.

Nick counted slowly, trying to calm the Creature.

The searchlight grazed the top of his head, but his dark

hair helped him disappear into the shadow cast by the hedges and the light swept on past him and into the next yard.

Shut the fuck up! he wanted to shout at the dog.

But he didn't, and a few minutes later the dog was shushed. Nick waited a bit longer before heading back down the street, his ears attuned to the distant sirens.

Inside, he burned for revenge.

Josh had been right to fear his fellow students.

But no one had expected so much hate.

Inside, Nick burned for revenge. And the Creature lusted for the flesh of those who had wronged him.

Nick decided he would satisfy both.

Payback. And bloodlust.

LUPO

They were sitting in the living room of Lupo's cottage. Arnow didn't seem comfortable, looking around as if maybe the place was too *normal*, too much of an up-north cliché to be true.

Dried-out largemouth bass and barracuda-shaped muskies were mounted on the walls and on either side of beams that crossed the wooden slat ceiling. Photographs of fishing trips past alternated with cozy built-in bookcases stocked with decades-old reading material that ran the gamut from kids' books to novels and humor and even a small stash of near smut, remnants of the days the cottage had been leased out to fishing and hunting expeditions, in the days before Lupo became its primary year-round renter.

Lupo's touch could be seen in the framed photographs of Jessie Hawkins that dotted the shelves here and there and dominated the mantel.

Lupo popped two Rhinelanders and gave Arnow one.

The ex-sheriff took a swallow. "I have just what you might need for that job."

"Silver ammo?" Lupo said. "Been there, done that. It burns the hell out of my hand, but if I can stand the pain, eventually I can squeeze off a couple rounds."

"This is different." Arnow pulled something out of his pocket and handed it to Lupo. He drank beer while Lupo examined the object.

It wan an ornate dagger, eight or nine inches in length, sheathed in a sort of light wooden scabbard.

"What the hell?"

"One of the council members, Daniel Smith, tried to defend himself against those three Wolfpaw guys with this. Hurt one of them real bad."

Lupo started to draw the blade and a painful jolt surged through him as if he had touched a live high-voltage wire.

He dropped the dagger and staggered back, startled as much as hurt.

"Silver!"

"I thought so. Either smelted from silver or plated. Silver, but . . ."

"But?" Lupo rubbed his hand, the pain echoing through his muscles.

"But you were able to hold it before exposing the blade. Try again."

"What the hell . . . ?" Lupo picked it up off the floor. The blade had disappeared into the scabbard when he'd dropped it.

Nothing.

"How did you know?" He held the covered knife gingerly, as if it might turn into a snake and sink its fangs into him.

"I didn't, not until you grabbed it just now," Arnow said. "I remembered somebody, maybe Davison, mentioning something about a sacred dagger. Sounded like bullshit. They'd given it to Smith and he held his own against those wolves. At least until they overwhelmed him. I wondered about it, that's all. I lifted it from the evidence room."

Lupo barked a laugh. "So you're a criminal now?"

Arnow smiled sourly. "I doubt they'll be looking for it. Anyway, I'm sure Davison told me more details I probably ignored. Enough of it came back."

Lupo examined the grip—it was covered with delicate etchings. He raised an eyebrow. "Is that a swastika in there?"

Arnow nodded. "Definitely. One on the other side, too. But notice how it's not prominent. There's a lot of stuff around it . . . looks like blades stabbing it."

"That's a stretch," Lupo said doubtfully.

"Maybe, but I swear Davison said something about it dating back to World War II, when it was used to fight against Nazi wolves. That's one thing I remember."

"Weird," Lupo said.

His mind suddenly started to whirl.

He was instantly transported back to when he was a kid and his grandmother, Maria Saltini, had filled him with fantastic stories of witchcraft and magic from her youth in a mountain village near Venice, and then how she'd talked to him about the German occupation after the famed Italian surrender, and the stubborn partisan resistance that arose almost overnight. She had told him more than he could even remember. He recalled also how she'd hid Italian-American newspapers from him that he later snuck and read anyway—tabloid-style articles about supposed wolf-man attacks in Sicily and other parts of Italy—but in the seventies.

Why would she have hidden them from him?

But then, she'd forbidden him watching *Mission: Impossible* because a commercial she'd seen apparently depicted torture.

His memories prickled, and he wondered what he could ask his grandmother *now*. And what she would reveal.

He shook his head, still holding the knife. He set his can aside and examined the wooden scabbard and the symbols carved on its oil-shiny length. The wood itself was something like balsa but heavier, denser. The scabbard was carved with precision from a single long piece of the wood.

Some of the symbols on the knife grip seemed ancient, smoothened by time and decades of handling. They had taken on a sheen caused by countless handlers.

He felt the dagger tingle in his hand, but the silver did not hurt him at all. He squinted.

There was a light aura shimmering around it.

"You see that?" he asked.

"What?" Arnow squinted. Shook his head.

"It's *glowing*."

"Nope, I don't see anything."

"You take it," he told Arnow. "This thing makes me nervous."

"I went through some trouble to get you that. Keep in mind, it'd be easier for you to carry it than a silver-loaded pistol, right?"

Lupo thought about it. "You're right. Damn it, though, Tom, what the hell does it all mean?"

"Too bad your friend Sam Waters isn't around to tell us about it. I got a feelin' he woulda known everything we need."

Lupo almost blurted out that he could ask Sam the next time he saw him, but caught himself. *What kind of information could a ghost divulge?*

"Maybe Davison?"

"Maybe, but then I gotta let him know I ripped it off from the sheriff's office. He trustworthy?"

"Well, he's one of us—he knows what the hell he saw. No need to go and convince him like we did you."

Arnow made a face. "Guess not. Who else?"

"Well, I guess Bill Gray Hawk and his family saw more than they should have, but his wife left him and took the kids, and they disappeared. They sure as hell weren't accepting anything they saw. Pure denial."

"Probably better for them. You think Jessie knows anything about the knife?"

Lupo's pulse quickened. Arnow seemed to want to involve her no matter what.

Arnow seemed to guess Lupo's response. He drained his beer. "She's part of it already, man. You said Wolfpaw might be on your trail, which means they'll find her, too. We're better off together."

"Yeah, I guess. But I don't think she knows anything about this weird knife. She would have told me. I remember something about it when Smith used it, but wouldn't they have taken it?"

"Maybe they were flustered when he hurt their commander. Maybe it got tossed and they couldn't find it. Maybe our side just got lucky and stumbled on it." Arnow checked the beer label. "Not too bad."

"There are better brews around, and great micros, too, but this stuff is local, cheap, and plentiful." Lupo drained his. "Another one?"

"Nah, thanks. I'm not the beer drinker you guys are around here."

"Yeah, I remember. You're a brandy man."

Arnow frowned and wrinkled his forehead. "So what's your next move? What next?"

"I leaned on Dickie Klug a little, down there in Wausau. He's connected to Heather somehow. Can't be sure, but he might have been the one pulled her out of the lake. Anyway, if he's connected, he's also a weak link. We can turn him; he might set her up for us. Then we move in and do it."

"Do it? The silver?" He started to shake his head furiously.

"No other way, Tom. You remember how it was. We could never have asked the feds to silver up. You think the Wausau cops are gonna be any more receptive? We have to put her down like a rabid dog, man. You see what she's doing. Deep down, you know I'm right."

"Shit, Lupo, you're talking about murder."

"Execution, Tom."

"That's supposed to make it better? Make it easier for me to accept? It's still against the law. Even when you're right, the law doesn't give individuals the right to carry out sentences. Justice or no."

"Sure," Lupo said, "it sounds good when you put it that way. But does the law account for people like me? Like her? Monsters? You know the rule book isn't complete, now that you've seen this secret world of ours. An incomplete rule book means we have to write the ending."

"Nice analogy, very literary," Arnow said, "but it's not as black-and-white as all that."

"I agree, Tom. I'm Mr. Gray Areas usually. But we're dealing with a race of creatures the law can't account for, and since they are harmful to humans, they need to be dealt with."

"Are you harmful to humans?"

"I have been."

There didn't seem to be much to say after that, so for a while they drank in silence.

JESSIE

Nick's call had been strange, curious really. His tone, mostly, as if there was somebody else there. He'd asked when she was coming home. As it turned out, she had just decided to sign out and head home, with maybe a little stop at the Great Northern first, for good luck, when her phone had buzzed.

Now she pulled onto Circle Moon Drive and through the pine trunks she spotted Nick's Maxima sitting on his drive. There was another car there, a nondescript blue sedan. Looked like a rental. Who did he have with him?

She made the slightly longer drive to her own place and dropped off her medical bag—she still used one, as she made house calls on the rez when needed—and freshened up a little. Then she drove her Pathfinder around the winding road and finally reached Nick's more remote cottage.

Her pulse quickened when it suddenly occurred to her the other car might belong to those Wolfpaw people Nick had aggravated.

Shit!

She reached behind her seat and hefted up a short-barreled Remington shotgun with a military pistol grip and pumped a shell into the chamber.

No point being stupid.

It wasn't a silver-loaded shell, but it would have to do.

She pulled up a ways down the drive, where a clump of pines was likely to mask her SUV, shut down, and headed for the door while keeping a sharp eye on the windows.

She stepped carefully to avoid crunching gravel or twigs underfoot, keeping to the sandy soil and the sparse spring grass as much as she could. The windows were blank reflectors, the images of distorted trees rippling across their surfaces. Anyone—and *anything*—could have been watching her from the windows and she wouldn't have been able to see them. The door was the same. Keeping the shotgun at the ready, she stepped closer to the door and tried to plan her entrance.

Before she could take two more steps, it opened.

She brought up the shotgun.

Then she breathed again. And lowered the shotgun.

Nick was there, smiling at her. Relief washed over her like a cleansing wave.

Keeping the shotgun aimed low, she swept into his arms, laying her head on his chest. She embraced him tightly for an endless minute, and he leaned into her neck, and she smelled him and felt safe and sexy and very happy. Very, very happy, remembering their last time together.

And then she glanced inside and spotted Tom Arnow, standing near the fireplace, clearly embarrassed.

"Tom!" She knew she was suddenly blushing hotly.

"Jess—Dr. Hawkins," he said, also obviously embarrassed about stumbling over her name.

They shook hands formally after she released Nick and he took the shotgun from her.

"It's great to see you," she said, meaning it.

"You too," he said.

Then they were forced to get down to business when Nick closed the door and stepped back inside, placing the shotgun on the cocktail table, a vivid reminder that they weren't here for pleasure, but indeed had an agenda and a mission.

Beer and a soda were handed out and then they sat, and Nick brought her up to speed on what they had been up to.

"Did Sam know about this knife?" she asked. They'd become such good friends, just saying his name made her heart ache.

"Don't know. He never mentioned it that I can remember. It's weird Davison seemed to know all about it. But then Sam did tell us about all these 'defender' myths, legends. Sounds like the tribe had some sort of tradition stretching a ways back, before I ever came along."

Arnow listened intently, but had nothing to offer. Jessie smiled at him, hoping he didn't think they were nutcases. He'd seen too much, hadn't he?

She said, "Sam did say something about that crooked shaman, the one who infected his son, going over to Europe and melding together whatever he had learned here, from his own people, and whatever they had going over there."

Nick nodded, snapping his fingers. "Right, he said the shaman had figured out how to bring the two traditions together, join whatever supernatural powers were at work. So, what do you figure was involved in the European tradition?"

"There were lots of werewolf sightings and reports in the Middle Ages," Jessie recalled.

Arnow snorted.

"Yeah, I know it sounds ridiculous," she said. "But they were serious. Hundreds of people were tortured and executed for being werewolves. Belief is a powerful thing."

"So then the tradition goes way back," Nick said, pondering. "Some of it was caused by diseases or mental illness, though."

"Sure, and it was a good way to get revenge on some neighbor you hated. Accuse him of being a monster." Jessie shook her head. "People always learn how to take advantage."

"But so how far back does this knife go?"

"It's hard to say," Arnow agreed. "But it definitely has a recent history. I think more properly it's a *dagger*, like those carried by the SS and other German units. You know, with 'Blood and Honor' etched into the blades. This is different, though. You see the symbols carved on the sheath. There are older, worn-off carvings below that, but the swastika and what's around it looks pretty recent. And the etchings on the grip are a mystery to me."

Jessie said, "You think it's a Nazi dagger like those other ones?"

"I don't think so. I did some online research before flying up here," Arnow said.

"Yeah?"

"Yeah, 'cause I remembered this knife thing, but there was so much other stuff happening around that time that we didn't really look at the knife, just collected and tagged it. But now it seems to have some major importance, doesn't it? I did some Googling and got something you may find interesting."

"You been holding back?" Nick said.

"A little. Wanted to see if you knew."

"Knew what?"

Arnow waved at the empty cans. "Let me hit the head, then we can start on some new ones. And I'll tell you what I know about the Werwolf Division."

Lupo was startled. "What?"

"Yeah, gets your attention." He used the washroom upstairs following Nick's directions.

Jessie reached across and squeezed Nick's hand. He smiled at her and brought it to his lips, brushing it with a gentle kiss.

After he returned, Arnow continued. "Far as I can tell, this division was created toward the end of the war—when they realized all was lost—to harass the occupation forces they expected would take over their fatherland. It was like a secret nest of saboteurs and assassins, and their mission was to kill and disrupt. Kill soldiers, officers, political appointees, German collaborators, anyone who helped the Allied occupation."

"And the werewolves?"

"Probably just a name. The Nazis loved that stuff—symbolism, mythology, the occult. Hitler was a big fan."

"Sure," Nick said, "I remember reading about it as a kid. Loved all that stuff."

"Maybe you were drawn to it because—"

"Nah, no way." Nick waved off the rest of the sentence. "I was always into weird stuff."

"Whatever. Anyway, if those Wolfpaw guys were related to somebody in the Werwolf Division, then maybe there were actual werewolves in the ranks, and the dagger came through those channels. Or maybe it was meant to fight against them."

"A sort of anti–Werwolf Division weapon," Jessie said, nodding. "Maybe the Allies had their own counterterror units."

"You bet they did," Arnow said. "There's a ton of history there, if we were to spend the time going through it all."

"We don't have time for that," Lupo said.

"No, we don't."

Lupo turned the dagger around in his hands. "This thing makes me nervous. You hang on to it."

"For now, sure," Arnow said, and reached for it.

The air around them had turned grim. Jessie watched Nick carefully. Something was going through his thoughts, leaving a cloud behind. She'd gotten good at reading his moods, if not the reason for them.

Arnow put the dagger away, and they discussed the animal attacks. And whether Heather Wilson was behind them.

Nick added, "I think it's time Tom and I pay Mr. Klug a visit down in Wausau. Time to lean on the weasel a little more."

"I'm up for it," Tom said, nodding. "Let's do it."

CHAPTER NINETEEN

LAURA ARNOW

She caught her reflection in the car door when she clicked it closed after Freddie and Jill had climbed in. She smiled wanly, and even in the glass she looked tired, worn down.

The driver looked at her over his shoulder. His turban seemed to have grabbed Freddie's attention. But Jill was breathing in hitches, trying to avoid crying. Laura Arnow gave the driver the address.

"You'll be okay, Jill," the faded old woman in the glass said. "Gramma will take care of you."

She hated that reflection. *I have to get some sun*, she thought. *I need a manicure.*

"But I wanna stay with you!" Jill's lips trembled, threatening to send the little girl into a full-fledged crying jag.

Laura shuddered. *Jesus, anything but that.*

Brett had insisted they shed Freddie and Jill.

"Love the kids!" he'd said loudly in that salesman's voice she suspected lied more often than it didn't. "But not for the wedding. We decided on this Vegas thing and I got limited time off work, babe. Can't take them to the wedding chapel or the drive-through, or whatever we do. And sure enough not later, eh? They'll be safe with your mother till we get back."

She saw the driver was still patient but edging toward losing it with all the time-wasting. Finally she got the kids settled down in the cab and headed off to her mother's. She waved halfheartedly at the back of the car, where two little heads bobbed in response. *Finally!*

Now it was time to get ready for her trip to Vegas. Time to turn that faded old lady in the reflection into the glamorous babe she had once been—and could be again. She went to get ready for Brett.

Laura had been prepared for certain parts of being a cop's wife, but not others. The danger, the worry, the hours—all that, she could handle. And she had. But Tom Arnow had been so committed to the Job that he had started to pay less and less attention to her. After trying food and gifts and romantic getaways that inevitably turned awkward, she'd tried ordering risqué undergarments from Frederick's, trying to get the magic—trying to get Tom—back. Apparently the crotchless panties and nipple-cutout bras made the wrong impression on Tom, who pulled even further away.

Then she realized that Tom had developed feelings for a fellow cop. She confronted him and he confessed the feelings, which had gone nowhere, but instead of understanding and forgiving, something had snapped inside Laura and she had taken the kids and left him immediately, almost as if he had cheated. As far as she was concerned, *feelings for* was a euphemism for *adultery*, and that was it.

She'd felt neglected while trying to see him through his bad times. Eventually she found herself using those risqué undergarments on random men she met through her own job, a career in real estate she'd interrupted and then picked up again when the kids were older and she felt stifled.

Feeling guilty, but still with needs to satisfy, she had allowed herself to get so far away that eventually she barely knew Tom at all. Which was sad, she admitted, because he had always been so decent and a great father. She'd filed for divorce, perfectly happy to give up custody—and then the universe had a laugh at her expense.

Tom had been an exemplary cop, but he'd been drawn into an Internal Affairs investigation of graft and corruption in the Chicago PD. He'd been innocent, but was part of a group of off-duty friends who were all guilty of shakedowns and taking bribes. Though exonerated, Tom had been under the microscope for weeks when she filed, and when the custody hearing took place, his name was in the news along with the dirty cops.

In a dirty trick, fate granted Laura exactly what she hadn't wanted—the baggage of the kids, who would have been better off with their father.

She'd put up with it for a long while, doing the nurturing-mother thing, but she knew it was over when Freddie and Jill walked in on her once as she gave one of her men friends a sloppy blow job in her kitchen. Right then she'd decided to find some hot guy to latch onto and shed the kids. Tom would take them. Tom would do anything for his kids. While Laura felt the same way in a general sense, she also realized that she drew lines between her and them, that now there were things she wouldn't do, or give up.

Good old Brett. He'd come along about a year before. At the real-estate company Christmas party, all the women lusted for him. But Laura could still clean up pretty good when she wanted to, and Brett had given her good reason. Brett Singleton was one of the best salesmen in company history, a member of the ten-million-dollar club. They'd hit it off, much to the dismay of the other women in the office. He was attractive and bright, very well-off, and sexual—in fact, he was outrageous sexually, and she could barely keep up. But she liked it, liked it *a lot*.

One thing led rapidly to another, and a Vegas wedding was set. And then she had gone to see Tom, determined to convince him to file for custody of Freddie and Jill so she could marry Brett. She intended to promise him they wouldn't fight it.

Imagine her shocked surprise, finding that Tom had closed his office indefinitely and headed back up to that backwater he'd almost gotten killed in, Eagle River.

She'd had a "what the fuck?" moment.

So now she had another. She'd flown back to Chicago and dumped the kids on Gramma, got them into the cab and on their way, and Brett called and told her he had to postpone the Vegas trip.

"Got a hot property nobody wanted during the bust," he said in the macho voice that told her he could be heard by *somebody*, so he had to look good. "But now they're beating down my door and the price is creeping up with the economy upturn."

"So what about our *wedding*, Brett?" She fought to keep the whining tone out of her voice. He had promised!

"Babe, it's just a couple days until this thing comes together. Three to five at the most. These people wanna pay almost what it went for before. I'd be crazy to pass up the chance. They'll get a deal with somebody—might as well be me, honeychile."

She cringed. Hated it when he started to do bad dialects. Sometimes he thought he was funnier than he really was. But refilling the coffers—could she really be against that? She wanted him to buy her *things*. He *owed* her things.

"Okay, sweetie, take as long as you need."

"Weren't you gonna get rid of the kids?" he said.

She frowned. Did he have to make it so obvious? The kids and Brett hadn't exactly bonded. The opposite, really. "Well, yeah. I sent them to Gramma's just now."

"That's just temporary, though, right? We gotta get 'em back after the wedding?"

"Yeah," she said cautiously. "Tom's left town for a while. Back to Eagle River. I had to use Gramma 'cause we were about to leave."

She heard his fingers drumming on his mahogany desk. She could almost hear the gears. "Well, now you got some extra time, babe. Maybe you can give it another try, convince Tom to be a father again."

So you don't have to be, she thought.

"Sure, Brett," was what she said. "I'll drive up tonight."

"Bring the kids with you. Then he can't refuse."

She shut her eyes hard until they hurt. Was he really telling her to dump them? She still wanted to see them grow up, just not on a daily basis.

"Call me when you get back. We'll celebrate, just the way you like."

Champagne, coke and Ecstasy, and lots of rough sex. She licked her lips. It was no contest.

"Sure, baby, I'll let you know when I get back."

"I'll be waiting."

"And then we can go get married?"

"Right." He sounded . . . distracted.

"Okay, Brett, I'll call—"

Click.

She stared at the phone. Was that some woman's voice she'd heard in the background, just before he hung up?

She stared at the phone a long time. Then she packed Freddie and Jill's bags after all. And called Gramma.

DICKIE KLUG

He hung around her doorway until he glimpsed her coming into her lobby, then followed her as she crawled from street to empty street.

It didn't take much for him to figure out that she was trawling, trying to help him spot a tail by making herself visible. By making herself bait.

Dickie did his best to melt into the shadows. He didn't spot anyone on her trail, although he tried every trick he could think of from movies and television shows he had watched. He kept to shadows, stayed across the street, stopped when she stopped (and stared into windows no matter what was on display). Downtown Wausau at night was no humming hive of activity, so anyone following the statuesque blonde would have stood out.

Now and again Dickie felt eyes on his back, but whenever he tried to see if anyone was tailing him, it always turned out that it was some innocent bystander, passerby, or office worker leaving work late. Even though his neck hairs tingled a couple times, he was pretty certain no one was following him.

And no one followed Heather Wilson, other than Dickie himself.

She made a long rectangle and swung around the straight roads around city hall and headed back toward her building, never giving any indication she had spotted him at all, but giving him one last chance to identify anyone on her.

When she disappeared into her lobby, he decided to call her and let her know she was tail-free. But he'd left his phone at home, so he doubled back toward his much more modest building.

Walking the empty streets, he started to feel jumpy. There were footsteps, he thought, behind him. He'd stop, and they'd stop. Or was that an echo?

He was jumpy, that was for sure.

Jumpy!

Even still, he started to sweat in the chill air. He'd lost the edge he used to have when he'd stake out seasonal homes for days on end, before breaking in and cleaning them out of all valuable consumer electronics and other goods. He'd been in good shape then, but working for the woman—*the monster!*—had slowed him down, turned him into something of a slug. *A couch slug.*

His belly shook like Jell-O now as he hustled his butt inside. Up the stairs, puffing, he stepped inside his place and before he could close the door behind him, he felt someone behind him, someone who had climbed the stairs as swiftly and silently as a ghost.

Fuck, not that fuckin' cop Lupo again!

He had a split second to come up with a reason he hadn't left, as the cop had ordered.

Or had he made an appointment with the escort service? They'd threatened to cut him off after the last one complained about his rough treatment, but he knew they secretly *all* liked it rough.

He whirled and instead of Lupo or a hooker, there stood a lean but muscular gray wolf half again as large as any German shepherd he had ever seen.

"H-How . . . ? Wha—?" Dickie stuttered as he tried to recover his composure, for clearly this wasn't anything to do with the cop.

But was this his mistress?

Suddenly the wolf blurred slightly like an old-fashioned antenna-television image and he looked more closely, and it wasn't Heather Wilson at all.

But those eyes!

He seemed to fall into the wolf's iridescent eyes. They rolled like a kaleidoscope, if he had known what that was like. They were as deep as mysterious sacrificial cenotes deep in Belize, as endlessly deep as the Marianas Trench.

Dickie didn't stand a chance.

He was still staring at the wolf vision when it stepped through his doorway.

"Noooooooooooooo!" he screamed, holding up his hand as if it could ward off the wolf's approach.

Its leap took him down backward, smacking his head hard on the polished old floor, but he barely felt the impact, because razor-sharp fangs were already ripping through his throat and severing his vocal cords so that his scream died as a gargle drowned in arterial blood.

His eyes glazed over, and the wolf tore most of his face off, chomping down on the oily skin with relish. Then it dug into his clothing and after tearing the cheap materials had his slippery entrails out to snack upon.

When finished, the wolf casually let a pungent stream fly onto the floor and over the prey's carcass.

DiSanto

He was watching Killian making his computer smoke, printing over a dozen documents on the common squad-room printer. DiSanto heard the telltale whine of the printer's power-up just before it spit out a new sheaf of papers. He maneuvered himself closer and closer, keeping an eye on Killian's back in his office. Near the printer, he knew he was out of Killian's line of vision anyway. He ducked and snagged a couple sheets off the top.

Sure enough, it was a list of links leading to stories of recent animal attacks in Wausau. And a couple at the bottom of the list that included Eagle River.

Shit, and Milwaukee, too?

DiSanto wasn't sure what that was all about, but it sure seemed like a list pointing to someone looking for connections to all three.

DiSanto knew the only connection had to be Nick Lupo.

Whatever the reason, Nick was involved in these attacks—investigating them, of course—and Killian was going to get on his ass about it.

DiSanto slid the sheets back onto the tray as more sheets came tumbling out.

Fuck the order!

He edged out of the squad room before Killian could come for his documents, digging the cell out of his pocket before he hit the bathroom.

LUPO

He pushed the door open, Glock in hand. Arnow hung back in the staircase, holding his own pistol, a SIG P250 .40-caliber semi.

What were the chances Klug would just leave it ajar like that?

None, none at all.

Both cops had agreed wordlessly and drawn their weapons.

The smell of blood, copper pungent, hit them first. Then it was the butcher-shop smell—meat, bone, melted fat, coagulating blood, and something else.

Lupo swept the room with his gun, backed up by Arnow, but it was empty.

The source of the smell was scattered throughout the loft in chunks, pieces of bloody meat and strung-up intestines. Dickie Klug's severed head was propped in front of the television like a flesh sculpture. Ragged teeth marks made it clear it had been gnawed off the rest of the body, which had then been sloppily dismembered.

"Jesus fucking Christ," Arnow said, looking around.

Lupo's nose twitched.

"Urine," he said. "That's what that other smell is, the one that's overlaying all the rest of it."

Arnow passed his free hand over his face as if he could scrape off the stench of the messy death that had found Dickie Klug.

"What does it mean?" he said.

"I guess it's a taunt. Marking the territory, making the prey hers."

"*Hers?* You think it's Heather?"

"I can't tell," Lupo admitted.

"What about in your—that *other* shape?"

Lupo shook his head. "It's like we're not able to connect human scents to wolves'—maybe it would make us all too territorial, lead us to kill each other at first blush. Even if I Changed right now, I'd probably get the wolf's scent, but couldn't connect it to its human. Same thing in reverse. Hints, occasionally. Unless I just didn't get the memo."

"Those Wolfpaw assholes . . . you said they knew more than you."

"They had an advantage over me. I bet they weren't infected like I was. They might have been born that way."

"Jesus."

"Yeah, I still feel outclassed, believe me." Lupo made a quick check of the rest of the loft, but he'd already sensed there was no one there. "I'm sure I'm catching hints of Heather's scent. But I already know she was here, using him as a kind of manservant."

Arnow said, "Like in the movies, a human to do stuff they can't do?"

"Yeah, but usually in the movies it's a vampire, needs somebody who can go out in daylight. Here, I figure he helped her rope in some of her kills, maybe all of them."

"Was it really her did all this?" He pointed at Klug's head and made a face.

"Had to be. No reason for Wolfpaw to be after this dickhead. I leaned on him, but I was hoping to use him to get to her eventually."

"Shit."

"I'm sorry man, I know you kind of hoped I was wrong."

Arnow's face was a mask of sadness. He shook it off in typical cop fashion. "So, we have two problems. Heather chopping the hell out of people and those guys probably after you. They're gonna hit you in Eagle River, aren't they? How do we manage two fronts?"

"That's why I wanted you here, Tom. And now there's three of us. We're gonna meet our other ace in the hole. I ran into a Wausau cop who's already made Heather as a suspect, but who thinks the animal attacks are faked. I think the two of us can convince her otherwise."

"*Her?*"

"Sheila Falken. You'll like her."

"Right, if you say so. What do we do about *this* now?"

"I'm gonna call her to meet us here. We can decide if we want to turn it into a crime scene or just walk out the door."

"What?" Arnow looked at him in surprise.

"What do we gain calling it in? We might be able to connect Klug to Heather, probably through some crappy job she got him, or this place. I'm sure she paid the rent. He was barely a notch above trailer trash; he couldn't swing this place on his own. But that won't help us get her. Maybe we can find a way to use the knowledge that he's off the board. Literally."

Arnow nodded slowly, thinking about it. "Might work, if this cop Falken goes for it. But it'll make us outlaws."

Lupo looked at him sideways. "I got used to that shit years ago."

"Not sure I wanna know."

Lupo called Falken's cell and gave her a sketchy account of what they'd found. He asked her to meet him there in Klug's loft, after convincing her to not call it in yet. He gave her the address and put away his iPhone.

The charnel-house smell of the place was clearly bothering Arnow. Lupo understood, but he had done so much hunting as a wolf now, he wasn't affected. He cracked a couple windows and let some chilled air into the place.

While they waited, they searched carefully for anything that might be useful, information in the form of papers or notes or anything at all. But Klug had no desk, no computer, no papers other than what lay crumpled in a small plastic bin, and basically nothing that indicated he did anything other than watch television, masturbate, and cash checks issued by some third-party entity probably hired by Heather Wilson.

"He likes company, the pro kind," Arnow said. He held up a shiny business card with a kissy red lip logo in the corner and a number for the Class Act escort service. "Is this burg large enough for an escort service?"

"Wausau books a lot of sales and paper- and lumber-industry-related conventions. Nothing too flashy and not as many as Appleton, but they're working on it. But wherever you got conventioneers, you get escorts—even if they have to drive in from farther away."

Lupo didn't like talking about escorts. It reminded him of his old friend and neighbor Corinne, and how Martin Stewart had used her murder to send him a message that he was gunning for Lupo. She'd been an escort who was edging into more and more serious porn work, and he hadn't realized until too late how he felt about her.

Arnow nodded.

They poked around some more, but found nothing useful. There was a single knock at the door and Lupo let in Falken. She was wearing an oversize leather bomber jacket and tight black jeans, her hair pulled back in a sweeping ponytail. Her makeup was muted, just enough to play up her natural beauty and high cheekbones.

"Falken, meet Arnow. Arnow, Falken," said Lupo, who always felt awkward introducing people.

They grinned at his discomfort.

"With an intro like that . . ." she said.

"Yeah, we must really be something." Arnow shook her hand and it was a strange tableau, very collegial, as they stood among the ruins of a human being.

Falken wrinkled her nose at Klug's severed head. "Jesus," she said. "Somebody doesn't fuck around."

"Yeah," Lupo said. "And if you look carefully, you'll spot the teeth marks."

"What?'" she said, crouching immediately to check. "What the hell?" She looked up at him, puzzled. "An animal attack? In here? In a loft?"

Lupo said, "This is where we have to decide what to do with what we know. We call this in right now, the whole story blows up in the news and becomes a circus. It'll keep us from getting the perp."

"You agree it could be Wilson?"

He nodded. "I think so."

"But how is she faking these attacks?" Falken stood up again and tilted her head. "I just don't get it."

"First of all, we know this guy was a kind of employee of Wilson's. Unofficial. But she paid his rent."

Arnow stepped in. "Wait, you're still jumping to conclusions. If Heather did this and the others, then we'll deal with her. But if she didn't, then it's somebody else." He gave Lupo a knowing gesture and face. "It's not like there aren't other possibilities."

Lupo sighed. "He's right, there are other possibilities. Falken, we've gotta get to this eventually. You're not gonna like what I have to say."

"Try me."

"It's possible the attacks aren't faked. They're done by people. People who can turn into wolves at will. Ask Arnow here. He's seen it. I have, too."

Falken started to smile, then changed her mind. "You're

making fun of me, right? People who turn into—You talking *werewolves*? Like in the fucking movies?" She started shaking her head.

Lupo sighed.

It was going to be a long night.

CHAPTER TWENTY

LUPO

Falken was looking at them as if they'd grown goiters the size and shape of magic elves.

Her shit-eating grin was insult enough, representing the kind of condescension best practiced on the strange and gullible by the intelligent, pragmatic realists of the world.

"She's not faking the animal attacks. Is that what you're saying? She *is* the animal?"

"We can't prove it yet, but we have good reason to believe so, yes." Lupo thought the serious approach might convince. "Not long ago, Wilson was bitten by another of the beasts."

"Uh-huh," Falken said.

"It was one of those mercenaries the local authorities ended up calling terrorists. She was sleeping with him. She put three silver-tipped bullets into him and I finished him off."

"Silver bullets?" Falken rolled her eyes. "Look, guys, I think you've gone—Your little joke's gone far enough."

"So you don't believe us?" Lupo said, glancing at Arnow. He wasn't helping.

"Not really," she said, shrugging.

Arnow sighed. "He's not kidding. I've seen it." He cleared

his throat. "It sounds incredible. It did to me, too, but I know what I saw."

She looked back and forth at them, clearly trying to process the weirdness into something she could use.

"Who else has seen this so-called transformation?"

"There are others," Lupo said. He'd been about to mention Jessie, and Sam, though he was gone, and Davison and the Gray Hawk family. He nearly offered his own Change for her benefit as he had done for Arnow, but—he wasn't sure why—he held back. Some things are better left as surprises. And besides, they'd have to prepare the situation with precautions in case his Creature turned on them.

On the other hand, without proof their explanation did indeed sound far-fetched at best. *Crazy* at worst.

Arnow glanced at him and shrugged. He wasn't willing to spill to this stranger the details of what he had seen, because he knew the chances she would believe them were almost nil anyway.

"It doesn't matter how many people you have willing to corroborate," Falken said. "You've heard of mass hysteria and mass-induced hallucinations? I think there's your explanation."

"The problem is that while we try to convince you, Heather can kill pretty much at will. She's obviously out of control."

Falken rounded on Lupo. "And your answer is to execute her? Without charges? Without a trial? Are you crazy? It's death row for you and anyone who helps you. You care about these people who agree with you? If you do, you'd better not drag them all down with you."

Lupo waved her off. "If you aren't willing to listen, then there's nothing you can do to help us."

"But now that I know what you're planning . . ."

"You'll what?" Arnow said. "Turn us in?"

"Wouldn't you?" She stuck out her chin at him.

After a pause, she added, "No, of course, you wouldn't. You didn't before. You're already implicated."

Lupo wanted to grab her by the shoulders and shake the truth into her, but he stayed away.

It was exactly the kind of impasse he'd hoped to avoid.

HEATHER

She'd been trying to call the idiot for hours to set up another tailing session. She wanted to know if someone was following her, and the best way was to have Klug stumble around behind her. Either he'd see the tail, or Heather herself would spot someone trying to shake him.

But he wasn't answering, so she drove to his place . . .

That was a laugh! He couldn't have afforded the door on "his" place.

From where she parked down the street, she saw two men step out of Klug's doorway. She ducked below the dashboard and peered stealthily through the steering wheel.

It was Nick Lupo.

And the second man was in the shadows at first. He was tall and slender but muscular. Light caught him.

Tom Arnow!

She felt a tingle. Arnow here? She'd sensed he had a thing for her back when he was sheriff of Vilas County. It was short-lived, because she had had her hands full with two lovers, and then she'd almost died. But now, she rather wished she'd . . .

What? What would she have done differently?

She had her needs and wants and tended to indulge herself.

This was bizarre. What were they doing to her? Were they trying to frame her for those murders? She'd been trying to work that story, secretly, but had hit a brick wall. Now here were these two people from her past.

Well, not completely the past . . . She chuckled.

What the hell were they up to?

And more importantly right now, what were they doing at Klug's place?

Then a third person showed up from out of the shadows. Shit!

Heather melted down into the seat and crawled into the leg well, keeping to the shadows.

New developments indeed.

ARNOW

The cop, Sheila Falken, had pretty much taken them to task, stopping just short of calling them insane vigilantes.

Jesus, maybe she's right.

He was giving Lupo way too much latitude in making his case, and it was only Lupo who seemed convinced Heather Wilson had gone rogue, even if she had become a werewolf.

Arnow had some doubts about the lack of logic it would take to do what Lupo supposed she had done.

For instance, why would she shit in her own backyard? At the very least it was stupid, and he'd never thought she was stupid. Though he had to admit he couldn't know whether something like this Change would alter a person's thinking patterns. Maybe it did make people different, more savage.

Fuck, he'd seen plenty of savagery from all of them.

Lupo was heading back to Eagle River, but Arnow thought he'd poke around the Wausau area and check on the animal attacks. He should be able to talk to someone, anyone, who had some insight. Maybe he'd find that Lupo was wrong after all.

Even after all the Werwolf Division stuff, he hesitated to include Heather in that. If Lupo was right as far as she was concerned, they had much more trouble to worry about than just Heather.

He headed for the police department, a recent-vintage neomodernist, pseudo-Federal building on Grand. It was one of those long, low school-like institutional buildings adorned with an abstract two-and-a-half-story atrium entrance. Arnow walked inside and made for the desk sergeant. Lupo had given him some names and when he showed his badge, the cop didn't question it, even though it was outdated.

Maybe they should be more careful around here, he couldn't help thinking.

He asked for the cop Lupo had met at the crime scene, Dell'Onore. The desk sergeant crooked his thumb back at a row of desks and a grizzled old uniform who sat hunting and pecking through some sort of online report. Arnow approached him from the side.

"I remember liking the paper reports a whole lot better," Arnow said.

Dell'Onore turned a twitchy eye on him, looking over old-fashioned glasses. "Do for you?"

Arnow introduced himself and started to ask a question, but Dell'Onore interrupted him.

"Yeah, I remember your name. You were sheriff up in Vilas while back." He held out his hand. "Looked to me like you got shit on by everybody. Crap that happened was pretty out-there, wasn't it?"

You don't know the half of it. "Sure was," he said. "Kinda reminds me of what's going on here."

Dell'Onore glanced around the mostly empty squad room. "You got that right!" he said forcefully. "Nobody here's got any fuckin' idea."

"You do?"

"What's your interest?" the cop said, suspicion dripping from his gravelly voice.

"I think what I dealt with and what's going on here are connected. The animal attacks."

"Fuckin' animal attacks, my ass," the cop spit out. "I know a setup when I smell one."

"So you think they're being faked?"

Dell'Onore looked at Arnow as if he'd grown a third eye. "Well, what the fuck you think? I see the Mod Squad here bullshitting around, and there's a Milwaukee cop skulking around, too, and they look like they got some idea, but then they don't get it."

Arnow wiped a hand over his eyes and nose, rubbing some of the fatigue from his features.

"What's your theory?" Arnow asked. Could it be the old guy would know something?

Dell'Onore lowered his voice to a whisper. "I think it's the government."

Great. Yeah, sure.

"I can't figure out why. But why are they covering it up? We keep getting told to shut up about it."

"Local politics?"

"Maybe. Maybe not. I haven't figured out why they keep assigning Sheila Falken to these. She ain't done dick about 'em that I can figure. She stalks around the crime scene like an elephant and files a report and that's it."

Arnow nodded as if he agreed. "Tell me more."

"It's time for my coffee break," Dell'Onore said with a huge grin.

"On me, sure, let's go," Arnow said.

KILLIAN

His stomach rumbled and he shifted in his seat.

Give the breakfast burrito and the lunch burrito a little room to breathe.

He should have gone for no beans.

I like beans, he would say, *but they don't always like me.*

It was a fifty-fifty proposition, but he liked the odds

anyway. Until his stomach and irritable bowel syndrome and reflux kicked in and declared him a loser.

He swung his Altima onto the freeway and hoped the belly gas would settle down. Talk radio had already reached saturation point, and the signal thankfully faded to occasional snatches of bad country music. Good thing he had GPS or he never would have attempted this kind of personal surveillance.

It was part of his job. He was the department's IA officer and it was up to him to root out bad or crooked cops. The MPD had had its share of scandal, and they took his investigations seriously. Problem was, he couldn't tell whether Nick Lupo was a bad cop, a crooked cop, or something else. Maybe a profiteering cop? Killian couldn't quite interpret Lupo's mixed messages. As soon as you thought you'd spotted a blot on his record, you flipped the page and that blot turned him into a hero. Somehow.

He wove through traffic whistling some old Irish ditty through his teeth.

Let's see what you're up to this time, Lupo. What's got your attention up north? Again.

He belched a little.

Oh-oh, here it comes.

He was conscious of the fact he was following Julia Barrett's footsteps, and look what had happened to *her.*

But she was stepping out of the bounds of her job.

I'm actually doing my job.

Damn those burritos.

He belched operatically for the next fifty miles.

FALKEN

Nick Lupo convinced her to follow him back to Eagle River, where he could introduce her to Jessie Hawkins, the reservation doctor. If anyone *could* convince her about this were-wolf stuff, he thought his girlfriend could.

She laughed without humor.

She drove behind his Maxima in her unmarked Impala, thoughts swirling in her head. She worked the cell out of her handbag and dialed one-handed. No one answered at the other end, and she clicked off and resigned herself to this change in her plans.

She kept his taillights in sight through the more crowded highway portions of the ride, then when the traffic thinned out she rode behind him and relaxed, knowing how long the drive would take.

Thoughts swirled through her mind and she let them.

Things were winding up, tighter and tighter.

She felt she was close.

She was close, but then what?

She stared at the lights of his car and tapped the steering wheel tunelessly.

LUPO

He had called, and Jessie was out on a series of house calls and not expected back for a couple hours. He was famished, as he hadn't had enough time to eat—or hunt—for too long. They could wait for Jess at his place. Meantime, they could eat.

He was never all that well stocked at his cottage, so he pulled into a local sandwich shop and she followed him in. They carried out a couple subs with the works. He could have gone for a super-rare steak, but figured it would have looked strange.

He led her to his place on Circle Moon Drive.

They unwrapped the food and spread it over the table.

"Beer?" he asked, and she nodded while chewing.

He put out two cold Rhinelanders.

She gazed around curiously at his environment. Judging, he figured. It more resembled a vacation getaway, not really a home.

At some point during their lunch, he'd looked into her eyes. They were a deep-water-pool blue, almost like tropical ocean water. Her dark hair, the shape of her face, wide mouth, and those limpid eyes, they all reminded him of somebody on television.

Lupo and Caroline Stewart had watched some TV while lying in bed, between bouts of lovemaking. He had been so young, and she had been so giving, like a teacher as well as a lover. But they'd found time to watch and mock the glamorous soaps of the early eighties. *Dallas* and *Dynasty*—both were good for a laugh. But now as he looked at her, Falken reminded him of someone on *Dallas*, the actress Morgan Brittany. Except Falken was more muscular, and probably taller.

They ate and made small talk. He wasn't sure why, but she made him uncomfortable. When she drank from the can, she glanced at him over its rim.

He cleared the sandwich wrappings and popped two more beers. She surprised him by leaning forward slightly and brushing her lips against his cheek.

"What's that for?"

"Just being friendly," she said, her eyes wide and fixed on his. Then she grabbed his face in her hands and locked lips with him before he could turn away. Her tongue dug through his lips and met little resistance, meeting instead his tongue and caressing it wetly.

They held the pose for a full minute and Lupo felt himself responding to her sensual assault.

But then he pulled back firmly, though gently, shrouding himself in thoughts of Jessie as if she were an antidote to the sexuality that came off Falken in waves.

Besides the fact Jessie could enter his kitchen at any time, he figured he suffered enough guilt already for his slip with Heather. Did he want to compound his sins with Falken, a fellow cop?

Jesus.

She stepped back and he thought he was safe.

Then, in one quick move, she slipped out of her shirt and he was surprised to see her breasts were bare. No, wait . . . They were mostly bare, held up by some sort of underwire bra thing that gave support and helped her large, engorged nipples thrust out at him.

He couldn't deny the lust he felt. Damn it, his response betrayed him. *We men really are pigs.*

She reached down and took hold of him through the fabric of his jeans, her long fingers cupping him sensually.

When she went for his fly, he pushed her away.

She groaned, annoyed. Her eyes seemed to stare in the distance.

"Falken?"

She started to sink to her knees, her fingers reaching for him.

"Falken?" he said, more forcefully. He reached down before she could tilt the balance fully her way, grabbed her biceps, and pulled her up. Her nipples brushed his trousers and shirt, and he almost surrendered. Her eyes flashed lust and anger, a volatile mix.

"Falken!" he said sharply. "Sheila! Stop."

His hands were still digging into her bare arms. Her breasts were full and very attractive. He noted the scar of a removed tattoo just under her left arm.

Weird place for a tattoo. If that's what it was.

She opened her mouth and he expected her to berate him. Her eyes reflected a simmering rage.

She pulled her arms out of his grip and bent at the waist to retrieve her shirt. She was completely unashamed of her nakedness, which was exciting in itself, but Lupo stepped back, too.

He realized that the Creature had been hovering near the surface, hungry and lusting, and he suppressed his own urges and beat down the Change that might have bubbled up uninvited.

Falken's eyes blazed as she buttoned up her blouse. Finally she could speak. "I'm sorry," she said in a clipped tone that indicated maybe she wasn't sorry at all. "I thought I read your signals."

"We got our signals crossed, Sheila. It's my fault. Maybe I led you on."

"Maybe you did," she allowed, nodding, shedding some of her anger. "Maybe you did, Nick Lupo. Maybe you didn't. Either way, Jessie Hawkins is a lucky girl."

He didn't know what to say to that.

She smiled. "You may want to wipe the lipstick off your face before she sees you, though." She started to let herself out. "I'm heading back home. Call me when you and Arnow and anybody else on your team figure out what you want to do. About this *wolf* thing you guys are so fond of."

She left him there, wiping his face, embarrassed at how close he had come to screwing up. Again.

From the Journals of Caroline Stewart
January 15, 1982
Last entry

I never thought I'd question Nick's motives.

He seemed to tormented, so tortured, so guilt ridden. He needed help, badly. He sought help, my help. He wanted to learn about his condition and tame it. I fell in love with him while helping him, while trying to help him understand this horror he lived with, all the while trying to come to grips with it myself.

But now I have reason to believe he has neglected to tell me he has used his lycanthropy to his advantage at various times in his life. Not just using the increased physical abilities or sharpened senses he has mentioned, the same ones that will help make him a great cop.

No, I think he has managed to use the Creature within him to achieve his own ends, in some cases to punish enemies and defend friends. Which sounds noble and so forth, I know, but which makes him all too likely to have blurred the lines between the duties of the judge, jury, and executioner.

None of which should be Nick Lupo.

But I think he has more blood on his hands than he ever confessed, and I think he has decided it's not a crime for him to pass judgment on the guilty—and execute them.

This is not a good mind-set for someone who will carry a badge and gun for the good of society.

Jesus, Nick, why?

What am I going to do?

I've had thoughts of unpacking the family silver and— and what, Stewart? What will you do with it?

That, I'm afraid, is the question I don't want to face.

But I may have to . . .

1978
BRAD SCHNEIDER

School sucked all week.

Brad's kegger had achieved the status of legend within hours of the fuzz's raid on the Wiener Woods.

All week teachers and administrators tried to make sense of what had happened in the shadow of their school building, while also attempting to round up the ringleaders.

Surely *somebody* had put the rest of the sheep up to all the violence.

But who?

The community was outraged.

The police had nabbed several dozen teenagers in various stages of drunkenness, drug-induced insanity, or some combination that rendered them about as useful as zombies.

One kid, Josh Gowan, lay in a hospital bed, comatose.

Another, Sherry Ludden, required around-the-clock care in a psychiatric facility. The word *rape* was used gingerly in the local media, but hovered over everything. All told, at least a dozen jocks and thugs had taken turns with her before the cops had come to ruin everything.

A couple of the other girls rounded up also claimed to have been raped, but the authorities had their doubts, figuring them more likely sympathetic to the perpetrators than to the victims. They were sure some of them had been willing participants rather than victims.

Brad chuckled in his seat at the rear of the study hall.

"Mr. Schneider," the teacher in charge called out, "kindly refrain from bothering anyone. This is a *study* hall, and you will now *study!*"

Nobody was giving up the group's leadership, however, or the incident's planners.

Brad gave Mr. Smart Fuck the finger under the desk.

Nobody would ever give up Rollie or him, not if they wanted to survive.

The faggot kid had survived, but he'd heard it was a close call. He almost chuckled again, but held off. Too bad they hadn't been able to finish the job on him.

The chick had been a good, tight fuck. Her struggling body had really helped get him off, and he figured everybody who lined up behind him had shot his rocks off pretty good, too.

This would become legendary.

School would never be the same. The newspaper talked about how it was forever tainted. They were gonna raze the Wiener Woods.

Brad and Rollie had sure made their mark!

Sure, now his girlfriend Susie was pissed off at him for going too far. Secretly she was probably jealous 'cause he'd had the hots for Sherry. Maybe this was the only way he could get her and it had been worth it, even if now Susie said she didn't want anything to do with him.

She'd change her mind. Chicks all wanted the same thing, and now he was the big thing around here. He was the Man. No more worrying about his curved dick. Everybody was afraid of him now.

He'd become the godfather after all.

After the interminably dull study hall period, Brad ran into Rollie out in the hall.

Rollie had managed to avoid the dragnet, too. His hold on the minions had already made itself known with a quiet threat here and there and some payoffs. The Hawthorn money spoke and people listened.

The two manipulators put their heads together in a quiet meeting. They'd had almost no time to gloat about their great success.

"Meet out behind the diamond tonight? I got some good shit," Rollie whispered, taking a chance on being overheard. The hallways kind of resembled prison cell blocks now.

"Man, you got it. But listen, we better stay away from here. I got a better idea. You know the dirt mound behind Red Arrow Park, where the BMXers do their shit?"

"Uh, yeah."

Brad said, "That ain't far from my house. I'm on a tight leash, so how about meetin' there? Same time, same bat shit. We'll be all alone, on a school night." He hawked up a wad and spewed it all over the hallway floor.

"Yeah, sure."

"Bring the shit," Brad warned. "We gotta celebrate in style."

They parted, never noticing how the door to the reading center behind them was open just a few inches, a shadow barely visible behind its frosted glass.

After skipping two out of three classes, Brad headed for the park, lusting for Rollie's weed.

Rollie always gets the best weed.

CHAPTER TWENTY-ONE

JESSIE

When Nick called to tell her he had a cop with him she should meet, she hadn't realized it was a woman cop.

Immediately, Jessie felt a stab of jealousy.

She hoped he couldn't hear the casino's drone in the background, because she was supposed to be doing house calls, not gambling again. But she'd finished early and the call of the slots was strong. Her last house call was a mere block from the casino, so it was natural she should pass it on the way back to the hospital. Before she'd known it, she was pulling into the lot. Then she was in the lobby. Then she was at her favorite slots.

She was embarrassingly predictable.

She sighed.

Well, after she was done here she could look for Davison and talk to him about that dagger business.

What a strange story. And Nick sure had gotten a faraway look on his face for a moment there. She wondered whether he had some memory he'd either repressed or withheld.

She lost a couple hundred dollars in quarters and gave up

even trying. If she went to a therapist, maybe she could explain this new compulsion.

Probably overcompensating for a lack of control when it comes to Nick and his crazy life.

Nah, probably it's just stupidity, losing money I don't have. And in this economy!

She snorted and headed for the lobby, ignoring the siren call of the jangling drone and the beeping of winners and losers.

ARNOW

When he saw the name and number on his cell's screen, he swore and almost let it go to voice mail. He was just turning onto Highways 39 and 51 to check out Wausau.

What does she want now?

He'd sent the check, every damn check, on time.

He clicked the green button, suppressing a sigh. "What, Laura?"

"Where the fuck are you?"

The scream took him by surprise. "Wha—? Nice to hear you, too."

Bitch.

"They tell me you're in goddamn Eagle River and I'm looking for you, and nobody's seen you. Except Sheriff Mc-Coyne, and he says you told him you were goin' to fuckin' Wausau."

What the hell? "I forget to file a flight plan? I didn't know you cared."

"Tell me where you are right now. We need to talk."

Arnow hated to hear *that.* Never pleasant, never ever.

"I'm in Wausau," he said sarcastically. "Like the sheriff said. Not coming back for a while."

"Goddamn it, Tom. This is an emergency."

"What's wrong? The kids—?"

"They're fine. But I'm not. Brett and I are getting married, but I need a place to keep the kids. At least until I get back. And I was hoping you would—" She paused. "They're *your* kids, too, Tom!"

"Back from where?" Arnow was trying to make sense of the woman's ranting.

"From Vegas. We're getting married there."

"Figures," Arnow muttered.

"You never gave a damn about me—" she began.

"Yeah, since you left me and fucked some random guys. Get to the point, Laura."

There was a brief silence. "We're not going to Vegas for a couple days yet, after Brett's deal closes, but Freddie and Jill need their father right now, and I went to see you in Florida, and instead you were here, except you weren't."

"Jesus, Laura, this is all news to me. I'm in the middle of a case. A dangerous case. Can't they stay with your mother?" He hated himself, but what else could he do right then?

"You fucking hypocrite!" she snarled. "You put me down constantly for not thinking of the children, then you pull this shit on me?"

Christ, it was so good she'd left him.

"Okay, okay," he said, thinking. "You're in Eagle River? With Freddie and Jill?"

"Where the hell am I gonna leave 'em? If you were home, we'd be there right now. We gotta talk about—about after I get married."

Shit! This was the worst timing. He sighed. Sounded like she wanted to talk custody. Maybe this Brett guy wasn't cut out to be a stepfather. "So, where can I find you?"

"I got us a room at this decrepit motel just out of town. Looks like they just put in plumbing last week. Toilet's plugged already."

He smiled grimly. *Serves you right.*

"Didn't you say you were headed to Vegas?"

Petulantly: "Well, not today! And I couldn't leave the kids on your porch. Can you be a father tomorrow? The next day?"

"You don't get it," he started, his anger growing. "It's not that simple. Of course I want to be their father, damn it."

"Yes it is that simple. You pick them up, I leave."

"Anybody connected with me could be in danger. I can't have them with me. You'll have to stay until this thing is resolved. Either that or take them back home."

He heard her grind her teeth. "How long?"

"Couple days, max. Then we'll talk."

She swore under her breath. "Fine. Two days. So what, do we stay here?"

"No, it's too dangerous for you out in the open like that."

"Then what the fuck—what am I supposed to do?"

He drove, thinking hard.

"All right, just stay put right there. I'm on my way. I've got an idea. I'll get you all squared away and when this is over you can go get hitched." *And get fucked.* "Just stay off the streets, away from windows. It's dangerous. I mean it."

He clicked off just as she started sputtering.

Was he exaggerating? Would anyone connect her and the kids to Arnow? Or to this case? Still, it was better to play it safe.

He scrolled his address book and dialed up Jessie Hawkins, who picked up on the third ring. Arnow explained the situation drily, leaving no doubt what he thought of his ex-wife and her new catch. His children, on the other hand . . .

If he played ball with his ex-wife and it led to getting his children back, then it would be worth all the previous vitriol. Maybe they'd stop contesting his custody appeal.

"Do you still have that cabin? Sam's old place?" he asked.

Jessie said, "Sure, Nick and I still use it. Sam left it to Nick in his will. It's remote enough and there's not much chance these Wolfpaw guys will know about it. They should be safe there. But how long? Will you stay with the kids once your wife goes?"

He hadn't thought that far ahead. If they wanted to re-visit the custody thing, well, that was all right by him. But not just yet.

Damn the bitch! This was the worst possible timing.

"I'll work something out, Jess. Thanks for your help."

"I'm on my way now to talk to Davison. How far out are you? I'll meet you when I'm done here."

They arranged to meet at the no-name motel where he would have the distinct pleasure of introducing his wife to the kind of woman he himself longed for. He couldn't stand Laura any longer, but he ached to see his children again. And to have them with him . . . well, it was going to be great.

Just not here, *not now.*

He tapped the accelerator and tempted the Fates and the state police both by edging up his speed as much as he dared.

ALPHA TEAM

Their new uniforms fit them well enough, except for San-tino, who was too wide for what had been provided. The rest of them mocked him mercilessly, until they got down to business.

Santino himself remained stoic about the mockery. He was in charge of this aspect of the operation.

Behind the security office was a large, half-empty storage room. Inside, three night-shift security guards had been herded, bound, and gagged. Their eyes were large as they watched the eight come in and out, their uniforms indicat-ing they had been replaced by these unknown men—men whose hard looks did not fit the generally genial attitude usually cultivated by the casino.

The captive guards had no chance to communicate with

each other or anyone else, but it was easy for them to deduce they were witnessing a casino robbery. The secure cash room would hold at least a million in cash almost any time of the week, two million on the weekend. The guards relaxed as they realized they were likely to survive the robbery.

Then Santino came to see them, still smarting from the mockery of his companions.

He locked the storage-room door behind himself and stood staring at the three men sitting on the floor at his feet.

Before they could even guess at his motives, he stripped out of his uniform and stood before them, naked and hairy. His huge erection bobbed before him as he considered the three.

In their eyes was the obvious question and its inherent horror. *Rape?*

Santino chose the most slender of the three. No use slaking his appetite too soon. He reached down and dragged the helpless guard across the floor as if his two forty were ounces instead of pounds.

He grinned widely and the men screamed into their gags. Their eyes were wide, locked into grotesque parodies of surprise.

The muffled sounds made Santino grin even more widely, and then the rest of his body followed his head and went over.

He transformed into his upright-stance form and leaned down like a giant bear and opened the guard's stomach with one swipe of his forepaw.

The screaming guards huddled together, traumatized, as their friend bled out and his guts came tumbling onto the floor. Santino turned toward them and growled an obvious warning. They shut up.

Then he dipped his snout into the twitching guard's belly and ate his fill. The storage room became a charnel house.

KILLIAN

He filled up in New London and wondered why people always said gas was cheaper up north. He paid and eyed the convenience-store offerings.

What the hell. He bought and nuked a fajita-steak burrito and blew on it all the way to the car. He couldn't quite tell whether his stomach clamored for it or rebelled at being forced to handle it, but it sure smelled good.

Finally he took a bite and smiled.

Now he was aiming for Wausau, where the animal attacks had taken place. He'd connect with the cops, find whoever was in charge of the case. The Wausau PD wasn't very large and their resources would be stretched thin already. He just wanted to touch base, see what they had to say about a Milwaukee homicide cop nosing around, too.

You had to wonder, what did Lupo know that no one else did?

And was this talking to dead people a ruse of some sort? Was he angling for an early retirement? Or was he certifiably nuts?

Killian aimed to find out.

He belched up the questionable beef taste and frowned.

JESSIE

She tried Davison's office at the tribal longhouse, but he wasn't there. It was a nearly new glass and chrome building that still stuck out as the only one of its kind among older, worn-out buildings. The influx of new money into the tribe's coffers would likely continue to fund such strange imbalances. Davison's secretary told her to try the casino.

Damn it, she'd just been there!

The elder was "observing and assessing," according to the older woman handling his phone. Whatever *that* was.

Sounded like an excuse to hang out in a much cooler environment.

Good work if you can get it.

Jessie shook her head as she left the sleek building that somehow managed to capture none of the tribe's character. Or heritage, or history.

She drove back to the casino with a wry sense of déjà vu and into the always-crowded parking lots and hunted down a slot, feeling the pull of the lights—always on, always beckoning, always tempting.

She understood the lure all too well.

Inside, she was pulled to the slots like iron to a magnet. *Again!* But this time she managed to find Bobby the security guard and he pointed to where Davison might be found, one of the administrative offices along the same hallway as the casino theater. She noted that Bobby wasn't very talkative today, dark circles under his eyes, his pleasant features tightened by some burden he didn't want to share. Or about which he assumed she didn't want to hear.

Trying to ignore the ringing, dinging, flashing quarter slots made her head spin. In her pocket, she barely realized her fingers were twirling her casino card.

But she persevered.

No more losses today!

Davison's eyes were haunted, she noticed after she was waved into his office.

"What can I do for you, Doctor?" he said, after their greeting.

She wondered if he suffered from PTSD since the battle on Cranberry Island. *Such a friendly-sounding name for a place that has seen so much savagery.*

She explained what Arnow and Nick had asked her to find out.

"Please, sit." He pointed to a leather armchair.

Is he looking at my legs?

He was reticent at first, but she smiled at him and re-minded him that he owed Nick Lupo. Finally he relented, and recounted his shortened version of the story she remembered Sam Waters telling her early on when they'd first met to discuss the possibility of a werewolf Defender of the Tribe.

Sam had spoken of the tribe's disgraced shaman, Joseph Badger. "You see, Badger blended the evil of the European werewolf mythology, what they call lycanthropy, with the many wolf-oriented stories of magic native to our tribe and others. Europeans feared their so-called werewolves and demonized even normal wolves, killing both animals and people they thought could transform themselves. There were hundreds of witchcraft and werewolf trials in the Middle Ages, and many executions. Here, on the other hand, the wolf represented heroic figures and was revered as a powerful totem. Joseph Badger concocted or learned enough rituals from both traditions and spent years perfecting them and creating his own set. His rituals worked, apparently. He must have tapped into some of the native magic we all know has lingered in these woods for centuries. It's the magic heard in the whispering of the trees and the birdcalls, but it also seems to run through the water and ground itself. You feel it, too, don't you?"

She *still* did. But now the pureness of the magic was tainted.

Davison made it all seem a lot less magical.

"But what about this dagger you gave Daniel Bear Smith?"

"Last I heard, it was impounded as evidence," Davison said, tilting his head a little and looking at her with a curious expression.

"If it were to be . . . *liberated* . . . ," she suggested, not sure whether to beat around the bush.

He nodded, satisfied with the nonanswer.

"We don't know for sure where Joseph Badger found the

dagger, but when he returned from his European trek—where he learned some of the rituals that eventually led him to recreate the wolf strain here among us—it was already considered a holy weapon."

Jessie was fascinated to learn that lycanthropy wasn't as unknown among her people as she'd thought. She had never heard anything about it from her father, or her mother's family. Davison gave no indication whether he himself had believed before seeing Nick and that evil Tef kid turn into wolves on the island, but he clearly believed now. Nick and Tom Arnow had bargained for Davison's confidence.

"Perhaps he purchased it, or it was given to him," Davison continued. "Perhaps his intentions weren't completely evil. He surely knew he was walking a narrow path atop a precipice. As we all know, it swallowed him up."

"Sam Waters finished it."

"Yes."

"And the dagger survived? Sam didn't know anything about it?"

"Indeed he did know of its existence, but we didn't know very much about its history. Its markings make it clear it was used throughout World War II. The swastika seems to indicate it was used against German werewolves. Badger once told me it was a 'werewolf's werewolf killer,' because it could be used by a werewolf against another even though the silver should have made it impossible."

"How can that be?" Jessie asked, shifting her long legs.

He smiled, glancing down. "We never knew. We just gave it to Daniel on the off chance it would help. Apparently it didn't—"

"Only because he was overwhelmed," she pointed out. "There were three of them. He did manage to wound one severely."

"Perhaps."

"Nazi werewolves?" she said, shaking her head. "Seems rather—"

"Far-fetched?"

"Yes, I guess so. Why didn't Sam ever mention it, I wonder?"

Davison smiled grimly. "The man had his own demons. He hunted down and killed his son, his flesh and blood. He found that a silver-loaded shotgun did the trick for him. We took the dagger and stored it securely, secretly, in case it would be needed someday, no one really quite sure why we would even need it."

Jessie nodded.

Davison continued. "Anyway, whatever magic the thing possesses seems to be in the wood the scabbard was carved from. Badger thought the markings went back hundreds of years, though he could never prove it."

"Is there anything else you can tell me that will help us?"

"I'm afraid not, Doctor. You said it's no longer in lockup. What about Sheriff McCoyne? Does he know something's afoot?"

"No, there's no good reason to involve him. He'd be difficult to convince."

"Yes, he would." Davison looked around as if worried someone lay in hiding nearby. "Anything else I can help you with?"

Jessie noticed for the first time that the man was sweating profusely. It wasn't hot in the office. She had to wonder . . . But then he stood and she knew he was dismissing her.

"Thank you," she said as he saw her to the door.

He glanced down the hallway, then nodded and gave her a small wave.

She walked away, looking for Bobby. Maybe he knew some scuttlebutt that would explain Davison's weird behavior.

But Bobby wasn't anywhere to be found.

And it seemed there were fewer guards in the casino proper, and far fewer faces she recognized among them.

She decided she'd ask Bobby the next time she saw him. She wanted to make it to that motel about the same time as Tom.

She managed to make the door without wielding the card and sinking further in debt. But it was hard.

WAGNER

The good doctor was on a mission, and Wagner followed her easily across the crowded casino floor, down the deserted administrative hallway. Gaming card in hand, Wagner appeared to be just another tipsy, obsessive tourist searching out a bathroom.

Approaching the closed door marked with Davison's name, Wagner hovered in the hallway long enough to hear a snatch or two of the conversation within.

The words brought a smile, and confirmation that two of those who knew about the existence of lycanthropes were in that office.

Wagner's plan was almost ready to put into action.

It would just take a bit of luck in the timing. But most of the elements were in place already.

Wagner left the casino. Any business with a Wi-Fi connection would suffice to trigger the plan.

BOBBY AND ALPHA TEAM

He'd been sent home.

The reason they gave—the *excuse*—was that they were overstaffed. But he knew it was bullshit. Between the layoffs and the disappearance of several other guards who should have been on shift, the casino was woefully undersecured. Bobby would have staked his life on it.

Sure, there had been those new guys, a bunch who looked like mobsters and didn't seem to know the ins and outs of casino security. They stood by and watched effectively enough, but didn't seem to have the training to make them interact with the clientele in the mostly positive, subtle way casinos generally demand.

So Bobby Burningwood sat in his living room not watching his TV for a few minutes after being dismissed, and—being home alone and with nothing to do but think—he'd thrown on a light leather jacket and jeans, tucked his father's old snub-nose .38 into the back of his pants, and headed back to the Great Northern. He undid his braid and let his long, black hair cascade over his shoulders. They'd likely not recognize him quite as quickly.

Not really knowing what he should look for, he sidled into the casino and saw that the security counter wasn't manned.

That's weird.

He wandered in, hearing the long—almost infinite—C chord made by the machines. It was a sound he had come to love. People still lined up at the slots and poker machines, but the crowd looked a bit smaller today. *Maybe they were taking in less cash*, he thought.

But then he stopped and reversed his thinking.

Two customers were chatting on cell phones, one in front of a poker machine and the other about ten feet away at a progressive ten-dollar slot with a huge payout. Both spoke loudly over the hum around them, and both seemed engrossed in long conversations.

One of those guards—Wilcox, it was—stood nearby, facing that same row of slots. His flat, square features were expressionless. And he watched with a vague disinterest as the customers flaunted their phones in front of him.

There it was, proof something was badly fucked.

One of security's main tasks was to confiscate cell phones that hadn't been turned in at the door. Voluntary phone check didn't grab everyone, so the guards made sure, if a cell phone was used, to courteously discourage the user and, in most cases, to confiscate the offending phone and issue a receipt. The phone could be claimed upon exiting.

Bobby knew there was no way anyone had ever trained Wilcox in casino security.

And now Bobby remembered that he'd spotted other illogical behaviors in the rest of those new guys. But he hadn't quite put two and two together, preferring to just see a bunch of numbers.

He walked toward Wilcox, intending to confront him about the lapse, but something in that expressionless face warned him off.

Instead, he headed for Davison's office. The elder had been spending more time at the casino lately, and Bobby had seen his old Jeep Grand Cherokee parked in its slot outside. Check with the highest-ranking guy—that made sense.

Outside Davison's office, he was about to knock when he heard a noise.

Sounds like a muffled scream!

From down the hall. Storage B.

What the hell?

Bobby dug at his lower back and slid the .38 out of his waistband. He'd made sure the cylinder was full. Not much of a weapon, the old Smith & Wesson, but under twenty feet it would do the job. Close in, he could hit the bull's-eye six out of six times. He pressed the trigger enough to feel ready to complete the needed pull. The double-action would do the rest.

He approached the storage B door stealthily, wondering where everybody was. *There should be more traffic back here, damn it.* He stood listening at the door and thought he heard some snarling sounds, as if a wildcat had found its way into the room.

The fuck?

He turned the knob and the door cracked open. The light was on.

And just like that, Bobby saw the depths of hell.

CHAPTER TWENTY-TWO

JESSIE

She was walking out of the casino entry, waving at a stolid guard who didn't bother to wave back, when a striking woman in a light leather blazer approached her just outside the door.

"Dr. Hawkins?"

"Yes?" she said, resisting the urge to check her watch. She was supposed to meet Arnow and his family at the motel soon, and she didn't want to be late.

"I think Nick Lupo may have mentioned me. I'm Detective Falken, Wausau PD."

I'll be damned! Can Nick ever meet any homely women?

She scolded herself for the rebel thought. But this chick was gorgeous, and Nick had been spending a whole lot of time either hunting Wolfpaw, shadowing Heather Wilson, or with this woman. Was that perfume she thought she'd smelled Falken's?

"Yes," she said, keeping her feelings under her vest. "What can I do for you?" Didn't mean she had to be smiley-huggy with her, did it?

"Nick told me he was going to bring us together. I just happened to drive up on my own and figured I might as well catch you. At the hospital they told me you were finished with house calls for today and to try you here." Falken looked around as if to question why a prominent community doctor would be caught slumming in a casino.

She'd have to have a talk with the staff, Jessie thought. Maybe it wouldn't do to have them send *everyone* to the casino when she wasn't to be found.

"Yes, I had an appointment here, last one of the day," she said, white lying furiously, glad she didn't have her gaming card clutched in her fist.

"Sure," Falken said. "That's what they told me. So, is there somewhere we can talk? Nick said when we met we could compare notes. He and Sheriff Arrow—*former* sheriff Arrow—seem to think they have the answer to my animal attacks at home."

Her animal attacks? Brother!

"Yes, we have information to share. And it takes some effort to present it and the proof you'll probably require. We'll need to have Nick and Tom with us. Right now I'm going to meet Tom, as a matter of fact. His wife—*ex*-wife—dumped his kids on him. To get married, would you believe it? Anyway, they're at the motel and I'm showing them Nick's cabin, a place remote enough to keep them safe while we handle—uh, help you handle this streak."

Jessie realized with an internal groan that she was babbling. This cop didn't care about Tom's family troubles. She had to figure what to do to help her and then get her on her way. She was a little too good-looking to be hanging around Nick.

First there was Heather Wilson. Now here was Falken. What was her name, *Stella? Sheila?* Anyway, Jessie snapped her mouth shut and waited to see what Falken wanted.

"Maybe I can take the opportunity to find a place to dump my stuff, too, and then we can meet whenever Nick and Tom want. Where's this motel?"

Jessie chuckled. "It's not Zagat rated, believe me." *Understatement of the century!*

"That's all right, all I need is a bed."

I'll bet! Jessie thought.

"Just follow me," she said. "I'll get you there and you can check in. I'm sure they'll have vacancies. They don't even fill up in the high season, just during the snowmobile races."

Falken seemed to come to a decision. She nodded once, decisively.

"Why not? Lead the way."

FALKEN

Shortly afterward, when Jessie Hawkins had gone to meet the ex-wife and wait for Arnow himself, Falken was in one of the shabby rooms overlooking the parking lot and took a call. She looked at the display and frowned. It was Dell'-Onore. He was a pain in the ass. His "Mod Squad" comments had bugged her for a while now.

"Yeah, Dell, what is it?"

"Hey, Falken, you know that Milwaukee cop who's been interested in your animal attacks?"

"Yeah?" She tried to keep the impatience out of her voice.

"Well, another damn Milwaukee cop was just here. An IA guy, name of Killian. He's lookin' for your Milwaukee cop, chasing him down for some infraction or other. Wouldn't tell me squat."

"Nick Lupo? So what do I care?" she said.

She kept an eye on the lot, waiting for Arnow to show.

"So when I told him that cop was up in Eagle River, and you were in charge of the attack investigation and currently up in Vilas, too, he wanted to talk to you. He's driving up."

"How wonderful to have more people to the dance," she exclaimed. "You have his number, I assume? Good, call and tell him to meet me—meet *us*—at the casino. He'll have to drive a ways north to the reservation, but you can't miss it. Do that for me, Dell?"

"Anything for you, schweetheart," the old man ground out.

"Shut up." She clicked him off.

This was interesting.

ARNOW

He was vaguely embarrassed as Freddie and Jill leaped all over him like eager puppies while Laura stood aside, fuming.

"Dad! Dad!"

"Daddyyyy!"

Meeting Jessie at the motel had been necessary because he couldn't find his way to the old cabin, but having her watch him made him feel like a very bad dad. If Laura's eyes had been a twelve-gauge side-by-side, he'd have had a hole in his gut by now.

"This is very inconvenient, Tom," she said through gritted teeth. "I hadn't planned on staying very long." She glared at Jessie as if she'd stumbled into a brothel.

Jessie seemed to take it all in stride. She looked great in worn jeans and a light leather baseball jacket. She told him Falken had shown up and gotten a room here, which was convenient for when they'd meet with Lupo. Right now, he wished he could explain to Jessie, *Laura wasn't always like this. My job got to her, made her nuts.* He wasn't sure that was it, but it gave him an out, and he took it.

After calming down the kids, he loaded up their bags.

"Can we go fishing, Dad?" Freddie said.

It broke his heart.

"Yeah, go fishing!" Jill picked up the theme.

"Wish I could, sport," Arnow said, eyes lowered. *I can't even look my kid in the eye.* "Maybe soon," he told his daughter. "There are some bad people Dad has to help catch and make you and your mom safe."

"But you're not even a cop anymore!" Freddie protested.

"Once a cop, always a cop, Fred. We'll go fishing as soon

as we can." It sounded weak, even to him. Jessie gave him a wan smile.

Was he a bad dad?

"Damn it, Tom," Laura said. Fortunately, she left it at that, the disgust evident in her twisted features. When she scrunched up her face like that, hate pouring out of it, he wondered what he had ever seen in her at all. He ignored her now, which he knew infuriated her even more, but she held her tongue because Jessie was across the room, whispering with the kids. Tom noted how quickly they, especially Freddie, had taken to Jessie.

Apparently sensing the tension, the doctor led the kids outside. Now alone, Laura tore into him.

"What the hell's going on? What are you doing back here, this hick town?"

He stared at her. "I told you, I'm on a case. Why are *you* here?"

Laura couldn't meet his eyes. "I need you to take them while we're on our trip. And maybe . . . maybe we can work out something. The judge . . ."

"Your new guy doesn't want them, does he?" Arnow said, disgusted.

"It's not that," she started. "It's just—"

"No, it's a deal," he said, interrupting her stammering. "I want my kids."

She nodded. Maybe there was some sadness there.

"But like I said, I can't do this for a couple days. Your trip can wait, right? So you stay with Freddie and Jill until I'm finished here and I'll take them to Florida with me and we'll start the paperwork."

She seemed about to say something sarcastic by the curl of her lip, but thought better of it. When she spoke, her voice was soft. "Okay. We'll go where you want."

Once everything was loaded up, he packed all of them

into his car and followed Jessie's Pathfinder through the hilly, circuitous route to the cabin, which was set deeply in a pine grove on the edge of the rez. Laura sat in a silent huff beside him. He tried to point out landmarks for the kids, but there weren't many out this way.

He glanced up as a glint crossed his vision—a reflection from the mirror? He slowed and kept an eye out, but there wasn't a car back there. He was just jumpy. He sped up to catch the Pathfinder and even though he glanced in the mirror occasionally, there were no cars coming or going the entire way.

Sam's cabin—a bit fixed up since Lupo had started to use it—loomed up at the end of a long, winding path through the pines that went from blacktop to gravel to grass ruts. Now Arnow remembered the place.

"Jesus, Tom!" Laura burst out. "We're in the middle of nowhere!"

"That," he said, "is the idea."

He pulled up next to Jessie and tried to look happy. "Race you to the door!" he shouted as Jill and Freddie piled out in a tumble of clothes and teddy bears. Out of the corner of his eye he saw Laura talking to Jessie, gesticulating with one hand.

Probably telling her what a jerk I am.

He ignored her accusing stares and basked in the presence of his children until it was time to go. It would be great to have them back and Laura far away.

He waved as Jessie pulled away. When he got into his car, he took his silver-loaded .357 Magnum Colt Python out of the glove box and set it on the passenger seat. Suddenly he felt as if he were being watched from the surrounding woods. But that was impossible. He shook his head and put the thought out of his mind. But still he felt the cold comfort of the gun's proximity.

BOBBY AND ALPHA TEAM

The blood.

That was the first detail he noted.

There were splatters of it on the off-white walls, long patterns of lines and splotches. There were puddles of it on the concrete floor, large puddles oozing in all directions. Three-dimensional droplets in fanciful patterns.

The blood was the first detail.

The second was the scattering of body parts. A leg here, an arm there. A tangle of—what were they, *intestines*? Was that Jimmy's head? A squashed, dented balloon upside down in the corner.

Jesus!

Bobby was mired in molasses for one long second; then he jerked back and started to back out through the door. When his field of vision widened briefly, he saw where his buddy Jimmy's torso had ended up, a bloody hole where somebody had done the slaughterhouse surgery.

And then he saw—and heard, for the first time—the other guards trussed in nylon rope and dumped into the other far corner, their eyes wide-open. They were screaming into their gags, and that was the noise he heard.

And suddenly he saw the animal, jaws dripping blood, staring at him from just inside his peripheral vision.

He continued his backward motion, now bringing up the Smith and squeezing the trigger—

And then he felt a gun barrel jab him in the back of the head *hard*, sending him sprawling into the room. He slid on the bloody floor, arms windmilling, and went flying in one direction while his gun went in the other.

Wilcox came in behind him and shut the door.

"Well, hello, Bobby," Wilcox said. "Great of you to come back for a little overtime. We're working extra shifts, too."

Bobby's eyes twitched from Wilcox to his tied-up friends to the wolf, *that impossible fucking wolf* . . .

He tensed his muscles, preparing to try and leap at one of his attackers, maybe Wilcox, but the big man smiled as if he had gravel in his mouth and shook his head.

"Too late, Bobby, much too late," he said.

And then the wolf pounced.

Bobby managed to sidestep the great animal, but the growling dervish flipped in midair and reached out with an improbably long snout and took a chunk out of Bobby's neck as he flew by.

Bobby felt no pain, but the curtain of blood he saw spreading before him told him all he needed to know.

He landed on his belly near the gun and scrabbled wildly for it, but before he could manage to grip it in his blood-slick hand, the wolf was back, landing on his arm and tearing through his bicep with one rapid bite.

Bobby screamed as the indescribable agony seemed to overshadow whatever the wolf had done to his neck.

But then he realized that his life had already mostly leaked out of the jagged tear in his neck.

He wondered briefly about Doc Hawkins and hoped she wasn't here tonight. Then he thought about his wife and family and died, his eyes frozen in puzzled horror.

Nearby, the other captives waited their turns with glassy-eyed stares.

The wolf dug in.

LUPO

Heather Wilson called him and he almost didn't answer.

"Look," she said, "I'm sorry about what's happened between us. I'm sorry I'm such a bitch. I just—"

Her voice dropped in volume. He heard a tremor in it.

"I can't seem to help myself," she whispered.

"What are you talking about?"

Was she confessing?

"I was always into feeling good, know what I mean? I'm— I've become worse than even I thought was possible."

Lupo was sitting in the Lifeson diner, hoping to choke down a sandwich—rare roast beef, he planned to order— before heading home.

Where the hell was Wolfpaw? Why were they waiting so long to come get him?

She was sobbing quietly on the line. If she was faking, then the tears indicated top-notch acting ability. Still, she earned her expansive living on television. Who was to say anything she said and did was honest?

"Where are you?" she asked.

"Why, Heather?"

"I want to talk to you."

"We're talking now," he said, coldly.

"I need to see you when I talk. Look, I know what you are. I saw—well, I saw too much on that damned island."

He was silent. Where was this going?

She hesitated so long, he thought she might have hung up.

"I know what you are, also because now I'm like you. I am—" She stopped, as if gathering courage. "I am like those monsters you—*we*—had to kill. I have killed, Nick Lupo. I've got blood on my hands."

A confession then.

"Go on," he said, waving off a waitress with a "come back later" motion. He hated doing that.

She went on. "I'm telling you this honestly. I'm begging you to listen. I've done some bad things recently, but . . ."

"But . . . ," he prodded.

"But I'm not responsible for all those so-called animal attacks they're half covering up."

"You're not?" *Yeah, right.*

"I've taken a few, I admit it. Early on, after . . . after that night, I didn't—I didn't know what to do, how to live. There's no manual, is there?"

He ignored that. He'd had his own lessons to learn. Some he'd never learned, God knew. "So you used Klug?"

"Yeah, he was perfect. Easy to buy off. Easy to intimidate. He helped me."

"Okay. Now what?"

"My point is that I'm sure you're tailing me because you think I'm guilty of all those attacks. And—"

"Yeah?"

"I'm *not*. I'm not the one who's doing it."

"I can't ask Klug. He's dead." Lupo waited to hear what she had to say about that.

"I didn't do that, either! Why would I kill the one person who was helping me?"

"Maybe he wanted too much? Blackmail?"

She snorted derisively. "He was sure the type. But I didn't do it. He was afraid of me. He'd never have crossed me."

Lupo sighed. "So, what do you want me to do?"

"Meet with me. Let me explain."

"Fine. Where are you?"

"In a motel here in Eagle River."

Jesus. She wasn't kidding around. She sure seemed to like motels, he thought nastily.

Trust her? Well, at worst he would defend himself in wolf form. What could she do to him? And what if she was being truthful? Then who was killing all those innocent people around Wausau? And *why*?

It really didn't make sense for her to do it. He'd been convinced by the geography. But what if the geography had been meant to convince? What would someone else have to gain by framing Heather?

"Okay." He told her where he was and how to find the diner.

He finally had his beef sandwich, but it stuck in his throat. It was embarrassing, but his pulse involuntarily raced at the thought of seeing Heather. First Heather, then Sheila Falken.

What the hell was wrong with him?

He had Jessie.

No wonder she was spending her time in the casino. Time and money. She was sending up a distress flare, and he'd been ignoring it. Wolfpaw consumed his thoughts. And the animal attacks. How were the two connected?

Damned if it made any sense.

Maybe Sam could help him. But he was nowhere to be seen.

He settled in to finish his food and wait for Heather.

LAURA ARNOW

The cabin was shuttered and now she was going from door to door, checking the locks.

Goddamn it, she was supposed to be in Vegas, getting hitched and then getting her brains fucked out amid endless champagne and whipped cream. Something romantic just *had* to happen in her life. She'd been a good cop's wife for as long as she could handle it, but then finding out that Tom had grown closer to that bitch—*that female cop bitch*—had thrown a switch in Laura's brain. She hadn't realized it right away, but she'd started to feel the need to be good to herself. She'd started to withdraw from the marriage, and while she still thought of herself as a good mother, here she was now with the kids even though she wanted a break—a *long* break—from being with them. During the trip here, she had convinced herself that she forgave Brett for forcing the custody issue, ignoring his pressuring her to find a way, or else—

Or else what?

But her anger kept simmering, occasionally intensifying to a rolling boil.

That bastard Tom had managed to strand her in this lousy cabin, in the middle of *fucking* nowhere with two antsy kids who got into trouble every five minutes—

Shit! Where were they?

Laura had been about to bolt the doors when she realized the kids were probably not inside at all.

"Freddie?" she called out.

Silence. Not even the scrape of a shoe. Or a creaky floorboard. No answering shout. Freddie was a good kid, but he got distracted easily. Probably got that from his father.

"Freddie?" She waved an arm helplessly. So much like him. He'd probably slipped out and got himself involved in watching a caterpillar or something icky. Maybe he was playing hide-and-seek with Jill, even though she was younger.

"Jill?" Laura tried it, but if she couldn't even find Freddie, then it was a foregone conclusion the two troublemakers were together. The question was, *where?*

Lord, not outside?

She made a quick sweep of the downstairs, which wasn't hard, and then climbed to the loft.

No, neither Freddie nor Jill were anywhere to be found.

Laura stamped her foot.

Damn it!

If she got her hands on those—

Angrily she undid the bolt and threw open the front door.

"Fredd—"

Her voice died in midname.

There was a dog sitting on its haunches on the porch.

In its jaws was a bloody scrap of blue tie-dyed T-shirt.

Freddie was wearing a blue tie-dyed, the one he likes that he won't ever let me wash—

Her eyes focused tightly on the blood.

Freddie? Where was Jill?

It wasn't a dog at all.

She screamed.

The surrounding trees seemed to lean in and absorb the screaming until there was no sound but that of the breeze through the ramrod-straight pine trunks.

Then the howling started.

CHAPTER TWENTY-THREE

WAGNER

The laptop equipped with a satellite Wi-Fi card connected easily to the necessary servers. With the appropriate software open and the parameters carefully set, Wagner powered up the phone and spoke the message. On the screen, sound waves flowed into one screen and then flowed out of the other, altered. Faders on an automated virtual mixing board took care of the auditory details.

The calls, both prerecorded and live, took a few minutes.

ARNOW

He drove the route to Sam's—now Nick's—cabin and was halfway there when his cell buzzed. He worked it to his ear and said, "Hey, Lupo, what's up?"

"Listen, Tom, I need to meet with you."

"I'm heading back out to the cabin. I want to check on the kids. I tried Laura's cell, but got her voice mail. The idiot's got her phone off, can you believe it? Have to tell her to keep it on and charged. Anyway, I'm closer to them than to you, so I'll turn around as soon as I check on them and make my way down to you."

"All right. That sounds good."

"Uh, Lupo, *where*? Where do we meet?"

"Let's make it the casino, about two hours from now? Dr. Hawkins will be there. And everybody else will be, too."

"Developments?" Arnow was intrigued. He checked his watch.

"Yeah, you could say that." Lupo's voice faded momentarily with the signal.

"Me, too," Arnow said, smiling. "Got something of interest . . ."

"Really? What?"

Arnow shook his head even though Lupo couldn't see it. "Not yet. I'll tell you in person. Your cop friend gonna be there?"

"Falken? I'm calling her next."

"Just talk to me first," Arnow said.

"Will do."

He clicked off.

Wonder what that's all about. Weird time and place for a meeting.

The pines were every bit as claustrophobia inducing as he remembered. *Give me Florida anytime*, he thought. He was done with the North Woods. He'd liked it until the goddamned wolves had ruined it for him. Now he couldn't wait to head back down to the sunshine and heat. Here it was spring and still cold. *Shit!*

The tree trunks set so close together gave him the creeps as the sunlight began disappearing. He just wasn't too keen on this remote location, even though it was logical to stash Laura and the kids as far away as possible from the action.

As the shadows lengthened, the spaces between pines grew darker and slowly went black. He thought he saw eyes, *red* eyes, glaring at him from the undergrowth just like in the cartoons.

Made him wonder about that intriguing dagger he'd stolen

from the cops, which he had kept with him. Why hadn't Lupo taken it when he offered it? The way he had stared at that funky dagger, it was almost like Lupo'd seen it before. Or it meant something to him he wasn't willing to share. Arnow was sure now he'd bagged it and boxed it himself, and then it had disappeared into the black hole of the evidence room.

So much shit had been covered up, there was no way Lupo could have seen it.

So maybe he'd heard of it. From Sam, maybe, or one of the other elders.

Christ, where the hell is the road?

He suspected he might be driving in circles. Some of these roads looked unused for years. They made useless loops and crisscrossed, so you could do the same figure eight over and over before you realized it.

The area actively gave him the creeps now. He shifted the silvered-up Python closer on the passenger seat. He could almost imagine a pack of wolves surrounding the car, approaching, leaping onto the roof and breaking the windows, reaching inside with their bloody snouts, snarling their anger. And going for his throat when they were within range. He could take a few with him, but how many would be in a pack?

That last bullet, the sixth, would be for me.

Suddenly there it was, the almost-hidden turnoff to the private road. Gravel and dirt crunched under his tires as he nosed onto its narrow length gratefully.

By the time he pulled up to the cabin, however, he knew something was wrong.

Deathly wrong.

"Laura?" he called out as he cautiously climbed out of the car, quietly. No echo, no response. "Freddie? Jill?"

The silence mocked him. The pines seemed to laugh at him. The breeze tittered as it slipped through the trunks and across his skin, leaving him cold.

Ice cold.

The door was ajar.

He blinked and it was like taking snapshots. Dark splotches on the porch. Smeared by skid marks.

Snapshots.

The images came like clicks through a slide show, unbidden but inexorable.

He moved through it all like a ghost. Blood coated the inner log walls like paint, long dribbles here and there, tendrils reaching across the floor toward where he stood.

He found most of the remains in the main room, the three bodies posed, their roughly severed heads lined up from large to small.

Oh my God . . .

A lancing pain pierced his forehead like a hunter's arrow.

They were supposed to be safe here. They were supposed to be a family again. Why, why had Laura brought his children into the middle of his damnable case?

No, it was Lupo's case. *Damn him!*

He sank to his knees, a strange sort of keening sound whirling about, surrounding him. It was his voice, but he didn't know it. His brain had partially shut down. He was as close to insanity as he had ever been, and he felt himself falling off the edge and into it, embracing the darkness that waited for him down below.

The keening became a full-throated scream of anguish and rage.

LUPO

She walked into Lifeson's and turned every head there. Males drooled, females snarled. Some recognized her from Wausau television; most just lusted.

Lupo knew the feeling. He could smugly claim to have

"been there, done that," but it made him feel sleazy and unfaithful, so he suppressed the feeling.

She marched up to him, every bit as formidable as he remembered. As a wolf, she would be extraordinary. She would be suited to the body. If not a wolf, then it would have been a tiger.

"Thank you for seeing me," she said, sitting.

"You're welcome. But I'm not convinced that means you're innocent."

"Look, I told you, I'm *not* innocent. I took some, uh, game in my early days. But then I started to realize that would call attention to me, and I stopped."

"You still had Klug helping you?"

"Well, how could I get rid of him?"

"The way you did, tearing him apart."

"No! I could have, but I didn't! He cost me less alive than now, dead. Another murder victim in my territory, and I don't have somebody to help me."

Lupo noted how she said *territory*. She'd ceded Eagle River to him, apparently, but claimed Wausau as her own. Maybe this indicated that she hadn't been the rogue wolf. *Why shit in her own backyard?* Arnow had said, or something to that effect.

"Suppose I believe you," Lupo said. "Then who's killing all those people, and why?"

"Maybe to frame me, I don't know." She flared her nostrils in frustration, ignoring the admiring glances from all around the room. The waitress brought her water, but she waved off anything else. "But I thought it was *you*," she whispered after they were alone.

"Jesus! Why would I—?"

"You and Sheriff Arnow. And that cop," she spat out.

He shook his head. "Not us. We hovered around you because we all liked you for the killings."

Her best camera-friendly sad look hit him in full.

"It wasn't me. It's all I can say."

"All right. Let's go with it for now. Go back to your motel and wait to hear from us. We'll work it out somehow. Just don't do anything stupid. *No hunting.*"

She nodded. "Thanks. I get it. Lay low. Promise me you'll consider alternative perps?"

He stared into her limpid eyes. He nodded. He was already considering alternatives, and their possible motives.

Perhaps his eyes were opening.

They shook hands awkwardly and she left.

Lupo stared at the ceiling.

ARNOW

There couldn't be *that* many silver Lexus SUVs in the North Woods. When he saw one pass him going in the opposite direction, even through his tear-bloated eyes, Arnow just knew it was Heather.

He stood on the brakes, screeched through a tight U-turn, and got on her bumper. But then he pulled back and gave her some room.

Better to follow her and catch her when she stopped. Why pressure her, risk a high-speed chase, and kill either her or some innocent driver?

Even through his rage, his better cop instincts took over and he lay back, keeping his rental car within sight of her very visible vehicle.

His vision was tinted red, as if his eyes were wrapped in red gauze. *Bloodred.*

Rage twitched along his veins and muscles and made his nerves tingle.

The Python, its silver slugs ready in their chambers, waited patiently near at hand.

In his mind, he saw himself executing the monster she had become, the monster who had slaughtered his family.

His *children*!

He wept as he drove, and when she pulled into a motel lot out in the middle of nowhere, he stepped on it and roared up behind her, adrenaline making his extremities sing with hate and a finely honed rage.

He was out of the car before he knew it, Python in hand, grabbing her by the hair as she climbed out of the Lexus, kicking her to the asphalt and grinding the barrel into her scalp.

She screamed first in surprise at being assaulted out of the blue, and then in silver-tinted agony as the heat of the slugs in the Python's cylinder reached her skin and began to scorch, peeling a layer of scalp and hair from her head. The slimy mess slid off and into Arnow's hand.

He was raging now, screaming words that made sense only to him, and then accusing her of killing his children.

"Nooooo," she gasped out. "Talk to Nick! No, I didn't do it, don't know anything about it!"

"I don't believe you!" he shouted. He was almost out of control. His finger tightened on the trigger. One slug and the silver would explode in her brain and burn it to a cinder. And he wouldn't stop at just one.

"*Wait!*" Heather shouted, her last-ditch effort.

He hesitated.

"I wouldn't kill children," she said with urgency, her voice breaking. More of her skin sizzled and burned as if held onto an open grill or burner. "No children, never any children."

Perhaps it was the repetition of the word *children*, but Arnow suddenly saw himself as just the kind of vigilante he'd always despised. He backed off, pulling the gun away from Heather's skull. The stench of burning skin and hair surrounded him and made him retch.

Heather sagged to the cracked asphalt, her face screwed up in pain but refusing to cry out any more.

"I deserve that," she whispered, "but not for your children,

Tom. And not for all these other killings. Ask Lupo. I just convinced him."

"He's soft," Arnow muttered. He watched as Heather's scalp slowly began to heal itself, now that the silver was no longer near her head.

"No, he's being logical." Heather sat up, clearly heartened by the fact that he hadn't killed her when he could have. Not yet, anyway.

"Come inside," she begged, nodding at the door in front of which their vehicles were still idling. Nobody had stepped out onto the lot, so apparently there hadn't been any witnesses. "Let me call him for you. Check for yourself. He agreed to look at alternatives."

"Alternatives? My children were slaughtered like animals!" Arnow howled.

"But not by me, Tom." She added, "I'm sorry . . ."

Roughly he pulled her up and shoved her toward the door.

He couldn't help noticing that her head looked almost as good as new. Her hair was still patchy where he'd ground the gun moments before, but it was rapidly revitalizing itself . . . or whatever.

He followed her into her cracker-box room.

"Start talking," he snarled.

"For one thing, I was trying to help. I was trying to figure out who was framing me for those murders!"

"Go on," he said as he waved the Colt. She shrank from its heat.

"I talked to Nick Lupo. He believes me now. You can call him."

"I will. And?"

"And there's something weird going on you should know about right now."

Her face was losing its panic-induced twistedness and was settling into her natural beauty. Even though her makeup was smeared and her hair and scalp still smelled of the burn caused by the silver slugs, Heather Wilson was reverting to her poised anchorwoman persona.

"What is it?" he said, and his voice was infinitesimally less hostile.

"I talked to Nick, and afterward I retrieved a voice mail from him that didn't make any sense. He never mentioned it. In fact, it was left at the same time I was talking to him."

Arnow made an effort to slow his breathing and process the information.

"Call him now."

"I did, just before you caught up to me. Cell service must be out. Couldn't get him."

"What did the message say?"

"Sounds weird, but it was his voice. Asked me to meet him at the casino in two hours. I had the phone off, though, so I never heard it coming in."

Arnow wiped his free hand through his hair. He had talked to Lupo, but was it Lupo?

The rage had eaten him up only moments before, but now he was beginning to feel something deeper and infinitely worse. Grief.

He was not sure how it happened, but at first she turned and touched his face, tracing where the tears had coursed until there weren't any left, and then her hand had strayed down and touched his chest, where his heart pounded like a hollow log.

Her face came closer to his, the skin and hair now completely repaired, restored to their original luster.

His hand dropped the Colt to the carpet.

He kicked it away.

He didn't need it anymore.

She looked into his eyes and he saw some kind of eternity there, something he'd noticed on Lupo once in a while. She made a noise in her throat. She was choked up.

"I never—I would never have attacked your children."

He brushed her words aside, but didn't stop her hand from caressing his arm, his side, his chest.

He grunted when she came closer and hugged him. Let her put her arms around him, lay her head on his chest. If she was the killer, the rogue werewolf, then he was dead.

But the fact was, he didn't care.

If he was dead, then so be it. He'd lost any reason to live, anyway.

He surprised himself—and her—by pulling her closer and responding to her touch, which began to heat up between them until she was peeling off his clothes.

And he let her.

If she'd looked into his eyes, she would have seen an unhealthy, intense glow that he himself couldn't explain. Their hands roved over each other's flesh, and when he took her right there on the floor, tears were flowing down his face.

They rocked in an increasing rhythm of lust and rage and relief and pure calculation, each sealing a bargain with the other as if their rutting were a metaphor.

In the middle of their violent passion, Arnow lifted Heather and turned her around and entered her from behind more as if it were a wrestling move than anything to do with sex or love or passion. And he leaned down over her shoulder and spoke directly into her ear, more insistently when she shook her head, and then finally with vehemence until she nodded her agreement. He increased his rhythmic motion and then backed off, and then he felt her begin to Change under him, her skin turning to fur in patches that raced along her long, lean muscles.

Through the fear and uncertainty, Arnow closed his eyes and refused to watch as Heather fulfilled his request and became the monster of nightmares. He heard the snarling and squeezed his eyes closed all the harder, until the pain lanced through him like lightning along his nerves—and he passed out onto the cold motel carpeting.

Jessie's call was strange. Her voice was flatter than he was used to. She was the type who always had some laughter tucked back there, somewhere, no matter how grim the subject. She was well-adjusted, that was certain.

He smiled grimly. She had to be, to put up with him and the trouble he caused. His smile changed to one of fondness.

Love, idiot. It's love.

Even though Heather had caught him in her web, it had been a brief capture. Had a "pull the Band-Aid off the scab fast" sense to it. He wasn't smitten anymore. He could be—he *was*—happy with Jessie. Now to prove it.

He thought about Jessie's call.

Uh-oh.

Maybe she'd learned of his night with Heather. Maybe she'd intuited it. He *had* been acting strangely lately. It was the whole Wolfpaw situation. She just didn't understand how it felt to him. She knew other humans existed, end of story. When Lupo had met Wolfpaw, through Tannhauser's gang, it was like a cosmic kick in the balls. He hadn't known others like *him* existed, and it had caused a ripple effect in his life.

And now that he knew they were out there, getting closer, and he had led them here . . . well, he wasn't feeling happy about that. They seemed to have decided not to come. At least, not yet.

What are they waiting for?

Since talking to Heather, he'd been mulling the possibility that *Wolfpaw* was responsible for all the killings.

Why?

Why not?

To get at him?

To *attract* him?

Maybe their motive predated his recon of the compound?

When he looked down from the spot on the ceiling, Sam was seated across from him where Heather had sat.

"Thinking hard? Must hurt."

Since when had Ghost Sam become a wiseass?

"It's not like you're helping," Lupo muttered. He saw a couple heads turn.

"Hey, I'm here," Sam said.

"Where have you been?"

"Keeping busy. Lots to do over on this side."

Jesus, I can't even be haunted by a serious fucking ghost.

"I'm as serious as a heart attack, Nick. You just need to rearrange what you know. And then you'll see that you already know everything you need."

"That's fucking helpful, O Riddler."

But Sam was gone.

Lupo paid and left a large tip. He checked his watch. Still time before making that meeting with Jessie. She must have info. Maybe she had Davison on tap to give them more on the dagger. He dialed his cell and, when Arnow didn't answer, left him a voice mail about Jessie's call. Should he call Falken? Suddenly he wasn't so sure about placing Sheila and Jessie in the same room, not with Jessie's recent bout of jealousy.

He headed out, wondering if he had time to shed his clothes and hunt. The food had only teased his appetite.

He felt the Creature clawing its way to the surface.

It wanted food.

It wanted action.

It wanted blood.

1978
NICK

He had been in place for an hour when the two manipulators showed up, one entering the park from the east side and the other appearing almost magically over the rutted BMX hill on the southwest side.

They met near a stand of maples and sat with their backs to a large trunk, concentrating on their bag of weed and rolling papers. They chuckled smugly as they rolled their joints and reminisced about the mayhem they'd caused.

Nick huddled in the undergrowth less than twenty feet away from the meeting place. He had surveyed the area and pegged the best place with the least likelihood of being spotted from the street by a wandering cop car.

Nick smiled grimly at how well he had predicted their hidey-hole. In fact Rollie and Brad were more or less invisible from anywhere in the park except where Nick lay in waiting.

He remembered well how not that long ago he had enraged the Creature and caused it to claw its way out of him when he decided to punish a bully named Leo. It was dangerous, luring the Creature out and letting it run amok, because he was never sure he could bring Nick Lupo back once he had been replaced by the wolf's animal rage.

Today Nick didn't care.

He started to fix images from that night in his mind, remembering Josh and his broken, battered face, and Sherry's screaming as jocks lined up to fuck her squirming, bucking body, laughing all the while at her struggles.

Nick felt the Creature stir deep down inside him, where it resided until the moon's call. And increasingly, until Nick's call, akin to poking it with a stick.

Today the stick was the image of the smug *bastards*, Brad and Rollie.

They chattered and smoked, chuckled and patted themselves on the back for their importance. Nick heard them mention Sherry Ludden.

"Man, when I turned around and you were stickin' it to her good, that was better than those crappy loops Manny got hold of for that party last month. I could see your pecker goin' in and out."

Brad laughed like a hyena. "Yeah, I wish I coulda got a film of it."

"You fucked her in the ass, too, right?"

"What could I do? The guys flipped her over. Too good to pass up that tight little virgin hole."

"Man, you know you got quite the curved dick?" Rollie said, after toking. He handed Brad the roach.

"Fuck you, man, it's the length that counts," Brad protested.

"That's what I would say, too," Rollie said.

"I said fuck you and lay off my dick."

They both laughed uproariously.

The pot was making them giddy.

But their laughter was doing it, enraging the Creature. The wolf might not understand the words, but Nick did and as he felt the rage rising within himself, he also sensed the Creature stirring, coming to life and climbing closer to the surface.

"—that fag gettin' what was comin' to him was the best, man!"

Mocking laughter.

Smug, hateful chatter.

Nick gave himself over to the wolf.

The wolf rose out of him before he could finish stripping out of his clothes.

A howl was ripped from his altering throat.

And then he was over—*just like that*—and his huge, muscular body was hurtling through the air.

He landed with his paws on Brad's chest, caving it in, and simultaneously his jaws tore into Rollie's face, ripping his bony nose to shreds.

The two boys squealed in their shocked, sudden pain. And then the fear set in.

The wolf grinned at them with its open jaws, then suddenly snapped forward and shredded the skin of Brad's cheeks and face while the kid screamed in terror.

Somewhere deep inside the Creature, what was left of Nick Lupo smiled.

His teeth firmly planted in the skin of Brad's cheeks, the wolf shook his head viciously and turned the smug bastard's face into hamburger.

Then he turned his attention to Rollie, who was trying desperately to roll away from the carnage, his arms and legs emptily grasping at grass and tree bark.

The Creature's jagged jaws clamped onto the rear of Rollie's thigh and tore outward, raising a curtain of blood from the severed femoral artery.

Then he turned back to the screaming Brad and went for the groin, sawing through the jeans and tearing through penis and scrotum, then moving up to the flailing kid's stomach and ripping through clothing and skin until the intestines unraveled and squirted out onto the dirt.

The Creature then stood panting, watching the two screaming kids dying, blood and gore drooling from its jaws.

Then he howled, long and loud, crowing his victory.

Before their eyes closed for the last time, Nick Lupo returned and stood before them, making sure they saw him and understood why they had been punished. He made sure they understood what he was, and what he had done to them.

Naked, he crouched just out of their reach and watched them bleed out, their cries for help and mercy growing fainter by the second.

Nick didn't care what dog or other wild animal would be blamed for this, but he considered that a blight on the school had been exterminated.

Huffing with exertion and strange exhilaration, Nick watched until the light went out of their eyes.

He had thought he'd feel better watching them die, but he

had to admit there was nothing—no feeling at all—inside him. He was hollow. His revenge was hollow. And yet the wolf was satisfied.

Something about it did feel *right*.

He collected his clothing and set off for home as twilight fell.

CHAPTER TWENTY-FOUR

JESSIE

Once again it seemed there were fewer security guards on duty than normal. One at the door stared at her and didn't return her smile. Then she saw not a single blue shirt where there should have been at least a dozen.

She'd ask Davison about it, if he was here. The elder had been spending a lot of time here, his secretary at the longhouse had told her. And he was here now.

Nick's voice mail had been patchy, likely due to his cell signal fading. They still didn't have perfect cell-phone coverage in the northern areas of the county. But the message had sounded important. Maybe he had spotted somebody from that Wolfpaw group or had figured out their next move. The fact that he wanted them to meet in the conference room meant it was more than just her.

Regretfully she passed up the slots and headed for the administrative offices, past the darkened theater entrance.

Where was Bobby? Not around again. She hoped he hadn't been laid off.

The casino drone filled her head and she almost thought she felt the gaming card pulsating in her pocket.

No, not today.

There were fewer people than usual gambling. Several rows of slots lay empty and unused, their jingles calling out to nonexistent spectators. *That's weird.* She'd been inside at two in the morning or later and had seen more gaming going on. *Dinner hour?*

Another security guard—burly, in a tight-fitting uniform—stared at her as she walked past. She was sure she'd never seen him before. He muttered into his shoulder mike.

Her neck hairs began to tingle.

Something was wrong. The whole thing *looked* wrong.

Shit, now what?

She wasn't prone to premonitions, but sometimes one of *those* feelings was borne out. Her original instinctive suspicion of her tenant Nick Lupo had certainly proven correct, if not in the way she'd thought. That was before they'd become lovers, which she had hoped would happen, but not predicted.

Out of sight of any of the creepy security guards, she ducked into one of the sparkling bathrooms. It was more like a suite with multiple toilets—she hadn't stayed in hotel rooms this nice. She looked around, then under the stall panels.

Alone.

She stared at herself in the long mirror. What to do?

She stripped off her baseball jacket and stared at the red blouse she wore underneath. Well, that looked different. What else could she do? She patted her pockets and felt her reading glasses tucked in there. Kind of a secret that she felt she needed them, a bit too soon for her pride, but . . . now they would help. She slipped them on and they did change the shape of her face a little. She took the glossy cascade of her hair, all chestnut highlights she loved to have Nick nuzzle, and rubber-banded it into a sloppy ponytail.

Too bad I'm not wearing anything reversible.

She remembered one of the Flint movies Nick enjoyed so much, which featured a reversible tux in one scene. *Ah, well . . .*

She untucked the red blouse and tied its tails under her navel Mary Ann–style. Thank God for all those *Gilligan's Island* reruns Nick made her watch now and again.

She stared at the package as it stood.

Rather different . . . but not enough.

She plucked her makeup out of her bag and applied a quick, heavy layer of royal blue eyeshadow and bright lip gloss. Popped a stick of gum into her mouth and tried chewing theatrically.

Now she might look different enough.

Her tingling sensation had increased. She felt sure this wasn't stupid, unfounded fear. There was something amiss here, and those security guards had something to do with it.

She packed up her bag and other belongings in her rolled-up jacket, then placed them in a stall, locking it from the inside and slipping out below the partition.

Still no one had come in.

She slipped out of the washroom and headed for the first row of slots. She held her gaming card like a lantern before her, chewing her cud like a movie teenybopper. She stood at one slot, then another, for a couple minutes, her eyes roving the place. Dead-eyed gamblers plodded here and there, the life sucked out of them.

Do I look like them? she wondered.

Any silliness she might have felt at playing dress-up dissipated when she peered through two unused slot machines and saw a guard approach another and both of them gaze at the small crowd scattered around them, obviously looking for someone.

Looking for me . . .

She just knew.

A chubby woman was chattering on a cell phone right in

front of the guards, and neither looked at her. And that was against the casino rules. The guards should have confiscated the phone. The woman ambled away still chattering, blissfully unaware. But then she held the phone away from her ear, looked at it, and listened. Shook it, looked at it again, and shoved it into her purse, disgusted.

Jessie was puzzled for a second, but forgot about it when the guard's glance slid over and past her.

She mimed playing, momentarily frightened into breathlessness, but then breathed in relief when a zombie woman came and played the machine next to her. The guard moved on, staring at people. *But not her.* From her position she could see almost clear to the administrative hallway.

The ubiquitous blue camera bubbles above—the infamous "eye in the sky"—caused her some concern, but she sensed that if they could have used them to spot her, they already would have.

Maybe it's a happy coincidence—my disguise is working and they're undermanned.

Covering exits might be more important to them than staring at screens.

The two guards meandered away, still scanning their surroundings, staring at the people who ignored them to concentrate on their next potential score. She gauged how long they were gone, disappeared behind a row of poker machines and their lifeless players.

She counted to ten, slowly.

Then she walked purposefully toward the hallway opening onto the main casino floor. Usually there was a guard hanging around, but not now. The hallway was still a public area, with more bathrooms and the employment office. She made for a drink station and veered off at the last second, entering the hallway as if the bathroom were her goal.

If she could see Davison, maybe all this weirdness could be explained. Maybe she was overreacting. But there were fewer guards, and Bobby wasn't around. And Bobby was *always* around.

At the end of the hall a double doorway led to the private offices. Fifty-fifty odds on finding it open. Hadn't Bobby once mentioned that it drove the guards crazy that certain staff continued to leave the doors unlocked despite the rules?

She tried the doors. The first was locked. The second . . .

Open!

She slipped inside and the smell hit her.

Shit.

She knew it well enough. It was a dizzying cocktail of blood, feces, urine, and acrid adrenaline, overlaid by a kind of wet, suffocating musk.

A shiver ran through her.

Forward? Or retreat?

LUPO

He was just approaching the casino lot when a car screeched around and blocked his way in. He jammed on the brake pedal and started to go for the horn, then spotted the driver's face. Arnow's arm waved furiously out the window, grabbing his attention.

He waved Arnow out to the street and pulled up behind him, outside the lot.

"What's the deal?"

Arnow appeared drawn and almost wasted away, as if he'd aged twenty years just since the last time Lupo had seen him.

"Did you make a call about meeting here?" Arnow said hoarsely as he approached.

"No, I called about Jessie's weird call."

What the hell?

"You didn't call twice?" Lupo shook his head. "Heather

claims you told her you believed she wasn't responsible for the killings in Wausau."

"She's responsible for *some*, the early ones, but she made a good case for not being stupid enough to do all those people in such a small area. And Klug didn't make sense. He was an asset to her. I think somebody did him for our benefit."

He examined Arnow more closely.

"What's happened? You look—"

"My family—" Arnow's voice cracked and he couldn't finish. He shook his head, as if denial could make it all better. Then he broke down and sobbed. "Dead, all . . . dead."

"Christ, your wife, kids? At the cabin?" Lupo let the news sink through him. *What about Jessie?*

Arnow nodded, his face a carved-granite outcrop. He'd used up his tears.

"Goddamn it! They've been ahead of us every damn step."

"Wolfpaw?"

"I think so." Nick pulled out his iPhone and dialed Jessie's number. But before it could even dial, the screen went blank. There was nothing. "*Shit!* Looks like they're using a jamming device. If she's here, there's no way to warn her."

"So they're here? Wolfpaw?"

"That's my guess now. Jessie'd noticed some strangeness going on with security in the casino." He grimaced. "Turns out she's been hanging around the slots a lot more than I thought." He slapped his thigh. "I kept looking over my shoulder, expecting them to follow me. I didn't figure they'd leapfrog us and set up a trap. They must want to terminate anyone who knows their secret. This means us, Davison, Jessie, Heather. And now Falken. The Gray Hawk family moved away, so maybe they're safe for now."

"You went and poked that rattlesnake, didn't you?" There was bitterness in Arnow's voice. No, worse, it was repressed rage.

"Yeah, I think I did."

Arnow made a face. His hands were fists.

For a second, Lupo thought Arnow was going to lunge at him, or throw a punch. Arnow's face betrayed the struggle within him, jaw muscles working, clenching and unclenching, his brow furrowing.

Lupo sensed the sheriff's muscles were twanging like rubber bands.

The crisis moment lasted a minute, then passed, fading away and leaving Arnow desiccated and worn, as if consumed from the inside out.

Lupo turned away. The man deserved to grieve and let his rage play out in private. But Lupo figured there wasn't much time for that now. He examined the casino entrance, far across the lot. There were fewer cars parked than usual. As he watched, a busload of gamblers arrived and pulled up. A blue-shirt security guard waved it down, spoke to the driver, and a minute later, the bus roared away.

"Looks like they're turning people away. Maybe claiming technical trouble. They can't keep everyone out, or sweep out whoever's in there."

"They gonna kill everybody?" Arnow cleared his throat of the hoarseness.

"Wouldn't make sense. If they're trying to squelch people's knowledge, then they'll want to keep this trap as private as possible. They're hoping to get us in there, but to deal with us in private. They're just limiting customers because there aren't enough of them to handle everyone." He waved at the cars in the lot. "Less than usual, but still a few hundred gamblers and staff. No, I think the odds aren't as bad as they could be. Maybe this is a small operation, somebody trying to cover his ass. Maybe the whole of Wolfpaw doesn't even know about it. Like a battalion commander keeping some kind of mess in-house."

"Sounds good—better than it could have been, maybe. But what about Jessie?" Arnow asked.

Lupo felt a shiver. "Shit, we have to assume she's in there. Either a prisoner, or not suspecting a thing. Maybe they're using her as bait, drawing us in there so they can shut us down. *Fuck!*"

"So what do we do, walk in the front door, guns blazing? Between us, we've got the guns, I bet."

"No good. Too much collateral damage. And anyway, I have a secret weapon." Lupo dug into his wallet and plucked out a white card with a tribal logo on the front. "Davison set me up a while back. We can infiltrate through the back. There's a zillion cameras, but they won't expect us that way, and I doubt they have the whole staff replaced."

"If they do?"

Lupo smiled grimly. "Then we're truly fucked."

WAGNER

The Wolfpaw agents were assembled in the conference room, except for the one who watched the front door and another who watched the camera feeds in the security office.

Wagner looked at the squad leader.

"Report, Wilcox. What about Hawkins?"

They were following informal protocol. "We logged her entering, but then she disappeared . . ."

"Explain how this is possible," Wagner said, suppressing rage.

"There are twenty-eight separate rooms in this establishment. We infiltrated and have terminated a small number of the security detail in addition to those who were 'laid off.' However this makes the space overwhelming for a small squad to secure. I've got just one guy on cameras. A dozen screens, but they cycle through the hundred fifty camera feeds. He can miss something by a fraction of a second."

"Have your men start a search. Find her! Don't forget,

this operation is about *containment*. We don't want to kill everybody in the casino. What about these others who were killed?"

"I take responsibility."

"Who did it?"

"My outside man at the moment, Santino."

Wagner tapped a finger on the conference table. "After the operation is finished, have him report to me."

Wilcox nodded.

"All right, spread out. Find Hawkins! I want her alive, however. If the phone calls don't get them here, then she will be our little tied-up lamb."

Wagner dismissed them and headed out into the casino.

JESSIE

Forward.

Anytime, somebody could come up behind her. Much better to keep moving.

She approached Davison's door. His truck was in the lot, so he had to be here. She heard no sound from inside, not a peep.

Gingerly, she tried the door. It opened easily and she was halfway through it when the stench hit her like a physical blow. She couldn't help it—she gagged, reaching up to cover her nose and mouth as well as anyone could with mere fingers and skin.

Davison was behind his desk. And on his desk, beside it, around it. All over the floor. Blood had even reached the ceiling. His head was impaled on an old-fashioned pen holder.

He'd been torn apart like a roasted chicken.

She felt her eyes tear up, but frankly she realized she had little or no time to mourn. He'd been mostly a good man, willing to sacrifice for his tribe. He'd done a good job marshaling the casino project when most of the old tribal board had been murdered. Now he had been murdered in the same way.

Jessie knew right then that Wolfpaw wasn't coming.

Wolfpaw was already here.

They had infiltrated casino security. With or without Davison's help, they had slowly insinuated themselves into the background. And now they were getting down to business.

Was this what Nick wanted to show her? Why he had asked her to meet him here? Did he know? Was he here?

She gasped.

The picture came into focus all at once, and she didn't like it at all.

She closed the door and headed down the hall. Still amazed there was no one around, she wondered whether anyone was being held prisoner back here. She opened every door, but found empty offices.

Then she opened a storage-room door and stepped back in horror.

It was like Davison's office, but ten times worse. Whoever had killed the security guards had done so as sadistically as possible. It was almost impossible to tell they had been human. The blue shirts, in tatters, were about the only clue as to who they were. Their blood had mingled in the center of the room, after having trickled from each corpse and body part strewn about.

She gasped again.

Bobby.

He would never wave at her again, or give her concert info, or show her into better casino seats.

Her heart screamed and cried, but Jessie backed out and tried to move on. She would have to mourn later. First, she had to survive—and warn Nick and Tom. Knowing not to carry her cell phone in the casino, she'd left it outside.

Jesus, what to do?

She had a silver-loaded Remington pump gun in her trunk. There was an exit back here, but how . . . ?

Then she risked heading back to Davison's office, pinched her nose shut, and set about searching his clothes. What was left of them.

His wallet hadn't been touched, and in it she found what she needed. His entry card. He'd let her in through the back door on more than one occasion, and now this was her only chance to get out. Clearly, she'd never make the front door.

She ignored the blue camera bubbles. Maybe there was no one in the security office.

Or maybe they were letting her do her thing.

Waiting for the rest of the gang to arrive, so they could spring the trap.

ARNOW

Amid the grief and the rage was the scorching desire for revenge.

Behind the casino complex, they approached with guns half-hidden in case civilians spotted them.

"Here!" Arnow called out, tossing Lupo the dagger.

"Why me?"

"It was made for you, Lupo. A 'werewolf's werewolf killer,' remember?"

Lupo nodded, still uncertain. He tucked the sheathed dagger into the small of his back.

Arnow kept his distance, knowing the silver in his two guns bothered Lupo even at a few feet away. The dagger against his skin didn't even register. *Weird magic.*

"Look," Lupo said, pointing. "Davison's car is here. There's Jessie's SUV. And shit, there's Falken's squad car. She's here."

Arnow nodded. He'd shared with Lupo what Dell'Onore had told him down in Wausau.

Maybe changes things a little, doesn't it?

Lupo had seemed strangely silent, as if the news were both expected and not.

However it went, it was Lupo's play. At least, until Arnow had what he wanted.

JESSIE

Outside, the cell phone was dead. Jammed? She knew the military had devices that could do it. Wolfpaw might as well have *been* the military.

Once the impostor phone calls had been made, cell service had been jammed. Now she remembered how the woman in the casino had looked at her dead phone— suddenly dead—while the guard didn't even care. They didn't bother with cell phones because they weren't normal security, and they knew the signal would be killed at any time.

She yanked one of the Remington Model 1100 twelve-gauge short-barreled pump shotguns Nick had given her from the trunk and made sure she was loaded for wolf. Six shells in the tube magazine, plus she dumped more shells into her pockets. She cranked the pump and wrapped her hand comfortably around the pistol grip. She'd been around guns all her life.

She tucked the gun as out of sight as possible and swiped herself in.

The hallway was blocked by a double door she didn't even remember. She opened it carefully and ignored the camera bubble, then made her way past the storage room where Bobby and the other guys had been massacred.

She wished she could get whoever had done that in her sights.

Maybe I will.

Why was she still undiscovered?

Maybe they wanted her here.

Were Nick and Tom already prisoners?

Jesus, how to find out, except to look behind every door?

She opened several doors and saw nothing of interest.

Then she opened a conference room door and two guards were waiting, their handguns pointed at her.

LUPO

Lupo and Arnow made their way down the hallway, acutely aware that it was a narrower entrance. According to Lupo's memory, their hallway was parallel with a wider one that housed all the main offices. This was more a service-access tunnel, with doors leading to mechanical systems and staircases down into the basement rooms.

No security at all back here seemed to confirm Lupo's theory.

They moved carefully toward a T intersection, where another narrow hallway would connect to the other larger one and lead to Davison's office. Arnow kept his silver-loaded Python and conventional .40-caliber Glock away from Lupo. He seemed distracted, and winced occasionally from pain he hadn't bothered to mention. Lupo wondered how things had shaken out between the ex-sheriff and Heather Wilson, but this was no time to discuss it.

He needed to find Jessie, if she was here!

A door opened up ahead and both tensed, sidling up to the wall to see who it was before opening fire.

There were still innocent people here, after all. It would be difficult to confirm a bad guy in a fraction of a second. Any security guard could turn out to be Bobby Burningwood or one of his group, not a Wolfpaw bogie.

The door opened slowly—whoever was behind it was careful—and it was Falken, her compact Glock held down low, near her thigh.

She saw them and her eyes widened.

Lupo motioned a question, then another. *You okay? You see anything?*

She blinked for *Okay* and shook her head on the other. She raised an eyebrow: *You?*

Lupo chanced a whisper from across the hall. "Think Jessie's here, somewhere. And it looks like Wolfpaw infiltrated casino security."

"I saw her outside a while ago," Falken said. "But—"

Gunfire erupted somewhere down the hall, in the bigger corridor.

Small arms—pistols. Then a shotgun. More pistols, maybe 9-millimeters.

"Jesus! Jessie!"

They loped in that direction, the three now watching each other's backs as they passed dangerous doorways.

JESSIE

The guards fired first, but she was already backing out of the room, so their slugs hit the jamb and sent up splinters she felt in her cheek and neck.

Reflexively she fired back, the boom of the shotgun loud in the enclosed space. She missed, taking out a chunk of the conference table between them, and they returned fire again.

But she was in the hallway now and running.

There was another hallway crossing into this one, so she took it.

She heard the guards shouting behind her.

Then one of them snarled and she knew he had Changed into a wolf.

She half-turned and realized with a sense of awe that he had half-Changed, into a biped wolf! His hand still had a pistol, but it was more paw than hand!

Christ, can they do that?

Blindly, she fired while on the run. Two rounds, and one of them hit its target, obliterating the wolf's head in a cloud of blood and bone. The body went hurtling to the floor, the stench of burning flesh and fur immediately apparent throughout the hallway.

Her shoulder was now sore and battered by the shotgun's recoil.

She turned forward and almost fired again, holding up pressure on the Remington's trigger just a fraction of a second before shooting Nick in the face.

Clearly, he'd almost done the same thing.

Jesus!

Tom Arnow was there too, leveling a hogleg silver handgun, which boomed twice and took out the second security guard in a gush of blood and guts.

Jessie hoped he'd used silver slugs.

Given the sudden stench of sizzling human and non-human flesh and fur and hair, Tom's gun was indeed loaded the right way.

The Wausau cop, Falken, hunkered behind them, her Glock also in hand.

After sharing a quick wordless hug with Nick, Jessie followed Nick and Tom and Falken down to the main corridor. The gunfire might or might not draw more Wolfpaw guys, depending on whether the administration area was soundproofed to keep casino noise out and any operational noise out of the casino.

Jessie handled the shotgun with relative ease thanks to a life of outdoors and up-north living. But she couldn't help seeing that werewolf's two-footed stance, gun in hand. *Paw.* She had to tell Nick. If it came as a surprise, it could lead to all of them getting killed.

"Where now?" she asked Nick's back. He had taken point and didn't hear her.

She followed, then Falken, and Tom brought up the rear. She heard Tom dumping his brass and reloading his two empty chambers.

"Where are we going, Nick?"

He stopped. "Jessie, you back up and leave the way we came in. Here's my card."

"I have Davison's," she said.

"Is he—?"

"Yeah. But I'm not leaving. Whatever you're doing, I'm doing with you." She was aware that her gun and Arnow's were likely causing Nick's skin to sizzle and pop. He was gritting his teeth against the pain.

"Jess," he began, but then there was a slamming of doors behind them.

"Connecting passages?" Arnow asked.

"Not sure, but I bet."

"Great, so the exit's cut off in this hallway," Nick said. "Looks like you stay with us after all, Jess." Then he looked straight at Falken. "Here's what we're doing. We're an eradication squad. We're eradicating a kind of cancer that has invaded our world. I have the same illness, but this other type is aggressive and fatal. It has to be cut out. We have to cut these Wolfpaw thugs off our body."

"At least we got two."

"How many you think we're dealing with?" Nick asked Jessie.

She shrugged. "More than two, less than twenty. If there were more they would have covered the casino better."

"Right, that's what I thought. Everybody check weapons. Falken, too bad you're packing a nine-millimeter. We don't have any silver slugs for you."

Falken shrugged, eyeing them one by one.

"No more time," Nick said, and right then three guards burst out of a doorway behind them.

But they appeared only half-human, with fur-covered arms and legs. The other half of each body was wolf—especially the heads, with their snarling, snapping jaws full of fangs. Their eyes glowed with unnatural ferocity.

Before any of them could fire, another doorway crashed open to cut off their escape in the opposite direction. Two more guards, now in hybrid form, blocked the hallway.

There was no way out of the corridor, except through the wolves.

Any second and gunfire would erupt. But the wolves were too close. Some of them would get through.

Jessie leveled her shotgun and waited for the word from Nick. Her hands trembled.

LUPO

In one swift motion, Lupo whirled and dug the edge of his silver blade into Falken's neck.

Arnow snatched the Glock from her hand.

Jessie gasped in surprise.

"Back! Step back, or your commander gets it!" Nick's voice carried to both knots of half wolves. "Back off!"

Falken chuckled without mirth, as much as the pressure on her neck allowed.

"How did you know?"

Nick stared down the wolf-men, who were approaching inch by inch. He pressed the blade into Falken's neck, and the smell of blistering skin almost overpowered them all. Falken hissed in pain, but didn't crack.

"Tell them to back off!"

"Back off, Wilcox," she said, her voice gurgling.

"How did you guess?" Falken said again. The pain was evident.

"That it was *you* killing all those people and framing

Heather Wilson? Dell'Onore told Tom here about your two years in Iraq, working for Wolfpaw." Lupo's voice turned into a snarl. "So those three bastards were friends of yours? I didn't figure you for the sentimental type."

"If you'd have let me fuck you, you might have changed your mind."

"That's how you get what you want, isn't it? You started fucking Heather, too, didn't you, even while you were framing her for those indiscriminate murders."

"Couldn't bring myself to waste the opportunity. She would have made a great ally—too bad she's an *idiot*."

"Plus you had that funky tattoo removed from under your left arm. I racked my brain trying to figure that out, then it hit me. You guys still like to ink your blood group under there?" He drove the dagger deeper into her skin, scorching it. The flesh turned black and curled.

"An unfortunate obsession left over in the elders," she gasped out in pain.

Smoke curled around Lupo's hand, too, as the dagger's silver blistered him.

Jessie was dumbstruck by the revelations. The nearby threatening guards were almost easy to dismiss temporarily.

"But why?" she whispered hoarsely.

Lupo fielded it. "Falken mostly wanted revenge. But Wolfpaw—whoever *they* really are when you scrape off the layers of shit and shell corporations—they needed to cover their ass. Those three who made a mess of Eagle River were loose cannons who opened up their secret to everyone. Some of the Wolfpaw people wanted to shut down our group, who knew about werewolves, but by then there were two of us. Heather killed some people early on, but figured out soon enough that it was better to resist the urge. But she liked it, and she might have continued. Falken here just made sure Heather looked like she *was* murdering people, hoping to draw all the werewolf killers to this place and finish us off."

"Sounds great," Falken said with some difficulty. "Now let me go before my men make hash out of your intestines."

"Fuck yourself, Falken."

"That's so juvenile, *Lupo*. You even know what your name means?"

"Shut up about my name," Lupo said, grimacing.

"That knife starting to smart?" Falken said, laughing silently.

It was true. He could barely hold the unsheathed dagger.

Her own skin was being seared by the silver blade, and it was clearly all she could do to keep talking. The silver edge dug into her neck, parting the skin layer by layer, causing rivulets of sizzling blood to wash across her chest. Silver was like liquid fire in the veins and bones of a werewolf— Hollywood had got *one* thing right.

But she was damned tough. Lupo had to give her that, at least. He'd gotten over the beauty. Inside, Falken was a bigger monster than many he'd met.

"You killed too many innocents, Falken. And you plotted against my friends."

"Aw, so sorry." To the guards, she suddenly barked an order. "Get them! Forget about me. Get them now—"

Lupo slit her throat with one flick.

Her voice died in an obscene gurgle. A cascade of hot blood gushed over her and Lupo.

He jerked his clenched fist—first in one direction and then the other, until he was almost holding up her sagging body by the knife's grip alone—and nearly severed her head.

At the same time, even though shocked, Jessie opened fire on the two wolf-men on one side of them, the silver shot ripping chunks of flesh from the torso of the nearest one. The silver in the loads burned the wounds from the inside and he hopped in a Saint Vitus's dance as she pumped another round into him.

On the opposite side, Arnow's Colt Python boomed twice

and one guard went down, while the second howled in pain. The third one growled furiously and lunged at them, but Lupo threw Falken's headless body at him. As the wolf ducked the corpse, Lupo pirouetted like a nimble-footed samurai, opening the guard's torso from sternum to pubis with one true slice of the silver-edged dagger.

Lupo kicked the dying Wolfpaw guard aside and invoked the Change, bringing the Creature to the surface in the usual visualization that gave his DNA orders to realign and make the Creature dominant.

The Creature roared its anger at having been suppressed when clearly his input was needed. Instinct took over.

Lupo's wolf went for the guard named Wilcox. The squad leader morphed instantaneously, and the two wolves met in midair, savaging each other with fangs and claws.

Meanwhile Jessie turned and barely had time to squeeze the Remington's trigger again before the last wolf-man could reach her.

The blasts punched through his chest and he looked down in pain and surprise, the intense heat beginning to sear him from the inside out. But his jaws were snapping mere inches away from her face, so close she could smell the rankness of his last human meal.

And then Jessie put her last shell into the center of his head.

The twelve-gauge buckshot blew his head apart and dropped his scorching body like a sack. He continued convulsing as he hit the floor, fluttering back and forth from wolf to human until he went still and simply bled out.

ARNOW

With all the attackers down except the one Lupo was battling, there was a moment in which he felt the need to curl up and sleep.

Lupo's wolf body was still raging through the air, snapping and biting, drawing blood from a dozen places on the Wolfpaw guy's chest and neck, and it was clear that Lupo was having the best of it for the moment.

Suddenly a roaring body bowled him over and he saw that another guard had arrived to join the fight.

This guy was huge and horrendously powerful. He swatted Lupo's wolf off the back of the other and turned to face Arnow on two muscular paws, his mouth full of slathering, slashing fangs.

Arnow reached down for the discarded dagger and went in low, surprising the wolf. The blade sank in a few inches and the gush of boiling blood brought Arnow some relief.

It was as if this wolf represented the horrors Arnow's family had been forced to face in their last moments. Intellectually he knew that Falken had probably been the one, but she was done for and this guy was handy.

The nasty wound may have surprised the guard, but he still possessed a survivor's instinct and was nimble enough to evade Arnow's other thrusts.

The wolf turned and fled, making for the door at the end of the corridor.

Arnow flashed on a thought. Maybe this meant there were no more reinforcements. He had to be the last.

Arnow's rage was like a sentient being, and it had taken over.

So the ex-sheriff gave chase.

Behind him, Lupo's wolf scrabbled for footing on the blood-slick tiled floor and followed.

JESSIE

She picked her way over the bloody pools throughout the hallway. Cordite and blood and fried skin and fur made for a stench she could barely have described. Nausea washed over her in a sour-tasting wave and she fought to keep from vomiting. Reaction was just setting in, starting to claim her alertness and replacing it with a dull haze.

She forced herself to focus as she reloaded the Remington.

Was the casino still operating? Were zombie-eyed retirees still pressing buttons and flushing away life savings? It seemed incredible that the gunfire and death so close to her might not have been even noticed in the gaming rooms, but the cavernous place was solidly soundproofed, and the security department had been understaffed for days now. The whole battle had taken less than a minute or two off the game clock. Guards out in the gaming halls might not have even noticed yet that something had happened.

She remembered Bobby and felt tears burst out.

Suddenly one of the half-wolf/half-man hybrids she'd shot earlier leaped up with crazed eyes rolling in his skull, driven insane by the silver shot drilled into his torso.

Now he wanted nothing but to take her with him.

He reared up in a crippled attack on legs that would barely hold his weight.

Coldly, her voice roaring nonsensically, she shot him again, the Remington hot in her grip.

This time the wolf-man hit the wall, his back blown out, painting the light-colored drywall crimson, smearing his life's blood crookedly on his way back down to the floor. He lay still, his fur smoking. Then he began to flutter back and forth—until he was a dead human.

Jessie stepped over him, desensitized to the carnage.

Nick. She had to follow Nick and make sure he was all right. *And Tom.*

What the hell did Nick know about Falken's tattoo? Under her left arm?

Besides trying to figure out what it meant, Jessie couldn't quiet the screaming voice that asked her to find out *how Nick had known about it.*

Gripping the Remington, she approached the outside doors.

And heard gunfire from the parking lot.

KILLIAN

That Wausau cop's phone call had sent him to the Great Northern casino.

It was all the way in hell north of even that tourist trap they called a town, but his GPS had come through again, sure as shit. When he pulled into the lot and drove around looking at cars, he'd spotted Lupo's well-worn Maxima.

That damn Milwaukee cop was here, constantly getting himself into trouble and neglecting his own duties in the city that paid his salary, had paid for his disability, and now seemed to be the last thing on his mind.

Killian had spent most of his career making bad cops pay, and he'd had a bad feeling about Nick Lupo from the start. That guy had *stuff* to hide.

He pulled in not far from the Maxima, felt the hood. Still a little warm. So the bastard hadn't been here for long. The Wausau cop—what was her name?—might be looking for him now. He headed for the rear of the massive building. There had to be an entrance there, somewhere.

He spotted it just as the double doors burst open.

Caught in midstride, Killian could only watch as a man-shaped wolf—*or whatever the fuck he is!*—flew out the doors, blood streaming and fur smoking, and headed for the nearby tree line.

The doors burst outward again and a blood-spattered pursuer who brandished a sleek blade gave chase. Moments later, another body hurtled out the doors, this one a full-fledged black wolf on four legs.

Killian remembered to go for his piece, struggling to draw the Glock as he witnessed this bizarre procession.

He barely realized when he sagged to the ground, almost as if he could have folded a blanket of earth over himself.

Then all he could do was watch.

LUPO

He overtook Arnow easily on four legs and leaped, bringing down the wounded guard in a flying tackle he started as a wolf but ended as a human.

He smelled Bobby Burningwood's scent on this guard's uniform. His rage ratcheted up and threatened to consume him.

The guy's face was twisted in excruciating pain and Lupo could tell he was trying to Change, but the wound Arnow had dealt him seemed to prevent him from doing so.

Lupo grabbed his head to keep him from biting, holding his jaws out of reach. "Any more of you?" he shouted, in a frenzy now.

"A million! And they are coming for you, *chico*," he snarled.

"You killed some good men, you bastard!" Lupo smacked his head into the ground and let it bounce.

"Fuck you!" the guy spat, eyes crazed.

"Then see you in hell." Lupo gave the guy's head a quick, strong twist and broke his neck with a tremendous snap.

"For Bobby and his men, you sonofabitch."

Arnow materialized beside him. "Make sure," he said, and handed him the dagger.

Despite the heat scorching his hand, Lupo grasped the glowing weapon and disemboweled the dead Wolfpaw soldier. A gush of heat blasted him as the silver seared the guy's insides.

No way he'll ever get up again.

When Lupo turned, wheezing, his hand starting to blister, Arnow had the Colt Python half-leveled at him.

"Tom?"

Arnow wouldn't meet his gaze, but the gun never wavered. "It was all your fault. All of it."

Lupo stood silent, his hand on fire. Arnow was right.

But then Ghost Sam leaned in and whispered in Lupo's ear. He hadn't been there a second before.

Lupo listened to Sam's quiet voice, his heart heavy, and knew he was hearing the truth.

He just knew.

Maybe he sensed it. Maybe he smelled it. Maybe Arnow was telling him, in his own way.

Heather Wilson bit him today.

Even Ghost Sam seemed sad.

Lupo threw the well-balanced dagger in one snap-motion and the sharp blade plunged into Arnow's chest just below his neck with a terrible sizzling, sucking sound.

Arnow stared down in surprise at his boiling blood gushing over the blade. Then he tottered sideways and sprawled to the ground.

Lupo sobbed helplessly.

Ghost Sam was gone again and it was only Lupo and that pit bull Killian, who'd managed to find his way up here after all.

Bastard.

Lupo growled and stalked to where Killian still seemed to recline against a car as if suffering from indigestion. He snatched the Glock from Killian's hand and racked the slide.

Killian winced, closing his eyes, a silent prayer on his lips.

The moment lengthened impossibly as if stuck in molasses.

Lupo turned suddenly and put a single bullet into Arnow's chest where the dagger had gone in. Then he yanked out the blade and tossed it among the nearby trees.

His face had become demonic.

Killian was nearly catatonic. His eyes followed Lupo, but

the rest of him seemed to have disappeared in a past long gone, or a place far away.

Lupo snapped his fingers and got his attention, then spoke in a low, clear tone. "I was fighting the dead guy when this other guy came up and was about to shoot me. You dropped him. End of story."

"U-Uh?" Killian stuttered. His eyes were wide.

"You're stuck, Killian. Tell it my way. No one will believe it your way. I'll visit your padded cell weekly." He tossed the Glock at Killian's feet. The big cop flinched and shrank away.

"Nick!"

The shout startled them both.

Lupo stared hard at the IA cop. His eyes might have glowed red.

Then he turned to meet Jessie, who was running up. She saw Arnow's body, dropped the Remington, and—sobbing—collapsed into his arms.

JESSIE

It was later. It felt like much later.

She drove. Nick, exhausted, had slumped over and laid his head on her shoulder.

It wasn't a long drive, but she was unsure. Her hands trembled on the wheel. The street signs seemed foreign.

So much death.

She'd shed more than a few tears for Tom Arnow. Who'd have expected that other cop would show up, misjudge the situation, and shoot Tom? He thought he was saving a fellow cop, sure, but what a terrible way for Tom to die after having survived a massacre.

Nick had been masterful, telling Sheriff McCoyne about how the fake guards were interrupted while robbing the casino cash room. The bags of money strewn all over the hall made it a done deal.

Apparently the thieves had been sadistic psychopaths. They'd tortured the captured security guards and the tribe's chief elder, Rick Davison.

Rich DiSanto had arrived, late as usual. He'd been in touch with Nick while following Killian, and Nick, predicting a face-off, had suggested he bring the rez cops with him. Bill Rogers and John Deer, the ranking officers, had followed in a rez SUV. If he hadn't stopped to recruit them, DiSanto would have been there in the thick of it, too.

Though then he would have had to be briefed on Nick's secret. Nick wasn't sure the younger cop could handle it.

Heather Wilson had disappeared.

Jessie wasn't sure what *that* meant, but Nick seemed unsurprised.

The mercenary wolf Nick had left for dead had vanished, too, and that was bound to cause them trouble eventually, since he'd left no trail. They hoped Wilcox had died in the woods. Nick would keep searching until he could be sure.

The circuits between Wausau, Milwaukee, and Eagle River had burned up. Not only had a cop shot an ex-cop, but a Wausau cop had also been killed while heroically foiling a robbery. Falken's funeral would be attended by thousands of cops from all over the Midwest, probably the country. Nick thought it was all right, even if a farce.

Sometimes it's best for people to believe what they want to believe, he'd said.

She felt him there, soundly asleep on her shoulder as she drove. His presence was solid, comforting.

And yet.

She wondered if she fell into that camp herself.

People who believe what they want to believe.

She wondered how long the reprieve would be, this time.

Wolfpaw, the mercenary outfit, might have reason to intensify their efforts. Especially now.

The intense darkness outside was barely diminished by her headlights. For the first time, this land she had loved since childhood seemed frightening and oppressive. For the first time in a long time, she felt doubts.

In the headlights, the road curved in front of her, tall pines lining both sides like ranks of silent sentinels.

Her eyes blurred, but no tears came and she didn't wipe them.

LUPO

Nick Lupo sat in the leather club chair near the fireplace in his rented cottage in the darkening night.

His blinds were open. But today's sun had long since stopped filtering through. The tree line across the channel had robbed him of the last few minutes of sunlight, allowing him only a glimpse of the bloodred disk as it dipped behind the trunks and disappeared.

"Us and Them" played softly on the iPod dock, Rick Wright's jazz chords clean and crisp and infinitely sad in the evening air.

On the end table next to him lay the silver dagger in its magical scabbard.

The werewolf-killer weapon's aura was vaguely visible in the half-light. The silver smelted to the blade was inert, however, and would remain so as long as the blade was sheathed.

Lupo looked around at the familiar surroundings, fixing them in his head. There were several framed photographs of Jessie over the fireplace. He had taken one down and it rested in his lap, where he could see it.

He had reached the end of his road.

Much blood had been spilled, and it had been his fault.

And then he had spilled the blood of a friend, betraying a sacred trust. And doing so for his own benefit.

He had let Jessie down, and he had let Sam Waters down, and he had let Tom Arnow down. And now Griff Killian was caught in the same web of lies he had tried to escape his whole life.

There was only one solution for the problem of what he had become. What he had always been, if he faced up to it.

He had always been a coward when it came to solving this greatest of all problems. But now that he had caused so much pain, he felt the pressure on his soul and he wanted nothing more than to atone. There was only one good way to do it, and he was ready.

And Ghost Sam hadn't shown up to talk him out of it.

He took the sheathed dagger from its resting place and turned it over in his hand, seeing the symbols carved deeply into the scabbard's outer surface.

He wondered which of them had been carved by his grandfather.

He wondered what his grandfather would have thought if he'd predicted this exact moment.

That was the problem with destiny. Someone always felt compelled to fulfill it.

Nick Lupo slowly drew the blade from the scabbard and the white heat began to scorch his hand and his arm.

Bram Stoker Award–Winning Author

JOHN EVERSON

Night after night, Evan walked along the desolate beach, grieving over the loss of his son, drowned in an accident more than a year before. Then one night he was drawn to the luminous sound of a beautiful, naked woman singing near the shore in the moonlight. He watched mesmerized as the mysterious woman disappeared into the sea. Driven by desire and temptation, Evan returned to the spot every night until he found her again. Now he has begun a bizarre, otherworldly affair. A deadly affair. For Evan will soon realize that his seductive lover is a being far more evil . . . and more terrifying . . . than he ever imagined. He will learn the danger of falling into the clutches of the . . .

Siren

"Superbly effective. Modern horror doesn't get much better than this!"
—Bryan Smith, Author of *The Killing Kind*

ISBN 13: 978-0-8439-6354-0

✂

☐ **YES!**

Sign me up for the Leisure Horror Book Club and send my FREE BOOKS! If I choose to stay in the club, I will pay only $8.50* each month, a savings of $7.48!

NAME: _____

ADDRESS: _____

TELEPHONE: _____

EMAIL: _____

☐ I want to pay by credit card.

☐ **VISA**   ☐ **MasterCard.**   ☐ **DISCOVER**

ACCOUNT #: _____

EXPIRATION DATE: _____

SIGNATURE: _____

Mail this page along with $2.00 shipping and handling to:
Leisure Horror Book Club
PO Box 6640
Wayne, PA 19087
Or fax (must include credit card information) to:
610-995-9274
You can also sign up online at www.dorchesterpub.com.

*Plus $2.00 for shipping. Offer open to residents of the U.S. and Canada only.
Canadian residents please call 1-800-481-9191 for pricing information.
If under 18, a parent or guardian must sign. Terms, prices and conditions subject to change. Subscription subject to acceptance. Dorchester Publishing reserves the right to reject any order or cancel any subscription.